THE INQUISITOR'S HOUSE

ANNIE LAURIE WILLIAMS, INC.
18 EAST 41st STREET, NEW YORK CITY
TELEPHONE MUrray Hill 5-7565

ALSO BY ROBERT SOMERLOTT

THE FLAMINGOS

THE INQUISITOR'S HOUSE

ROBERT SOMERLOTT

NEW YORK / THE VIKING PRESS

Copyright © 1968 by Robert Somerlott

All rights reserved

First published in 1968 by The Viking Press, Inc.
625 Madison Avenue, New York, N.Y. 10022

Published simultaneously in Canada by
The Macmillan Company of Canada Limited

Library of Congress catalog card number: 68-29712

Printed in U.S.A. by Vail-Ballou Press, Inc.

For the Señora Nell Harris Fernández
. . . and for others who remember a trip to a ghost-place,
Real Catorce

ONE

THE MAGICIAN

1

At the last moment of the Day of the Dead, November 2, 1903, when the bells of a dozen churches were chiming midnight, an explosion of uncertain origin damaged the second story of a mansion which had stood for more than two centuries not far from the Governors' Palace in the ancient Mexican city called Guanajuato. The blast, accompanied by an astonishing and lovely cloud of pure white fire, turned the stone structure into an incinerator or, more accurately, a crematory, for five of its six human occupants were instantly dispatched to Kingdom Come or to other destinations less agreeable but equally final. There was a muffled roar, a slight trembling of the thick walls, then an unearthly radiance flashed in the upstairs living room, bathing in brief flame those five people who sat in a circle around a marble-topped table.

Their departure from this world was sudden and apparently unexpected. At one moment they were intensely alive and—if we trust the testimony of Tomás D'Aquisto—at the climax of a peculiar search which had led each of them, by differing routes, to this unlucky meeting place.

Each of them must have been haunted at various times by a fear that this search was endless. Then the end came, although surely it was not in a way they could have foreseen. Yet, as Tomás D'Aquisto longed to believe, what happened that night may have been not an ending at all but a beginning. For years afterward D'Aquisto struggled to force his rebellious and cynical intellect to accept this conclusion, and the hopeless effort cost him his peace and eventually his sanity.

Whatever the truth is, we know that the lives of those five were snuffed out like candles. They were arrested by death, caught in their final poses and attitudes with ten blackened hands still clasped together on the white table —not so white after the ashes had settled. They seemed to have been quite undisturbed by the holocaust which filled the cavernous room, then quickly extinguished itself. Their positions the next morning were so oddly natural that one police investigator wrote a report stating flatly that the five victims had been murdered earlier in some obscure way—an undetectable poison?—and the explosion was a disguise for this crime. The man's superior, Captain José Guzmán, had the good sense to dismiss that notion. He knew his assistant was an avid reader of Edgar Allan Poe and had even gone so far as to rewrite both *Murders in the Rue Morgue* and *The Mystery of Marie Roget,* tacking on his own far-fetched solutions. The captain, after one initial mistake, concluded that the dead perished in a flash fire tremendous in heat, merciful in brevity. Gaslights had been recently installed in the house, and escaping gas which had somehow collected was clearly the culprit. The whole thing was easily explained.

Yet all those who examined the scene were troubled by a vague suspicion that the matter was not quite what it appeared to be. There was an oddity of timing: a fatal accident at the stroke of midnight somehow suggests arrangement and design. When such a midnight falls on the

Day of the Dead, latent superstition and a longing for romance are inevitably aroused. A hidden agency must be at work, and the imagination rejects the dullness of coincidence. (This oddity of timing plagued Tomás D'Aquisto; it was simply too eerie to be natural. But he could not quite bring himself to accept the alternative explanation.)

The victims, despite the heat they had suffered, were uncannily preserved, reminding observers of ancient Indian mummies which line the famous caves on Guanajuato's outskirts. They were shrunken by death, yet they remained disturbingly lifelike: three women and two men leaning forward in their scorched leather chairs, heads bowed as though in prayer or communion. None had turned away, none had raised up his hands to shield himself. It seemed that death had overtaken them at a moment when they refused to be interrupted. Or else—and the clasped hands suggested it—these five had entered into some unbreakable pact and the fate they met so calmly was its natural consummation.

No one knew for sure. Even the Bishop of León, who was sojourning in Guanajuato at the time and who maintained a formidable staff of informers, could not make up his mind as to what attitude to adopt. And some attitude *had* to be adopted, once the identity and prominence of the victims became known. The poor bishop—"poor" in the sense of pitiable, for he was far from impoverished—pondered, prayed, and discussed the affair with several political cronies but remained in a quandary. His conflicting thoughts were jotted down in a diary called *Daily Meditations,* a journal he kept faithfully for seventeen years, which is still preserved in the archives of the León cathedral.

> After breakfast of red snapper, prayed Divine Guidance about what happened on Day of Dead last. There are rumors, and no one knows why such strangely assorted people had gathered. Did they plot mischief against the

government and hence our Holy Church? Or were they practicing the abominable heresy of spiritism, as some are saying?
If so, it is a hideous scandal and an excellent sermon topic.
The Hand of God suffering not a witch to live. But if not so,
stern remarks might antagonize Certain Persons. [Here the
bishop's capital letters refer to government officials, not to
the Persons of the Holy Trinity.] Great caution advisable.
Tread lightly. . . . Today's text: "The Lord is my light and
my salvation, whom shall I fear?"

The bishop, who had flourished under the dictatorship,
knew the answer to this question. The sermon he finally
preached was learned and ferocious but so conservative in
its moral that it embarrassed almost nobody. Placing the
blame for the tragedy squarely on illuminating gas, he
warned the poor against coveting dangerous newfangled
inventions. "O my children, luxuries of this world are Satan's snare for the unwary. . . . Retire at sunset pleased
by a day of honest labor. Rise at dawn to earn your bread
by the sweat of your brow, sure of your reward in heaven.
O dear children, be content with your lot . . . be content . . . be content. . . ." What he said mattered little,
for the poor returned to their unlit hovels remembering
not his words but the gleaming jewels in his miter. And
not everyone was pleased by his attempt at diplomacy.
The following week he received a sharp message from the
newly formed electric company and another from the
manufacturer of illuminating gas. Even the holiest men
cannot appease all viewpoints, try though they will.

Doubts and rumors about the explosion persisted, and
Tomás D'Aquisto, the man who could have cleared much
confusion, wisely fled the city and did not speak until long
afterward. Yet even if he had told as much of the story as
he knew, who would have believed him? How could he
convince anyone of things he himself doubted? He was
known as a trickster, an illusionist, a man who had become
famous throughout the world for his skill at deception.

Such a man may be amusing, at times even confounding, but is hardly to be taken seriously.

Investigation continued while Captain Guzmán collected every available fact. He learned that the explosion, at the moment of its occurrence, had attracted little attention. The foundations of the old city were honeycombed with tunnels and mineshafts and at all hours underground blasts rattled the china teacups of Guanajuato's numerous millionaires. This subterranean thunder, which would have been alarming in most places, was a comforting sound in Guanajuato, audible proof that the Indian miners were faithfully toiling in those black noxious caves, shattering the rock whose yield of precious metals made the city—or at least a handful of its inhabitants—legendary for riches. The labor of the miners, a stunted mole-like race of men, was supposed to be unceasing, and in Guanajuato silence would have been ominous. Indeed, silence in the mines always preceded the gory and futile revolutions which had so often erupted in that bitter land, times of upheaval when the scarred walls literally dripped blood.

Moreover, the Day of the Dead, the most bizarre of all holidays, was just ending, and for twenty-four hours the city had been subjected to a bombardment of fireworks, Roman candles and skyrockets zooming from churchyards and crowded cemeteries where thousands had gathered to visit, dine, and drink with their buried relatives; booms, roars, and thunders rang through the tortuous streets all day until at sunset a thick haze, blue and sulphurous, hung above the gorge to which the city clings. The fogged sky and stinging aroma resembled the aftermath of battle.

Thousands of pesos had gone up in smoke that day, but the aristocrats did not begrudge the money, having learned that entertainments were cheaper than revolutions. As Roman despots once diverted the poor with circuses, so the patricians of Guanajuato dazzled the Indian toilers with fireworks and festivals. They could afford to give these baubles: for three hundred and fifty years this infertile gorge and the naked hills towering above it had poured forth a seemingly endless flow of silver and gold—wealth to build the vast and dreary monuments of Madrid, to equip the Armada, and at last to drown Spain in a flood which was not less deadly for being golden. Two centuries later Spain lay destitute, while Guanajuato remained swollen and rich. Its untitled barons, under the rule of the dictator, commanded not only wealth but the power of life and death over the rabble who slaved in the mines or scrubbed the tile floors of the palaces. Often, as in the old days, men were forced to kneel to kiss the hand that had lashed them, mumbling thanks for the wisdom of punishment.

So on the Day of the Dead, Guanajuato's fiery displays were magnificent, the poor ogling each new spectacle with wide-eyed delight, while the rich buried their noses in scented handkerchiefs and the sensitive plugged their ears with beeswax pellets. The din continued until the next morning, and it was small wonder that one additional explosion at midnight aroused scant notice. Its noise, fumes, and eerie white light added little to the hell-breath hovering over the city.

There was one survivor of the doomed house, a hunchback known as Little Brother, a grotesque dwarf slightly more than a yard tall and astonishingly ugly. He was a stranger to the city, having arrived only a few weeks before with his employer, a handsome and reticent woman who called herself Señora Laurier. Obviously Little Brother had Indian blood and was Mexican, and obviously his employer was not. Señora Laurier was European, a lady of wealth and elegance, according to the agent who rented her the mansion in which she later perished.

That night Little Brother, hair singed and clothes smoking, dashed from the blazing building to stand gibbering in the street. He gazed at the house as though hypnotized, then, flapping his tiny arms, he leaped up and down like a great flightless bird struggling to rise in the air. Crying out, he fled, plunging down the dark streets and alleys, still uttering mad gibberish, and as his little feet pounded the cobblestones the black silk slippers he wore were slashed to ribbons. In terror he darted this way and that, striking his head against the corners of buildings, colliding with alarmed passers-by. The city, to those who have not grown up in its twisting streets, is a labyrinth, and three times Little Brother, as though under malicious guidance, found himself once more at the scene of the explosion, and each time he screamed at the sight of the house and the fading glimmer within. Still he tried to escape, but at that moment a troop of children returning from a graveyard entered the street, their faces masked by the hideous death's heads appropriate to the holiday. Little Brother, in demented panic, mistook the grinning paper skulls for some terrible reality. Unable to bear more, he hurled himself down on the stones, rolling over and over, kicking the air and gnashing his teeth to the accompaniment of guttural noises, for all the world like a dog that has eaten poisoned meat in the marketplace. The children were startled, then fascinated, and, believing the little man was performing a show for their holiday amusement, they danced around him, a squealing, cavorting pack of imps, pressing close to pinch his hump in hope of luck and money. Hours later Little Brother was still lying convulsed on the cobblestones when he was seized and carried away by the dictator's police.

Survivors of a tragedy are sometimes less fortunate than the apparent victims, and this proved to be true for Little Brother. The police thought, briefly and mistakenly, that the blast had been an act of revolutionary terrorism. Such outrages against law and orderly conduct of business were increasingly frequent, and Captain Guzmán leaped immediately to a wrong conclusion, partly because his nerves were on edge. Only a few days before, the dictator himself had visited the city to attend the opening of the new opera house, a building whose spendthrift adornments outdid the finest theaters in all the Americas. The world had been combed to decorate its interior, and the première performance, sung by a company of imported Italians, was dazzling and gala. Gala for everyone except Guzmán and his men, who were assigned the thankless task of guarding the "Hero of Peace," who was in constant danger of assassination. For three nights Guzmán had had little sleep, so when the explosion occurred he was already jittery.

There was another, much stronger reason for Guzmán's mistaken and cruel treatment of Little Brother. Although two of the victims were using assumed names, all were quickly identified and one turned out to be none other than Major F. Patricio Donaju, a prominent and glamorous officer of the *rurales,* that savage body of men who served as state police but who were actually the dictator's private storm troopers. Donaju had risen to fame on far more than his blazing red hair and insolent eyes, although these alone were enough to flutter the pulses of many influential wives in the country.

He was magnificent—nearly two meters tall, broad-shouldered, narrow-hipped, and graced with the agility of a tiger. As a horseman, it was claimed, he could outride the devil himself, and the barracks reply to this remark was always, "Why not? He's Satan's twin brother." The major had fought a dozen well-publicized duels, usually over card games, although he did not need a reason. These contests, against opponents reputed to be invincible, always ended in the death or the utter humiliation of his adversary. There was a story that he had once compelled a Prussian engineer to lick the soles of both his boots from heel to toe, and Donaju's subordinates, who idolized him, boasted their major used "German shoe polish." They also loved and quoted his remark that no saber was properly tempered until it had tasted the blood of one human and two Indians.

For a time Donaju bore a peculiar nickname. He was called "the Smiler" because of the engaging boyish grin which lit up his freckled face. It was when he smiled that he was most dangerous, and those acquainted with him knew that his ironically winsome grin was equivalent to the buzz of a rattlesnake. Yet it was so cheerful and disarming an expression that several men had met death at his hands, perfectly deluded until the last surprising second. "The Smiler," attractive and ruthless, was a god in a society that worshiped masculine brutality above all things. When the god died, someone had to atone. Little Brother was the first man Captain Guzmán could lay hands on.

Since the death of a "fellow officer" was involved, the hunchback was questioned under tortures that would appall the imagination if we were not so accustomed to such things nowadays. The methods of the dictator's police were crude, and today they strike one as quaint. A generation was to pass away before a better-educated world would create precise scientific procedures and devices for the infliction of pain. But although the Guanajuato police lacked modern equipment, they nevertheless had experience, talent, and energy. Little Brother's howls, echoing from the cellar of the Governors' Palace, chilled the blood of the army of clerks and copyists who worked at long tables on the floor above. Over their inkstands they glanced uneasily at one another, as though suspicious of hidden enmity and betrayal. Each, as he listened, tried to assure himself that his politics and conduct were above doubt, and silently they congratulated themselves on the lightness of their own skins, confident that they had the advantage of looking more Spanish than Indian.

The police learned nothing from Little Brother. All efforts were useless, all customary methods failed, and when they at last decided he was insane and released him, more or less alive, they fumed at their own helplessness. Although they had resorted to draconic measures, he had not even understood their questions, much less answered them.

Captain Guzmán should not be judged too harshly for his cruelty to the dwarf. He was, after all, only an ordinary man doing his duty as ordinary men have always done. The night after releasing Little Brother he wrote a letter to a certain Señor Francisco Nava, a boyhood friend now high in the state government. The letter conveys some idea of the hardships of police work when the circumstances are not routine.

9 November, 1903

Esteemed Panchito,

I hope when this reaches you you'll be enjoying yourself in Chapala and that the whitefish will be biting. After you left for your vacation, I again tried to question the hunchback. We did our best but learned nothing more about Donaju's death. Ruben and Jorge assisted me at the informal interrogation and, believe me, they did a day's work! Tonight Ruben's hands are so swollen he can't get his wedding ring off his finger. Too bad because he was supposed to meet a little dove in Marfíl who doesn't know he's married. (He says she's a virgin. Where were you? Ha, ha!)

Anyway, the hunchback did nothing but mumble and yell. At first I thought it was one of those Indian jargons, but it wasn't. He kept making crazy gestures and somehow, the way he moved his fingers, they seemed to be *talking*. Weird. You know how superstitious Ruben is? He thought these motions were hex signs and got panicky. He had the fellow's wrists in the "wives" and he squeezed so tight he broke some bones and we wasted a lot of time reviving the prisoner. Ruben's a fine man personally, but these superstitions are a problem. But how can we get good officers—educated men like you and me—if we don't increase salaries? Always the same problem. The public never appreciates the police force.

Panchito, I'm almost convinced that what happened was

really an accident. Naturally when a man like Donaju is involved you start suspecting a plot. It's hard to believe he could die any other way. A list of just his *worst* enemies would include half the country. Frankly—and for God's sake don't quote me—I never liked him myself, and was thankful he wasn't stationed in Guanajuato. I'm not prejudiced, and I know some good people with a little mixed blood, but I just can't stand Irish Mexicans. It was a sad day when we let those gringo traitors stay here. Maybe Donaju was an exceptional Irishman, but they're all a little crazy. Besides, they have a peculiar smell—and it's *not* my imagination.

Strange thing, but so far I can't find one man who knew Donaju well. Not one friend. Acquaintances, yes. Fellow officers, of course. But no one knows the least thing about him personally. And, believe it or not, *no women!* Not one! Everybody thought he was the great lover, but I begin to doubt it.

I still haven't learned why he was in that house with those other people. Two of them, by the way, were foreigners. There's some talk of some spiritist nonsense, but I just can't connect that with a man like Donaju. Another victim, a woman, has also turned out to be *very important.* The story I heard about her seems completely incredible and since I don't know yet *who is involved,* I won't write more about it.

How I envy you at the lake! Kiss the girls for me. *Abrazos.*

I remain yours truly, your attentive, very affectionate and constant servant,

Pepe

P.S. There was one eyewitness and since you're interested in the case, I'm enclosing his testimony. "Burro-witness" might be a better description. The man is an idiot.

Attached to Guzmán's letter was a two-page summary of the statement given the police by Pablo Sanchez, a candy vender in the city of Guanajuato. This man, who seemed stupid to Guzmán, actually had a keen eye for detail. During his questioning he was at a serious disadvantage, for two conflicting desires battled in his mind, a longing to talk and an instinct to keep silent. From his own sad experiences and from the misfortunes of others he knew there were only three possible answers to make to a policeman. The first was "I didn't see anything." The second was "I don't remember." And the third was dependent on the other two. If you could simply not avoid answering, you had to discover what the questioners wished to hear and then assure them of that as quickly as possible. A poor man's job was to flatter the police, not to inform them. If he had been able to stick to this safe course, things would have been easy for him. But Pablo Sanchez was a dramatic and imaginative man who loved to tell a story. He had just seen an unusual and startling thing, and it was impossible to resist talking about it. So his answers alternated between safe denials of all knowledge and wild flights of superstitious fancy.

That night at a few minutes before twelve he was happily returning home from a graveyard where he had had one of the most successful days of his business career, selling skulls made of sugar whose white foreheads were cleverly decorated with pet names of various children. He had also created some wonderful innovations on the traditional merchandise of the holiday—crossed bones made of peanut brittle and corpselike hands molded in white wax and filled with red cherry syrup. Before midnight Sanchez had sold his entire gruesome stock and he left the graveyard and entered the dark city, his pockets jingling with copper coins.

Instead of walking directly to the two-room house he shared with nineteen members of his family, Pablo followed a circuitous route, detouring through back alleys and lurking in the deepest shadows of great buildings. Each time his keen ears caught the sound of a police whistle and a whistled response he waited until the coast was clear, thanking the saints that tomorrow he would be finished with this childish game of dodging and hiding.

Pablo's problem sprang from that eternal curse of mankind, taxation. His taxes as a vender were, to him, enormous, and by any standard they were not small. The state gouged more money from peddlers than from all the ranchers and mine-owners combined. A week ago his taxes had mysteriously fallen due three months early, in the nick of time to pay for decorations honoring the dictator's visit to the city. To meet this crushing and unexpected bill, he had been forced to sell his only pair of factory-made trousers, so now he was a fugitive in trouble with the law. Not because of indecent exposure—the white Indian bloomers which he and most of the poorer workers wore covered him well. But a new law clearly stated that no man could enter the city proper without wearing trousers made in a factory. Violators were fined to their last centavo, and revenue poured into the government coffers. For three days and nights Pablo Sanchez, in his decent but illegal bloomers, had been avoiding the police, a difficult feat for a man forced to earn his living on busy corners. Tomorrow he would buy new pants, but tonight he crept through the darkest of the dark streets.

Alerted by a nearby whistle and the flicker of a lantern, Pablo pressed himself flat against the wall of the nearest building, which happened to be the Alhóndiga de Granaditas, a huge stone granary whose evil history had become a Mexican legend. It was to this grim pile of masonry that the Spaniards of the city had fled during the savage revolution of 1810, and it was within its walls that they were later butchered. Pablo, when lawfully clad, often passed it and recalled this part of the story with considerable satisfaction. But tonight, cringing against the stone foundations, he remembered how the heads of four patriots had been hung up to adorn the building after the revolution failed, and how these fearful heads gazed sightlessly at the city for ten years. The darkness, the nearness of the police, and his having spent the day at the graveyard combined to

arouse his active imagination. He believed for a moment
—or later claimed to have believed—that the heads still
hung there. Looking up in the moonlight fogged by smoke,
he found himself staring into the blood-stained face of Father Hidalgo himself, his beard grown long in death. "I
was frozen," he later told Captain Guzmán. "I knew then
it was a terrible night and the worst would happen, because I shook so that I believed my bones would fall
apart." Pablo, seeking refuge, ran toward the church of
San Roque, but turned away in fright when he saw a uniformed man there. He ran until he was breathless, then,
forgetting all caution, sat down on a curb, gasping. "I
crossed myself and sat very still, saying three Hail Marys.
The big house across the street was dark. Then I heard a
sound like the wind blowing in the canyon. Suddenly all
the shutters of the balcony doors burst open, though no
one touched them, and there was a great light, brighter
than the sun. For a second I was blinded, then I saw five
ghosts sitting in a circle. They disappeared in the white
light. I couldn't move, I thought my hour had struck. A
devil ran from the house and I saw him with my own eyes,
I swear. A small devil breathing smoke. I hid in the doorway of the Casa Suárez, telling my rosary. It was there
your men found me. That is the whole truth, I swear by
the Virgin, and I hope the esteemed captain will forgive
my bloomers. I lost my fine factory-made trousers while
running to escape the devil."

Pablo Sanchez not only embroidered the truth, but he
omitted part of it, instinct telling him that something
should always be concealed from the police. While hiding
in the doorway, only a moment after the "small devil" had
vanished, Pablo heard the furious hoofbeats of a horse galloping through the street, then saw its iron shoes strike
sparks from the cobbles. Pablo's teeth chattered as he saw
the figure astride its back—a tall thin man wearing a black
hat and a billowing black cape. The horse reared as it

reached the smoking house, and the rider leaped down. Only then was Pablo sure he was human, for the man pressed his hands to his face and Pablo realized he was weeping. He threw back his head, and in the moonlight and the flickering glow of the ruined house agony showed on his face. In grief he cried out a strange and puzzling thing. "God, why couldn't I have been with them? Why couldn't I have been there?" Then he mounted the horse and plunged away into the night.

The rider was Tomás D'Aquisto, once widely known to the world as Zantana the Great, a magician, a fakir, a performer of tricks and feats of conjuring.

2

Captain José Guzmán fervently hoped that his involvement in the case would end with the funerals of the victims. He was a busy man, charged with controlling a hundred thousand resentful people—a people whose outward docility and humble manner did not deceive him for a moment. They touched their sombreros respectfully while their hearts smoldered with hate and the desire for vengeful rebellion. The horror of their history was enough to make any official sleep with one eye open and a rifle within arm's reach. Guzmán's concern was with the living; he had no time to worry about the dead, who were, after all, harmless at last.

When he received a message from the governor demanding a full investigation, he shouted obscenities so imaginative that his subordinates listened in awe. Striding about his office, the short stocky captain was a figure of bristling indignation as he twisted his drooping mustache and at last crushed the governor's note under the heel of his boot—an unusually high heel, for Guzmán was self-conscious about his lack of height and always stood "tall from the waist," which gave him a barrel-chested but rather sway-backed appearance.

But although Guzmán was outraged, he was not surprised. Ever since the explosion female tongues had been wagging, and speculations about it, now spiced with the titillating gruesomeness of a Gothic romance, enlivened the monumentally dull tea parties and the duller *meriendas* which upper-class ladies of Guanajuato inflicted upon each other. Guzmán was chagrined to discover that his own wife, a woman whose stupidity was among the world's wonders, knew more about the affair than he did.

Margot Laurier, she informed him placidly, was certainly a spiritist medium and quite probably a witch, who had conducted séances not only in Mexico City but in such glorious places as Madrid and Paris. Nor was this all. Major Donaju ("Ay, how handsome he was!") had not been the only important person attending. "There was a woman from Mexico City called Doña Dolores Cortés, a real *somebody*. All the best people in the capital attended her funeral, and the dictator himself sent a spray of calla lilies." Señora Guzmán's eyes glittered with envy. Dying was a small price to pay for such a social triumph. "How I'd love to know what went on in that house! I mean the *details*."

There was no mistaking the lechery of her tone as she thought of Major Donaju sitting in the dark. Guzmán glared at the fat blowzy woman he had married and slammed down his coffee cup hard enough to crack the saucer. When leaving the house, he kicked at the family dog and later that day not only curtailed his wife's charge accounts but also fired her hairdresser.

The women were not the only ones talking. Pablo Sanchez repeated and elaborated his wild tale in every cantina and *pulquería* of the city, and soon passers-by crossed themselves when they approached the infamous mansion. Also, the American Embassy asked for details about the death of Dr. James Edwards Esterbrook, whom it described as a "prominent citizen of Massachusetts," a remote, frozen place which Guzmán thought was inhabited by wild cowboys and scalp-hunting Sioux. Still more troublesome was the flood of letters from private individuals asking for "any information you can give me about the last moments of my beloved friend, Doña Dolores Cortés." After such a prelude, the governor's request was not surprising.

So Guzmán sighed, shrugged his thick shoulders, and went patiently to work. His labors finally produced a remarkable seventy-page report with the unwieldy title *True Facts Concerning The Untimely & Heroic Deaths of Major Francisco Patricio Donaju & Doña M. Dolores Cortés With Official Conclusions*. It will be noticed that Guzmán gave only two of the five victims title billing. There is even less equality in death than in life, and to assure a proper memorial it is essential to die in the right place, preferably on home ground. If the explosion had occurred in Boston, most attention would have gone to the "distinguished physician Dr. James Edwards Esterbrook, late of this Commonwealth." But the unfortunate doctor perished too far from home to receive his due publicity. Still, he fared better than two of his companions. Captain Guzmán portrayed Margot Laurier as an international swindler with seditious connections, and in so far as was possible he ignored Elvira Campos, feeling that the presence of a common harlot on the scene lessened the dignity of his main characters.

Despite Guzmán's diligence, the report was long delayed. Not only was information hard to find, but weeks went by before he could bring himself to believe the "true facts" about Doña Dolores Cortés. For a time the unhappy man thought himself the butt of a gigantic practical joke and he could not fathom why some of the most influential men in the country were conspiring to make a fool of him.

If ordinary citizens of Guzmán's bailiwick had told him the fantastic tales he was hearing about this woman, he would have clapped them into jail without a second's hesitation. But the men he interviewed in Mexico City were bankers, judges, and even cabinet ministers. Who was he, a worm of a provincial policeman, to call them liars? If such personages had told him that Mount Popocatepetl was made of Chihuahua cheese, he would have been compelled to nod his head solemnly and murmur, "Sí, señores. I have often smelled it myself." So he sat in their offices, balancing his sombrero awkwardly on his lap and trying to maintain a proper air of respect, while each one told him the same incredible story. He longed to point rudely to his right eye and say, "I'm Columbus! You'll damn well have to show me!"

When speaking officially with important persons, Guzmán usually had trouble keeping his mind on the questions that were supposed to be his business. There were so many other things to remember! He knew he must never spit on the floor or flick cigar ashes there, as he did in his own headquarters and at home. He had to be careful where he scratched himself and realized he must not dig his ear with his little finger. Such preoccupations crowded all other thoughts from his mind, and he always finished in a state of amnesia. But now, probing the history of Doña Dolores Cortés, he listened intently, doubting but goggle-eyed, like a child who is old enough to scorn fairy tales but is nevertheless fascinated by them. After each interview he looked again at a small tintype photograph of this woman, trying vainly to reconcile the gentle but plain face with the story just told him. She was elderly, with wide-set eyes, intelligent in expression yet shyly sweet—a lady, a gentlewoman, a virginal maiden aunt as sheltered from the world as velvet flowers under a glass bell. "Why do they lie to me?" he asked himself desperately. "They are lying or the camera was! I am not taken in. I have my eye-teeth!"

So that fragile lady nearly proved to be a reef upon which the whole investigation foundered. (She would have thoroughly enjoyed Guzmán's bewilderment. Her chief delight lay in confounding the pretentious, and she was one of the world's great specialists in doing it.) Yet eventually Guzmán was compelled to belief and could no longer doubt the sincerity of the woman's mourners and their unconcealed grief.

Dimly Guzmán realized that this gray spinster, who had never set foot on a stage, was the most magnificent actress Mexico had ever produced. She was incomparable, a genius to rank with Bernhardt and Duse. But Doña Dolores needed no theater for her performances; the world was her private playhouse, and in it she assumed whatever role she chose. Like many great actresses, she had one star vehicle which was an audience favorite, and she repeated it often. Yet her versatility seemed limitless and she could shed one personality for another as skillfully as a repertory artist can play a dozen characters in a dozen nights. Those who met her became unwitting and unsuspecting actors in an outrageous make-believe with which she gulled and exposed the most celebrated men of her country. And they loved her for it—an idea utterly incomprehensible to Guzmán. In the captain's experience, men who were duped invariably responded with anger or even hate. Doña Dolores made fools of hundreds. She laid bare their avarice, revealed how little pride they possessed, still they loved her, and some, at the mere mention of her name, swallowed hard and blinked quickly. Guzmán shrugged again, accepting what he could not understand.

After the hurdle of believing in Doña Dolores, the rest of his work was routine. He gathered and sifted data, traced meetings and connections as well as he could, then turned to the most important task of police work, which is not investigation but creative writing. Being a successful officer, Guzmán had, of course, that natural talent for producing fiction which is mandatory to the profession. His *True Facts* is a masterpiece, and many who are today engaged in law-enforcement could profit from studying its technique and content. Surprisingly, it is almost entirely Guzmán's own work, although he hired an impoverished professor from the University of Guanajuato to polish the language and correct the spelling, since Guzmán himself spoke the dialect of the Mexican *bajío* region and frequently confused "v" with "b" and "s" with "z."

The report is nearly perfect. Its turgid prose, congealed with lumps of official jargon, has the boring ring of manifest truth, and its stylistic devices are marvels. When Guzmán has absolutely no evidence to back up a point, he writes, "After carefully weighing all pertinent data, it became apparent beyond all possible doubt that . . ." This, in the manuscript, means he is taking a shot in the dark. All facts he cannot discover are "immaterial to the case" or "beyond the subject of our inquiry." When he has seized upon an unsupported belief which suits his purpose, he entrenches it behind the barbed wire of "Having ruled out all other possibilities, we are forced to conclude that . . ."

Guzmán's unerring eye never strays from the target. His task, he knew, was not to discover truth but to provide explanations, and while doing this to create villains and heroes for public entertainment. He was dealing with two highly connected victims. They must be glorified to the full satisfaction of their admirers; the others could shift for themselves.

He tells us first (and quite correctly) what his wife had told him: a spiritist meeting was in progress. After commenting gravely about the idiocy and impiety of such a thing, he continues: "Carefully weighing all pertinent data, it is apparent beyond all possible doubt that the tragedy was caused by an explosion of illuminating gas and was entirely accidental in origin. This is according to expert opinion." Guzmán was his own expert; the sputter and hiss of gas lamps always made him nervous, and he had never trusted the things.

Having explained the cause and the occasion, a lesser man would have ended his report, and such a man would never have risen above the rank of sergeant. Guzmán became a major six years after writing his masterpiece. (He still held that rank when a band of tattered rebels strung him up naked and dead on a eucalyptus tree.)

Only the highlights of Guzmán's virtuoso performance need be given here: Major Donaju ("a keen-eyed officer and certainly no believer in ghosts") became aware of the nefarious activities of a spiritist charlatan called Margot Laurier. Precisely when his keen eye fell on her is not clear, but perhaps it was in the capital, where she had once lived. That, however, is not "material to the case." The major set out to expose this fraudulent medium who was not only a swindler but "an undoubted plotter against the Mexican government. . . . The daring major acted alone, confiding nothing of his undercover work to his fellow officers." (And that, thought Guzmán, is God's truth! The red-haired hero remained an enigma. When men best acquainted with him attempted a description, their words seemed to apply not to a person but to a machine. They were familiar with Donaju only as workers at a country depot are familiar with a locomotive which arrives daily on a certain schedule, consumes a given amount of fuel, makes identifiable sounds, then departs for unseen destinations. People did not know Donaju; they only knew about him, and the sum of their knowledge was not a man. How could a person as flamboyant as the major live for nearly forty-five years and keep his private life such a secret that until he died no one realized there was anything hidden?

Where did he go when he disappeared in the evening? Whom did he visit on his unexplained journeys?)

Donaju's suspicion of fraud and subversion easily explained his presence at the séance; now Guzmán had to account for Doña Dolores. "The major met this esteemed and lovely lady seven years ago. Since they seem to have had no subsequent meetings, it is apparent that deep mutual regard flowered quickly between these two remarkable and patriotic people." So when the major was on the verge of exposing Margot Laurier, he naturally called on Doña Dolores for expert help. She was, after all, an unimpeachable authority on hoaxes and impostures. (The captain, recalling the lady's powerful friends, stated the matter more delicately than this.) "Together they attended the séance, expecting to unmask Señora Laurier, but tragedy chanced to intervene. Thus, though their deaths were accidental—and *certainly* require no further police investigation—they nevertheless gave their lives in the line of duty, loyally serving our beloved country and its well-beloved President, His Excellency Don Porfirio Díaz, the Hero of Peace."

The supporting characters in Guzmán's drama are quickly dismissed. Dr. James Esterbrook is a respectable but gullible American being bilked of his dollars. The whore Elvira Campos is "either a duped client or perhaps an accomplice. Her exact role is not material to the case." Little Brother appears as a half-wit servant who was "painstakingly" interrogated. Guzmán's choice of that adverb is to be applauded.

The captain encountered difficulty in keeping Tomás D'Aquisto off stage, for the magician had been seen and recognized in Guanajuato that week and it was commonly known that he had called on Señora Laurier at least once. D'Aquisto was a minor international celebrity, the foremost vaudeville conjurer of his generation and not a man to be ignored. Much worse, he was still alive and might at any moment step forward to contradict anything Guzmán invented about him. How did he fit in? Guzmán did not know, although he learned that since D'Aquisto's sudden retirement from public performance he had devoted his energy to the exposure of spiritist and psychic chicanery. He had challenged the world's practitioners of occult art by offering three thousand English pounds to anyone who could materialize the wispiest fragment of a dead soul or establish provable communication with Them. A score of fakirs more greedy than wise accepted this bait, and one by one D'Aquisto revealed their tricks, catching many an embarrassed ghost with its cheesecloth and phosphorous showing. Surely his visit to Guanajuato involved Señora Laurier.

But the magician had disappeared, vanishing as mysteriously as he once did from a locked cabinet in the middle of a stage, so Guzmán solved the problem by mentioning D'Aquisto several times, but always vaguely, leaving him as a misty eminence hovering above the city like powder smoke on the Day of the Dead. He also included a brief biography of D'Aquisto in one of the report's many appendices. (The appendices were invaluable. They made the report even duller and so bulky that many people admired it but wisely refrained from attempting to read it.)

The remarkable document ends by demonstrating the link between spiritism and rebellion. Guzmán performs astounding feats of logic and handles evidence as dexterously as D'Aquisto could juggle a pack of playing cards. "It is well known that one of the most seditious rascals plaguing our country today is prompted to treachery by the unholy advice of a Ouija board!" (He refers to Francisco I. Madero, later a president and martyr of Mexico, who was indeed advised by a planchette that he would attain his country's highest office. He and others who eventually forced the dictator from power were fascinated by automatic writing and other such practices.) "These traitors, lacking scientific logic, turn naturally to mysticism. Although no Ouija board was actually found on the table at the scene of the accident, its earlier presence is inescapably inferred from all other circumstances. Such paraphernalia are the stock-in-trade of mediums, and the lack of anything being found clearly shows that something had been removed—either by the feeble-minded servant or Unknown Accomplices. Besides, if there were not traitorous goings-on, why would Major Donaju and Doña Dolores Cortés have been investigating? Their presence cannot have been coincidental; a scientific mind will not accept this or any other coincidence. Effect follows cause. Thus, having eliminated all other possibilities, we are forced to the conclusion that . . ." And so on.

The captain, in the fashion of his day, blindly worshiped a scatterbrained goddess called Science. In this he emulated the brutal clique surrounding the dictator, a group calling themselves the *cientificos*. But his rejection of coincidence is mere whistling in the dark or perhaps is a boot to cover an Achilles heel, for near the end of *True Facts* it becomes clear that the magic word "coincidence" is the very Pater Noster of the scientific religion and the New Universe simply cannot operate without it. Guzmán writes:

> Certain circumstances have aroused the imaginations of superstitious individuals, and we shall now quell these rumors once and for all. The fact that the explosion occurred at midnight, a time stupidly called the "witching hour," is mere coincidence. Accidents happen at every second of the day and night; some must take place exactly at midnight and by chance this one did. That this particular midnight was on the Day of the Dead, a holiday fraught with superstition, is only further coincidence. That a séance was in progress means nothing: séances are not excepted from the Laws of Chance.
>
> It is true that the scene was a mansion whose dark and evil reputation dates back to the days of the Inquisition. This has

caused much foolish babble. An accident must happen *somewhere*, and we are confident it can be mathematically proven that a house two hundred years old will be the site of four times as many fatal accidents as a house fifty years old, and two hundred times as many as a house one year old. That is plain logic.

The only eyewitness was an ignorant man totally unfamiliar with the appearance and behavior of exploding gas and who happens, by unlucky chance, to be a man suffering psychic delusions. It is mere bad luck that there was not a more reliable witness.

All this is the simplest Science and it astonishes us that everyone does not grasp it immediately. However, some persons always incline toward eerie nonsense, rather than accepting the clarity of obvious and provable facts.

Guzmán was sincere—or rather he achieved sincerity after the manuscript was completed. During the investigation he was often troubled by a strange doubt, a nagging voice inside him which could be ignored but not silenced. Whenever he rode past the ruined mansion he paused to gaze uneasily at the gaping windows of the second story, now merely holes in the stone face of the building, and although they were open it struck him that they did not seem to admit sunlight to the room beyond. The room, Guzmán thought, where They had gathered, held their peculiar rite, and died so suddenly. (The victims had become "They" to him, and "They" were inseparable, joined in a unity he felt but could not explain. He found it increasingly difficult to consider one without considering all who had formed that circle. Perhaps the sight of the clasped hands had impressed him more deeply than he had realized.)

From childhood the captain had known the grim history of this house, but until now he had seldom recalled the hair-raising legends connected with it. A moneylender named David Espinosa, one of the early Jews to emigrate to Mexico, had built it as a residence and counting house only a generation or two after the conquest. The massive *cantera* blocks of its walls were quarried below the town, then borne two miles up the steep slope of the gorge on the naked backs of Indians, many of whom died beneath their burdens—as many always did when a new palace was erected or a cathedral raised to the glory of God. The moneylender prospered with the young city, and soon half the Christians of Guanajuato were hopelessly in his debt, an intolerable situation which quickly ended with the arrival of the Holy Inquisition. The inquisitors seized Espinosa, his family, his property, and his wicked account books. They found and appropriated a fortune buried in two cryptlike vaults in the cellar. The unlucky Jew had dug these rooms as strongrooms; now they served as dungeons for himself and his sons and daughters. Despite the most ingenious and prolonged persuasion, the inquisitors' gains were entirely material. They could extort nothing else from Espinosa—not a confession, a conversion, or the salvation of his deluded soul. But one of his daughters went mad under torture and shrieked out a long admission of unspeakable rites practiced in the house, a fearful list of crimes and sacrileges ranging from lewdness with the devil to the sacramental drinking of Christian blood. The shocked city could hardly wait for a public burning, but this was denied them. Somehow poison was smuggled into the dungeons, and the family cheated the town of its entertainment.

The Inquisition's existence in New Spain was brief, but during those years the house continued in use, and although it was later sold to a noble Spanish family, the name "House of the Inquisitor" clung to it. Other stories evolved, stories of curses, of violent death mysteriously overtaking heirs and owners; and the grisly tales of the Inquisition were repeated to each new generation.

Guzmán was highly susceptible to accounts of antique torture, although in his daily work he frequently witnessed the inflicting of pain and sometimes administered it himself. The pleas and whimpers of suspects left him utterly unmoved. Such things were routine—not pleasant, but indispensable for the preservation of law, order, and property. Afterward he could eat a hearty supper with a clear conscience, chewing his *carne asada* blissfully, unmindful of the toothless mouth of a captive he had questioned in the afternoon. Present duty, which is always just and necessary, is very different from the terrors and cruelties of the past. Inhuman acts, in aging, acquire a romantic flavor of horror and mystery which sets them apart from more familiar atrocities.

Guzmán, scowling at the mansion, shuddered inwardly at thoughts of black-hooded judges, of hot pincers and autos-da-fé, just as the electrician of a death chamber may be sickened by a tale of the guillotine or a modern general may be honestly appalled at the fiendishness of Genghis Khan's pyramid of skulls and see no parallel between this and so common an event as an air raid. To Guzmán, his own headquarters was merely a workshop. But the House of the Inquisitor, with its grotesque carvings and menacing gargoyles, inspired his imagination. If ghosts existed (preposterous idea!), this was surely a place where they would congregate—bleeding specters floating from the cellar at night or, in more fleshly form, creeping up wet stairs to leave distorted handprints behind. "It ought to be haunted," Guzmán said, half aloud. No wonder the explosion had aroused so much idiotic superstition; no wonder some people crossed themselves as they passed the sealed entrance. He cursed Margot Laurier for choosing to hold her doomed séance in such a building and on such a night. "Fools!" Guzmán exclaimed. But he began to avoid the street on which the troublesome house stood.

He had other difficulties. Often when he was working on the report a clear, hard-etched memory of the faces of those five would flash into his mind. He remembered them as he had first seen them in the harsh morning light, their expressions so disturbingly calm and unsurprised. Or was it merely that? Had there been a look of expectation and even of relief? The more he pondered, the more certain he became that they had been relieved to die, just as the tortured captives once imprisoned in the same house had welcomed death as an ultimate mercy. To welcome death . . . It seemed perverted to Guzmán. How could such a thing be? He was sure his own desire to survive, whatever the suffering, was unquenchable. In a few years he would learn otherwise.

Even after all available material had been gathered and Guzmán had begun his actual writing, his uncomfortable misgivings continued and were undoubtedly increased by the conditions under which he had to work. His office was confused and noisy. Loud-mouthed men in russet uniforms tramped in and out all day long with their spurs clanking; there was the clatter of rifles being racked against the wall and there were always the idiotic jokes and questions of his subordinates. Finding it difficult to concentrate, he often wrote at night, sitting alone at a desk in the cavernous reception room of the Governors' Palace. This wing of the huge building was unused after sunset and utterly deserted except for a servant who slept on the floor below. Its silence and darkness were awesome, and Guzmán's oil lamp made only a tiny island of flickering light. A more sensitive man or a man less familiar with the vast palace would have felt an immediate sense of isolation and foreboding. But Guzmán was not troubled at first. Then, as he became more deeply involved with the subject of his report, he began to notice that the vaulted stone ceilings echoed and re-echoed the least noise, giving a strangely lonely and hollow quality to even the scratching of his pen, the clearing of his own throat—Not sounds, he thought one night, but the ghosts of sounds. When he laughed at himself for being fanciful, his laughter came back with a peculiar mocking echo, and the idea continued to bother him. That week a vague apprehension invaded him. It was almost—he scoffed at the notion—a fear.

One night he sat alone with a jumbled collection of newspaper clippings from which he had gleaned facts for a short biography of Tomás D'Aquisto. He had just completed this entry, basing its bone-dry prose on the style of the *New Madrid Encyclopedia,* and now as he reread it he had no premonition that anything unusual was about to happen.

D'AQUISTO, TOMÁS. Born Lisbon, Portugal (?) in 1848 (?) of unknown parents. No information about early life. No Lisbon police record, but the subject once said that he was arrested in that city at the age of seven (?) as a pickpocket and cutpurse. Toured Europe as an apprentice to Carlos Cantari, a stage magician of prominence. After Cantari's death, the subject made his debut as Zantana the Great, eventually appearing in the largest theaters of Europe and the Americas, performing astounding feats of illusion, including demonstrations of apparent telepathy. Offstage he denies any psychic power. Has executed fantastic escapes from chains, chests, etc., and his seemingly miraculous reappearances strongly indicate that the subject is double-jointed or physically abnormal in some other way.

In 1873 he married his stage assistant, Miss Miranda Downey of London (?), who died suddenly after a performance in 1890. The subject retired from the stage then and has since been an exposer of spiritist fraud, assisting the London police in the famed "Green Ghost" swindle.

D'Aquisto has no permanent address. For reasons known to the Guanajuato police, his present whereabouts cannot be revealed in this report.

Frowning, Guzmán crossed out the last sentence. Where the devil had the man vanished to? No trace. No trace at all. It was positively uncanny. The captain held a photograph of the magician near the lamp and studied it closely, glaring at the enlarged picture as though he could force it to speak. The magician's face, Guzmán decided, was dramatic and disconcerting. Its harsh features compelled the attention but were in no way appealing. There was something cruel and Moorish about the narrow nose with its flaring nostrils. Could D'Aquisto be an Arab and not really Portuguese? Gazing at the thin sardonic lips, the captain thought of a Barbary pirate. Yet, at least in the photograph, the man's complexion was starkly white, a paleness which made an arresting contrast with the black tilted eyebrows. A face carved from white flint, a man capable of all treacheries, of any evil. Guzmán, fascinated and repelled, was unable to take his eyes away. Then suddenly his head jerked and he cried out, "Who's there?"

Beyond the rim of lamplight the darkness was empty and silent. Yet he was certain he had caught a glimpse of a man, in fact of the magician himself, standing only a few yards away, watching him. "Who is it?" he shouted again. No answer came and he peered into the gloom, which he was sure concealed an intruder who had approached as stealthily as a puma. With a shaking hand he lifted the lamp high, faintly revealing even the farthest corners of the room. "Some trick of the light," he said at last. But the impression, though fleeting, had been absolutely definite: a tall, gaunt man in a cape. Not a fingertip cape such as Guzmán himself wore, but a cape that fell to the knees and had a winged collar. The magician—dressed exactly as in the photograph.

Guzmán stood behind the desk, bewildered and alarmed. How could the man have crept up so quietly, and—far stranger—how could he have disappeared in an instant? Then an explanation occurred to the captain and he sank into his chair with a mutter of relief, assuring himself that an optical illusion had been caused by his staring too fixedly at the picture. His eyes had simply transferred the image, projecting it against the darkness in the way of a magic lantern. "Amazing what the human eye can do!" he told himself. "I could have sworn—" He was overwhelmed with gratitude that a scientific mind could so quickly solve all mysteries and provide explanations that were truly marvelous.

He glanced once more at the spot where he had believed the intruder to have stood and decided at once that further work that night would bring eyestrain and probably a headache. In the few minutes it took to gather his papers he convinced himself that he had not really believed in the silent watcher for a second. "Remarkable, but I realized even then it was some sort of illusion." He picked up the pistol he had unconsciously drawn and replaced it in his holster.

This was the first but not the last of his unnerving experiences. On other nights when the wind swept down from the high slope of the Sierra Madre, rattling shutters and causing the lamp flame to waver, he found himself imagining another darkened room, a circle of chalk-faced communicants hushed in the presence of the dead whose amorphous shapes hovered above them. The impression was so vivid that he almost believed himself to be among them, and, closing his eyes, he strained to hear whispered words. When such moments came upon him, he dropped his pen and rang a bell to summon the servant for some unnecessary task, and always the approaching footfalls, the shuffling of sandals on tile, had an unnatural sound. As the soft steps drew near, Guzmán felt a tightening of the muscles in his throat, then swallowed quickly when he was sure that the man emerging from the blackness of the corridor was indeed the servant and not another visitor. While he ordered the lamp to be refilled or its shade cleaned, he inwardly cursed himself for a coward. "Jittery as a woman! Superstitious as an Indian! This is nonsense, nonsense!" Once he suddenly banged his fist on the desk so hard that the startled servant dropped the lamp, smashing it, and no more work could be done that night. Although Guzmán berated the man and slapped him on both cheeks, he was secretly delighted to have an excuse to leave early. He went straight to a cantina, got roaring drunk, and challenged all other customers to test his bravery. As an act of self-discipline he forced himself to work one more night in the reception hall, then finished the report in his office, despite the interruptions.

Gradually his confidence grew, and when at last he studied the completed manuscript of *True Facts*, so learnedly and admirably edited by the professor, he was swept away by its patriotism and the force of its argument. Captain Guzmán discovered to his amazement that he had accomplished an almost impossible task: alone and unaided he had completely convinced himself of something he did not believe at all.

The governor was enthusiastic about the thickness of the report and even read several pages of it. "Astounding! What a mass—that is to say, a wealth of detail!" He promptly ordered a thousand copies printed at public expense, which was not really unusual, for during his term of office more than five hundred different books were financed by the state treasury, earning the governor a reputation as a patron of authors and libraries. The fact that his brother owned a printing company was what Guzmán would have described as "coincidental."

The captain, basking in the promise of quick promotion, gloated when he heard praise of the report's several appendices. ("My dear José, you not only left no stone unturned, you upended every pebble on the beach.") One of these is a series of biographies of no less than seventy-four people. To gain wordage, Guzmán included even Doña Dolores' cook and the collateral descendants of Major Donaju to the second degree. In composing these entries he employed a variety of styles. Some, based on the encyclopedia, are like his account of Tomás D'Aquisto.

Others read like the program notes which are written to amuse impatient audiences during intermissions; still others, those of his principals, are cast into more detailed form and today would be called "case histories." These last are more or less factual, but they suffer the failure of all such attempts. Case histories, even the best of them, resemble their human subjects only as the dregs of a wine bottle resemble a vineyard. The lives of all these people slipped from Guzmán's fingers, as elusive as the ghosts he imagined in the Governors' Palace.

Guzmán soon forgot his doubts and questions. He suppressed all memory of those moments when, despite the halter of science, he had longed to plunge toward the supernatural and toss aside all he called reasonable. With a mind as simple and unfettered as that of Pablo Sanchez the candy-seller he would then submit to what his emotions, against all logic, told him was true. He forgot this, and even forgot that he had once written another version of *True Facts*, a complete version that was only three sentences long. At the time he did this he told himself it was only a joke, that he would present it to the governor, who had a sense of humor, and watch the consternation on the man's face, then, with a loud laugh, whip out his real report from behind his back. But this did not happen. Somehow the presence of the peculiar page in his desk made him uncomfortable and one day he suddenly seized it, crumpled it, and tossed it into the charcoal brazier which warmed his office. The words he burned were these: "*No man knows what happened in that house and no one will ever know. But I think those five strange people—and they were indeed strange—were destroyed by the Dead they had summoned. I think they pressed too far and so they were . . . obliterated . . . sent to join those they were seeking. . . .*"

3

Few men have had the privilege—or the misfortune—of coming face to face with the devil. Martin Luther suffered such an encounter and drove the fiend from his chamber by hurling an inkwell. Saint John the Theologian also observed Satan and later described him as a seven-headed sea monster with ten horns. In Saint John's account the devil spoke blasphemies in Greek. Since reports of this kind are rare and astonishing, they always command a large audience.

Pablo Sanchez quickly discovered this. In the cantinas of Guanajuato he repeated his story, embellishing the tale with every trick of the actor's craft, rolling his eyes, shuddering, arching his fingers into claws and twisting his face into grimaces which grew more hideous with each glass of tequila the entranced listeners bought him. The story changed with each telling and at last the dripping blood of Hidalgo, the mysterious white light, the hunchback, all the things Pablo had really seen or believed he had seen, became mere preliminaries to a bone-chilling climax: the entrance of the devil, galloping up to observe his handiwork. "His cape was like the wings of a bat—a vampire bat! And the horse breathed fire!" Pablo was now sure that Tomás D'Aquisto was Satan himself and felt foolish when he secretly recalled that he had first mistaken the strange horseman for a human being, a blunder in identification, for upon reflection he realized that D'Aquisto must have been the devil.

Pablo arrived at this conclusion by the same logical method Captain Guzmán had employed: the process of elimination. Since the event was preternatural, the devil's presence was mandatory. The hunchback was a mere imp, Pablo himself was not the devil, and there was only one other observer of the scene: the dark rider, who, therefore, had to be Satan. There was simply no other possibility. Guzmán, who thought the candy-seller to be a creature of pure instinct and superstition, would have been astonished to discover that Pablo's reasoning was as scientific as his own.

Also, the devil's entrance was necessary for purely literary purposes. Pablo was gaining fame as a storyteller and he basked in the respectful attention of his comrades. But the story of the Inquisitor's House had to compete with a hundred other ghostly legends that were current in the city. One was especially popular, a grim tale of the Weeper, a female specter who haunted the murky byways and alleys at night, sobbing piteously as she recalled the cruelty and deceitfulness of men. In life she had been mistress of a rich man and had borne him sons, believing that one day he would make her his wife. But when she learned the truth, that he was marrying another, she turned into Medea, first murdering her own sons; then, in the presence of her betrayer, she drove a dagger into her heart, and ever since has prowled the city's darkness, searching out male victims, appearing often as an enticing young girl but sometimes as an old woman begging charity. Whatever her guise, any man who followed her was lured to his death, and many of Pablo's friends had suffered narrow escapes.

Against such formidable competition Pablo presented the devil, and his success was immediate. "When I saw him I crouched in the doorway, terrified, trying to say 'My Jesus, mercy!' for I thought the end had come and I remembered my sins. Then, when I made the sign of the cross, the devil gave a horrible cry—like this, '*Ayiiii!*' The ghost horse reared and they raced away toward the caves where the mummies of the Old Ones are buried." The eyes of the men gathered around him widened as they thought of those caverns near the town where long ago the Indians had placed the bodies of their dead, setting them upright in a grim line. The cold dryness of the mountain air had preserved the corpses for generations, and they remained as one of the wonders of the country. Pablo continued in a hoarse whisper. "I think there is an entrance to hell through those caves, and the devil passes in and out at his pleasure. How else can we explain things that happen here? Has there ever been a city nearer hell than Guanajuato? The devil will have no surprises for a poor man who has lived in this town!" His listeners, dark-faced men whose thin bodies shivered under ragged serapes, nodded gravely, understanding the political meaning of Pablo's words. They glanced over their shoulders to make sure no strangers were in the cantina, then nodded in silent conspiracy, their passive faces giving no sign of the flame of vengeance and rebellion that burned within.

Pablo never attempted to describe the anguish he had heard in D'Aquisto's voice that night and never repeated the words the magician had spoken—they were incongruous, they did not fit the rest of the tale, and eventually he forgot them. But once, years later, while attending mass at the Valenciana church, his eyes fell on a painting of the martyrdom of Saint Andrew, a gaunt body stretched on an X-shaped cross. The saint's pale face, twisted in agony, was so uncannily like D'Aquisto's that suddenly the scene in front of the Inquisitor's House flashed through his memory, the recollection more vivid than the experience. He gasped as his faith in the story he had told so often now faltered. Stripped of fantasy, he recalled exactly what he had witnessed. Was it possible that he had not seen Satan, but only a grief-stricken human being at a moment of unbearable pain? Looking quickly away, he fixed his gaze on a statue of the Blessed Guadalupe, whose plaster smile mocked him. "It was the devil!" he muttered angrily. "I saw him ride toward hell!"

꒛ 38 ꒦

But if D'Aquisto was bound for hell that night, then hell is not the brimstone vault which seethed in Pablo's imagination. It is only a familiar and lonely place whose worst torment is its terrible privacy, a region of the mind that no man shares with another, and hours spent there mark the face as indelibly as baptism is said to mark the soul.

Standing alone in the street, watching tiny tongues of fire lick the walnut beams of the Inquisitor's House, Tomás D'Aquisto shook with grief, cursing fate or luck or God—whatever force had led him to this spot, to the threshold of discovery, and then had barred the door. At a glance he knew that none of the five in that house still lived; they had gone, eluding him at the last moment, taking with them the knowledge he longed for and which had again been denied him. He saw in that instant a future as hopeless as his past had been. Against all reason he would go on searching, driven by the unanswered riddle as long as his life continued.

The stench of death by fire, sweet and dreadful, invaded D'Aquisto's nostrils. It was unbearable to stand helpless, viewing the scene of his defeat, and he was overwhelmed by a sudden compulsion to flight, to escape this city which was now hateful beyond all places. He leaped into the saddle and rode like a madman, spurring the horse until blood flowed, plunging through black streets and across dark plazas while straggling pedestrians, returning late from their graveyard picnics, flung themselves against walls to escape, crying out in alarm and shouting curses after him. He heard neither them nor the furious whistle of a night watchman who mistook him for a fleeing desperado and fired three shots at him. The bullets went wide of the mark, but now the horse bolted in panic, iron-shod hoofs hammering the stones of a boulevard leading from the city, past a silent church at the edge of town and a cemetery where bonfires still blazed and guitar music echoed thinly among the marble and granite tombs. They raced into open country, charging blindly down a narrow trail which snaked the rim of the gorge, a precipice where the land fell away to naked rock. D'Aquisto clung to the animal's wet neck, letting it take him where it would, relief surging through him as he put distance between himself and the city. At last, when the horse could go no farther, they halted in a hawthorn grove near the ruins of an abandoned hacienda. D'Aquisto dried his mount's lathered flanks and led the horse inside the crumbling walls, where they could spend the night sheltered from the mountain wind. They remained there until dawn, the horse too exhausted to be frightened by the howling wolves on the nearby slope. D'Aquisto did not sleep. Wrapped in his cape, he lay staring up at the stars, which glittered icily in the clear air of the plateau. Gradually his anger at his failure in Guanajuato subsided, leaving behind a sense of deadness and futility. "Where do I begin again?" he asked himself. "Where next?"

With the first light the magician and the limping horse started a slow, aimless journey northward toward a barren land whose settlements were scattered and whose roads were infested with bandits calling themselves rebels and with rebels who were forced to live as highwaymen. D'Aquisto gave no thought to the hazards of the road or the difficulties of survival. His future meant nothing to him, and he rode like a man in a trance, his eyes wandering the arid mesas, feeling nothing as he watched a hawk soar in the empty sky. It did not occur to him that day that he had left money, clothes, and baggage in a room in Guanajuato. He carried some gold pieces, and tucked in his belt was a brass pistol which looked like a toy but could be fired with deadly accuracy.

Early that afternoon he met a pack train bound for Guanajuato, and the muleteers sold him food for his horse. When they questioned him about his destination he shook his head silently, and after he left they pointed to their temples, murmuring, "*Loco. Muy loco.*" He slept that night in a dry gully.

As the next day wore on his mind began to reassert itself. He became conscious of soreness, of thirst, and aware of the dry wind filling his nostrils with grit. Against his will he suddenly longed for a glass of brandy and a clean bed; the demands of survival and even the desire for comfort were rekindled in him. He was astonished by his own fickleness. Only yesterday he had wished for death, believed he was beyond despair, and imagined riding into a vast nowhere to disappear forever. His love of the theatrical gave a temporary grandeur to such emotions, but now he found himself thinking dreamily of hot onion soup and a steaming plate of the polenta he had loved in childhood. D'Aquisto frowned, annoyed at being plucked from the depths of pure tragedy by the mundane growling of his stomach. The awakening of his appetite changed his thinking, and he began to see the disaster at the Inquisitor's House in a new perspective. The grief that had seized him that night now appeared exaggerated, a self-dramatization. "After all," he said, "it was not a tragedy, but only another negative experiment. And there will be others."

What were the victims to him? He had detested the red-haired major, a swashbuckling sadist whose demise was of undoubted benefit to humanity. The whore Elvira Campos was a worn-out creature bound to the major by a mutual hate stronger than any love could have been. The Boston doctor had interested D'Aquisto only as a curiosity, a Yankee eccentric with an evil twist of character, another of those peculiar New England mystics who should have been born in Tibet, not Massachusetts. The distorted passions of these three were within the scope of D'Aquisto's imagination but beyond his understanding. For the other two women, Margot Laurier and Doña Dolores Cortés, he felt a genuine sympathy, but friendship with the former had been denied him and he hardly knew the latter. They were part of an experiment, nothing more. His grief had been not for any of them, but for himself and for loss of the answer he had hoped to learn.

Now D'Aquisto scanned the horizon for any sign of an inn or at least a hospitable ranch house. The desolate hills, parched by autumn, seemed to stretch on endlessly, their scarred slopes spiky with cactus and jagged with sharp protrusions of gray rock. "The end of the world," D'Aquisto said aloud. Yet he did not consider turning back: Guanajuato was still abhorrent to him; the bleakness of the country fitted his mood. In the west the sky flamed vermilion and the blunt peaks of the Sierra Madre had darkened to a wall of slate as D'Aquisto approached a cluster of adobe huts near a muddy stream, a wretched hamlet whose dog packs greeted him with ferocious snarls but retreated at the sound of his voice and skulked after him as he rode on toward a building much larger than its neighbors. A faded signboard said: THE DRAGONS OF THE QUEEN. HOTEL & CANTINA. TRAVELERS WEL—the latter half of "Welcome" had been blasted away by a shotgun.

Halting uncertainly, D'Aquisto studied the gaunt inn with suspicion. A skinny sow with a brood of sucklings nursed near the half-open door, and in the fading daylight a few chickens pecked at a garbage heap. The Dragons of the Queen did not inspire confidence, and D'Aquisto remembered a story that the whore Elvira Campos had told him only a few days before. At one time she had been an inmate of a roadside hotel which must have resembled this one—an isolated backwoods inn where solitary travelers were sometimes done to death in their sleep for the sake of their money and possessions. The landlord continued this practice for years, selecting victims who would be little missed or those whose whereabouts (like D'Aquisto's) were difficult to trace. These unfortunates simply vanished, as did many travelers on badly patrolled roads. On rare occasions, when the authorities investigated, it was always decided that the victims had been waylaid by highwaymen either before or after reaching the inn. Such investigations were a farce; Major Donaju headed the rural police in that district, and the murderous landlord divided his gains with him. Donaju knew that the patio of the inn was a secret graveyard, but he was not a squeamish man. In fact, on the night of his last visit to the Inquisitor's House he had worn a beautiful gold watch that had once been the timepiece of an unlucky and unsuspecting wayfarer. (Elvira Campos had recounted the details of these crimes in a flat, listless voice, and her utter indifference to the horrors she had witnessed appalled the magician more than the events themselves. He realized then that, although she still moved, breathed, and spoke, she had really ceased to live long ago. It was well she had perished in the fire. She had no further interest in the world, and only the dead had been able to arouse her.)

Night was coming swiftly now, and D'Aquisto, chilled by the rising wind, ignored his misgivings, dismounted, and entered the uninviting hotel, a square, squat building of two stories with an unpaved courtyard which was flanked on one side by a line of dingy bedrooms and on the other by a thatch-roofed stable. Inside the door and to D'Aquisto's left was a murky barroom whose mud walls were blackened by the smoke of rushlights, reeds floating in lard, serving as candles. The inn appeared to be deserted except for three men who sprawled at a rickety table drinking pulque from a leather bottle as they played a silent game of dominoes. The rushlight flickered on their brown pock-marked faces, and as D'Aquisto's eyes became accustomed to the gloomy dimness he saw that they were dressed in *charro* costumes, the fringed, flamboyant clothing of Mexican cowboys. But their outfits had long ago lost all traces of elegance; they were worn, seedy, and patched. Intent on their play, the men were not aware that a stranger had arrived until D'Aquisto cleared his throat and said, "Good evening, gentlemen."

Their heads snapped toward him, and one man's hand dropped to a holster strapped to his belt. No one spoke while they eyed him warily, as alert and hostile as a trio of jaguars. "Good evening," he repeated firmly. "Is the landlord here?"

"What do you want of him?" It was the largest and best-dressed of the men who spat out the question, his guttural Spanish tinged with an Indian accent.

"I want lodging for myself and shelter for my horse. This is, I believe, a public inn?"

The man stood up, a barrel-chested giant, taller than D'Aquisto, his heavy face covered by thick stubble which spread upward to the line of his cheekbones. "I am the landlord, and we have no rooms. All are filled. *Adiós, compadre.*"

The insolence of the tone galled D'Aquisto, and against good judgment his pride rose to the challenge. "A pity. But I congratulate you on your success. I did not think your hotel would be so popular." The magician abruptly sat down at the nearest table. "I want a drink before going on. Brandy if you have it. Otherwise tequila will do." D'Aquisto was accustomed to having his orders obeyed, and for a moment the eyes of the two men locked; then the landlord nodded reluctantly.

"A drink, then. But the cantina is soon closing." He shouted toward an archway at the rear of the room. "Juana! *Ven acá!*" A young slattern shuffled into the room, a baby clinging to her swollen breast. "Give the señor a tequila before he leaves." Turning his back on D'Aquisto, the landlord resumed the domino game, paying no attention as the woman served D'Aquisto a glass of clear liquid, a dish of salt, and a slice of lemon on a cracked saucer.

The magician downed the tequila in two long, fiery

gulps. Then, humming a little tune, he began to toss the empty glass idly in the air. In a moment he had added the saucer and the lemon slice and was dexterously juggling the three objects in time with his own music. The domino game stopped as one by one the three men at the next table became aware of his performance. The magician hummed louder and faster; then, miraculously, the tequila glass vanished. So did the lemon and the saucer.

"Landlord!" D'Aquisto spoke sternly to the wide-eyed man. "You have taken away my drink, and I was not finished! Give it back!" Reaching out, apparently empty-handed, he removed the lemon slice from behind the landlord's ear, with a quick gesture found the glass under a sombrero on the table, and discovered the saucer floating in mid-air.

"*Dios!*" exclaimed the landlord. "He's the devil's own son!" And he stared at D'Aquisto with childish awe and delight.

The magician pointed to the man on his left. "No wonder you are winning the domino game! Look at this!" From the man's pocket he produced the double six, double five, and double four. "A foxy player for sure."

A quarter of an hour passed while D'Aquisto held his audience spellbound, performing a series of sleight-of-hand tricks most of which were so simple that he had not used them for years. "And now," he said at last, "I must be on my way to find lodging for the night."

As he buttoned his cape the landlord seized him with a heavy hand. "On your way? Jesus, Mary, and Joseph, would you insult my hospitality? There is room for you here." He turned to one of his companions. "Miguelito, take the señor's horse to the stable." D'Aquisto found himself clamped in a crushing bear hug, and the landlord's bristly stubble chafed his cheek. "Forgive me, *amigo!* I thought you were a spy! This inn is out of the way, and strangers who come here are usually snoops or troublemakers. Permit me to introduce myself. I am General Jesús María Valles." He preened himself, expanding his chest and thrusting out his chin to give D'Aquisto a better view of his savage mustache. "Of course you have heard of me. I am none other than El Lobo, the wolf of Guanajuato."

Recognition was obviously expected, and D'Aquisto, who knew nothing of this man, murmured politely, "Ah, yes. I am honored. Perhaps you have heard of me. I am Zantana the Great." The magician awaited the reaction which always followed the announcement of his famous professional name, but his host looked blank, then nodded vaguely. "A pleasure . . . a pleasure."

Food was brought, an unappetizing dish of roast goat and onions which D'Aquisto devoured, mopping up the last trace with a tortilla. "This brandy is excellent." He examined the label of a vintage Napoleon.

"*Gracias.* The dictator of Mexico serves no better." Suddenly the general roared with laughter. "In fact, you might call this a gift from him. For myself, I prefer pulque or tequila. At heart I am a man of simple taste—I think all great leaders are like this."

After eating, D'Aquisto was more than ready for bed, but this was not permitted him. For three hours he performed, repeating his tricks and illusions over and over while El Lobo, the wolf of Guanajuato, howled in delight, pounding his thighs and shouting, "More! More!" A score of sinister men had now gathered in the cantina, cutthroats armed to the teeth, who stared at D'Aquisto in open-mouthed wonder. In the course of the evening he learned that the Dragons of the Queen was not a public inn and Jesús María Valles was not a landlord but the bandit general of a huge stretch of barren territory. He controlled the roads, the mountain passes, and the springs, and was so securely entrenched that the government let him alone, finding it easier to tolerate a brigand than to fight another rebel.

Before midnight D'Aquisto was on the point of collapse, but his host, roaring drunk, showed no sign of halting the entertainment. Tequila in El Lobo's stomach was like steam in a locomotive, and he charged about the room, bellowing, dancing, and trying to imitate the magician. He juggled an empty bottle with a loaded revolver, which exploded when he dropped it, shooting the high heel off a bystander's boot. "You are a genius!" he cried, slapping D'Aquisto's back. "I love you, *compadre*, you son of all the world's whores! Show me again how you make the ace of spades turn up every time!"

At last the weary magician was led to a room at the rear of the inn. An old man who seemed to be El Lobo's body servant brought a jug of water, a fresh bottle of brandy, and an extra serape for the rope bed. He watched the magician warily, then backed out of the room, taking D'Aquisto's boots for polishing. Before tumbling onto the straw shuck mattress, D'Aquisto barricaded the door and placed his small pistol within quick reach. The bandit's affection appeared to be genuine, but at moments a look of malicious cunning had flickered in his eyes and it seemed wise to take precautions. D'Aquisto did not feel any real threat to his safety, yet when he recalled El Lobo's calculating expression he muttered, "There is some plan in his mind. He's up to something."

Despite exhaustion, sleep did not come easily, and when at last it did he was troubled by dreams of alarming reality. He relived his journey to Guanajuato and his adventures there, becoming in the nightmare two people, a participant who spoke and acted, yet at the same time a spectator removed from the scene, watching the events as one watches a stage. He felt again the jerking motion of the train he had ridden from Mexico City, sitting uncomfortably upright on a horsehair seat, irritated by the airlessness and sham splendor of the coach; the gilt scrollwork was sooty and the ornate brass lamps were in dire need of polishing. He drew Margot Laurier's letter from his breast pocket and read it for the tenth time. ". . . If you wish to come to Guanajuato, we will try once more, although I warn you your trip may be useless and you know I promise nothing."

From their first meeting in London he had felt that this woman was no fraud. She might be deluded, even a little mad, but there was no deceit in her. Her sincerity had caused him to travel five thousand miles to this barbaric country whose discomforts were proverbial and whose typhus-bearing fleas bit more fiercely than any in the world.

The train was crowded, and five special cars had been added to accommodate the dictator and his party, who were bound for Guanajuato for the dedication of the country's newest and most elaborate opera house. Soldiers and bodyguards, bristling with arms, patrolled the aisles of every coach, keeping sharp eyes on the hordes of venders and beggars who swarmed aboard at each stop. Midway in the journey they halted briefly at a dusty provincial depot and two new passengers entered: a tall red-haired man in a uniform of russet suede, and a woman whose tawdry plumes and bejeweled pumps were a mockery of fashion. D'Aquisto inspected her gloomily, reflecting that a whole herd of ostriches had been decimated to create the purple outrage she wore for a hat. From its brim a thick veil drooped, almost swathing her face in a style more than a century out of date. D'Aquisto reminded himself that in a savage land one should expect the inhabitants to dress like Hottentots.

The newcomers entered separately, the woman staggering a little on her unaccustomed high heels. They searched in vain for space at opposite ends of the coach, but were at last forced to share the empty seat across from D'Aquisto. Although each studiously avoided looking at the other, the magician was somehow certain that they were actually traveling together. Their pretense of not being acquainted was badly acted and unconvincing. The woman sat rigidly, her hands so tightly clenched in her lap that the white of her knuckles showed through the lace gloves. Her shoulders jerked at the scream of the whistle, and when the train rumbled forward she gave a faint cry of alarm, moving as though to rise. Her companion's hand shot out, gripping her arm. "Sit down," he whispered. "You're attracting attention!" D'Aquisto, watching them from behind a magazine, suspected that the woman had never been aboard a train and its sudden sounds and motion terrified her.

A thought occurred to the magician: perhaps he recognized these two, knew them from a story he had heard in London. The woman he could not have identified, but the man—surely this was an officer named Donaju. The red hair, the cool and pitiless eyes fitted perfectly with Margot Laurier's description. D'Aquisto observed them with new interest, but during the remainder of the trip they exchanged not a word or glance except once, when the woman, apparently trembling with a chill, tugged at the man's sleeve and whispered a few words in an insistent tone, and he gave her a capsule which she quickly swallowed.

Long after midnight the train chugged into the ramshackle depot at Guanajuato, and they departed separately, the woman lingering behind, pretending to search for a missing article in her beadwork bag.

D'Aquisto had indeed recognized this peculiar pair, and he was to meet them again in the salon of the Inquisitor's House the night of Margot Laurier's first séance there.

Tossing restlessly on his bed at the Dragons of the Queen, he relived in his dream every detail of that evening, his mind creating again the long narrow room, the gilt mirrors draped in dark velour, the glass bells filled with waxy lavender flowers as funereal as the small shrine to the memory of the medium's late husband. Five guests arrived individually at spaced intervals, according to the medium's instructions. She had no wish to attract attention, and apparently those who came shared this reticence. No introductions were volunteered, there was no conversation, and the only greetings were brief nods or a murmured "*Buenas noches.*" One by one the hunchback ushered them into the salon, indicated a chair at the circular table, and offered chocolate, which all refused. The silence and anonymity of the guests lent a vague atmosphere of guilt and conspiracy to the meeting. All had come of their own accord and with the common purpose of attempting to communicate with the dead—a purpose which, D'Aquisto thought, was at worst merely foolish or useless, at best perhaps noble. Yet there was tension among them, a tautness of nerves and muscles, a refusal to recognize each other, as though they met shamefully, under compulsion to share a secret vice. Every face seemed to say, "We are together because we must be. Beyond this we do not know each other."

D'Aquisto had no trouble identifying the four guests; Margot had described them to him, telling what little she knew of their lives. On his right was Doña Dolores Cortés, a genteel spinster whose restless eyes belied the quiet of her face. ("She is of a good family," Margot had said. "Not rich, but she seems to know every important person in Mexico. I have no idea how.") On his left sat Elvira Campos, whom Margot, avoiding the word "whore," had called a "lady of the gallant life," a Spanish euphemism that made D'Aquisto smile. She was haggard, hollow-cheeked, faded before her time, and her only remaining beauty was the luster of her hair, blue-black and luxuriant, falling in a soft cascade to thin brown shoulders. She wore a dress of coarse gray cotton, like an Indian woman's, but when D'Aquisto noticed the endless clenching and unclenching of her hands he recognized her as the gaudy passenger on the train from Mexico City. Her companion of that day, Major Donaju, sprawled in a chair opposite

D'Aquisto, staring fiercely at the figured ceiling and announcing by his insolence of manner that he was not really in the room at all. Did he always wear a hunting knife and pistol? Did he intend to shoot any specters that might appear? The last to arrive was the Yankee, Dr. James Esterbrook, a small handsome man whose sensitive face suggested a poet, not a physician. He nodded quickly but confidently to the others, yet his eyes were apprehensive—haunted, thought D'Aquisto, then chided himself for a romantic notion.

As they awaited Margot Laurier, he considered them carefully. A diverse group, they had nothing in common except a stubborn refusal to let their dead go, and he tried to imagine the intensity of love which ignores the fact of death and forever persists against all reason in seeking some communication. He, of course, was different. He was a searcher for the truth, an impersonal observer, not a participant. But even as he told himself this, the memory of his wife, Miranda, suddenly flooded over him as it had so often lately. He closed his eyes, picturing her face, hearing again the clear low tones of her voice. More than twelve years had passed since her death, yet he could not remember her without a feeling of pain, of helplessness, and a longing to make amends—some final apology. If one could undo what had been done . . . He looked up quickly as the hunchback spoke in the still room. "Madame Laurier is ready. You will please join hands."

Impressions of the next hour whirled and kaleidoscoped in his mind: the darkened room, the flicker of a black candle in a red cup, Margot Laurier quietly entering to take her place in the empty chair between the major and the doctor. . . . Her white dress shimmered faintly in the dimness as she whispered to herself no louder than the breathing of the guests or the night wind outside the closed shutters. . . . He was aware that there was music somewhere near, and the gleam of a gold disk that hung above the table held his eyes as it swung slowly to and fro. The medium's silk dress rustled, her white shoulders swaying in rhythm with the disk, pale lips moving, her eyes dilated and enormous. . . . Then that moment when, startling in the hushed room, a voice had spoken. (Whose voice? And in what language? Each one who heard it had lied to D'Aquisto, as he himself had lied to them.) In his dream he heard it once more, felt the sudden grip of Doña Dolores' hand. Across the table, Major Donaju and the doctor sat rigid, frozen, not realizing that Margot Laurier had emerged from her trance, that her eyelids fluttered and her lips formed small inarticulate sounds. Then Elvira Campos cried out, collapsing on the table, burying her head in her arms as she sobbed. D'Aquisto, unable to believe what he had heard and unable to endure more, rose so violently that his chair fell backward with a crash on the marble floor. "What was it?" he demanded. "Who spoke?" But he knew the answer, and it was unbearable.

No one replied. Donaju seemed paralyzed, his face ashen, and he still clasped the medium's hand in his own while, wide-eyed, he stared blankly across the table into the darkness beyond. "What did you hear?" D'Aquisto felt himself shouting at a circle of stone statues, but one by one their eyes turned toward him, mute and accusing. "There was a voice! Surely you heard a woman's voice!"

Suddenly, shockingly, Doña Dolores laughed, a hollow, frightened laugh, echoing in the salon. "You are mistaken, señor. There was nothing. Nothing!"

Her words awakened the spellbound major, who now recovered a trace of his bravado. "If you heard something, tell us what it was."

D'Aquisto hesitated. "A woman's voice."

"Not a woman's!" the major exclaimed, then abruptly ceased speaking. He stood up, casting a look of defiance at the others. "Nothing was said to me! This gentleman is imagining things." But his tone was unsteady and his shoulders trembled as he strode from the room, spurs clanking, the hard heels of his boots unnaturally loud on the floor. Elvira Campos, aroused by the noise of his departure, leaped from her chair and ran after him, still weeping, still holding her hands to her face. "Wait, for the love of God!" she called as she vanished into the hall. A second later there was the sound of a blow and a woman's faint whimper of pain.

D'Aquisto, too wrought up to care what had happened in the hall, turned to Dr. Esterbrook and said in English, "What did you hear?"

"I—perhaps some sound. What did you think it was?"

But the magician looked away, unable to bear repeating the words he had heard so clearly, unwilling to identify the familiar voice, which, he believed, had spoken an accusation for him alone. "I couldn't understand what was said," he muttered. "It was so quick."

Margot Laurier had also risen, and now she said, "You must excuse me. I—I am not feeling well; perhaps that is why our séance was a failure tonight. But we will try once more as soon as I am able. I will send messages to all of you. And now, good night."

Her dismissal was abrupt and final. No one looking at her could have doubted her illness, for her skin was without color and a feverish perspiration gleamed on her forehead. As she turned to leave, James Esterbrook halted her. "Madame Laurier, it is important that I speak with you privately. Tomorrow, perhaps? I must—"

She shook her head. "It is not possible. Please do not try to see me until I send word. It will be soon, I promise. *Au revoir.*"

A moment later D'Aquisto found himself in the street outside, and behind him he heard the rattle of bolts and chains as the hunchback secured the great carved doors. Doña Dolores and the doctor mumbled their good nights and hurried away in opposite directions, vanishing into the twisted streets, which were now shrouded in a thin mist drifting down from the mountains.

The magician stood alone, head bowed, his fingertips pressed against his temples. He felt the coldness of the night on his cheeks and he breathed deeply, drawing in the chill air as though its coolness would cleanse his mind of illusions and calm the pounding of his blood.

"I was mistaken!" he said aloud. "The others heard nothing!"

But why had they been afraid? Why had they sat awestruck, dazed, and unable to speak, if they had not heard that voice which had spoken to him? No one else could have known that it was Miranda's voice, every tone and inflection exactly as it had been in life. D'Aquisto leaned against the damp wall of the Inquisitor's House, his knuckles clamped over his mouth to hold back a hoarse cry. Her words, the words he had denied understanding, rang again in his mind, as piercing and clear as they had been in the darkness of the salon. "*I loved you*," she said. "*Why did you destroy me?*"

4

The nightmare D'Aquisto endured in the Dragons of the Queen faded sometime before dawn, and he slept deeply until midmorning. When at last he awoke he was surprisingly refreshed, cheered by the brilliance of the winter sunshine, and eager to continue his journey. With slight annoyance he discovered that the servant had made a mistake and instead of returning his boots had left a pair of thin straw sandals outside the door. He put them on quickly, for the floor tiles were like ice blocks against the soles of his feet, and went to the barroom for breakfast.

While he waited for someone to serve him, he congratulated himself on the performance he had given the night before. No wonder those backwoods louts and cutthroats had been fascinated! In Paris or London he would have been paid five hundred pounds for giving such a show. It was a display his audience would remember the rest of their lives.

Now the inn was deserted except for a slack-jawed young man who lounged near the entrance, a shotgun propped against his shoulder, and the Indian sloven who had given D'Aquisto food the previous evening. She saw him through the kitchen door and rushed to his table, waving her brown arms and rolling her eyes tragically. "Ay, señor," she wailed, "I have terrible news for you. Before dawn this morning burglars came over the wall."

"Burglars?" said D'Aquisto sharply.

"Burglars, thieves! While we slept they stole the señor's boots and horse!"

D'Aquisto slammed his fist on the table, his face crimson as he roared in anger. "Do not worry," the woman went on. "Even now the general and his men are pursuing the criminals. Your property will be returned in no time." After this obviously rehearsed speech, her tone became wheedling. "Meanwhile, would the señor like *huevos rancheros?* The eggs are fresh this week."

The magician had no choice but to accept the woman's story. He stabbed savagely at the mess of scorched eggs and limp chilis. After choking down what he could, he set out to explore the hamlet surrounding the inn and soon became aware that wherever he went the young man with the shotgun would appear. The thinness of the straw sandals made walking difficult on the stony ground, for every pebble and thorn poked the tenderness of his feet. His inquiries about buying new boots or even stout huaraches met with no success. The villagers spoke a gibbering Indian tongue and seemed not to understand even the simplest attempts at pantomime. They smiled cheerfully and shook their heads, no matter what he asked. Nor could he find any animal that could be ridden—not a burro, much less a horse. Giving up hope of finding another mount, he returned to the inn, seething with frustration and infuriated by the smug, vacant smile on the face of the young shotgun-bearer, who was now shadowing him openly.

At sunset Jesús María Valles and half a dozen of his henchmen galloped into the courtyard of the Dragons of the Queen, the hoofs of their horses raising a blinding cloud of dust. El Lobo, in high good humor, greeted D'Aquisto with boisterous cordiality and was utterly unfazed by the anger in the magician's voice. "An outrage!" he agreed blithely. "A painful embarrassment to think that such a thing could happen to a guest and friend of El Lobo! When we find the culprits we will shoot them like coyotes."

"My horse is a valuable animal. I bought him in Guanajuato only last week. I must have him or another immediately. Also, I need boots to continue my journey." D'Aquisto glared at the bandit. "I shall expect to be provided with both in the morning."

El Lobo's face darkened. "I much regret that is impossible. My men love their horses more than they do their wives. No one would dream of selling his horse. And you know how fond a man becomes of his own boots. I am afraid you must wait here until yours are recovered." The bandit grinned, displaying an irregular set of sharp yellow teeth. "Meanwhile, we will have some good evenings together, no? Perhaps your misfortune is my good luck!" He led the unwilling magician to a table in the cantina, called for brandy, then spoke in a comradely tone. "I am a man of culture and appreciation. But what surrounds me? Idiots! My men are good men, but can they amuse me? No! They are chickens' asses, all of them. You, *mi amigo*, are different. We have much in common, and your coming here is a miracle!"

As D'Aquisto slowly comprehended the truth, he realized the enormousness of the error he had made and cursed himself for the brilliance of his performance. The straw sandals and lack of a horse bound him to the Dragons of the Queen more securely than any chains or fetters, from which he could easily have escaped. Two and a half days of hard travel lay between him and Guanajuato, most of it through country controlled by El Lobo's men. To set out on foot was impossible, and a plan for horse-stealing began to form in his mind. The bandit seemed to read his thoughts, for he said sternly, "Rest assured that the criminal who robbed you will be punished. We shoot horse thieves with no questions—although often we bury them in anthills for a few days first."

"Indeed?" said D'Aquisto, rejecting his previous notion. "I should enjoy watching that happen to the guilty party and will pray for the opportunity."

Although El Lobo had the grace to look uncomfortable, his good spirits returned quickly. "Years ago I saw a fakir like yourself in Mexico City. You are cleverer than he was, but still he did amazing things." The bandit leaned toward him, awe in his face. "He pulled a rabbit from an empty sombrero! Would you believe it?"

"Yes," said D'Aquisto wearily. "I have pulled thousands of rabbits from thousands of hats. Also birds, cats, hamsters, and long red underwear."

"I knew it!" cried El Lobo. "Today while searching for your horse, we happened to catch a rabbit! Tonight you will show me how the trick is done. I have longed to master such a thing, and you will teach me."

D'Aquisto glanced at the bandit's rough, clumsy hands. "I will do my best. And I will consent to stay a day or two more. But no longer! Is that clearly understood?"

"Clearly!" said El Lobo.

Despite the bandit's word, Tomás D'Aquisto was doomed to spend a long and frustrating captivity at the Dragons of the Queen. It was during this time that he began to write the manuscript whose completion (and it was never completed) became an obsession for him. He called his book *How Are the Dead Raised Up?*— a title taken from his favorite passage in the apostle Paul's first letter to the Corinthians, a portion of scripture which almost seemed to refer to the magician himself. "But some man will say, 'How are the dead raised up and with what body do they come?' . . . Behold, I show you a mystery. . . ."

The question mark at the end of his title did not save it from being misleading, for the name suggests a manual of instructions, a guide for conducting successful resurrections or at least an effective séance, and D'Aquisto had no advice to give on these practical matters. On the contrary he spent hundreds of pages showing how such things could *not* be achieved; he revealed the mechanical devices of fraud by which mediums bilked the gullible and the pathetic, unmasking such charlatans as Andrew Jackson Davis, whose gauze ghosts were so convincing that even after the fakery was exposed the victims still believed fanatically. He had only contempt for floating trumpets and jiggling tables—tricks so crude that even as an apprentice he would have shunned them. He wrote, "If the dead can be summoned at all, it is not by hocus-pocus. They come, if they ever come, in their own way—a way no one has yet explained."

"*If they ever come . . .*" His manuscript is riddled by doubts he could not resolve. Despite his conviction that he had heard Miranda's voice, that she had spoken to him plainly and clearly, he was unable to conquer that skeptical part of his mind which always doubted. Nowhere in his book does he say that he believes in ghosts, nor does he claim that there is any provable communication between the living and the dead. D'Aquisto passes himself off as a Socrates who merely asks questions, refusing to admit that he has a favorite answer concealed in his sleeve. It was as though a blind man who secretly challenged the existence of the stars had written a thousand-page treatise on astronomy.

Yet he longed to believe. He wrote:

> There are two questions. First, is there a soul that survives the body's death? Second, can such a surviving soul somehow cross the barrier to speak to those still living? If the answer to the second question is "Yes," then the first is proved also. . . . Religion assures us of immortality, but the whole army of priests and evangelists cannot compel one agnostic to faith. But if a single ghost story is shown to be true, if we can find one genuine appearance of a specter, then all doubts are ended. One castle, truly haunted, silences all the atheists of the universe. And if tonight at midnight I meet a ghost on the staircase, I will know that I myself am in some way immortal.

This was the peculiar door through which D'Aquisto, a man who needed to thrust his hands into the wounds of God, sought to enter religion.

> Today in 1903 we live in a golden age when man has reached the pinnacle and perhaps the limits of scientific knowledge. We have proven that the world is composed of only eighty-two indivisible elements, and "spirit" seems not to be among them. The least belief in the supernatural is considered synonymous with ignorance, yet most men, even those who deny it, persist in an ancient faith. Who can walk through a lonely graveyard at night without a rising of the hair, a chilling of the flesh? The dead appear to us in dreams and although we shrug off such things or explain them away, we none the less wonder. Reason shouts, "No!" but an inner voice whispers, "Perhaps." Can the instincts of all men be utterly discounted? I myself will accept nothing until the last possibility has been explored. Learned men who have con-

fused the unknown with the impossible have been the greatest fools of history. . . . Further, I have witnessed things
and have heard stories I am at a loss to account for. Recently
in the Mexican city called Guanajuato certain odd events occurred, events involving five diverse persons, all of whom, it
appeared to me, were at least briefly in communion with
some force I do not understand. . . .

The magician wrote these words by the light of a candle
which El Lobo had given him after he complained that
the rushlight was harming his eyes and making it difficult
to give his nightly performance. In the hours before dawn
his room at the Dragons of the Queen was no less dismal
than the drafty hall in the Governors' Palace where Captain Guzmán was struggling to write another version of
the same story. Like Guzmán, the magician listened to the
howling gale outside and rested his head in his hands as
he realized he had written the first of several lies that were
to mar his manuscript. There had been not five persons
involved but six, and the sixth was himself.

In the few days that passed between the first séance and
the explosion he had managed to learn more about the
lives of the victims than Captain Guzmán discovered in a
half-year of searching. They were gone now; he could
write down what they had told him. But he could not bear
to reveal himself, to expose his own conduct and admit the
vanity that had cost him so much. So his manuscript remained forever unfinished, the heart left out of it.

During the long nights of writing, the remembered faces
and voices of those five returned to him again and again,
until eventually it seemed that the lonely room was somehow inhabited, that they peered over his shoulder, correct-
ing their own words as he recorded them. Of these
memories none was so vivid as that of the medium,
Margot Laurier, whom he had met for the first time seven
years before.

The huge and well-publicized reward he had offered to

anyone who could materialize genuine spirits or transmit real communication from beyond the grave had attracted dozens of charlatans, scores of people who professed various psychic and spiritual gifts. They converged on him, drawn by money as schools of piranhas are drawn by blood; men, women, and even well-coached children clamored for a chance to prove they could summon the departed. Some were dramatic in the extreme: an Irish mystic guaranted to materialize all six wives of Henry VIII, with or without heads as the client preferred; a hag calling herself the "Queen of Spanish Gypsies," although she spoke with a marked Lancashire accent, offered to conjure up the ghost of Cleopatra. (D'Aquisto let her try it, and Cleopatra proved to be a London streetwalker who became violently ill after being doused with phosphorescent paint.) One by one they tried and failed as D'Aquisto duplicated their tricks down to the last rattle of a ghostly chain. He found grim satisfaction in exposing them, yet this pleasure was mingled with disappointment and sometimes rage. It was appalling to discover that those who claimed knowledge of such a sacred mystery as death were invariably tawdry money-grubbers, the most ignorant and callous creatures he had encountered since his childhood in the Lisbon slums. They were without science, philosophy, or conscience, and after two futile years D'Aquisto realized with bitterness that his project to find the truth was a failure. He had offered the reward in good faith, not intending that it should be only bait to lure frauds to their exposure. Yet that was what it had become. He had hoped to be a seeker of truth, not a mere spiritist detective, but those who approached him were all alike. Their devices and their "spirit controls" varied (although Iroquois maidens and Tibetan lamas haunted many a bogus scene), yet, underneath, all aspirants had two things in common: a determination to extort money and a smug assurance that their obvious frauds were undetectable. There were no exceptions until Margot Laurier called at D'Aquisto's London flat.

It was a bleak, dreary afternoon in February, a day when lamps had to be lighted at four o'clock—the weather which always made D'Aquisto long for Egypt or at least Italy and wonder why he remained in this dismal country whose drawing rooms were as dank as the bottoms of cisterns. He was suffering from a head cold acquired the previous week during a drafty séance (did the chill of the tomb have to be so realistically created?) and was in no mood to receive a visitor who had announced herself as still another clairvoyant and spiritist. He would not have bothered with her except that she had written far in advance and he had confirmed the appointment.

When he entered the dim sitting room where she waited, he was startled by the appearance of his caller. The young woman—no, not really young; it was an illusion of lamplight—was utterly different from the usual candidates who came there. She was perhaps in her midthirties, but she gave an impression of girlhood. An aristocrat, he decided at once, a woman so confident of her bearing that she could ignore fashion and wear a simple black dress in a season that demanded bustles and flounces. Her hair, pale enough to be called ashen, was swept back from her forehead and bound with a plain grosgrain ribbon as though she had planned that nothing, no ornament, would detract from the odd beauty of her features—a face which, except for its lack of repose, might have been painted in Siena: slanted eyes, long-lidded and almost luminous, high cheekbones, and full lips that were strikingly vivid against the whiteness of her skin. She wore no jewelry except a thin wedding band.

They exchanged greetings and made the necessary remarks about the weather without which no conversation in England could possibly begin, and D'Aquisto was immediately aware that she was not the cool, poised beauty he had believed her to be. Several times she glanced furtively toward the door, as though on the point of making an apology and leaving at once. A vulnerable woman, he thought. A woman who is trying to conceal fear and does it badly.

"Your letter said you are a spiritist. A medium?" he asked.

She hesitated, considering her answer carefully. "I—I have been told so." He waited for her to continue, as they always did, to describe psychic miracles she performed, but she added nothing. The small room was silent except for the heavy ticking of the mantel clock and the faint hiss of the coal fire on the open hearth. For a moment D'Aquisto's mind wandered from the business at hand and he enjoyed the quiet pleasure of sitting alone near a beautiful woman. Her femininity created an atmosphere, an enjoyment he savored, remembering many nights when he had sat with Miranda, sipping brandy near a fire, listening to midnight strike. The long silences between them had been more meaningful to him than any speech, and now, as he gazed at Margot Laurier, he recalled those times with a pang of loneliness.

She sat with her face slightly turned away from him, lost in thought as she studied the flame on the hearth, and when at last she spoke again there was a strange tension behind her words. "I have heard a great deal about you."

"I am flattered, madame."

"I understand you have attended—that is to say, investigated many people who claimed they had contact with the spirit world?"

"That is so."

"I read a newspaper article about it. Is it true they have all been fraudulent?"

D'Aquisto sighed. "So far that has been the case—except for a few who were sincere but quite deluded."

"Then you are an expert on such matters," she said

slowly, looking directly into his eyes for the first time. There was a hidden appeal in her voice, a quality of pleading he could not understand.

"I have been interested in these things most of my life, and during the past few years I studied and investigated. I may not know what is real, but I always know what is false. I'm a cynical man and not easily deceived."

"And people have tried to deceive you? I remember a story about a medium you exposed. Something about a green ghost."

"Ah, yes!" He repeated the tale, unconsciously emphasizing his brilliance in the affair, telling how his shrewd nose had instantly detected the odor of acetone and potassium permanganate which had been used to produce the mysterious fire that so impressed the medium's victims. Under her adroit questioning he went on to other stories, telling of steel springs hidden in the legs of séance tables, threads that descended from chandeliers, and ghosts created by Linnebach projectors. At last D'Aquisto became aware that he had talked steadily for nearly an hour, while she had said nothing. It startled him to find that she had neatly reversed his usual role of questioner, for he prided himself on his subtlety at drawing others out. He quickly concluded the story he was telling. "So you see, the tricks they attempt are really childish, and I have not yet found one who was genuine."

Now he would turn the conversation to her. "I keep hoping. Perhaps there is an exception, perhaps you yourself are quite different. . . ." He waited, dreading what would surely follow—the quick assurances that she was unlike all others who claimed psychic power, her inevitable tales of a strange talent which had been manifest since early childhood. Then, like the others, she would present him with written testimonials from clients who, through her control, had held conversations with dead sons or daughters, mothers or fathers. The clients would be prominent men and women, physicians, attorneys, ladies of nobility, who were more easily duped than a cockney charwoman. D'Aquisto regretted that the moment of pleasure he had enjoyed would soon be spoiled forever.

But this did not happen. Nodding thoughtfully, she considered his words and, to his irritation, seemed to be judging him. Then, glancing at the clock, she fastened the clasp of her fur cape. "I have taken too much of your time. Forgive me for disturbing you." Rising quickly, she said, "My coming here was a mistake. I thought this before I met you, and now I am sure of it. You have been most patient with me. And now good-by."

As she moved toward the door the sharpness of D'Aquisto's voice halted her. "Just a moment, madame!" He knew that if she left with no explanation he would spend hours wondering about her. "You are leaving rather abruptly. Since you came at your own request, I think you must tell me why."

Again she studied him intently, as though his face could reveal the answer to some question that tormented her. "I have said my coming here was a mistake. There is nothing to be gained by talking further. Good afternoon."

D'Aquisto's vanity, always sensitive, was stung by her refusal to answer, and he struck back instantly. "Very well. If you will not tell me, then I shall tell you. You intended inviting me to a séance, as many others have done. You are an attractive woman, clearly intelligent, and I assume you have a profitable business as a medium. But if you could convince me, if I said you were genuine, there would not only be a reward, but new clients would flock to your door."

Color flared in her cheeks, but she said quietly, "You are mistaken."

"I think not. Upon meeting me you decided I am not

easily fooled. So you are leaving, not caring to risk an investigation which would prove you a fraud. I think this is wise of you."

D'Aquisto, pleased by the self-flattery of this explanation, was astonished to realize she was staring at him with an expression that could be described only as contemptuous. "You are insolent," she told him. "You are not content to be a magician but think you are a mindreader as well. You could not possibly understand my reason for coming here."

"Oh, indeed? You are at liberty to tell me the reason and find out."

Her voice rose suddenly. "I am not interested in any money you offer, nor in what you call 'clients.' I neither want them nor need them!"

"Admit it," he insisted. "You are afraid I would discover you are a fake."

"It is the opposite!" She stepped toward him, her lips trembling and her eyes wide. "What if you discovered I had a power that was *real?* What then? That is what I am afraid of! But you cannot possibly understand this." Her poise, her effort at control had vanished, and D'Aquisto saw before him a woman on the edge of hysteria. "Things happen which I can't explain. You talk of fakes and frauds —can you imagine how happy I'd be if I thought it was all some kind of trickery? Only that!"

The unexpected violence of her words struck D'Aquisto like a blow, and for a moment he could not comprehend her meaning. "Are you saying that you came here hoping I could show that you have no psychic gifts? You *want* to be called a fraud?"

"Yes, that's why I came! And you have talked of nothing but wires and springs and ghosts made of cheesecloth. What would you do if you came to my house and found none of those things?" Margot Laurier suddenly buried her face in her hands. "You cannot help me. No one can!"

D'Aquisto was baffled. He stood watching helplessly, unable to decide whether this was a woman in real terror or an accomplished actress giving a superb performance. In either case he was intrigued by the novelty of a self-professed medium claiming to want her psychic power disproved and doubting that he could do it. He looked at her in bewilderment, not knowing how to proceed; then, remembering he was in England, he said, "Please sit down, madame, and I will ring for tea."

While the fog of the London night sealed the windows, D'Aquisto listened to Margot Laurier's story, drawing it from her by gentle questioning. There were many intervals of silence when, lost in her own memories, she seemed to forget his presence. D'Aquisto, at such times, waited impatiently, aware of every sound, the fire's hiss, the unbroken rhythm of the clock, the drip of melting snow on the brick sills, and the rumble of iron-rimmed carriage wheels on the pavement outside. Then his guest would speak again in a soft voice whose intensity was compelling. With no effort toward drama she brought an exotic world into the English sitting room.

She was born, she told him, into a genteel but impoverished French family. Her father, Léon Duval, gleaned a precarious living as a minor diplomat and a perpetual hanger-on at the court of Napoleon III. In 1860 Duval took his wife and infant daughter to the remote country of Mexico in hope of improving his fortune, thus becoming a member of the horde of foreign predators, especially Frenchmen, who invaded that bankrupt and chaotic madhouse, spurred on by Napoleon's delusion of cheap conquest and endless booty. First came businessmen and investors, then the inevitable soldiers to guarantee the profits. Margot Duval became conscious of the world during the glittering and tragic reign of Maximilian Habsburg, the puppet emperor whose Mexican throne was propped up by French bayonets, and one of her earliest memories was of parading through the vast corridors of Chapultepec Castle as a train-bearer for the Empress Carlota on a night when that grim fortress twinkled with five thousand candles. Beneath its façade this tinsel world was rife with superstition, necromancy, and faith in the occult. The young Empress, who eventually ended her tortured days in her beloved Belgium after sixty years of madness, was an avid believer in astrologers and sooth-sayers. Anyone with a glib tongue and a mysterious manner could easily gather a following by passing himself off as a crystal-gazer or a sand-diviner. Members of the spurious Mexican nobility spent evenings casting the I-Ching or dealing and redealing the tarot pack, and once the empress suffered a physical collapse when her wish card (for her husband's long life) turned up ominously between the Drowned Man and the Ace of Swords.

The castle itself could have nurtured such beliefs, for it stood on the rubble of an ancient palace built by the Aztecs, those practitioners of the most gruesome religion man has thus far invented. The country's millions of Indians and mestizos were only nominally Christians; they had adapted Catholicism to a pagan faith of their own. Idols were concealed behind the altars of the most magnificent cathedrals, prayers were chanted to both the saints and the rain gods, and peons trembled in terror at stories of voodoo curses and the evil eye. In Margot's childhood reports of witches stoned to death in nearby villages were common, and neither she nor the other blue-clad little girls at the convent school ever doubted that these unfortunates had perpetrated hideous crimes conceived by the rulers of darkness.

The handful of foreign courtiers and administrators who reigned over Mexico formed a tiny island in the midst of an ocean of Indian humanity which threatened daily to rise and engulf them. Such a flood was surely coming, but meanwhile they exquisitely performed a grotesque and doomed comedy of manners, like the proverbial passengers who waltz while their ship founders. (Indeed, as they patterned their dazzling quadrilles in the fairyland gardens of the castle, some of them were literally dancing on their own graves. The Emperor himself, while sailing toward his certain destruction, filled the idle hours by writing a six-hundred-page treatise on courtly etiquette.) Precarious societies have always clutched at superstition as at a lifeline, and so the inmates of Chapultepec bolstered their courage with favorable messages from the stars, from dreams, and from spirits.

When rebellion flared once again across the pillaged land, the fragile aristocracy was swept away in a tide of blood and cannon smoke. The Emperor, no longer debonair, slumped inelegantly before the volley of a peon firing squad, and most of the foreign invaders fled for their lives; but a few, among them Léon Duval, clung to a little of their new-found wealth by paying huge bribes and committing last-minute treacheries. Also among those survivors was a young French opportunist and confidence man named Pierre Laurier.

The Habsburg court had vanished, but wealthy merchants and landowners still provided an eager market for the occult, and Laurier devoted himself to this demand. At the age of twenty he invented a new system of astrology which patriotically used the Aztec calendar and zodiac. He had a genius for learning secret information: his horoscopes warned crooked customs officials of impending audits and advised cuckolds to "beware of a short man with a Prussian goatee who has designs on your wife." Moreover, he was a handsome young gallant with dark sideburns and a mustache shaved pencil-thin in the latest Paris fashion; his black curly hair made an intriguing contrast with pale blue eyes, giving his face a mystic, almost ethereal appearance. Certain matrons, not really superstitious, paid well to attend his séances for the sheer pleasure of holding hands with him in the dark.

Despite these outright frauds, Pierre Laurier was not entirely insincere. He worked diligently at preparing his horoscopes, struggled with every muscle of his well-knit body to throw himself into a genuine trance, and studied every available book on spiritism and the black arts. There was something in all this, he told himself, and it was hardly his fault that the weak faith of his clients had to be bolstered by material means. He did not *want* to fool them; they themselves demanded it.

In 1873 Laurier, then twenty-seven, met Margot Duval. He was enchanted by the fifteen-year-old girl's virginal innocence and resolved to marry her. The match delighted Margot's mother, who had become a widow that year. The family was impoverished, and Madame Duval longed to return to Paris, where she might remarry if she did not have the handicap of an adolescent daughter. Margot, for her part, was enraptured with her glamorous older husband. A compliant, feminine youngster, she worshiped his dominance, and even the dankness of the huge house he rented in the oldest quarter of the city did not mar her bliss. She had no clear idea how he earned his seemingly ample income, except that he called himself a "scientist" and sometimes used the title "Professor." Guests often called late in the evening, and he entertained them in an upstairs dining room which he had decorated with Indian masks and grotesque Aztec statues whose evil grins horrified Margot. She was never invited to these gatherings and never introduced to his friends, but, having been brought up in Mexican society, where stricter husbands virtually kept their wives in purdah, she accepted this as quite natural.

At the time of their marriage the astrology business was going badly. Last year's superstition is even more outmoded than last year's ball gown, and Pierre Laurier, casting about for some novelty, became fascinated by the work of Mesmer and the new French psychologist Charcot. Hypnotism had caught the public's fancy, its practitioners were reaping fortunes both in "scientific circles" and in vaudeville, but Pierre could think of no way to utilize this fad. It was a field almost unknown in Mexico; only a few intellectuals were familiar with the marvels of animal magnetism; and Pierre himself, for all his book-learned knowledge, had never seen a demonstration. Yet he felt sure that a fortune awaited a man who could somehow combine this new mystery with spiritism. But how?

Strolling in the Alameda one afternoon, Pierre met an old acquaintance who had just returned after a year in Paris. As they shared a bottle of wine at a nearby restaurant, the man began talking excitedly of a remarkable evening he had spent at the home of a physician. "It was positively uncanny! The doctor is a Mesmerist, and he put this young woman into a sort of waking sleep. When he told her she was an old lady, her voice cracked and wheezed. Then he said she was a little child, and—would you believe it?—she laughed and cooed like a baby!"

"Amazing," Pierre agreed. "Tell me, could she speak clearly? Answer questions?"

"Certainly. In fact, she gave an astonishing demonstration of memory." Suddenly Pierre's friend looked uneasy. Frowning, he toyed nervously with his wineglass. "Interesting, of course. But it was somehow—I don't know—ghostly."

Pierre pondered this new information, and the next morning, as he was admiring the adolescent beauty of his bride, a daring plan flashed into his mind. That night in their bedroom he seated her on a low stool and placed a candle on a pedestal a few inches higher than her eyes. Taking a gold coin attached to a chain from his waistcoat pocket, he commanded her to watch its slow pendulum-like movement. At first the attempt was unsuccessful; she was frightened by the strange intensity of her husband's face and the monotonous, whispering voice repeating her name so softly and compellingly. But gradually she succumbed, lost consciousness of the room, and when at last she emerged from the trance had no recollection of having moved or spoken. Nor did she realize how much time had passed until she saw in amazement that the tall candle had burned to a stub. "What happened to me?" she cried.

Taking her in his arms, he kissed her breasts and eyelids. "Nothing. It was merely a scientific experiment. You want to help me in my work, don't you?" Then he embraced her fiercely. "You are an angel, and I love you! We're going to be rich, my darling, rich!" When she asked how this would happen, he chuckled and took her to bed.

Despite her faint protests, the "scientific experiment" was repeated the next night and the next. As her mind became conditioned to the unvaried ritual, she succumbed more quickly, and at last the mere sight of the swinging coin prepared her for what Pierre called the "magnetic sleep." He was always jubilant after these sessions, but sometimes she noticed a fleeting expression of awe pass over his face as he looked at her.

Two weeks later Pierre gave her a sheet of paper covered with fine writing. "Memorize this," he told her. "I am having guests tomorrow evening and I want you to know some things about them." The first item concerned a man named Miguel Ramos, a well-known jeweler in the city. "His only son, Pablito," it said, "died of typhus eight years ago at the age of five. The child's pet name was Little Monkey, and he called his father 'Papacito.' Ramos carries the child's portrait in his watch case. In a second-floor closet of Ramos's house there is still a rubber ball, a toy horse with blue glass eyes, and some alphabet blocks. *Important:* the child loved cinnanmon candy and used to search his father's pockets for it. *Key Question:* 'What does Little Monkey like?' *Answer:* 'Little Monkey likes cinnamon.'"

Margot dutifully memorized this and three similar paragraphs about other men, although she could not imagine the purpose. Such painful and sentimental details were hardly things one mentioned to a guest. She did not know at the time that Pierre had obtained this intimate information by bribing household servants.

The following night she was told to remain in the bedroom until she was summoned, and to dress herself in a gown Pierre had bought that day, a filmy garment of white silk which vaguely resembled a confirmation dress. At nine o'clock a new servant her husband had employed, a hunchback called Little Brother, tapped on the door and without a word led her to a darkened dining room. Pierre and four older men sat in the dimness, their faces almost indistinguishable in the light of a single votive candle glowing in a red cup. As she entered, they leaned forward, silent, expectant, and their breathing was hoarsely audible in the stillness.

"Sit down," said Pierre softly, and she obeyed him. Little Brother withdrew soundlessly, and a moment later she heard the faint tones of a violin played in the adjoining room. "Look at the coin, Margot. It moves back and forth . . . back and forth. . . ." Even in her confusion and fright she could not take her eyes from the shining object he held before her. As she gazed at it all other awareness faded and she felt herself moving swiftly down a long corridor toward a faraway light. She floated, moving over a stone floor, but the light receded, became a pinpoint in the blackness, and then her mind and her body seemed to fold into themselves and she thought of a flower closing its petals, its stem shrinking, and then she was a seed buried in warm dark earth.

A voice called her name sharply. Her eyelids opened

and she found herself lying in their bedroom, gazing up at the brown velvet canopy, while Pierre, sitting on the edge of the bed, stroked her cheek. "What is it? How did I come here?" Yet she was not frightened but filled with a deep contentment.

"In a dream," he told her as he undid the pearl buttons of her dress. He was in a gay mood, laughing and exhilarated, as he kissed her and nibbled at her ears. "Tomorrow, angel, I will give you a present. An emerald half as big as one of these buttons! The best jeweler in Mexico has promised it! Will you like that, my darling?"

"Oh, yes, Pierre!" But she did not really care. Her deepest pleasure was in having pleased him so much, although she did not know how and was too overcome by drowsiness to savor even this. Her heavy eyelids closed, and as the cathedral bells rang midnight she drifted into a deep, dreamless sleep. Then, at some hour between midnight and dawn, she heard the bells once more, fainter, farther away. Her consciousness stirred softly, yet she felt herself neither awake, asleep, nor in a dream. Again she moved through the stone-floored corridor, not floating now but thrust forward at a giddy and terrifying speed while a wind tore at her hair. The distant light grew in size and brilliance until it was a blinding white sun, and when she tried to shield her eyes from it the rays pierced the flesh of her hands. The light vanished, the wind ceased, and she stood rooted in a cavernous place surrounded by utter silence. Suddenly a voice cried in a shrill, mawkish parody of a child pleading, *"Papacito, where's the cinnamon? Give me the cinnamon, Papacito!"* The words echoed and re-echoed around her and when she covered her ears they rang inside her head, a hundred thin voices crying at once. She screamed, she struck at her face, trying to drive them away. Then they were gone and she felt Pierre's arms holding her.

"Margot, wake up! You're having a nightmare!"

"Was it that? Was it only that?" Weeping, she clung to him, trying to lose herself in him, to draw strength from the warmth of his body. He consoled her, speaking comfortingly, stroking her as if she were a kitten.

"Do you want to tell me about it?" he asked.

"No, no."

After lighting a lamp, he poured two glasses of brandy, and for more than an hour he talked to her. A beautiful world lay before them, he said, his eyes shining with his dream of the future. Soon they would have their own carriage; later they would travel, she would see France, she would be the finest-dressed woman in Paris. She listened dumbly, nodding but not understanding. As dawn was breaking he made love to her, and never had she given herself with such urgency and need, yet afterward when, fulfilled, she sank back on her pillow, she could not shut from her mind the terrible memory of the crying child.

Sleep came at last, and she slept as the dead are said to sleep, not hearing Pierre when he rose late in the morning, not feeling the brush of his lips on her forehead before he dressed and left her. She was undisturbed by the household clatter, which usually aroused her soon after dawn, the scrape of the servant's broom, the clumping of a burro delivering charcoal in the patio, the cries of street hawkers below the window. Then at noon a ray of sunlight, finding a gap in the bed curtains, struck her eyelids.

Margot sat up quickly, fully awake but for a moment uncertain of her surroundings. She had no clear memory of the previous night, yet was filled with an elation as though this day held some special promise. She felt a tingling excitement such as she had known in childhood when she awakened at dawn on Three Kings Day, unable to sleep because she knew that the Magi had come in the night and left her gifts.

She swept aside the bed curtains and let her bare feet

dangle over the edge of the high mattress as she looked around her at the familiar room, which now seemed to have an unfamiliar aspect. Perhaps, she thought, it was the peculiar light, the narrow beams filtering through shutter slats into the dimness, cool yellow reflecting in the oval mirror above the bureau, sparkling on her tortoiseshell combs and brushes. From the canvas ceiling the flock of painted cherubs and saints gazed at her—sly voyeur angels whose unblinking stares caused her to blush when Pierre made love by candlelight. Each hovered at his customary perch, peeping over cloud banks, peering curiously between the strings of harps. But their faded pastels had taken on new brightness, and the gilt of their wings twinkled. This morning they were charming confidants who shared a delicious secret with her. The dull objects in the room, the water carafe, the carved pineapples on the bedposts, displayed a beauty of shape and color, a new gloss, as though the pewter candelabra had turned to silver during the night, and she exclaimed, "I've never noticed before! I've never looked!"

She felt buoyant, transformed by a new sense of utter freedom and utter happiness, unable to understand why the least breath she drew was pure delight, and unable to remember any gaiety approaching this, although it was a little—but only a little—like what she had felt on the night of her thirteenth saint's day, when she had secretly drunk a third glass of champagne and scandalized her mother and her *dueña* by showing her knees as Indian women did when she danced the *jarabe*. But then she had been giddy, edges and corners had softened, blending into each other, and there had been a film between her and the world. Now there was no film, no giddiness, only a perfect vision of a room cut from crystal.

"Have I conceived?" she asked in wonder, feeling that Pierre's act of love must be the source of this novel happiness. In the convent where she was educated the nuns had spoken of childbearing, woman's eternal duty and Eve's eternal curse, as an ordeal which began with the "blood of defloration" and ended in the "pain of bringing forth." But the girls whispered among themselves that the dried-up sisters damned sweet grapes which were beyond their reach, and in truth a bride was literally kissed by an angel at the instant of conception. Afterward the world glowed, and this was how women knew they had proved success-ful. To Margot this seemed delightful but unlikely; yet today she could almost believe it. A beautiful change had taken place, and surely Pierre was the source. Whether or not she carried his child, he had somehow liberated her, given her joy she could not have imagined.

She sprang from the bed and danced across the room, laughing as she plunged her hands into the water basin, splashing, letting the coolness ripple between her fingers. From the street she heard a drum rattle and the whistling music of a fife and realized it was after noon, for at this hour each day a company of unkempt soldiers straggled past the house on their way to guard duty at the old prison.

"I've slept all day!" she exclaimed. "I'm lazy as a nun!" And this too pleased her. She ran to the window and threw open the shutters, letting sunlight pour over her, not caring that she wore only a thin nightgown ripped at the shoulder.

The house stood in the oldest quarter of the city; its street had once been fashionable but now was the haunt of pickpockets and diseased beggars called *leperos*. Today the squalid scene beneath the balcony neither frightened nor depressed Margot. "I could fly now!" She rose on tip-toe, stretching her arms toward the iron rail, unconscious of the gapes of passers-by, unaware that the soldiers had turned back to whistle.

Whirling back into the room, she brushed her hair from crown to waist, smiling at herself. "I am different today. I am someone else!" Suddenly memories of the night flooded over her and, dropping the brush, she stared into the mirror, wide-eyed, amazed she had not remembered until now. She recalled the darkened room, the aroma of incense, and the silent circle of men whose faces were hidden from her. Now, as she closed her eyes, the gold coin sparkled and spun before her, drawing her, compelling her again toward blackness and dazzling light, no longer terrifying. The voice of the child brought no pain but a peculiar sweetness, harsh yet inexpressibly lovely.

It was Pierre who had brought her this new happiness, and, turning to the rumpled bed, she knelt to press her lips against the sheet and whispered, "I love you." Words poured from her, words she could never have spoken in Pierre's presence, words recalled from childhood prayers and now addressed not to God but to her husband.

Suddenly she glanced over her shoulder, sensing she was not alone, that someone had entered the room and stood near her. Little Brother, a tray of chocolate in his small hands, gazed at her.

"Perdóneme, señora. I have intruded upon my lady's prayers." He spoke with the proper humility of a servant but did not lower his eyes.

"Haven't you the sense to knock before entering? I shall speak to the señor about this."

"Forgive me. I rapped three times, but you were too deep in your prayers to hear. I understand this. I too am devout in my own way. When I worship, I lose myself. But my lady should be temperate in her devotion. Too much adoration is a heavy cross even for God."

"You talk like a Jesuit! Take my chocolate downstairs and get some rolls. I will eat in the small dining room."

In the doorway he hesitated. "You were magnificent last night, señora. Magnificent!" Then he was gone, and despite her annoyance with him she smiled at his praise. Perhaps Pierre was right when he said that a dwarf brought good luck to his master, although she had also heard that the presence of a hunchback attracted the devil's eye as surely as a lone tree drew lightning.

Quickly she bound her hair, dressed, and went downstairs to the room where her breakfast awaited her, a dismal place whose only windows faced a sidewalk. The shutters were always closed, for it was disturbing to eat while street urchins peered through the bars, eying the food and whining for leftovers. But today Margot could not bear dimness and she unfastened the bolts to let light into the room.

As she sipped the chocolate there was a commotion at the front of the house, and a moment later Little Brother rushed to her, carrying an envelope and a tiny mahogany box. "Señora, it has arrived already!"

"What has arrived?"

"Messengers from the jeweler, Señor Ramos, were just now at the door."

Breaking the wax seal of the envelope, she opened a note addressed to her: "Accept, señora, this gift from myself and little Pablo." Pablo? Then she remembered the name of the dead child.

Inside the box, gleaming on white silk, lay an unset emerald, a cold green brilliance whose like Margot had never seen.

"It is worth a fortune, señora." Little Brother's voice was filled with awe. "Shall I lock it in the strong room?"

"Not yet. I will keep it a moment. Oh, it is lovely."

Alone, she gazed at the stone, touching it with the tip of her finger, remembering Pierre's promises of their future. The emerald seemed the proof, the assurance, and cupping it in her hands she stood, her back to the window, letting light strike the shining surface. Its radiance held her gaze, held it as the gold coin did, transfixed her eyes; and suddenly she longed to enter again that strange country she had discovered. How easy to go on, deeper and farther, to cross the landscape where figures like herself shimmered in a mist as they beckoned her to return to them. She was only a step away from an invisible threshold, and the emerald grew in her hand, as the walls of the room wavered, seemed to give way and dissolve. . . .

A voice, soft but insistent, whispered inaudible words, and something lightly brushed the back of her dress. Bound in the spell of the half-dream, she turned slowly toward the sound and touch. A shape loomed in the brightness of the window, a man who seemed a creation of her mind, as though she had crossed the threshold of the trance and he stood beyond it, awaiting her.

He pressed against the bars, a skeleton wrapped in rags. Two warped arms reached toward her, spotted palms upturned, the fingers opening and closing convulsively, imploring her. The tip of one finger almost touched her face, but she was unable to move or cry out, held by the eyes that stared into her own, hollow and sunken. The head twisted and in horror she saw that one cheek had been eaten away, revealing the black hole of the creature's mouth, where a tongue flapped as it tried to speak.

Screaming, she whirled away, fleeing the room, unaware she clutched the emerald to her, running blindly into the courtyard.

Little Brother was shouting. "What is it? What is it, my lady?"

Leaning against a stone pillar, she gasped for breath. "At the window. A beggar, a *lepero*, I think—I don't know. Oh, God, send him away!" The dead, she thought. Is this what the dead are? Fleshless, disfaced, but with hands to reach out, fingers to clasp, arms to hold? She was still trembling when Little Brother returned to her side.

"There was no one there, señora. He must have fled when you cried out."

"Are you sure?"

"Yes, señora. I even looked into the street. Believe me, there is no one."

"He was—horrible."

"I bolted the shutters. It would be better if you did not open them again. One never knows. Now I will bring you some brandy."

"Do you believe in warnings?" she asked. "Does God send special signs of what may happen?"

"No, my lady," said the hunchback. "Our misfortunes surprise us from ambush. There are no warnings."

"Yes, you are right. I was thinking foolishness." She looked once more at the emerald, twinkling in the sun but cold in her hand.

5

This was the beginning of the story Margot Laurier told the magician Tomás D'Aquisto in London, a story that would eventually lead him halfway across the world.

He listened eagerly, losing himself in the tale, unaware that the fog against the window pane had turned to sleet, unmindful of the distant striking of public clocks. D'Aquisto had no doubt of the medium's sincerity. His ear was keen in the detection of lies, and he discerned none in Margot's story. She told the truth, or at least what she believed to be the truth.

Yet he felt a twinge of disappointment. Where were the familiar intriguing phenomena of spiritism? The pianoforte played by ghostly fingers, the eerie chiming of bells, spectral rapping in darkness, and luminescent objects suspended in mid-air? There were none of these marvels. Her story was internal, and she told only what she had felt, seeming to have no idea of what the jewel merchant, for example, had seen and heard to move him to such generosity.

D'Aquisto found himself longing for her to describe the clank of chains, to produce affidavits of witnesses who had observed the materialization of a departed grandfather or the incredible appearance of an Indian maiden in full tribal regalia. "I am a vulgarian who wants baubles," he told himself sternly. "I want tricks and trappings that I can call signs and wonders. Underneath, I am a stage performer who delights in melodrama, and this woman does not deal with theatrics."

But he did need tangible proofs. "Madame Laurier," he said, "apart from your inner experience, what has occurred at your séances? Has there been materialization? Ectoplasm? What comes during your trance?"

"I am told that the dead come." She looked away from him.

"But what phenomena—"

"I know nothing of it! Nothing!" She rose from the chair, her slender hands clasping and unclasping. "I will give you the names of others, those who have attended me. You must come to a séance and speak with my husband. Pierre knows more than I, but he will not talk with me about it. Perhaps if you questioned him—"

The magician cleared his throat. "Forgive me, but do you feel that your husband's word is—well, quite reliable? From what you have told me, he is a—a—"

"Charlatan? Yes, he was once that." The nervous hands clenched, then were still. "Now he is nothing, a dying man."

"He is ill? I am sorry."

"Yes, he is ill. But if you could speak with him, show him that there is nothing strange in the séances. Explain perhaps that I am mad and my madness in some way communicates itself—"

"You are superb, Madame Laurier!" The magician smiled. "For years I destroyed the claims of frauds who pass themselves off as genuine. Now I am called upon to prove that someone who claims no special power indeed has none. An astonishing twist!"

"Will you investigate? Will you—"

"To the best of my ability. I will attend a séance. I will speak with your husband and other witnesses. You may count on my honesty, and, frankly, I have a certain reputation as an observer. But you must promise me one thing: if I begin, you must allow me to continue to the end. There can be no withdrawing. Will you give me such a promise?"

"I will."

When she sank into her chair, he realized how exhausted the woman was and how fragile. "Later we will talk more of these matters. Now you must join me in a glass of sherry, and we will speak of small, pleasant things."

"You are most kind, Monsieur D'Aquisto."

"Ah, but I am not! That, too, is one of my famous deceptions."

It was remarkable how powerfully she reminded him of Miranda. His wife had been even paler than Margot, her blond hair almost white. Silver, he thought, as he poured the wine. That silver hair and strangely translucent beauty had been the source of Miranda's great effect upon audiences when she assisted him on stage. He remembered her theatrical billing, small type beneath the bold letters of his own name: *with Miranda, the Silver Enchantress.* The type could have been a little larger, he thought; Miranda had earned it—in fact, she had earned much that she was never paid.

"I think you will find this sherry quite special," he said. "It comes from my favorite vineyard in Portugal. Portugal is the country of my birth, or at least the country of my first memories. I am not sure exactly where I was born. But then, who is? In this matter we must all rely on hearsay. . . ."

Years later Tomás D'Aquisto, straining his eyes in the candle-smoked room at the Dragons of the Queen, described this meeting in his manuscript.

During our first interview in London, the medium made no attempt to conceal the financial motives which prompted her husband to launch her spiritist career. She herself had no initial interest, did not believe she had a special gift. On the contrary, she suffered misgivings and fears.

The morning after her first professional séance, she saw, or thought she saw, a Lazarus-like creature whose decomposed features suggested resurrection after burial. This figure appeared at a window and since at the moment she was in a state approaching a trance she was uncertain about its earthly reality, not knowing whether he was simply a diseased beggar or a phantasm of her mind. She regarded the incident as an occult warning, a preternatural writ to "cease and desist."

She did not, however, heed this premonition, being blindly devoted to a husband who, to his later misfortune, insisted upon her continued work as a medium. Eventually her trances became as addictive as opium, a physical necessity for her. I am certain, and her husband confirmed this, that she could not have renounced the séances, no matter how great her determination. Indeed, only a year before our first interview she and her husband had suffered a terrifying experience in a Mexican city named Guanajuato, and afterward she resolved to forsake spiritist practice. Nevertheless, she returned to it almost at once and I think the necessity of earning a living was not the sole reason.

In fact, one of the startling characteristics of occultism is this addictive quality. I have never known a medium, even the most spurious, who wholly gave up spiritism, except for a few who turned to equally mystic cults, Christian and otherwise. Once a man's mind has been seized by the Unexplained, caught by its hope and fascination, he is not likely to free himself.

This applies to both mediums and clients, and it is astonishing how they persist. Even after the Fox sisters, the American founders of modern spiritism, were fully exposed as tricksters, their clients were unshaken in their faith. The sisters themselves, although self-confessed fakes, soon resumed occult practice with success and, I am forced to believe, at least a trace of sincerity. The addicted do not reform, and many find curious fulfillment in known illusions. Stranger still, there are those who never gain satisfaction, yet always continue to seek. . . .

D'Aquisto was unaware that the last sentence was his own biography. Unlike Captain Guzmán, who could not compose a single paragraph without injecting himself into it, the magician eschewed self-revelation. Had he been able to discover a ritual for materializing ghosts, and in his heart that was what he devoutly but secretly yearned to do, they would have been phantoms not personally known to him. In daydreams he imagined himself officiating in an enormous white temple, chanting mystic words while music soared and shuddered. An awed congregation watched as he raised his hands toward swirling spires of mist, invoking, then producing the shades of geniuses. *"Behold! William Shakespeare! . . . Voilà! Monsieur Voltaire! . . . Mire! Miguel Cervantes!"* But only in private would he have summoned the one ghost whose presence he longed for.

During the nights in the Mexican inn he lay on his cot, listening for the first cockcrow, considering his manuscript, but although this work was to cover the entire field of spectral communication and be drawn from all the observations of his life, the events in Guanajuato dominated his thoughts, and he found himself obsessed by those who had died there, plagued not only by the cause of their deaths but by the manner of their lives: diverse people summoned to a common fate by some common quality. Their destruction, he felt, might have been acccidental, or criminal, or perhaps even— But he did not yet pursue the third possibility. They came to the mansion by choice, prompted by their own natures. What led them there?

He had entitled his manuscript *How Are the Dead Raised Up?* But there was a second question, implicit in the first: *Why do we seek them? Why do I?*

Some men could drop a final bread crust into an open grave, hear the rattle of a handful of gravel on a coffin lid, then turn away forever. They could walk home, stumbling perhaps, their shoulders hunched by a burden of grief, yet they soon let go of what was left behind. They resumed their day-to-day lives, eventually finding new love, new grief. But other men were not of this breed. They could not resign themselves that the last word had been spoken, that a neat line had been drawn beneath the sum of a life. Nothing more could be added or taken away, and whatever had been left unspoken would remain so forever.

"Why do we seek them?" he asked. And because he could not bear to examine his own heart, he turned his thoughts once more to those seekers in Margot Laurier's house, all of whom had refused to give up their dead. If a common reason existed, it would be hidden in their lives —in their lives and in the life of one other man, who should have been present that night but was not. The circle at the moment of its obliteration had been incomplete, the magician decided. Pierre Laurier belonged among them.

D'Aquisto first saw Pierre when he kept his promise to attend a séance at the Lauriers' London flat. "I will come incognito," he told the medium, "posing as another communicant. The presence of an investigator would influence others who attend, and I wish to observe the séance in its usual circumstances."

It was one of D'Aquisto's vanities that he could become inconspicuous when he chose, although this was, of course, quite impossible. His satanic eyebrows, the pirate face with its Moorish nose, the whole theatricality of his bearing could not fail to attract attention. For this occasion he decided to wear the garb of a petty civil servant or a clerk: a rather threadbare suit with elbow patches, brown bowler hat, and checked vest. "A typical Englishman," he said as he studied the effect in a mirror. "Indistinguishable from a million others."

The address Margot had given him proved to be in a rundown district where ramshackle dwellings abutted ramshackle warehouses near the Thames, that area where mists were thickest and the gray-white hours of darkness echoed with mournful horns and whistles of ships. Nevertheless, as he rode in a hansom toward this dubious neighborhood, he still felt that the color and pungency of Margot's Mexican story would somehow be re-created in London. He looked forward to a séance chamber made mysterious by feathered masks of Aztec gods and jade idols at whose feet incense smoldered, the exotic, the glamorous.

He was quickly disabused of this notion. The séance, he learned upon arriving, was to be conducted in a dreary room in a building whose halls reeked of burned cabbage. He found himself standing on a frayed carpet, a moss-rose pattern that was monotonously repeated in the cheap wallpaper. There was a settee with its inevitable pair of matching chairs adorned in fake needlepoint, and a glass-doored china cabinet shaped like a packing crate.

The four clients who waited there were as drab as their surroundings: two decent British ratepayers dressed in honest blue suits and accompanied by respectable wives, one woman tall and horsy, the other plump and bovine. When he entered, the simultaneous inclinations of four heads greeted him. Four pairs of reserved and suspicious eyes studied his person, and he seemed to hear four minds in unison pronounce the word "foreigner."

"G'evening" said one man. They then resumed their own conversations, the husbands discussing cricket scores, the wives comparing recipes for shepherd's pie.

"It's skimming the gravy that's the trick of it, Mrs. Higgins," said the big-boned equine creature, her nasal voice tooting from some region in the sinuses. "At least that's how my husband prefers it. Mr. Hobbs detests grease in the gravy, and so do I."

"Oh, quite, Mrs. Hobbs," her plump companion agreed. "I abominate it m'self! But if the meat is lean and truly nice, then—"

Gazing at them in unbelief, the magician considered departing at once. These were Margot Laurier's mystic communicants? Surely her entire story was a hoax.

Only Little Brother lived up to expectation. The dwarf, his face even uglier and more simian than D'Aquisto had imagined, solemnly accepted the magician's overcoat and bowler, murmuring a Spanish greeting in a voice so hushed that D'Aquisto had to strain to catch the familiar words. As he padded away, his soft slippers making no sound, the English clients glanced at him suspiciously, although all of them had been in this house several times and the hunchback was familiar.

"Lord, Mrs. Hobbs," whispered chubby Mrs. Higgins, "he truly gives me jitters! Looks like something at Madame Tussaud's."

"Medieval, Mrs. Higgins! Positively med-i-eval! But I suppose poor Madame Laurier has to have him to help care for her husband."

"Oh, quite. Such a shame!" Mrs. Higgins sighed comfortably. "I never cease to rejoice that I married a man who's teetotal."

The dwarf returned, bearing a lighted black candle in a silver holder, which he placed near the center of a table, indicating that the time had come for the communicants to gather.

"I do hope there's good news for you tonight," said the big woman, drawing up a chair.

"Thank you, Mrs. Hobbs. You're a love to think of that when your mind must be on your dear Nancy."

"Oh, we have such faith in Madame Laurier. George and I only live for Tuesday nights now. And Nancy seems so contented. Not lonely as she used to be."

D'Aquisto joined the table, seating himself between the two men. The hunchback extinguished the single gas jet.

"Clasp hands," said the gentleman on his right. "Concentration and all that, you know! Must give Madame Laurier what help we can muster."

The magician blinked at the candle. Hearing shuffling footsteps, he glanced over his shoulder and in the dimness saw a stooped man come into the room and settle into a chair in a far corner. Pierre Laurier, he thought, and again felt disappointment, for this shabby figure bore no resemblance to the dashing gallant of Margot's story. Pierre slumped in his seat, his face buried in his hands.

"Please to keep your eyes on the candle, sir," Mrs. Hobbs told him severely. "We must prepare and concentrate."

Then Margot Laurier entered, and involuntarily D'Aquisto expelled his breath. Even in the midst of this dinginess she was spectacular, a white cloud of gauze and silk against the blackness. She is floating, he thought. She does not touch the floor! Now he was aware of a violin playing, but could not tell when its faint music had begun. The medium halted near the table, a swan coming to rest after flight, her enormous eyes fixed on the yellow flame, the pupils dilating. Her lips moved, but the sound was too soft to be audible. A moment passed, then another and another. The magician found his pulse quickening; he leaned forward, intent, eager for whatever might happen, his faith restored. Suddenly, to his astonishment and irritation, he heard the nasal voice of Mrs. Hobbs singing—off key, tuneless, not loud but very clear.

"D'ye ken John Peel in his coat so gay?
D'ye ken John Peel at the break o'day? . . ."

Turning sharply, he glared at the woman, about to reproach her for this unforgivable interruption, but he saw that her lips were tightly closed; no sound came from her except heavy, harsh breathing as her broad flat chest rose and fell. He looked then to Margot, knowing now it must have been the medium herself who had sung in an imitation of another's voice, but the tune had ceased.

Mrs. Hobbs spoke, and this time there could be no mistake, although the grating voice was now strangely gentle, even sweet. "Nancy, dear! You remembered the song! This is Kate, darling, and George is here beside me." Her husband smiled, nodded happily.

As Mrs. Hobbs leaned toward the candle her face was transfigured; the sharp cheekbones, the jutting chin had softened; the hard features had taken on the quiet harmony of a Giotto madonna. Yet there was no grief in her smile, no yearning.

The magician, in attending numberless séances, had witnessed a vast range of expressions and attitudes by believers. He had heard sobs, cries of joy and ecstasy, had listened to unlikely and often banal conversations between the living and the dead, conducted of course through the agency of a medium. ("Aunt Lottie, we had a pot of brussels sprouts last night and I remembered how you relished them! Do you miss them—where you are?" And Aunt Lottie, via the medium, replied that in her present glorification brussels sprouts were neither taken nor given. "But lovely of you, ducks, to remember.") The magician knew the hope, pain, and comfort which could be inspired by nothing more than a few table rappings, a bit of feeble ventriloquism.

But never had he encountered the calm assurance, the pure pleasure now stamped on the face of Mrs. Hobbs. After her first greetings she made no further sound, did not utter. Nevertheless, she was *conversing*. Her brows lifted slightly, her head tilted as though to say, "Beg pardon? I didn't quite catch that, me dear. . . . Ah, yes. Yes, of course. . . ." Her husband, eyes closed, had assumed a similar posture, and each time his wife nodded, he nodded also. Yet the magician was certain they did not look at each other. Was it possible that they were the medium's accomplices and were exchanging signals by the touch of their hands? Their reactions at each second were identical; they gave every appearance of listening to the same speaker. But he could not believe that this pair was in league with the medium. They simply had to be what they seemed, a respectable couple, dull, less imaginative than most.

Margot Laurier, eyes still wide but apparently sightless, hovered near the table, swaying to some rhythm he could not hear. Slowly her arms raised, seemed to be lifted, until they were held high above her head; then, moving like great wings, they inscribed two invisible arcs in the air.

On the opposite side of the table plump Mrs. Higgins chuckled—a friendly, homey chuckle—and to D'Aquisto's consternation he saw that she too had joined a soundless conversation, her lips moving inaudibly, then her mouth puckering into a tight rosebud as she listened to a reply, the small bright eyes interested and quizzical. Beside her, Mr. Higgins sat in rapt attention, not intruding into the dialogue but obviously overhearing it with full enjoyment. Once he clicked his tongue in sympathetic approval.

The magician gazed from one face to another, searching for any sign of insincerity. Could it be self-hypnosis, some form of group hysteria that had seized his companions? Utterly absorbed, they paid him no heed and seemed oblivious to their surroundings. Yet they did not appear to be entranced, their mesmeric state, if it was such, did not resemble Margot Laurier's. At any moment, D'Aquisto was sure, Mrs. Hobbs could politely introduce him to the invisible Nancy, then resume her spectral conversation. It was uncanny, it was frightening, and he shuddered at the terrible naturalness of the scene. Only the flickering light and the white presence of the medium lent an atmosphere of the occult. Otherwise, four ordinary people had gathered to talk in a dim, ordinary sitting room. They did not mouth words, like actors in a pantomime, yet unmistakably they conveyed speech and hearing. It was as though D'Aquisto had been struck dumb, deprived of a sense which all others in the room possessed. He heard the violin, the breathing of the communicants, the scrape of a chair against a table leg, but he was sealed off from sounds that were apparently clear to others. Had he, not they, succumbed to hypnotism? Suddenly desperate, he wanted to shout and to pound on the table. I am going mad, he thought. There is nothing happening, nothing! And yet—

The medium sighed, a low moan, head drooping as her tense body slowly relaxed, the white hands fluttering uncertainly.

"She's going now," said Mrs. Hobbs sadly. "So soon, too." Then her voice took on its usual complaining whine. "Such a pity there was so little time. I like a good long visit."

The violin had ceased to play. Little Brother entered quietly, escorted Margot from the room, then returned to light the gas jet. D'Aquisto noticed that Pierre Laurier was no longer present, although he had been unaware of his departure.

"*Con permiso.*" The hunchback, leaning between D'Aquisto and Mr. Higgins, removed the black candle. The evening had come to its end. And now, the magician thought, they will talk for a moment. Now he would discover what had taken place.

The four of them rose in a group, the two men fumbling for note-cases, and D'Aquisto saw that Mr. Hobbs's blunt red hands trembled slightly. "We leave the fee on the table," he informed the magician. "Were you told? Madame never speaks after a séance. Too exhausted, you know."

"Oh, quite," said Mrs. Higgins. "Dreadful strain and all."

Brief smiles passed between the two couples, expressions of deep understanding. Then Mr. Hobbs became efficient, counting out the fee for the ghostly communication with the briskness of a man paying at a telegraph office. He drew a brass watch from his vest pocket. "Crickey! Past ten already." He took his wife's arm. "Come along, Kate. We must be on our way rejoicing. The shop opens early tomorrow, you know."

Little Brother waited nearby, his arms heaped with coats and hats. He addressed D'Aquisto in Spanish. "My lady has retired. She asks if it is convenient for her to call on you Friday afternoon at three."

"It is convenient." The magician was still badly shaken as the hunchback assisted him with his coat. The English couples were already going down the stairs, and he heard Mrs. Higgins say, "I do thank you for that recipe, Mrs. Hobbs. You said a wineglass of broth, didn't you?" Their voices trailed away.

For a moment D'Aquisto stood in the hall, unable to collect his thoughts, then hurried after them. The couples had separated, were walking in opposite directions, and D'Aquisto chose to pursue Mr. and Mrs. Hobbs. He caught up with them at the first corner.

"I beg your pardon, sir," he said. "May I ask you a question?"

"What's that?" They halted, surprised. "Lost your way? These streets are a bit tricky."

"No, it is not that. I should explain that I attended the séance tonight as a scientific observer and investigator of—"

"Investigator?" exclaimed Mrs. Hobbs. Both appeared horrified. "Are you from the police? Or that nasty research society?"

"No, no. Nothing like that."

"I'm afraid, sir, we cannot be helpful," said Mr. Hobbs coolly. "Come along, Kate. Mustn't loiter on a corner like this."

"One moment, please!" D'Aquisto blocked their way. "I do not wish to pry into your affairs. But could you tell me even a little of your experience tonight? I observed you during—"

"Observed us? Did you now!" Mrs. Hobbs bristled, but D'Aquisto realized that there was fear behind her anger. "Then you saw all that went on. Nothing! A very quiet evening, it was. Answer your own questions, Mr. Paul Pry!"

"Kate!" said Mr. Hobbs, tugging at her elbow. "We simply have nothing to say to this man. Come along!"

"Perhaps you misunderstand my intentions." D'Aquisto spoke soothingly, but angry tears welled in the woman's eyes.

"I understand well enough!" she cried. "You're another snooper, and nothing's sacred to you. We've been badgered before—you needn't think you're the first. We've been laughed at too. Well, you'll not get a word from us—nor from the Higginses either, I assure you. I knew you were a wrong 'un the moment I saw you. Put that in your book and blot it!"

"That's enough, Kate!" Mr. Hobbs, glaring at the magician, gripped his wife's arm. "I repeat, we have nothing to say. Stand aside and let us pass. There are laws about accosting people on the public pavement!"

D'Aquisto gave way, defeated, and they hurried on,

Mrs. Hobbs looking back over her shoulder, malevolence in her eyes. As they vanished beyond the white circle of the streetlamp he caught the words, "Hateful . . . hateful . . ."

The magician's attempt to question Mr. and Mrs. Higgins was equally frustrating. When he appeared at their home armed with credentials, including a note from Margot Laurier, they admitted him reluctantly, and here he encountered no open hostility, no refusal to talk. Instead they adopted the simple tactic of telling him a series of bald, barefaced lies.

Although they had consulted mediums for years, ever since the sudden death of Mrs. Higgins' mother, they denied all interest in spiritism. "Just a little diversion for Maud and myself," said Edward Higgins, chuckling uneasily. "Lot of humbug, of course. Can't take such a thing seriously, can you now?"

D'Aquisto, sighing, asked, "What do you feel during Madame Laurier's trances?"

"Feel?" Mr. Higgins winked roguishly. "Once I felt Maud's knee under the table. Ha, ha!"

"Edward, what a thing to say! You've never done that!" She blushed and giggled.

"I am speaking of communication," said D'Aquisto. "Do you have any sense of spiritual contact?"

"Oh, never! I'd be frightened to death!" Mrs. Higgins' eyes were saucers of false terror. "What an awful idea!"

"During the séance you appeared to be listening. To what?"

"To the violin, of course," said Maud Higgins quickly. "The little man plays nicely, don't you think?" She folded her hands to conceal their trembling.

"Always did enjoy a good fiddle," agreed her husband.

After trying other approaches, D'Aquisto wearied of this useless interrogation. They lied and knew he was aware of it, yet they remained bland. "One last question. You are acquainted with Mr. and Mrs. Hobbs. Can you tell me who is Nancy and what did the song called 'John Peel' have to do with her?"

"Well, we don't know them well," said Mrs. Higgins cautiously. "I think Mrs. Hobbs had a younger sister named Nancy, a girl they raised as a daughter. You must ask them."

"And the song? 'John Peel'?"

"I don't remember a song," said Edward Higgins.

"Nor do I," said his wife.

"Surely you heard it!"

"No, I didn't."

"Nor did I."

D'Aquisto rose, picking up his hat and coat. "Thank you for your generous cooperation."

"Delighted!" Edward Higgins showed him to the door. "I didn't recognize you the other night; then I recalled seeing you on stage. Jolly good show, too! Your wife assisted you that night. A mind-reading act. Quite remarkable."

"Yes. Miranda was extremely skilled."

"Lovely lady. Give her my compliments."

"She passed away a few years ago."

"So sorry. I believe I do remember reading about that. It was mentioned in an article, now I think of it. A piece in the newspaper telling how you'd exposed so many fake mediums."

"I have done that, yes."

"Good for you, sir! I simply cannot abide dishonesty!"

On the threshold, D'Aquisto hesitated. "Forgive me, but at the séance I had an impression you were more interested in spiritism than you have since indicated. I cannot believe that so honest a man as yourself would attempt to deceive me."

"Deceive you, sir? Why on earth should anyone attempt to do that?" Mr. Higgins smiled innocently.

The refusal of Margot Laurier's clients to speak was unique in the magician's experience. Believers in the occult were always eager to recount every detail of their mystic adventures, to describe blue lights, buoyant furniture, and other marvelous manifestations. The Laurier followers were the opposite: they revealed nothing. From the medium he obtained a list of seven people who had attended her séances several years before during another visit of the Lauriers to England. Four of these seven employed what D'Aquisto now called the Higgins-Hobbs Defense—outrage at his inquiries or obvious deception. Another woman, a spiritist gadabout who visited every medium in London and many on the continent, said she could not recall Madame Laurier, and D'Aquisto believed her. The two remaining witnesses were honest but not helpful. Their impressions were much like his own, a feeling that something extraordinary had taken place, but it had involved others, not themselves.

"All very eerie, don't you know," a prominent actress told him. "I went for a lark, a novelty. Séances were all the rage that season. Besides, that young Frenchman, Pierre, was quite persuasive. Good-looking Frenchmen often are." Her famous slanting eyes twinkled; D'Aquisto was a fellow performer, and she could speak frankly. "He was most awfully handsome, liquid eyes and that sort of thing. So I went, but it was all a bore. Dotty people sitting around a candle, listening, mumbling sometimes, and Pierre's wife looking like Ophelia gone mad. Nothing happened. No spooks, no cold hands in the dark."

"Yet you returned twice," said D'Aquisto. "Why?"

"Well, I'm not sure. It wasn't because of the Frenchman; one look at his wife and I abandoned that idea. But something was going on with the other people there, though I couldn't catch it. You know how it is when there's a song in your head and you've forgotten the tune? It almost comes, but not quite; you hear it but you don't hear it. It was rather like that. Eerie, too, somehow. The third time I was frightened, and I don't know why. I had to get away from that room and those people. I never went back, and when I remember it I get gooseflesh. Look at my arm right now!" She had a lovely arm; it was a pleasure to examine it.

D'Aquisto had two more conversations with Margot and spent a long evening with her husband, learning that Pierre would talk frankly and freely as long as someone provided brandy. From these meetings he pieced together the couple's history.

Years afterward, when he attempted to record and unite what they had separately told him, he was astonished at how vividly he recalled those interviews. He remembered Margot's subdued tone when she first spoke of Doña Dolores Cortés and Patricio Donaju, the trembling voice as she described the remote city of Guanajuato, a city which D'Aquisto never expected to see.

Always his thoughts and questions returned to Pierre Laurier. What had the man discovered? What had happened to him? Resting his head on the rickety table where he wrote in the Dragons of the Queen, he inwardly raged at the irony of Pierre's knowing what D'Aquisto had struggled so long and fruitlessly to learn. He ran his fingertips over the first page of the manuscript, the page with the words *"How Are the Dead Raised Up?"* If such a hypocrite as Pierre Laurier had found the answer to the magician's tormenting question, then there was no justice on earth.

"He was a fraud," said D'Aquisto aloud, and his mouth tasted bitter. "A charlatan. He deserved everything that happened to him. . . ."

TWO

THE CHARLATAN

1

When Tomás D'Aquisto thought of Pierre Laurier
a definite picture came to mind: a haggard, shambling
man whose hunched shoulders suggested a perpetual chill.
He remembered a soiled collar, a loosened cravat, and a
stubble that needed shaving. The magician, aware of Margot's devotion to her husband, found himself asking a common question: "What can an attractive woman see in such
a man?" But had he known Laurier years before in Mexico
City he would have been less puzzled, for of all the debonair gentlemen who strolled the boulevards of the capital
there was none more glittering than the young Frenchman, a gallant so handsome, poised, and charming in manner that the term *savoir-faire* might have been coined especially to describe him.

If the high point of a life is the period of greatest happiness, then Pierre Laurier's brief prime began when he
discovered that combining Mesmerism with the occult was
a profitable business. During the months following Margot's first séance he was a resplendent figure striding along
the promenades, jaunty, twirling a gold-headed cane,

while Little Brother, in a gorgeous new livery embroidered with silver frogs, trailed respectfully four paces behind. When he paraded through the gardens of Chapultepec in a white felt hat with a scarlet band, common folk gaped in awe, although some of his less respectful acquaintances murmured, "Behold, the prince and his jester are favoring the air by breathing it."

On Sunday afternoons he hired a carriage to drive slowly around the Alameda park, displaying himself and Margot to the crowds, often whispering, "There is no woman as lovely as you in Mexico—or in Paris." Pierre found the world aglow, radiant with the prospect of quick riches.

Laurier had devoted his life to a search for shortcuts: shortcuts to fame, to happiness, and above all to money. Industrious in all things except honest work, he was incapable of turning a square corner if an oblique one could be found. He had no desire to conquer the world, merely to outwit it, and this was to be accomplished by one grand *coup* or, failing that, a series of lightning thrusts. His confidence that he would one day achieve success by some master stroke rested on a faulty evaluation of his own talents. When he inventoried his abilities, he pronounced himself clever when actually he was devious; he mistook shiftiness for subtlety and admired the originality of his own mind, although he was actually a mere kleptomaniac of the ideas of others. It is hardly surprising that Laurier, for all his show of gaiety, was almost unacquainted with happiness and had never been fully contented for as long as two consecutive days.

His small triumphs never seemed worthy of his genius. Even his marriage had not fully pleased him for, although he loved Margot's virginal beauty, she was, after all, the daughter of a ruined family, and even before the Duvals' impoverishment they had been unimpressive. All his victories seemed petty afterward, but he did not suspect that this was because he delighted in the process of crooked-ness itself rather than in its rewards. Unconsciously he would have preferred seducing the ugly Duchess of Alba to marrying the beautiful Queen of Spain, simply because intrigue fascinated him.

Now, for the first time, he thought himself completely happy. The success of Margot's séance aroused his wildest hopes, and when the bereaved jewel merchant, after send-ing the promised emerald, inquired about a second chance to communicate with his son, Pierre was ecstatic. He had the gem cut in thirds: a piece for his creditors, a piece to sell for cash, and a piece he lent Margot, feeling she had been helpful in acquiring the stone. Little Brother was given a lordly bonus.

The hunchback was invaluable. Having a dwarf for a valet struck Pierre as a brilliant ploy, appropriately medi-eval and sinister. Moreover, Little Brother proved himself a genius at ferreting out scandal and prying into the his-tories of potential clients. He had demonstrated this talent on the day when he first attached himself to Pierre by ac-costing him on the street, tugging at his sleeve, and saying, "Señor, I will be your man."

Pierre laughed at the grotesque figure. "What the devil are you talking about?"

"I am Hermanito, Little Brother, and I will be your spe-cial servant. There is nothing I cannot do, *patrón*. I am a musician and a mimic. I have worked as a burglar, a cook, a tailor, and a professional witness. Besides, I can tran-scribe your letters in the Italian hand. I am nearby when you need me, invisible when you do not. I—"

"You're mad," said Pierre, walking away.

The dwarf pursued him, uttering a singsong litany which Pierre soon realized was a list of names, times, and places. "Señora Rosa de Gonzáles-Jérez, February seventh, in her daughter's bedroom . . . Señora Olivia de Segovia-Escobar, March third, in her box at the opera . . . Señora María Concepción de—"

Pierre, confounded by hearing a catalogue of his most secret amorous exploits, whirled on the dwarf, brandishing his cane. "Get away and shut up!"

Little Brother grinned, his mouth stretching like a chimpanzee's, and continued in a stage whisper. "Señora Mirabella, wife of General Juan Ortega-López, on All Fools' Day in an empty confessional at the Church of the Holy Rosary." He winked. "A dangerous gamble. Only two years ago the general caught one of his wife's lovers, a violin master from Sevilla, and he cut off—"

"I don't care to hear!" Pierre, sure that this was blackmail, fumbled for his wallet. Forgotten sins buzzed around him like a swarm of hornets. "What do you want?"

"I will be your man," the hunchback repeated. "There are few gentlemen I can work for, and you are one of them. I have studied and observed you, *patrón*."

"So I realize!" Pierre chuckled in spite of himself. "Perhaps I can use you. I can't pay much."

"Some day you will. I can wait. I am good at waiting."

"Very well, come along." And Little Brother followed him home, trotting as awkwardly as a three-legged dog.

The hunchback seldom spoke of himself and when he was questioned his answers were evasive, but Pierre learned that he was a native of the city's slums, the only child of parents who were deaf mutes and who had died in some violent way which Little Brother would not discuss. Each Sunday the hunchback prayed for their souls, offering up two hundred Aves and two hundred Our Fathers, silent prayers spelled out in the manual language of his childhood. When Pierre twitted him about his piety he said, "I remember my dead. Always."

After prayer he went to an obscure corner of the Alameda where for generations the dumb had gathered to hold soundless conversations, their fingers flying as a hundred speaking hands clamored at once, a place which aroused uneasiness in passers-by, who, in the midst of stillness vibrating with speech, could not escape the suspicion that millions of words shaped by the fingers had frozen in the air, hovering until one day they would melt, find voices, and all cry out together. It was here Little Brother culled bits of gossip, learned the best-kept secrets. The mutes did servile work in the city's mansions, and their employers were unaware that the deaf-and-dumb scrubwoman who washed the chamber pots and carried away nightsoil read their most fleeting expressions and, since she could not be deceived by voices, she knew their characters as well as she knew the vessels she cleaned. Little Brother, with access to this granary of information, was indispensable to the career Pierre was now launching.

When a second séance, although disappointing in attendance, was as successful as the first, Pierre envisioned thousands of seekers beating on his door, pleading for messages from their departed, messages he would dole out a pinch at a time, appetizers to whet but not satisfy their hunger.

Now he spent hours each day with Margot, toiling to erase the colonial twang from her French, changing her Mexican Spanish to lilting Castilian, and giving lessons in English, a language he himself was only now acquiring. He was astonished to discover the quickness of her mind, having thought of her only in the cliché terms of romance: she was a white flower, a little star, a gentle dove. Now he learned her ear was as quick as his own, her memory better than his, and her determination boundless. "She's intelligent!" he exclaimed, and this, though convenient, did not fully please him. Soon she would ask questions, and he did not care to explain the real nature of their business. He himself felt no guilt in swindling the grief-stricken. The clients were fools who deserved the penalties of foolishness, and he was merely the magistrate who fined them. But he was not sure of Margot's feelings.

To his surprise, she asked nothing. More séances were held, and still she accepted his remarks about "an experiment in the new psychology." Although relieved that she gave no hint of curiosity, he found himself puzzled. How much did she really know? Was it possible that behind her innocence there lurked a cunning?

"These experiments are not too much for you, my darling?" he asked. "Not too difficult?"

Laughing, she kissed his cheek. "Of course not! I love doing what you want me to do." It was the perfect answer of the perfect wife, yet not quite what Pierre wanted to hear.

Still, he had no real complaint and he boasted about her to his drinking companions. "My wife is a marvel! A jewel."

"Yes, I saw her in your carriage." His friends stifled yawns and invented excuses to leave early, since the one thing which could have interested them, her performance as a lover, was unmentionable. Had Pierre been able to speak of this, and secretly he longed to, they would have raised doubting eyebrows at his reports of Margot's total and abandoned lovemaking. An experienced mistress might give herself with such ardor, but a virginal wife of gentle upbringing? Impossible! Pierre, after his wedding night, had congratulated himself on having a passionate bride, although she was restrained and awkward compared to a dozen "gallant señoritas" he knew. "She can be taught," he told himself. "Her passion will deepen." And it had. Her love had become so intense that he, the possessor, was in danger of being possessed. The excitement was maddening, but afterward he was plagued by the suspicion that such passion was inappropriate in a pure girl, and when she cried out, "You belong to me!" the words had a disturbing fierceness.

Despite these dissatisfactions, Pierre continued for two months in euphoria, not suspecting that he was about to be disabused of his hopes.

One night, after spending lavishly in a tavern, he was startled to find he did not have money to pay his bill. Going to the door he shouted, "Hermanito!" and the hunchback appeared from the shadows where he had been waiting. "Give me all the money you have!" Pierre paid and walked home, grumbling about the price of cognac. The next day he took back Margot's emerald, made a quick visit to a pawnbroker, then repaired to the tavern to consider his finances, at last facing the fact that instant riches had not materialized and after four séances his circle of clients had changed slightly but increased not at all.

"Who could believe it?" he demanded of nobody. He was learning a lesson any clergyman could have taught him: the commodities of the spirit world, however glorious and beyond price, require marketing.

"Why don't the clients bring others?" He had no doubt that Margot's performance was superb. The first time he had heard the crying child he had almost believed it himself; he had felt his hair rise, his flesh shiver. Other "communications" had been equally impressive; only last week Margot, after answering questions about the dead daughter of a tannery owner, had suddenly filled the dark room with laughter so eerie that the man had sprung to his feet, weeping and shouting, "Emilia! Emilia, my darling, I am here!" Pierre, standing in the shadows, had felt an uncanny breathing on his cheek, and even in memory the illlusion was so disconcerting that he banished it from his mind and yelled at the waiter, "Bring me another cognac! Must I wait all day?" To himself he muttered, "We give them what the truth ought to be!"

Night after night during the next weeks Pierre sat brooding in the tavern, gulping brandy and pitying himself as he considered the hardness of human hearts. Why

was his house not besieged by clients? How could heirs be
so ungrateful to testators, widows so indifferent to husbands who had passed beyond? The world was infested by
thankless children who cared not a whit for the lost parents who had nourished them. Now there were séances
twice monthly for two different circles of clients, and those
few who came paid well. They were astonished by Margot's power, they left the house with glazed eyes, but no
one said, "I will bring my friends here!" They came alone,
they left alone, and Pierre could not understand it.

"Is it possible that she is *too* convincing?" he asked himself and wondered if he should add elements of obvious
trickery to the séances—ghosts flapping net wings or a
luminous hand on the ceiling. In his days as a fortune-
teller Pierre had learned that most men and women will
pay to be hoodwinked only when they are entertained at
the same time, and that truth and probability are the least
salable items in a soothsayer's stock. So he had spiced his
fortune-telling with hints of erotic adventure, smiling sen-
suously at female clients as he shuffled the tarot pack to
turn up the handsome Knave of Swords beside Lady Belladonna, governess of intrigues. He followed a rule: "The
uglier the client, the more glamorous the prediction." This
had served him well, and he realized it would now be-
hoove him to inject some melodrama into the séances.
"But the fortune-telling was only lies! The séances are
different, they are works of art, they are thrilling!" He
could not bear to cheapen them, to sacrifice the strange
excitement and fascination that gripped him during Margot's trance. "It is as though the dead come, as though
they really do!" For a second he was awe-struck to realize
how deeply that impression had taken root in his mind;
then, shaking his head, he tried to laugh at himself for
entertaining such a notion.

"We will go on as we are. Clients are bound to come,"
he said. "Besides, things could be worse." Like many who

have made this remark, he soon learned how bad they might become. His troubles had been shapeless, but then one night they took form and attacked him in concert.

He accepted an invitation to take supper with Rudi and Fritz, two German acquaintances engaged in silver-mining at a dreary village near the city of Guanajuato. Their infrequent visits to the capital were monumental sprees of guzzling black, yeasty beer in the city's dives and can-can palaces. He joined them at a tawdry restaurant whose sole attractions were its sham French dancing and the gigantic breasts of the waitresses. When he arrived there was a stranger at their table, an ascetic-looking American only a few years older than Pierre but whose hollow cheeks and slate eyes gave him an aged appearance. Americans, Pierre thought, are much too bony.

Rudi introduced them. "I present Dr. James Esterbrook, a physician from the state of New England. For two years he has worked near our mines. He is a great humanitarian."

"Humanitarian? *Enchanté*," said Pierre, suppressing a shudder.

The doctor's Spanish was poor and his French little better. They resorted to English, a tongue in which three of the four were awkward, and the one native speaker indicated no desire to talk. Pierre, who prided himself on the gift of congeniality, could induce no conversation with the man, and his restless eyes roamed the room constantly. "Have patience," Rudi whispered. "The doctor's wife recently died in a most horrible accident. We brought him here to console him, but it seems useless." For an instant Pierre considered Esterbrook as a possible client, then rejected the idea.

"What are you doing these days, Pierre?" asked Fritz.

"Experiments. Scientific work in the new psychology. I think the English word is parapsychology."

Esterbrook gave a flicker of interest. "Are you acquainted with the work of young Dr. William James of Harvard?"

"Naturally. Dr. James and I have many interests in common." Pierre's voice gave the proper implications of intimacy. "He attempts to demonstrate telepathy. I go beyond this to a higher matter. Could we say extra-earthly telepathy? Would this be English?"

The doctor frowned. "Do you mean spiritism?"

"Spiritism is an unscientific term." Flattered to have caught the doctor's attention, Pierre now said more than he intended. "If you refer to communicating with the dead, then yes. I am engaged in demonstrating this, and I have had amazing results. Proofs!"

"What utter nonsense!" said Esterbrook with such unexpected anger that Pierre blinked at him. "The dead don't come back. The dead are—dead."

"Who knows this?" demanded one of the Germans. "My grandmother used to go to séances in Munich and one night she saw—"

"Lies, all lies!" exclaimed the American, speaking so vehemently that Pierre decided the man was drunk. "I've dissected more cadavers than any of you have ever seen, and I tell you there's nothing there! Bones, fat, tissues— nothing more. There's nothing left to speak or hear or—"

"Monsieur," said Pierre sharply, "you have no cause to be hysterical. There are things beyond this flesh. I could show this to you. Yes, even to such a skeptic as yourself!"

"I'm not interested!" Esterbrook's eyes met Pierre's, then shifted away. "It is a morbid idea. Even if it were possible, who would want such a thing? Who could endure it?"

"I could," said Rudi. "Raise a pretty little ghost, Pierre. With blond hair and—"

"This is not amusing," said Esterbrook. "It is blasphemous."

Leaning across the table, Pierre employed the deep, ominous tone with which he impressed possible clients. "Has nothing come to you in your dreams, Doctor? Have you not heard a whispering in the night, felt a presence that cannot—"

"No! Why would I? This sort of talk is disgusting!" But his face had blanched, and his tongue passed quickly over his lips. As the physician arose to give an abrupt good night, Pierre noticed that he had developed a slight twitch in his cheek, the left eye almost closing as the skin below it pulsed.

"Thank God he's gone." Rudi lapsed comfortably into Spanish. "Let us drink seriously and then find women. Bring beer!"

A shabby line of girls, chocolate-colored mestizos, pranced onto a stage to perform a stumbling can-can, then made way for a Cuban dancer who writhed and rolled while the Germans stamped the floor. Pierre, sinking into a mire of depression, paid no attention. The American had insulted him, and he regretted not having slapped the man's face and demanded satisfaction. Who was this doctor to say that spirit communication was nonsense? And why had he objected so violently? It was as though the possibility of ghosts speaking endangered the doctor's person. Guilt, Pierre decided, drawing from his own experience. Some special guilt haunted Esterbrook. Few people regarded the dead with real fear or abhorrence as Esterbrook did, although there was scarcely a man who could honestly face them without apology. The catalogue of crimes and unkindnesses with which the departed could charge their survivors was endless, and perhaps if the dead returned they would not come to console their supposed loved ones, but swarm upon the living, screaming ghosts demanding atonement and vengeance. Could it be this way? The words he had spoken to the doctor returned to him. "*Has nothing come to you in your dreams . . . a whispering in the night . . . a presence. . . ?*"

Pierre lifted his glass, and his hand suddenly trembled;

the cognac trickled down his chin as the mottled face of an old woman thrust itself into his memory, the face of Tante Julie, a hag who had raised him. He had believed all recollection of her was buried in the deepest recess of his mind, that she would never again trouble him, yet now he saw her eyes bulge toward him, felt the beating of her fat, wet hands on his face and shoulders. Then the hands fell away, limp, but still her eyes rolled and bulged and popped while the slack mouth worked like the jaws of a netted fish.

Pierre leaped to his feet. "I want to dance!" he yelled. "Somebody dance with me!" The line of girls had returned to the stage, and, jumping onto the platform, he seized the nearest one, whirled her high, hopping and cavorting, kicking his heels and flinging his arms. "Can-can! Can-can!"

An hour later he staggered into the street, where Little Brother waited. "Shall I call a carriage, *patrón?*"

"No, I want to walk, I want air." He took a few steps, then called over his shoulder. "Go another way! Don't follow me. You are a shadow behind me, and I can't stand it!" The hunchback vanished into a side street.

Pierre reeled from doorway to doorway, clinging to walls, struggling to run from one dim pool of streetlight to the next, falling, tearing his green velvet coat. The stretches of darkness between the lamps were haunted, filled with voices and faces that spun and whirled as he tried to focus his eyes on them. Margot, clothed in white, towered over him, reaching out her hands, and he drew back from her, cringing as he saw her features dissolve, change, become the face of the old woman.

Pierre beat his own door with his fists. "Let me in! Open!" There was a grinding of bolts, and Little Brother, panting from his run home, admitted him. The hunchback did not speak, but in the dark entry Pierre stared at him, recalled his saying, "I remember my dead. Always." Pierre fled, stumbling up the stairs to the bedroom, where a candle end still flickered and Margot, white on the white pillow, lay sleeping, her pale hands crossed, and he turned from the bed as he would have turned from a coffin. Slumping in a chair, he forced himself to keep his eyes open until unconsciousness came upon him, and then in sleep he twice cried out, "Tante Julie! Tante Julie, I love you!"

2

In childhood Pierre had memorized the longer catechism in both the Good Infant's and the Pious Young Person's versions, so he knew that the torment of a bad conscience is among the worldly penalties of sin, and Conscience is not a vague region of character but a relentless angel with a goad. Later, upon discovering how few men are plagued by such proddings, he speculated that this breed of angel might be extinct, and he began to rank it with the phoenix and the unicorn. Memory, however, was another matter; if not controlled, it drove men to crucify themselves not so much for their crimes as for their failures and embarrassments. Realizing this, Pierre kept his memory well in hand. "I learn from the past, live in the present, plan for the future," he boasted, stealing words from a popular essayist. For years he had walled out the past, maintaining stout defenses. But the old woman he had resurrected in his mind was not easily reburied, and the wall across his memory, having been breeched, threatened to crumble.

Always a frequent customer of the city's cantinas, he now became a habitué, claiming a solitary table, ignoring former companions to brood alone, inviting the recollections he hated. The least thing could set a whole train of memories in motion. If an Indian carrying an ax passed the doors, he thought of the woodcutters of Sainte Marie du Lac and began tracing his childhood from this point. More often he deliberately looked at a certain chandelier to recall the house in Paris where he was born. A chandelier—Venetian crystal, he now believed—had hung at the foot of a staircase between two white columns. His mother, in fancy dress as Madame Du Barry, hair powdered and crowned with a nest of glittering birds, moved down these stairs. The house, in memory, acquired the grandeur of Versailles; his father, a debt-ridden wine merchant from Alsace, became its Sun King.

His recollections were unclear and fragmented. He knew he had been ill with fever, attended by a strange nurse, and when he asked why his mother did not come to him she said, "Say your prayers and don't talk so much. Your mother and father are sick. Half of Paris is sick." A week later he was still too weak to attend his parents' funeral or follow their coffins to Père Lachaise. For a while he lived with the nurse, and then one morning at dawn he was awakened and told to put on his best shoes, his scarf and mittens. "Your aunt has come for you at last," the nurse said. "You're going home with her."

"My aunt? Do I have an aunt?"

"She's your mother's aunt. I suppose they never spoke of *that* branch of the family. Small wonder!"

In the hall below stood a big bearlike woman. She had the bosom of a giantess, and her head, capped by a tangle of grayish hair, seemed too small for the huge body; it protruded above her globular shoulders as a turtle's head protrudes from its shell. Strapped to her back was a mud-splotched rucksack, and she carried a heavy stick such as peasant women use to drive away dogs. Pierre gaped at her in alarm, refusing to believe they were related. When she moved toward him, the broad hips lurching, he was too terrified to flee.

"*Poupée!*" she cried, her voice as enormous as her body. "You are a little doll! A little gentleman doll! Ah, Tante Julie loves you already!" A thick arm swept him from his feet, and he was suffocated between her breasts. "Do you love Tante Julie, *poupée?* You will, you will!" Weeping, he struggled against her but was helpless.

That morning they set out for the village of Sainte Marie du Lac, trudging muddy roads, begging rides on vegetable carts, sleeping nights on the stone and sand floors of farm kitchens or in barns when Tante Julie could not drive a good bargain with their host. The strange things she said increased his fear. "Look! See those hairy leaves growing by the fence? That's henbane, love. Henbane is the devil's own skin. Fowls die from it, but half a leaf in a stock pot does wonders for the gall bladder." Once at a crossroads she knelt to scrape moss from a stone. "A suicide is buried here. I'll get a good price for this moss in Sainte Marie. Suicide's moss is a marvel against cancer and rotting of the liver. Chew it, lad! It's better than saying ten thousand rosaries."

Tante Julie's stone-and-thatch cottage stood a league from the village, nestling in a cup of land surrounded by firs and hemlocks. This tiny hollow lay among hills whose rocky slopes were too steep for vineyards, and behind the hills stretched the shadowy Ardennes forest. The isolation and wildness contributed much to the awe the peasants felt toward the old woman. She was an herb doctor, a midwife for women and cattle, a brewer of potions to double a sow's litter and nostrums to enchant a young man into involuntary wedlock. Her work being akin to witchcraft, she was the bane of the local physician and the parish priest, whose threats and persuasions failed to wean her customers from her. It was at Tante Julie's knee that Pierre learned the facts of human gullibility and superstition upon which he later built a career.

The cottage resembled a farm-shed, one large room with a broken fence to divide animal and human occupants, and above it a hayloft for sleeping and storing fodder. The old woman—and soon Pierre—lived like the pig who wandered at will in the kitchen. They rooted for herbs and plants, were innocent of bathing, and slept when and where they chose. Also, they ate prodigiously, for Tante Julie, who would not spend a sou for any other purpose, begrudged nothing to her appetite or Pierre's. She was equally generous with her affection, which surged over Pierre like a deluge. Nor was her love reserved for the child alone. In the neighborhood lived several farmers and woodcutters who stole to her door at night, scratching like tomcats, drawn by Tante Julie's incredible breasts and round thighs. Her age and evil reputation did not deter them, for to these slack-jawed peasants she was a great female animal, a warm, fleshy bulk to couple with. Her visitors paid no money, but were required to bring wine and on these nights she would dance, drunken and elephantine, trumpeting bawdy songs at the top of her lungs.

> "A captain bold from Halifax
> Who dwelt in country quarters
> Seduced a maid who hanged herself
> One Tuesday in her garters. . . ."

Sometimes she dragged Pierre from the loft, forcing him to join the revel, shouting, "Ah, *poupée*, how Tante Julie loves you! Say you love her. Tell me, tell me!"

His only escape was to say, "I love you." Indeed, these words were a magic formula to gain all rewards and avoid all punishments. When she scolded him after some mischief, he had only to say, "But Tante Julie, I love you," and she melted, hugging him and weeping for happiness. "Little doll, you are what I always wanted. Say again you love me!"

For two years they lived in this state of nature, and in some ways Pierre learned to return a little of her abundant love. She pampered his every whim, flattered and cajoled him, calling him her treasure and her "little strawberry." Then civilization in the garb of the parish priest intruded upon their idyl. "You are a daughter of Satan!" he berated her. "I cannot stop your wickedness, but you will not corrupt this child! He is growing up like an imp, and you will send him to the village for a Catholic education or I shall consult the authorities."

This was the beginning of Pierre's downfall. Tante Julie distrusted letters and books, but to her horror he quickly learned to read, write, and cipher. He raced through the catechisms, memorized the Latin of the mass, and was appointed altar boy before his distracted guardian knew what had happened. "Oh, they will teach you that Tante Julie is wicked," she wailed. "Never believe them!" She need not have worried, for his faith had exactly the same substance as the thin linen surplice in which he paraded about on Sundays.

But a more subtle corruption had begun. Sainte Marie du Lac was a coach stop on the road to Strasbourg, and elegantly dressed travelers could often be seen pacing in front of the inn to stretch their cramped muscles. Whenever possible, Pierre loitered nearby, ogling their clothes, soaking up their gestures and delicate accents. Vague memories were aroused in him, and he said, "I was once like these people. I would be like them now except for Tante Julie." He began to glorify the house in Paris, elevating his father to nobility, thinking of his mother as a duchess, and when he looked down at his patched trousers he bit his lip to hold back tears. He was a changeling, an unknown lord among savages. He must escape Sainte

Marie du Lac and above all free himself from the old hag who held him captive.

The desire became an obsession, and whenever he felt tenderness or love for her he stifled it by reminding himself of the coarseness of her hands and mouth, comparing her vulgarity to the refinement of the ladies who arrived in coaches. Although he schooled himself to loathe her, he was never quite immune to her devotion. "Is my darling ill?" she would ask, the ugly face wrinkling in dismay. "Lie in the loft, sweets, and Tante Julie will bring your supper. Whatever you would like! A tart? Raisins?" Then he would despise himself for his involuntary gratitude.

When he reached the age of thirteen, the village school had no more to offer him, and he begged to go to Paris or even Strasbourg. His teacher wrote a letter urging his further education, pronouncing him a "lad of quick mind, sure to succeed if he overcomes the sin of sloth," and the priest countersigned this. For the first time the words "Tante Julie, I love you" failed to work magic.

"You would leave me, *poupée?* Oh, I cannot bear it!" She wept loudly, blowing her nose on her sleeve, huge sobs racking her thick body. "Not now, not yet." A look of cunning came into her eyes. "Besides, there is no money. Tante Julie is only a poor old woman. How could you buy clothes and books? Who would give you food?"

This was not true, and Pierre knew it. Under her dress a heavy belt encircled her hips, and from it, on a chain, a leather purse was suspended between her knees, a purse with a strong lock to protect the hoarded coins of forty years. Did she ever remove this purse? Pierre wondered. Perhaps when nocturnal callers came, although he doubted it, for their matings were of the simplest fashion, clothes hoisted or lowered but never taken off. He began to observe her carefully and secretly, although the notion of stealing her money and fleeing was still only a thought, not a resolution.

One night a woodcutter came bringing three bottles of wine and a skin of sour beer. Pretending sleep, Pierre spied upon them from the loft. Soon Tante Julie was cavorting about the room, her bulk shaking the cottage as she bellowed the song about the bold captain from Halifax and another ballad detailing the unnatural sins of Franciscan friars. The purse, swinging like a pendulum, struck her skirt front then back, making sudden bulges. The appendage seemed a part of her and Pierre muttered a word he had recently learned in the courtyard of the inn. "Obscene!" he said. "Obscene!" Blowing out the candle, she stood near the glowing hearth, hugging her lover to her with a groan, skirt and petticoats tangled at her hips. Pierre waited breathlessly for the clink of the purse dropping to the floor, or, better yet, she might toss it into the loft for safety. But peering into the darkness he saw the silhouette of the purse in its usual place, a grotesque plumbline among four arched legs.

A few minutes later the man slipped into the night and Tante Julie, after barring the door, heaved herself up the ladder to collapse on the straw. When he heard snoring, he crept toward her, determined to examine the lock even if he could not open it, but the touch of his fingers on her skirt was like the pulling of a trigger. She was aroused instantly. "Why, *poupée*, you're awake! Were you worrying about Tante Julie? She's all right, love. Go to sleep now."

His fourteenth birthday passed. He was now a slender dark-haired youth, rather small for his age, but the titterings of peasant girls told him that he was handsome, and this befitted a young nobleman. He was old enough to go to a city to search out work or apprenticeship, but such drudgery was repugnant. He could not imagine himself sweeping out stables or toiling in a cobbler's back room. Although he begged and hounded his aunt, the best she would say was, "You're still too young to go away, love. Maybe in a year or two. Tante Julie will try to save a little money for you. But these are hard times! Ah, I don't know!" And he thought: She means to keep me here forever. Reversing the true state of affairs, he imagined being forced to be her slave for a lifetime. On his birthday, an occasion she celebrated lavishly, she had given him no new clothes, and he decided this was part of her plot. Where could he go in worn-out shoes and a patched shirt?

Spring and summer worsened his situation, for he outgrew his trousers and his ankles showed nakedly. "New trousers? Maybe for your next birthday, love. Francs are scarce this year."

Then in midwinter his hopes soared. She returned from a shopping trip to a neighboring town coughing so heavily that she could hardly carry her parcels and rucksack. Despite ointments and poultices the cold grew worse, her fever mounted, and Pierre, who had always regarded her as eternal, suddenly realized she might die and solve all his problems. Still, he worried about her; he cooked porridge, bathed her burning face, and climbed the ladder twenty times a day to care for the sick woman. When all else seemed to fail, she at last sent him for the village doctor, who came triumphantly, hardly complaining about wading through snow knee-deep. "Make her a bed near the hearth and keep the fire going night and day," he told Pierre and wrapped a wool scarf around Tante Julie's neck. "She's a tough old devil and may recover if she doesn't take more chill."

The weather grew worse that afternoon, an icy gale howling from the northern forest. Pierre faithfully tended the blaze in the fireplace, his shirt drenched with sweat while Tante Julie shivered beneath two blankets. Delirious, she believed she was entertaining a woodcutter, and between spells of coughing and moaning she raved and sang. "'A captain bold from Halifax . . .' More wine! Hug me, hug me!" When she kicked the blankets aside, Pierre's eyes fell on the leather purse. Only a corner of it was revealed below her twisted nightgown, but this brown triangle held Pierre's gaze. He moved nearer, afraid to touch it, remembering how she had awakened before. Then, of its own accord, his hand reached out. "I will go to Paris. . . . Monsieur Laurier . . . they will call me 'Monsieur Laurier.' . . ." She stirred, wheezing and choking, and he retreated to the far side of the cottage to sit watching, eyes still glued to the leather pouch.

The heat and smoke in the room made him drowsy, and he fell asleep, not to awake for several hours. "*Mon dieu!*" He rubbed his hands as he hurried toward the hearth. "The fire is all but out!" Reaching for kindling, he hesitated. What if he had slept on, undisturbed by the chill that had invaded the cottage? Poor Tante Julie, still uncovered, would have died in the night—but who could blame him? He had fallen asleep, exhausted by caring for her. He could not be accused of neglect, for everyone knew he had been more faithful to her than a son, giving up his life for her, loving her and staying here instead of going off to the city. Of course he loved her—she had been good to him, taking him in as an orphan. A kind old soul; it was heartbreaking she should die like this. Blinking back tears, he returned the kindling to the basket. In Paris he would have a special mass celebrated for her, perhaps in Notre Dame. . . .

Pierre donned his sheepskin jacket and knit cap. The smoke of the black embers was stifling, so he opened a shutter, then sat once more, head bowed in sadness, while he waited for her hoarse breathing to cease. The cold was bitter, and he wondered if the suede gloves gentlemen wore really kept their hands warm.

He did not dare approach the straw bed until late the next morning, although hours before she had made a horrible noise and then was utterly silent. Now her features were set like the face of a gargoyle, but her ugliness, repellent in life, was pitiable. Making the sign of the cross, he tried to recall the Latin of the service for the dead and hoped that she had made a dying repentance during the night. Taking a butcher knife from the table, he sawed the purse from its chain, then hacked it open, too impatient to search for the key. Out poured coins of all shapes and sizes, far more than he had dared hope, francs of the Directory, Napoleons, gold Louis stamped with the famous head that was severed. A fortune, and he was the rightful heir! Nevertheless, he hid all but a few of the coins in a hollow tree near the cottage, concealed a number of other valuables under the coop occupied by the geese, and packed away the unopened rucksack she had carried on her last fatal trip to town. He would inspect this after she was buried. After returning to the cottage, Pierre forced himself to the unpleasant task of removing her belt and chain, planning to bury these under the floor. Then he would go to the village to inform the doctor. Kneeling beside her, he fumbled with the buckle.

Suddenly the corpse rose up with a hideous scream. Cold fat arms encircled his shoulders, and Pierre gasped in horror as he stared into the face only inches from his. The mouth gaped and blubbered; the eyes blinked and rolled crazily; then she flung herself upon him, crushing him with her bulk while the arms and legs flailed. Shrieking, Pierre fought the chill flesh engulfing him, striking blindly. His hands grasped the scarf at her throat, and he clung to it, twisting with all his strength, choking the life from the thing that covered him, until at last the rubbery fists ceased to beat his shoulders, the blue tongue hung limp, and when he heaved against the dead weight of the corpse it rolled from him and he was free.

Not entirely free, perhaps. In the Mexican cantina, twenty years later and five thousand miles away, the pressure of that cold flesh still bore down upon him and he shuddered, feeling again the horrible embrace. His recollections always hesitated at this point for the events that followed were pale to him and without reality. He derived no satisfaction from remembering how efficiently he had behaved afterward. The village physician had told Pierre to build a roaring fire, and Pierre obliged him. Tante Julie's cottage became her funeral pyre, and no one doubted the story of sparks leaping from the hearth to the straw pallet. Nor could a slender youth, not quite fifteen, possibly carry the invalid to safety. A week later Pierre departed for Paris, traveling grandly in the public coach. He was even adequately dressed for the trip, for in Tante Julie's rucksack he found two new pairs of trousers, a jacket, and three linen shirts. Gifts, he realized, for his approaching birthday. There were also a used Latin grammar and a blue-billed cap such as schoolboys wear in Strasbourg. Remembering this, Pierre was quite moved—not by sorrow or remorse but by the bloodless grief of sentimentality. And he said, with an unknowing precision, "She was a kind old soul. She should never have ventured out to catch her death of cold."

3

These were the memories that returned to haunt Pierre Laurier in Mexico, and weeks passed before he was able to entomb them once more. But at last the same shallowness that deprived him of prolonged happiness rescued him from prolonged misery. His nightmares became less frequent, and at last his energy returned; he was able once more to cultivate the superstitious rich, several of whom he persuaded to come to his house for a "scientific experiment in extraterrestrial communication." Few who attended cared to repeat the experience, and Pierre raged at Little Brother as if the hunchback were the personification of all Mexico. "It is this damnable country! What can these peons appreciate? Does a burro enjoy a symphony? If only we were in Europe. Paris or London!" He now thought continually of going abroad, of presenting Margot in salons where he was sure she would triumph. "Money!" said Pierre. "If I could only get my hands on enough money!" And then good luck, nudged by ingenuity, intervened.

Among Pierre's newer recruits was an ancient spinster, a mad old woman pining for marriage with a cavalier who had been moldering in the Loyola Cemetery for half a century. ("I visit Alberto each Wednesday and Sunday," she croaked. "I take him a poinsettia or a Castilian rose, and I feel terribly close to him.") One night in the spell of the séance she suddenly cried out that the long-delayed union was at that moment being consummated. Writhing on the chair, she tore at her shriveled breasts, ecstatic, babbling the suppressed lewdness of a lifetime, until she was overpowered by Pierre and two scandalized clients. Ghostly matrimony proved too much for her constitution, and a week later she was carried off by a thrombosis, but not before making a deathbed codicil to her will, a legal document witnessed by Little Brother and a senile priest. She generously remembered "Doctor" Pierre Laurier and his heaven-sent wife, who "guided me to final happiness and perfect bliss."

An hour after her funeral Pierre danced around Margot in the bedroom as he tore off and hurled away his black garments of mourning. "Sell the furniture! Buy steamer trunks! We will leave this ignorant sinkhole and never come back!"

So Pierre, Margot, and the hunchback embarked for the conquest of Europe, a continent notoriously difficult to overwhelm. But as the squalid port of Veracruz with its mud buildings and fever-bearing mists receded, Pierre stood alone on the deck of the ship, exultant, eyes aglow as he whispered, "Paris, London, Rome . . . Paris, London, Rome. . ."

His optimism was dampened within a month of their arrival in the French capital. Pierre, a Beau Brummel in Mexico, was merely another provincial dandy in Paris. He had no acquaintances worth counting and found no easy entry to the salons of the wealthy. His stock in trade, the hypnotic trance, proved to be a worn-out fad. The Parisians talked glibly of animal magnetism, they knew that in India Dr. Esdaile had performed more than a hundred surgical operations using hypnosis, and now Dr. Charcot was making the trance scientific and thereby dull—a medical not a mystic phenomenon. Nevertheless, Pierre soon arranged a séance sponsored by a middle-class widow who had relatives in Mexico. The four women who attended sat spellbound, and the hostess sobbed softly when Margot, in a strangely masculine voice, whispered an endearment, then said, "Ah, Céleste, go to Versailles. We will watch the fountains together as we used to do." Magnificent, thought Pierre.

Afterward the lady smiled feebly. "Most impressive, monsieur! I mean, really, one almost *believes* it! For a moment I—" Her hands fluttered as she toyed with the ostrich trim of her dress. "But it is all so grim! Now with a ouija board everything is delightful. One receives such charming messages. Does Madame Laurier use the ouija?"

"No," said Pierre. "We do not deal in child's games."

"Well, really!" The Lauriers were not asked back to the widow's house.

Yet Paris, as always, teemed with followers of the occult, and Pierre, sure he could gain a foothold, insinuated himself into first one group then another. He witnessed table-tapping, planchette-pushing, and—dreariest of all—automatic writing. Idiotic diversions, he thought, but respectable because of such prominent believers as Victor Hugo. He encountered the disciples of Baron von Guldenstubbe, a clairvoyant who recorded over two thousand messages from the spirits—ghosts who spoke no less than twenty different languages but unfortunately said nothing of importance in any of them.

Pierre attended a meeting of a society devoted to the study of clairvoyance and found the members in a high pitch of excitement over the Black Prophecy of the peasant Matha, who had correctly forecast the assassination of Prince Michael of Serbia and the accession and abdication of his successor, King Milan.

"We await news from the Balkans," the society's president told Pierre. "We need only the murder of the present Serbian monarch for complete fulfillment of Matha's prediction."

"You expect this to occur?" he asked.

"Of course, monsieur! After all, you know that a seer announced that the late Alexander of Russia would survive seven attempts on his life, and that is precisely what happened. The bomb that killed him in Saint Petersburg was the eighth attempt!"

"Hmm," said Pierre and left the meeting, skeptical. (His skepticism was unjustified. Only a few years later Alexander of Serbia and his consort, Draga, were seized in a closet where they had sought refuge and were butchered by traitorous guards, who hurled their remains into the palace courtyard to be dismembered by a howling mob. The Black Prophecy held true to the end.)

The prevalence of spiritists and mystic cults in the French capital astonished Pierre, although he remembered that when he had first come to the city from Sainte Marie du Lac séances were the height of fashion. The Empress

Eugénie, having fallen under the spell of the medium D. D. Home, had through him entertained enough distinguished ghosts to fill a ballroom at the Tuileries. Among her spectral guests were Rousseau, Pascal, Solon, and Saint Louis. Not omitting members of her own family, she received and conversed with the shades of Napoleon I and her late mother-in-law, Queen Hortense. Eugénie's only disappointment and social failure was the refusal of Marie Antoinette to accept repeated invitations to attend. Antoinette's ghost ignored all communications and absolutely declined to materialize.

The Empress's influence on fashion survived her reign, and Pierre found occult practice everywhere. But these believers, all dabblers and dilettantes, were not the type of client which Margot could hold. Sneering at their superstition, Pierre went out in search of more serious men.

At that time the clergy of France were fulminating against a certain Rosicrucian sect, accusing its members of black masses, witchcraft, and an attempt to revive the Bulgar religion, a phallic worship that had nothing to do with Bulgaria but dated back to medieval times in France, its principal martyr being Jacques de Molay of the Knights Templar, who, with his companions, was roasted alive on the Ile de la Cité for practicing sodomy—and far worse—worshiping Satan as a black cat. Pierre decided such a cult must harbor likely recruits for his circle and after great difficulty gained admittance to a shuttered house near the Boulevard Saint Germain, where he joined a secret meeting at midnight. He listened to incantations of the ancient Pharaohs, falsely swore his belief, and even allowed his forehead to be crossed with the blood of a ram. Afterward the group went on foot for a pilgrimage to the spot where their hero had suffered his final ordeal.

Shivering in the raw wind, Pierre stared up at the dark towers of Notre Dame, hardly listening to a whispered lecture on the Bulgar religion and the transcendent power of the male loins. Male loins held no interest for Pierre, and it was only when he felt his own being stroked by the cult's leader that his attention returned sharply. "Power!" the man whispered. "Power!" For once the clergy had spoken the unexaggerated truth. Pierre disengaged the groping hand and by this gesture became apostate to the Bulgars.

Meanwhile, money was running low. Four months of royal extravagance at the Hôtel France et Choiseul had all but exhausted the spinster's bequest, and Pierre, growing sour, recalled the reasons for his having left Paris years before. This was a jaded city, a place where all easy opportunities had already been seized. He faced the fact that after five séances he had acquired only two real converts —a Left Bank seamstress whose monthly salary would not pay their hotel bill for a day, and a pensioned civil servant without a sou who gave Pierre a cheap watch and some worthless cufflinks instead of money. Clearly it was time to find greener fields.

Pierre considered going to Vienna, having heard that Empress Elisabeth of Austria was currently being seduced by the ghost of the poet Heinrich Heine, whose spectral caresses she regularly enjoyed at Gödöllö, her estate in Hungary. Yet, attractive as the possibility of a royal client was, this sort of carrying on with spirits suggested the same shallowness he had found in Paris. London, he decided, and the conservative, practical English offered a better opportunity.

When the Lauriers crossed the channel, Pierre was confident that the journey would end in success, sure that in London, Margot would be an exotic novelty. He was quickly disillusioned, for in England the spiritist stage had already been pre-empted by shows more spectacular than the one he offered.

Eusapia Palladino, an Italian tigress, was at the height of her fame and powers, conjuring up whole circuses of poltergeists, lemures, and similar apparitions who lifted marble-topped chiffoniers, hurled horsehair chairs across drawing rooms, and delivered messages from the spirit world with the regularity of the postal service. Eusapia, a coarse peasant who seemed an unlikely medium, was subjected to every test skeptics could devise: her hands were tied, her feet were tied, she was laced in a Bedlam jacket; still wild manifestations continued. Several times she was detected in trickery—surprised once by an elderly gentleman who hid under a table for more than an hour to observe her foot manipulations, and again by a physician who noticed a strand of thread on her lips and later learned that Signora Palladino could perform more wonders with her teeth than most mediums could do with two free hands and an assistant. A few lapses by no means explained all her miracles, and Eusapia's weight-moving poltergeists continued to defy, or at least escape, detection. Baffled scientists, finding no way to square her with their dogma, at last decided that she was not really worth studying and turned their attention to matters less embarrassing.

But the ladies of England took up Eusapia's cult, sniffed the air and declared they smelled ectoplasm, agreeing that it was sulphurous although tinged with bay.

Margot Laurier disarranged no furniture, hoisted no umbrella stands, sent no coal scuttles flying through windows. Her effects were quiet and elusive: a faint laughter, a sound of weeping or prayer, a small cry followed by a few whispered words, or a vaguely remembered phrase of music. Her listeners were shaken, and this was hardly the effect a hostess wanted from entertainment at a weekend party.

Margot could compete with none of the marvels being

offered. She was not even a match for the otherwise color-less parson on the Isle of Jersey whose manse was frequented by rowdy specters who tripped and pinched guests, while Elementals blew chilly breath to knock tea-cups and cloisonné from the whatnot. (In attracting spirits the parson was rather like John Wesley, the celebrated founder of the Methodist Church, whose home, a century before, had drawn disorderly forces as a magnet draws iron—annoying phantasms who rang bells, smashed crock-ery, and created nerve-racking confusion that nearly drove the great preacher to his wits' end.)

In the midst of such hubbub the voices of quieter, more ephemeral ghosts were utterly lost. Margot's failure to conquer London galled Pierre because he had come with the misconception that the English were a people given to moderation. Within a month he discovered that beneath the stolid surface flowed a river of sheer lunacy, a very Mississippi of zaniness. No idea was so insane that some Englishmen would not take up cudgels for it. Pierre en-countered pyramidologists, followers of the Cosmic Con-sciousness, the cult of Joanna Southcott, theosophical cranks who endlessly quoted Madame Blavatsky's *Isis Un-veiled,* and a whole army of people who believed them-selves descended from the Lost Tribes of Israel and in-sisted that Queen Victoria was the ninety-seventh lineal heir of King David of Jerusalem, via the prophet Jeremiah, who had somehow fled to Ireland and presumably con-tracted a gentile marriage there.

"The English are utterly mad," said Pierre, "and there is no doubt whatever about it."

Margot attracted and held a small group of faithful be-lievers. All were sincere, and not one was wealthy. Be-cause of the lack of money, séances had to be held with a frequency Pierre found intolerable. The gathering of the intent circle, the lowering of lights and clasping of hands had become an ordeal. Gradually he had begun to feel an exposure to something not only unclean but menacing, and he delayed summoning the clients until he was down to his last shilling. Margot, on the other hand, looked forward to the meetings with such eagerness that he was at a loss to understand her. When too much time elapsed between trances she became depressed, drained of vitality, and complained of agonizing headaches.

One night when a meeting of the shabby faithful was held, Pierre did not join the table but stood apart, watching. Margot had made a dramatic entrance, although that night her hair was lusterless and her face white as chalk. Then, in the deepest moment of the trance, as the five communicants leaned toward her, gripping each other's fingers, laboring silently to help her reach the Other Side, Pierre saw color rush to Margot's cheeks; her fixed eyes shone in the candlelight. She draws life from this, he told himself. Sucks it in like blood. This notion so gripped him that later his body recoiled from the touch of her hands and her mouth. "Forgive me," he said. "I am tired tonight, I am not well."

She fell asleep quickly, and as he listened to her contented breathing he thought: I am unnecessary to her. She has something else. Even in the séances he knew he was dispensable, for the gold coin was now only a theatrical prop. She could invoke the trance by her own will, needing only the circle, the dimness of light.

Pierre rose and, shivering in the drafts of the bedroom, stood staring at the ashes in the grate. For the first time he considered abandoning spiritism, turning to some other field. He knew the séances were affecting him, shattering his nerves and leaving him with an unexplainable sensation of fear and unwholesomeness. Yet they compelled him, fascinated him, and he realized even as he pretended to debate the matter that he could not give them up. "It is only that we have not found the right place, the right city," he said. "We will try elsewhere."

The next week they departed for Rome.

Naples followed Rome, and Brussels followed Naples, but in every country the discouragements were the same. Margot never lacked her handful of believers, a small group, pathetic and dedicated, which could be collected anywhere, and the Lauriers during these years were seldom impoverished but never rich. Then, after ten months in Madrid, prospects seemed more favorable than before. The fads and fashions of Spain lagged two decades behind the rest of Europe, and Pierre was delighted to find that hypnotic spiritism was regarded as an exciting novelty. But then, when he had just managed to interest some members of the minor nobility, the police swooped upon the Laurier apartment. Stories of the séances had reached the ears of a priest, who promptly informed his bishop, who in turn spoke to the civil authorities, charging these foreigners with sacrilege and blasphemy. Although the papal anathema on the abominations of spiritism was still a few years in the future, it was none the less a crime to attempt communication with dead Spaniards. The police, with Iberian gallantry, merely confined Margot to the apartment, but Pierre and Little Brother were kicked down a flight of stone steps into a fetid dungeon, where they languished fifteen days in misery and filth. Being foreigners, they were not brought to trial. The police escorted the trio to the port of Cadiz, where they were ordered aboard a leaky cargo vessel bound for Veracruz. A month later, when they saw that city once again, it seemed endowed with a beauty neither God nor the Mexicans had given it.

4

They had returned to a country where names change rapidly but all else remains stubbornly the same. The dictator now called himself "President," and his reseizure of power each six years was known as "election." The capital had a new mayor, who, like his predecessors, declared himself appalled by the sight of festering slums on the city's outskirts. This time, however, something was done about them, for the man was a reformer in the true Latin tradition: he constructed a high mud fence around the worst eyesores so those driving by in carriages no longer suffered the view of human wretchedness. Apart from such externals, the Lauriers found the country unaltered, and Pierre set about gathering his scattered flock.

During the Lauriers' absence their former client the jeweler had become father of a new son, who was now five years old, and he had lost the need for spiritism but not his belief in it. He called on Pierre, greatly excited.

"Señor, it is the providence of God you have come back to Mexico in time! Last month I had business in Guanajuato and I spoke with the Conde Calderón, who is there selling some Mexican holdings before he returns to Spain. The Conde is most enlightened about the Other Side. When I told him of my experiences with you, he expressed great interest. Would you and Madame Laurier give a séance at his Guanajuato home?" The jeweler lowered his voice. "I will tell you in confidence that the Conde will entertain an important personage there. You have heard, of course, of Don Gregorio Gorgoni?"

"I believe so," said Pierre, his heart pounding wildly.

Who had not heard of Don Gregorio? The South American billionaire was a living legend—diamond mines in Africa, a ranch in Argentina said to be as large as the whole kingdom of Belgium; he owned railroads, factories, and banks. Was there anything this mysterious financial genius did not have a secret hand in? At last, thought Pierre, his luck had turned, the great opportunity had come. "I think we can accommodate the Conde and his guest," he said cautiously. "Although a journey to Guanajuato is notoriously difficult."

"*Muy bien!* I will write him at once!"

Two weeks later a private courier delivered a letter stamped with the Conde's crest. Would the Lauriers present a demonstration of occult power for the nobleman and his friend Señor Gorgoni? Would the Lauriers accept a trifling fee? (Pierre gasped at the munificent sum.) Could this demonstration be in both Spanish and English, since another guest, a Dr. James Esterbrook, was American? Pierre scowled at the vaguely familiar name that aroused unpleasant memories he could not quite identify.

"Inform the Conde we accept. I will send word about our requirements."

"*Sí, señor.*" The messenger saluted. "If the railroad bridge to the north has not been restored, His Excellency will send his private coach for you. Naturally there will be a government escort."

"Naturally." A government escort! Then the Conde was a personal friend of the dictator. The prospect was breathtaking.

Pierre and Little Brother combed the city for information about the Conde and the billionaire. Calderón, who divided his time between Spain and Mexico, was an aged sybarite and rakehell, the sire of countless bastards, the subject of endless scandals. He kept no mistresses but consorted with various whores from the worst vice pits of the slums, flaunting these Indian women, taking them to his mansion in the capital or to his homes in other cities. Once he even appeared at the National Opera with a pock-marked Tehuana doxy on his arm and disported himself so shamelessly during *Rigoletto* that the soprano halted on the high C-sharp of "Caro Nome" to stare aghast at his private box.

"A depraved character," said Pierre piously.

It was easy to obtain facts about Calderón, but the billionaire remained a mystery. His origins and activities were shrouded in a secrecy which, Pierre decided, must be purchased at a fabulous price. When he visited Mexico, arriving from unknown locations, he invariably called on an obscure woman named Doña Dolores Cortés, a respectable spinster who could not imaginably be his mistress. Large but orderly parties were given on these occasions, and gossip said that to be invited was like gaining entrance to Aladdin's cave. If the billionaire was favorably impressed by a guest, he would lend vast sums of money at nominal interest and with no security but the borrower's word. On a whim he would back the most improbable business ventures—buy a hundred paintings from an unknown artist or grant an endowment to an unpublished writer. Everyone knew these stories, but no one whom Pierre could question knew the billionaire himself. Pierre decided to trust to luck and Margot's uncanny intuition.

At dawn on the day of departure a coach with silver fittings, accompanied by five armed horsemen in the russet uniforms of the rural police, arrived at the door. The leader, a tall officer with red hair, swung from his saddle with a grace that reminded Pierre of a circus rider. Carelessly he tossed the long rein to a black Alsatian dog, which caught it with a snap of teeth and then sat beside the horse, pointed ears alert, head held at military attention.

"Señor Laurier? I am Captain Patricio Donaju of the *rurales*. Your servant, sir. You will depart in five minutes.

A second coach follows for luggage and servants. How many servants?"

"One." Embarrassed by poverty, Pierre added, "The Conde didn't mention a second coach, so I arranged—"

The captain's eyelids flickered, but he did not smile. "Good. We already have one passenger in that coach. I presume you're armed?"

"I have a brace of pistols. Do you expect trouble on the road?"

"*Quien sabe?* We have not yet rounded up the Indian cockroaches who burned the railroad bridge. I always count available guns—although those in civilian hands I number, more than count."

Pierre suppressed a sharp reply. He was wary of the captain; there was something sinister about the pale blue eyes with their green cast and the cold voice. Pierre suposed that a shark, if it could speak, would sound like Donaju.

Four hours later, when they halted for refreshment, Pierre inquired who, besides Little Brother, rode in the coach behind. "A woman I am delivering to the Conde," said Donaju, and there was no mistaking his meaning.

"Captain! I remind you that you speak in the presence of my wife!"

For the first time Donaju smiled, a lazy, friendly smile. But instead of the apology Pierre expected, he said, "I speak as I speak. If the señor does not like it, he has ways of obtaining satisfaction after his visit to Guanajuato. I will be at his disposal."

Margot interrupted quickly. "Please, gentlemen! The captain meant no offense and none has been taken."

"As the señora wishes." Donaju doffed his sombrero, and although the courtesy was mocking, Pierre wisely held his tongue until he was alone in the coach with Margot.

"Another insolent Mexican showing he's *macho*. Another savage. I presume he's some Irish soldier's bastard."

"Don't quarrel with him!" She hesitated, then said, "There's an evil thing in this man."

He had heard her use these words before. When certain people came to séances she made the remark, almost as though she sensed an unexplainable emanation. It was the same with houses and rooms. In most places, she had told him, the trance was a beautiful dream, but in others, a nightmare. Although he pressed her, she could not describe what she meant.

At the dingy inn where they spent the first night, Pierre caught only a glimpse of Little Brother's fellow passenger before the captain led her to a room and locked her in. "What is she like?" he asked the hunchback.

"A whore like any other. And an opium-eater. She sits dazed and says nothing."

"Is she beautiful?"

"Maybe she once was. I do not always recognize what other men find beautiful."

They completed the long northward journey, encountering only the hardships all travelers endured—lumpy beds, inedible beans smeared with chili, and stinging clouds of dust that whirl like dervishes over the treeless Mexican highland. Pierre kept his pistols ready, but the only bandit they saw was the corpse of a mutilated Indian boy hanging by the ankles in the plaza of Celaya, a scarecrow object.

"I detest such displays," said Donaju.

"I agree." Pierre's stomach was queasy. "It is horrible."

"You mistake me. It is ineffective. It makes martyrs of scum who should die unnoticed."

The next morning, as the coach ascended the mountain wilderness of Guanajuato, Pierre tingled with the joy of optimism. The horses were winded by the long, twisting climb, and Donaju ordered a brief stop on the crest of a ridge overlooking the old city. Pierre squeezed Margot's hand. "Ah, look! The town is magnificent! More Spanish than Toledo. I had no idea it could be like this. Look at those domes, the towers."

She gazed down at the city and the great gorge. "I wish we had not come," she said. "I wish we could turn back."

"What kind of talk—" Pierre stopped speaking and cocked his head, hearing a distant sound. "*Mon dieu!*" He ran to Donaju. "Captain, there is trouble in the city! I can hear musket fire."

Donaju, tightening the girth of his saddle, hardly looked up. "Musketry? I hear only fireworks—just as I would expect. You surprise me, señor. A man of your calling should have remembered what tomorrow is."

"And what is tomorrow?"

"The Day of the Dead."

When they arrived at the Conde's mansion the nobleman himself was not in, but they were graciously received by a middle-aged woman of genteel manner whom Pierre took to be an elevated housekeeper. He treated her as such, sitting down in her presence and ordering a cup of chocolate. For a while she encouraged his mistake, then, with a twinkle in her gray eyes, explained that she was Señorita Dolores Cortés, a guest and friend of the Conde.

Not only of the Conde, thought Pierre, leaping to his feet and implanting the most gallant of kisses on her hand. This, then, was the billionaire's Mexican hostess.

"The Conde will take supper with you this evening, señor."

"And the other guests?"

"Dr. Esterbrook, whom I have not met, lives in a village nearby, but he will come tomorrow night for the demonstration. Señor Gorgoni will also be present, but he usually arrives at the last moment—or indeed several moments later than that."

"I look forward to meeting him."

"Ah, yes. You may find him an exasperating man, but he

is wonderfully generous. People forgive him much because of that." Although she smiled pleasantly, Pierre suffered an uneasy feeling that his mind had been read.

"Will you attend, señorita?" Margot asked.

"I regret I cannot. The Conde has arranged the demonstration for midnight, and my health limits my hours."

"I am sorry." She was relieved that Doña Dolores would not join the circle. The señorita, for all her courtesy, aroused Margot's apprehension, causing a fear she could not define. Of the hundreds of men and women who had attended séances, only a few had affected her in any way. All others were anonymous spectators who watched, heard her words, but could not share her private journey, were blind to colors and shapes she saw, deaf to music she heard. Their gathering was necessary for her to achieve her private experience; she used them, but from them she felt nothing. Yet there were individuals whose presence brought an atmosphere that suffocated and absorbed her. These were the special ones, and their specialness had nothing to do with voice or appearance or manner; some other quality communicated the message she could feel but not interpret. Twice in the last week this sensation had come to her: first upon meeting Donaju, and now while talking with Doña Dolores.

"I am inexcusable!" the señorita said. "You are tired and I have not shown you your room. I fear it is gloomy, but in this house the choice is between gloomy and gloomier."

They followed her across a central patio and up a broad stairway to a balcony which encircled the interior of the house, serving as a second-floor hall. "A mausoleum," she said, opening the double doors of a vaulted chamber. "I am devoted to the Conde, but this house is a crypt and I am sure it is haunted."

"Madame Laurier will remain in the room until she is called tomorrow night," said Pierre. "Our servant will bring meals to her. Absolute rest and seclusion are re-

quired. You see, the labors of the trance are enormous."
This was pure staging. Margot, he felt, should be seen
only under suitably dramatic conditions.

That night, while Pierre took late supper with the
Conde, she lay on her bed, fitful and disturbed, both the
city and the house oppressing her. When she closed her
eyes the mansion's history unreeled in her mind, stories
and legends memorized from the pages Pierre had given
her in Mexico City. Tomorrow night the circle would seek
contact with those who had died in the Conde's house, and
there had been many of them. In the patio she had noticed
a stone stairway, narrow and moss-grown, which led, she
supposed, to the cellar where the heretic Jews had suffered
and perished. The room she now occupied must be the
chamber in which Calderón's aunt, thirty years ago, was
strangled by an insane servant. A portrait of this unfortunate lady hung above the bureau, an angular figure with
a rosary entwined in bony fingers—no ghost, Margot told
herself, but a harmless old maid long dead.

Today new emotions, unfamiliar doubts had awakened
in her. From the moving coach she had caught glimpses of
twisting streets shadowed by ponderous arches and fa-
çades, motionless clusters of dark-skinned women wrapped
in black shawls, and even darker men. The streets rang
with noise—bells, fireworks, the clatter of carriage wheels,
and shouts of venders, yet behind the noise she felt a silence hovering like a great cloud above the canyon. The
city, cut from the rock of the desolate mountain, called
another place to her mind, a city she had visited only in
dreams or on those nights when the pleasant world of the
séance became a nightmare landscape swirling with mist,
through whose folds she saw towers and walls and great
structures resembling temples and tombs. "I have been
here before."

Long after midnight Pierre, tipsy from the Conde's
brandy, found his way to the bedroom. She kept her eyes

closed, knowing that if she talked with him her fear would pour out, she would beg him to return to the capital, to leave this place by the first horses they could hire. Without undressing, he collapsed on the bed beside her and, although he soon breathed heavily, he too was troubled, turning on the pillow, mumbling in his sleep, repeating the name she often heard him speak in dreams. "Tante Julie . . . Tante Julie . . ."

She had wondered who this woman might be but could not ask. Margot knew nothing of his early life, but he had told her he was the heir of a nobleman and had been swindled of his title and fortune by the connivance of his uncle with a wicked priest. This pair plotted a hideous death for him, but, warned by a servant, he escaped France to flee abroad, disguised in the habit of a Dominican novice. She wept at this tale and kissed him, never revealing that she too had read this romance of Alexander Dumas *père*. He was childlike, and she loved him all the more for this weakness, but she asked no further questions. Now in the dark she pressed her lips against him and thought he spoke to her when he murmured, "But I love you. . . ."

The following night, as the hour for the séance approached, Margot waited in the shadows of the balcony. Across the courtyard she saw Little Brother making preparations in the *sala*, a second-floor drawing room that faced the street at the front of the house. He arranged chairs at a marble table, placed the black candle scented with bay and myrrh, tuned the violin he would play in an adjoining room. She saw him hesitate in the doorway, gazing thoughtfully at a great iron chandelier hanging on a chain above the patio, its dozen oil lamps glowing faintly.

To her left the entrance to the dining room was open, and she could view the Conde enjoying late supper with his guests—Pierre, Donaju, and the American doctor.

Calderón, Pierre had told her, used a hair dye, coated his time-ravaged face with tinted rice powder, and rubbed his cheeks with rose cloth. Now the candelabra near him cast unkind brightness on his features, and harsh lines showed through the white film. Although he was telling a story—the others were laughing—the thin lips barely moved and his crimsoned mouth seemed only a deeper wrinkle.

There was the clicking of a cane in the patio below as a squat, plump man wearing a shovel-shaped sombrero approached the stairway. Withdrawing to the bedroom, Margot heard the Conde, his voice crackling like tissue. "Ah, Don Gregorio! Welcome! Gentlemen, our honored guest has arrived—late, as usual. Let us go to the *sala* and place ourselves in Señor Laurier's hands."

As they moved toward the front of the house, Pierre was speaking. "A pity there are only four tonight. We would have better results with five at the table."

"You do not count yourself, Señor Laurier?"

"No, I will stand to one side to watch—a precaution for the safety of the medium." In his coat he had concealed a strip of luminous gauze, thin but very strong, planning to materialize a ghost if Margot failed to impress. "Perhaps Doña Dolores could be persuaded to join us?" He did not explain that each additional person increased the chance that Margot would strike a right chord, hit upon a sensibility.

"For the love of God, don't awaken Doña Dolores! She is a bear when she hibernates!" The billionaire barked and growled rather than spoke. "Calderón, you goat, I know you've got a woman hidden somewhere. Bring her out of the closet and put her at the table. We can stand the stink of her perfume."

The Conde chuckled. "An amusing idea. Captain Donaju, fetch up Señorita Elvira whatever-her-name-is."

"Elvira," murmured Donaju. "She has no other name."

At the mirror Margot examined her hair and dress and

bathed her eyes in a solution of belladonna to make the large pupils enormous. A moment later Little Brother appeared at the door. "It is the time, señora."

Quickly she moved toward the darkened *sala*, taking long, gliding steps as Pierre had taught her, the white silk of her gown billowing cloudlike around her. At the arched doors she heard a small gasp—the doctor? the Conde?—but she kept her eyes fixed on the gold coin Pierre held above the candle. "Stand near the table," he said. "You will sleep, Margot Laurier. . . . Sleep, and your spirit will pass to that realm beyond the living. . . . The coin is moving . . . the coin . . . the coin . . ." Suddenly she could no longer control her gaze. Fear and confusion welled up in her, and her eyes broke away as she searched the table for the source of her panic. The billionaire's features were shadowed by the black sombrero, she could read nothing from his expression, yet surely the alarm that gripped her came from this man. But not only from him; the sensation pressed upon her, surrounding her, and her eyes moved swiftly from one face to the next, resting an instant on each one: the Conde, the haggard woman beside him, Donaju, the taut sallow features of the doctor. . . . All of them, she thought, all of them.

"Margot!" Pierre's fingers snapped, and she compelled her attention back to the coin once more, struggling to submerge her mind in unconsciousness. The candle flared before her, a blinding brilliance, then receded, leaving her in grayness, a numbing sense of sleep, a knowledge of the passing of time as though she herself had become part of a great clock, a hand creeping forward, moving certainly and inexorably to a determined place. She sensed motion, then flight, but knew nothing more until at last she felt the sleep fading from her, the trance ending, the slow return to the world. Shaking her head, she forced open heavy eyelids, expecting to find herself in the bedroom with Pierre standing near her as usual, commanding her to awaken. Instead, she was alone on the spot where the trance had begun, still in the huge room lit by the black candle, which had now burned low, the Conde's *sala*—but the others had left, their five chairs were empty.

A storm had arisen during her hypnosis; torrents of rain poured on the roof and splashed on the balcony outside the closed doors, while thunder rolled overhead, re-echoing in the mountain gorge, shaking the walls of the house. "Pierre! Pierre!" she cried. Incredible that he had deserted her. Left her to awaken alone in an unfamiliar place. "Pierre! Little Brother!" She ran to the door and, finding it locked, screamed, striking at it with her fists, pounding and shouting. When no answer came she turned to a window and struggled to open the bolts. As the shutters swung back, the wind and rain struck her, drenching the white gown. Outside, a narrow iron balcony stretched the length of the house, overhanging the street, but its windows opened only into the *sala* and as she made her way along it, hand over hand on the cold railing, she realized she could not escape except by leaping to the cobblestones below. Shielding her eyes from the rain, she looked left and right down a long avenue of utter darkness broken only by lightning which streaked and zig-zagged the sky, flickering on silent buildings, spurting suddenly down the tower of a distant church to outline the cornices in blue fire. "Help me! Help me!" she shouted, but there was no one to hear, no lamps gleamed behind the shuttered houses; no beggars, no nightwatchmen huddled in the entrances. The dark-faced men and women had vanished as mysteriously as the occupants of the Conde's mansion, and the city had become the city of her nightmares, deserted, tenantless, a place visited only by the rain and the wind. Terrified, she retreated from the balcony, whimpering when she saw that the wind had extinguished the candle.

"Where have they gone? Where?" Leaning against the

wall, she forced herself to control her shaking body. A cruel and hideous joke had been played. Pierre and Little Brother must be imprisoned elsewhere in the house, overpowered by the Conde and his guests. Again she beat on the door panels, screaming that they would pay for this, cursing them, shouting Pierre's name over and over until she had no more breath.

At the sideboard her searching fingers found a matchbox and roughstone. When she struck it a tiny spark flared, then suddenly burst in an explosion of light, filling the room, dazzling her, and she cried out in fear, thinking lightning had struck the house. But the radiance dissolved, drew inward upon itself, forming and contracting into the wavering shape of a candle flame, and then she saw the Conde's face, a pale mask in the blackness. He whispered, "Is she waking now? The eyes are changing. It is fantastic!"

She heard a long, trembling note of Little Brother's violin, a note which died away abruptly, and knew that only now was she returning to consciousness. The vanished circle, her imprisonment, had been illusions of the trance, but, unlike visions of other hypnotic dreams, this was etched in her memory, vivid in detail. The empty chairs of her dream were even now more real than the five silent people who encircled the table, their hands still clasped, their eyes transfixing her. "What has happened?" She caught the edge of the table for support. "Pierre?"

"Señor Laurier?" Turning his head, the Conde peered into the shadows. "Why, he's gone. I was so intent I did not notice him leave. Remarkable! This was not at all what I expected."

Margot felt Little Brother's hand on her arm. "Come, señora, I will take you to your room," he said urgently. "Excuse us, Excellencies. The demonstration has ended."

"Where's Laurier?" Calderón demanded. "I want to talk to him. This was an incredible experience."

"The señor was suddenly taken ill. I think he has gone to his room. *Con permiso,* Excellencies, excuse us."

As he led her toward the bedroom she asked, "What has happened? Hermanito, tell me!"

"I was in the next room. I heard you speaking. Someone sang part of a song. Then Señor Pierre cried out—softly, but I heard him. He ran past my door, stumbling, and his face . . . his face . . . Señora, I do not know."

Their bedroom door was bolted, and there was no answer to Margot's knock, but through the thick panel she could hear a sound like the weeping of a child. When she rapped again, calling Pierre's name, a shrill voice cried, "Go away! For the love of God, go away!"

"Pierre, let us in!" No reply came.

At the crack of the door the hunchback spoke softly and cajolingly. "Señor, surely you are not afraid of Little Brother? You do not want to be alone. I will bring cognac and stay with you. Please, señor." The bolt rasped; then there was a sound of retreating footsteps inside. A draft came from the dark room, a musty odor of ancient masonry. In the faint light Margot saw Pierre huddled on the floor, head buried in his hands as he sobbed.

When she approached him he screamed, cringing from her, and Little Brother quickly closed the door to shut off his cries from the rest of the house. "Do not go near, señora." The hunchback lit a lamp, found a flask in the bureau, and persuaded Pierre to swallow some brandy. As her husband lifted his head, Margot stared in horror at the wet lips and dilated eyes. He had torn his shirt open and ripped the ascot from his throat. It lay on the floor beside him, a shredded rag of gray silk.

"You are better already, señor," said Little Brother. "See? There is light and you are not alone."

Pierre shuddered, his shoulders trembling as he clutched the brandy flask. "Tante Julie! Did you see her? She was there tonight, she sang her song—the one about the captain

—and she put her hands— Oh, God! I knew she would come, but I did not think tonight—"

"You are ill, señor. The señora and I will help you to bed, and in the morning—"

But he would not move from the floor and he recoiled when Margot stepped toward him. "Keep her away from me, Hermanito! Don't let her touch me!" Then for nearly an hour they could understand nothing he said as he babbled incoherently, his voice a monotone, his eyes vacant. But when he grew calmer a story emerged, the story of Tante Julie, told as he had relived it so many times. Margot found herself drawn into the nightmare, felt the old woman's embrace, the suffocating weight of her body; and the terror was strangely familiar, as though she had experienced this before, had shared this memory with him.

Unable to bear more, she cried, "None of this is true! You never knew such a woman. It is this house and these people—they have done something to us. Some trick—"

"No, she will always come back now. Always."

Little Brother drew Margot away. "Soon he will sleep, señora. You can do nothing now. Lie on the bed and try to rest. I will stay near the doorway."

Margot had no thought of sleeping, yet at last exhaustion overcame her, and the hunchback also slept, wrapped in a blanket. During the hour before dawn, neither heard Pierre's quiet movements as he made certain preparations, but both awoke suddenly, aroused by the thud of an overturning chair. Pierre's body, arms and legs flailing, hung from a crossbeam of the ceiling. While they slept he had fashioned a noose from the thin, strong gauze he had concealed in his pocket before the séance, the gauze that shines whitely in the dark and is used by charlatans to conjure ghosts. Although it bit cruelly into the flesh of his throat, it held him for only a moment, and as Little Brother leaped toward the swaying figure, the noose gave way and Pierre fell into the hunchback's arms. He revived almost immediately and, lying on the bed, he looked up at Margot, his eyes filled with pain, but he was calm now; the hysteria had spent itself. She realized he was trying to speak, and when she bent close to his lips she heard a hoarse whisper. "Why have you done this?" he said. "I loved you once."

In the morning Margot sent Little Brother to inform the Conde that her husband was too ill to travel today but they would depart for Mexico City tomorrow. She expected the nobleman to be difficult, for his curiosity had been aroused by the séance and it seemed likely he would want to question Pierre, but the Conde lived in mortal fear of contagion and took alarm at this sudden unexplained illness of a guest. With tact but absolute clarity he requested that the Lauriers confine themselves to their room for the remainder of their stay. Rail service to the capital had resumed, and he would make prompt arrangements for them to leave tomorrow.

"Did he mention the séance?" she asked Little Brother.

"No, señora. I thought several times he would question me. He began to speak but then did not. It was on his mind."

It was also on the minds of others. A note arrived from Dr. Esterbrook, a message phrased in correct but awkward French. He had been impressed by her "unusual gift" and wished to consult her privately. Having crumpled the note, Margot threw it away. Later, Doña Dolores Cortés tapped at the bedroom door, and Margot spoke with her on the balcony.

"The Conde informs me that you will return tomorrow to the capital?"

"Yes. My husband is ill. I must take him home at once."

"I am so sorry. I had hoped to speak with you. I—" The older woman hesitated, searching for words. "Señora, Don

Gregorio has told me about the demonstration last night. He was most affected, and I—I wondered if I myself might attend such a meeting in Mexico City. I—I am quite interested in—"

"I think there will be no further meetings."

"But señora! Surely—" A desperate expression crossed Doña Dolores' face. "I would not decide hastily, if I were you. Don Gregorio himself might wish to consult you. It would be worth your while to—"

"Don Gregorio is nothing to me. Now I must go back to my husband."

"You are an unusual woman, señora. Unusual in many ways."

Doña Dolores studied her—a hard, questioning gaze. She is like flint, Margot thought; she smiles graciously but there is a tigress behind the smile.

"I will speak with you in Mexico City," said Doña Dolores. "Go with God, señora."

"Go with God."

The third request for a séance was more disturbing. Margot had gone to the kitchen to fetch a cup of broth for Pierre, in hope that he would be able to swallow. On the stairs Captain Donaju confronted her. "I will call on you in the capital three weeks from tonight," he told her. "Expect me then. I do not believe in spirits, but you have aroused my interest. I am curious."

"You are insolent and I will not receive you, señor, not in three weeks, not ever. Please permit me to pass now."

When he gripped her arm she winced at the force of his hand. "I have told you, señora. I do not engage in arguments with women, so perhaps I should speak with your husband. He is a foreigner, and I suspect his business in Mexico is illegal. I could arrange to have him questioned —thoroughly. Do you think he would find the investigation agreeable?"

Pain shot through Margot's arm. "I have no choice,

then." Even as she spoke she knew that they could not leave Mexico too soon. Here there was no refuge from such a man as Donaju.

That night Margot kept watch at Pierre's bedside while Little Brother slept on a straw mat outside the door in case she should call him. It was an unnecessary precaution, for Pierre did not stir but lay as one drugged, not lifting his head from the pillow when, at a late hour, an accident occurred in the house—an accident that awakened everyone and brought guests and servants running to the patio in their nightclothes. Pierre, unaware of the commotion, did not hear the servants begin to wail and recite the litany of prayers for the dead.

The accident, which added one more legend to the mansion's evil reputation, took place long after midnight, for the Conde Calderón observed Spanish rather than Mexican hours. After enjoying supper and a great quantity of wine, he had sat in the patio with Captain Donaju, discussing the transportation of certain valuables to Mexico City and then to Madrid. "This visit," said the Conde, "will be my last trip to Guanajuato." They finished their brandy and had risen to bid each other good night when the iron chandelier above them crashed down. The huge fixture was attached to a pulley so it could be lowered to refill the lamps, and at that unfortunate moment the hook holding its chain worked loose from the dry mortar on the balcony.

The Conde, his head crushed by the chandelier, did not survive until the arrival of a priest and died in his sins. Donaju's arm was bruised, and the *rurale* guards privately congratulated him, for if the two men had not both taken a step forward at that precise second, the wake would have been held for their captain instead of for Calderón. In fact the leather chair in which Donaju had been sitting was sliced in half as by an ax. "You're a lucky devil," they said. "Satan's own grandson!" Donaju himself said nothing.

The Lauriers did not remain for the funeral. At noon a *calandria* arrived to take them to the depot, and Margot, holding Pierre's arm, led him through the kneeling flock of black-shawled women who moaned through their beads in the patio. The Indian mourners paid them no heed, yet Margot felt eyes resting on her and, looking up quickly, saw Doña Dolores on the balcony. Near her was the American doctor, who had come to pay his respects. Both watched the departure silently.

As they passed the hall, Donaju saluted her, and, turning her head to avoid his gaze, she found herself looking into the bleared face of Elvira Campos. These four, she thought. The Conde is dead. These four remain. She did not question the absence of Don Gregorio; the billionaire did not enter her mind.

An hour later, when the train bound for Mexico City began its tortuous passage through the mountains to the south, Margot sat alone in the coach while Little Brother took Pierre to another car where he could buy brandy. She watched her husband shuffle down the aisle, head bowed, one hand on the hunchback's shoulder and the other grasping the backs of seats—the slow, unsteady movements of an old man. She sat with her hands folded, her face rigid, knowing that she too had changed. "I am alone; they have destroyed him."

The train descended into the narrows of the river-cut gorge, crept along the rock shelf of the bank, plunged into shadow as the canyon walls sealed off the sun. The cliffs towered on either side, cliffs pitted with caves and quarries, the gray-green stone of the Inquisitor's House. She did not look back at the city but, closing her eyes, saw it as it had once appeared to her, the dark streets empty, the lamps unlit, its domes and battlements lashed by rain, a blind and voiceless city of the dead.

"It is finished," she said. "I will not see it again." But in this, of course, she was mistaken.

5

"We fled Mexico a week later," Margot Laurier told the magician during their third and final interview in London. "I was afraid of all of them, afraid they would prevent our leaving. The American doctor followed us from Guanajuato and he called at the house four times that week. Little Brother turned him away, but he kept returning. There was a letter from Doña Dolores Cortés, requesting a séance, and she mentioned some of her powerful friends. Was it a threat? I was never sure.

"Most of all I was afraid of Captain Donaju. While we were selling our possessions, preparing to leave, a note came from him, reminding me to expect him and another person soon. Of course the other person would have been Elvira Campos. They were in league; there was something they shared."

"You do not know what?"

"No. But—" Her voice faltered and she turned her eyes away from the magician. "I think it was something vile. There was money in the envelope, and I cannot explain this but I felt he was paying me to do something unclean."

"You have not mentioned the billionaire."

"The billionaire?" She seemed surprised. "I heard nothing from him; he does not concern me. But I knew the others were evil, I knew they had caused what happened to us—one of them, or perhaps all of them together. I hated them and I was terrified.

"So we fled, traveling by night to a village on the coast, where Little Brother arranged for a fishing boat to take us to Cuba. I thought Pierre might die during the journey. That was almost two years ago, and he is still not well, still cannot be left alone. Little Brother and I never leave the flat at the same time. Someone must always watch."

"Has he suffered any repetition of his experience?" the magician asked. "Has he believed himself visited again by this—this ghost?"

"No. But I am always afraid. Before every séance I wonder . . ."

"Yet you continue the séances?"

Making a helpless gesture with her hands, she shrugged. "I have no other way to earn money. Besides, now I have only the trance. Nothing else is left for me."

The magician asked her no more that afternoon, although countless questions intrigued him. She had implied that rare individuals possessed psychic auras, a quality she had sensed among all those present at the Guanajuato séance. Were those people what mediums called "receptives" or "parasensitives"? Had the convergence of their powers produced the eruption of some unexplained force? Clearly Margot Laurier held them responsible for Pierre's destruction, connecting them one and all with "evil." Had this "evil" manifested itself to cause the separate but simultaneous nightmares which she and Pierre had suffered?

There were many questions, but he would make his investigation slowly and painstakingly, even if it required several months, and he felt that during this time he would come to know Margot as a friend. He had been alone too much in the last years, making a cult of Miranda's memory. "I must give it up, living with memories," he told himself. What was done could not be changed; he must cease blaming himself, have an end to repentance.

He had made this interview brief because other matters required his attention. It was the seventeenth of February, an anniversary, a yearly occasion on which the magician performed a prescribed ritual: the keeping of a deathbed promise made many years before to the man who had shaped D'Aquisto's life, Professor Carlos Cantari. As the magician bade farewell to Margot Laurier, escorting her to the hansom he had ordered, his thoughts were of Cantari and of the vigil to be kept that night.

Several hours later, at ten o'clock, D'Aquisto donned his greatcoat, scarf, and gaiters. He put on a huge karakul hat, which gave him a cossack appearance, and took from a chest the black fur muff he used in bitter weather. Thus fortified, he ventured into the snowy street, yearning for Tangier or the Costa del Sol. The only sensible residents of this inclement island, he felt, were the migrant swallows that were now nesting snugly among the reeds of the Nile. Next year he would join them.

D'Aquisto crossed a windswept square, turned right, and proceeded a short distance to the arched entrance of a church, a forbidding medieval building he had selected several days ago. He knocked loudly on the door, then waited what seemed an interminable period for a sexton to draw the bolts.

"My name is Tomás D'Aquisto," he announced. "I made arrangements with the vicar to—"

"Yes, sir, I was expecting you. Come in out of the heathen cold—though, frankly, it's very little better in here." The magician agreed. The deserted sanctuary was chill and dark as a Siberian dungeon. Lighting a lamp from the flame of his candle, the sexton said, "I'll leave you to your meditations, Mr. D'Aquisto. The vicar told me to return at midnight to let you out and secure the door."

D'Aquisto shivered. "Midnight? Eleven-thirty will do very well. I shall meditate more briefly than I planned." Cantari's ghost, he decided, would forgive him. The professor had hated cold as much as D'Aquisto did. "Please light several more candles for me. I will pay extra."

"Right, sir."

As, one by one, the candles were lighted, the high Gothic arches came into dim relief, masses and bulks of shadow. Overhead the magician saw the white gleam of an icicle that had formed like a great stalactite beneath a leak in the roof. He was surprised at the absence of bats; the atmosphere demanded them.

After the sexton's departure, D'Aquisto seated himself in a pew near the altar and began his vigil. The story he had told the vicar when he arranged to use the church was true but incomplete. "Years ago I made a promise to a man who was more than a father to me," he had explained. "On the anniversary of his death, I go to some holy place to recall his memory." D'Aquisto did not add that his real mission was to await contact from Cantari's ghost, that the old man, dying, had said, "If there is a way I can come to you, I will come. Listen for me!"

Alone in the sanctuary, he thought of the man to whom this night was dedicated, smiling as he recalled their first meeting. D'Aquisto had been seven years old—or perhaps six or eight, no one was sure—when he stole Carlos Cantari's pearl cufflink and attempted to pick his pocket, perpetrating this crime on a crowded Lisbon street and employing a technique in which the urchin Tomás had been painfully drilled.

He was a scrawny ragamuffin then, less a child than a famished little animal whose hunting grounds were the streets and alleys of the Portuguese capital and whose den was the cellar of a fetid tenement. That morning he loitered in a doorway, watching for a likely victim— foreigners and strangers to the city were the best marks, the least suspicious of begging children. In the passing crowd the boy's hawklike eyes caught sight of an elderly man almost as dark as a Lascar sailor who wore a beautiful coat with brass buttons and new-style cuffs clasped by small pearls set in silver.

Tomás struck boldly, rushing from the doorway, seizing

the man's hand. "Oh, good sir, I am starving! I die of hunger!" Although this was very nearly true, it was said only to divert attention from the activity of the child's small, deft fingers as they unfastened the pearl link. His hideous grimaces served the same purpose.

"Charity, charity! Help me for the love of God!" The link was now safely hidden in his trousers, and he tugged at the man again, weeping, while a tiny blade honed to a razor sharpness sliced a button from the back of the victim's sleeve. "Take pity on a poor orphan, and I will pray for you." The child, accustomed to being thrust away without alms, suffered a terrible shock when his hand, slipping adroitly into the man's pocket, encountered a larger companion. The stranger was actually reaching for a coin! Tomás tried to leap away, but iron fingers gripped his wrist.

"Well, well! The rogues of Lisbon grow younger every year!"

After useless struggle he resigned himself to another sojourn in prison—a pity, since he had been released from jail only three days before. Not that it mattered greatly. The gruel fed once a day to prisoners was greenish and sickening, but the older convicts were kind to him and taught him various useful things. They were much gentler than the woman in whose cellar he lived, a hag who pretended to be his aunt but was really a Fagin employing a pack of infant thieves. He hated her but supposed he belonged in her care and could remember no one else.

"A cufflink gone!" exclaimed the gentleman. "And a button! I would never have noticed. Enormous skill! Clever misdirection of my attention, too. Who taught you this, boy?"

Tomás blubbered as he had been trained to do. "Oh, have mercy! I am a poor homeless orphan!" If only he had not dropped the little knife he could have stabbed the man's hand and fled.

The dark stranger stared at Tomás—a long, hard look of appraisal and amusement. "You have talent. A shame it is so misused. Well, come along, we must do something about you."

Tomás was led away, but not to a magistrate. The man took him to a marketplace restaurant and bought him a bowl of rich, steaming soup. He was given all the bread he could cram into his empty stomach and, encouraged by the man's kindness, cautiously answered a few questions about his life, explaining rather proudly that he had no parents and knew nothing of them, although he had been accused of being the bastard of a Barbary smuggler.

"I am Professor Carlos Cantari," said the man. "Now watch closely and you will see something marvelous." He picked up three spoons from the table and began to juggle them, faster and faster, higher in the air, until they clinked against the beams of the ceiling. Then he added a glass and the empty bread basket. Tomás had seen street jugglers but never anything so amazing as this.

"Oh, sir, it is wonderful! How I would love to do such a thing!"

"Then come with me," said Professor Cantari, "and one day you will."

He became Cantari's apprentice, then assistant, and was with him fifteen years, traveling the world as he learned the arts of juggling and illusion. Nor was Tomás the only child befriended by the professor. There were young Gilles from the wharfs of Cherbourg; Mario and Benito, the twins from Rome; and a nameless boy who never spoke and was called Cairo after the city where Cantari had found him. Later there was the little girl, Miranda, a Whitechapel waif so terrified by unknown memories that for nearly a year she cringed and wept when anyone spoke loudly.

The orphans served Cantari as best they could, but the professor had no real need of them. He cared for these homeless strays because of a sympathy that was not pity but love, and he never forgot his own early years. Born in India in the Portuguese colony of Goa, he had lost his parents from cholera while he was still a child, and he himself would have perished had he not been cared for by a *jogi,* one of the strange Hindu holy men who are both jugglers and soothsayers. From the *jogis* who wandered that vast land, Cantari first learned his art, and it was to them he owed his survival. It was also the *jogis* who aroused his love of occult philosophy, and many of its mysteries he passed on to the child Tomás.

Cantari and his waifs were a band of happy nomads, roaming three continents, going wherever audiences could be found. They learned one another's language, and their conversation was a Babel of tongues: French, Italian, Spanish, English and Portuguese words crowded into the same sentence as they unconsciously shifted from one idiom to another. All the children became educated, for Cantari was an intellectual, but only Tomás had the manual and mental skill to become the old man's successor.

They were gypsies, but they camped in good hotels, for there was always money. Cantari was a celebrated performer, not merely a juggler but an illusionist in the grand tradition, fully meriting the historic title of master magicians, "Professor." He was the equal of such "Professors" as Henri Robin and Colonel Stodare, who produced the astonishing living head which rested on a table, speaking and blinking, although apparently bodiless. No one, not even Wiljalba Frikell, surpassed him in pure sleight-of-hand, and he had the added advantage of varying his performance with truly beautiful feats of juggling.

Slowly and patiently he initiated the boy Tomás. At the age of ten, D'Aquisto was a "floating boy" who hovered six feet above the stage, stiffly horizontal, while Cantari announced in a mysterious Hindi accent, "He is supported by the miraculous element of ether, an invisible substance new to our century, although long familiar to the holy men of Lhasa. Sniff the air and you will detect its aroma!" They sniffed and they believed. The hidden steel brace that actually held Tomás in air was painfully uncomfortable, but he would have endured torture before letting the beloved professor suspect his misery.

Now, waiting silently in the church, D'Aquisto remembered those years of devotion. "Of all the children, I was his son, his favorite," he said, then added ruefully but honestly, "except for Miranda. But she was a girl and did not matter so much."

One by one, the children had left Cantari. The Roman twins succumbed to smallpox in Damascus; the French boy married and departed; the silent Egyptian returned to his own land. When the end came for the old magician, only Miranda and Tomás remained. It was they who sat beside his bed in the hotel in Naples, in an enormous room stacked with luggage, black trunks with silver lettering, and crammed with the devices and properties of his craft.

"They are yours now, Tomás," he whispered. "You must have the labels changed to *Zantana the Great*. It is a good name; it will draw crowds."

"What talk is this?" D'Aquisto kept his voice light as he blinked back tears. "In a few days you will be well. I have canceled your engagement in Rome, but you must be ready to appear in Venice the first of April."

"You will appear in Venice, Tomás. My engagement is elsewhere, I keep it with no regrets. You will carry on my profession, and you must take care of Miranda. She is still a child, and you are a twenty-year-old man."

Burying her head in her hands, Miranda wept quietly, and D'Aquisto was furious because he knew she cried not only from grief but from shame. She was fourteen now, and for nearly a year, unknown to the old man, D'Aquisto had been sleeping with her when he could not find older and more experienced women in the cities where they performed. She was haunted by guilt because Cantari believed in her virginal innocence. She was a fool, Tomás thought angrily. In a moment she would give the whole thing away, pour out a ridiculous confession of something that was not of the least importance. She should have been honored, not ashamed, that he occasionally shared her bed.

The dying man continued to speak. "You two know that all my life I have searched for the answer to what lies beyond death. You also know that I am certain of nothing." Suddenly his strength seemed to increase; he tried to sit up, and there was anger in his voice. "But it cannot be the end! Is the world like the Indian rope trick? Do we all climb to the top and absolutely vanish? Go nowhere? I refuse to accept this! It cannot be done. There is a plane of existence at the top of the rope, and we abide there." Sinking back to the pillow, he spoke softly, and they leaned close to catch his words. "Promise me this: each year on the anniversary of my leaving you, you will go to some quiet place, a holy place, and if there is a way I can come to you, I will come. Listen for me!"

They promised, clasping Cantari's thin hands, and at eleven o'clock that night, the seventeenth of February, the old man learned—as D'Aquisto liked to term it—the ultimate answer.

The promise was kept year after year by the magician and Miranda. Silently they awaited his voice in many countries and in strange surroundings, for to the magician the words "a holy place" encompassed a Calvinist meeting house, the Hagia Sofia, and the crumbling ruins of an Athenian temple. Without speech and without real hope they watched together. Now D'Aquisto waited alone.

"And he will not come," he said aloud, his voice echoing in the hollowness of the empty church. Always the vigil was futile, only a monument D'Aquisto raised to the memory of a good man. But, like many monuments, it gave consolation to the living. "I do this for myself," he said. "Cantari gave love, and he needed nothing, either then or now. When I wait here, it is for my own sake."

Yet he was unable to keep his thoughts on the professor, and they turned again and again to Margot Laurier, as he wondered if she too at this moment was attempting spectral communion. He pictured the dismal flat, the flickering black candle. Were the clients assembled for their Tuesday ritual? Did Pierre cower in a chair in the far corner?

Just before the chime rang eleven o'clock, he was moved by a premonition. "I must waste no more time," he told himself. "This is the opportunity to learn the truth, and I cannot delay. She is genuine, I feel it, I am sure of it!" Tomorrow he would devise tests and exact demonstrations, he would begin questioning every person who had known her. If necessary, it was well worth traveling to Mexico to gather evidence, to determine what had happened there. Finding the proof would be his dedication.

Suddenly the magician felt ashamed. In letting his thoughts wander he had committed an infidelity against Cantari, to whom these hours belonged, and, knowing he must in some way make amends for his temporary neglect of the professor, he tried to think of a symbolic restitution. Always before, the vigil had been conducted in solemn silence, a rite of concentration, and this had failed; he had never felt close to the professor's spirit. Why not another method? He smiled as he recalled a familiar story by a French writer, a story that had once charmed him. "Yes," he said. "I will do it!"

In an unlocked cabinet he found four collection plates, pewter circles framed in dark wood, and he carried these to the candlelit altar. Facing the black vault of the nave, he spoke softly. "Professor, I have listened once again and I cannot hear you. But perhaps you hear me, perhaps you are here. Do you remember what you once said to a boy in

Lisbon? 'Now watch closely and you will see something marvelous!'"

D'Aquisto spun the plates into the air, first two, then the third and the fourth, talking as he juggled them, a swift running patter such as Cantari had used with an audience. "You observe that I am talking and seem not at all worried about the plates. You always said the mark of a good juggler was his unconcern. Of course, I am really watching closely, and I have set a pattern, a rhythm, but only you could detect this. Look at them sail! Good, is it not, Professor? And I have not practiced in four years! Oh, if I had some real equipment I would give you a show! I would toss bells and torches and brands of green fire! I am better than your Indian *jogis*.

"Have you been proud of me? Did you watch me the night I introduced the 'Flying Angel' at John Maskelyne's theater here in London? I was sensational that night! I beat Maskelyne at his own game. Miranda floated from the stage like a cloud, like a spirit ascending to heaven, and for a moment I believed in it myself. I forgot the levers and the counterweight, I believed I was lifting her with the power of my words and my voice—by my magic. When I was a child and we performed the ether trick, did you ever feel such a thing?

"Did you long for the illusions to be real? I would die in torment if just once the least trick I perform could be a true miracle. One coin that truly disappears, one glass of water that changes to wine! I know I am vain. Am I also a fool for desperately wanting the show to be genuine? Am I childish to delude myself that miracles can be accomplished, have been accomplished? Am I alone in clinging to illusions or are all other men secretly the same, Cantari?"

The plates skimmed higher and higher, flashing silver in the shadowed arches, but his fingers grew numb, and twice there was a clatter on the stone floor when he lost his rhythm. "Even Zantana the Great gets cold hands, and I cannot always please you completely. But I hope you were proud of the way I used to perform the Chinese rice-bowl trick. After I multiplied the rice I poured water from the empty bowl. I was the first one to do it! Even Ben-Ali-Bey had never thought of it.

"Then there was my mind-reading performance with Miranda. You would have been astonished by it, Professor! Once in Dublin things went wrong, yet still Miranda gave the right answer. I was certain that I had conveyed the thought to her, through the air, without the code. But she denied it, said it was an accident. It was hard to forgive her for doubting my miracle. She may have been right, of course. At least, I am afraid she was right. Still, I have been remarkable. The world knows my name. I have justified your faith."

Another plate crashed against a corner of the altar, and D'Aquisto concluded his performance. "No, I cannot always please you completely. If you know all I have done, you realize this, and I count on your forgiveness." Gazing upward past the red glow of the vigil light, he whispered, "You can read my heart. You know I meant well, I meant to do better."

When D'Aquisto left the church he was at peace with himself. For the first time the appointment with Cantari had ended without futility, without despair.

The magician, aware he had caught a chill, remained late in bed the next day. Sneezing, he recalled the unheated church. "Loathsome as a tomb! No wonder so many poor souls are terrified into salvation. Where there is no heating method, death has a positive imminence. Near a fireplace, one never expects it at all."

At noon, when his valet brought breakfast, there was a newspaper on the tray, and, glancing at a column entitled Late Bulletins, D'Aquisto at first paid no special attention to the heading *Man Dies in Fall*. Then, though Pierre Laurier's name was in small type, it seemed to rise from the page to meet his eye. The brief account stated only that Mr. Laurier, a French-born citizen of the Mexican Republic, had plunged to his death from a window of the flat in which he resided. "The tragedy took place a few minutes before eleven o'clock last night. Although there were five witnesses, including the wife of the deceased and four guests, there appears to be uncertainty as to the cause of the fatality, and an investigation is being conducted. Cards found on Mr. Laurier's person suggest that he was a doctor of psychology. . . ."

D'Aquisto's immediate impulse was to rush to Margot Laurier, to offer help and whatever consolation he could give. Then, realizing that his presence would be an intrusion, he contented himself with writing a careful letter, urging her to call upon him freely and implying that financial assistance was available should she require it. This message was delivered by his valet, who returned with a brief answer.

"Thank you, my dear friend, for your kindness. But it is too late now. Nothing can be done, nothing is needed."

For three days the magician waited anxiously, scanning the newspapers but finding no further report. He wrote a second letter to the medium, this time sent it by regular post, and waited again, but this time there was no reply. Finally, unannounced, he went to the dreary building in the warehouse district and was hardly surprised to see a FLAT TO LET sign on its door. The landlady, a pleasant chubby woman, was talkative but not helpful. "Paid up and left, she did, same day as the poor chap was buried. Didn't say where she was going, just went off, looking like a sleepwalker, and that nasty dwarf carrying her luggage. I'm not one to pry, but I've since wished she'd left an address. I've been fair hounded to death, I have, by people seeking her."

"People named Higgins and Hobbs, I suppose," said the magician.

"That's the names. Oh, they carried on like you couldn't believe! Seemed to suspect I know where the woman's gone and won't tell them. Now I ask you, why should I deceive them? Why should I do that?"

"Why, indeed?" Here, at least, was a small grain of justice.

From the landlady D'Aquisto learned enough of the circumstances of Pierre's death to reconstruct the scene in his imagination. Apparently she had eavesdropped when the police were asking questions.

"They were having a little social gathering that night with those Higginses and Hobbses. A concert of sorts, violin music and what. In the midst of it, Mr. Laurier was seized by a kind of dreadful attack. Why, I heard him screaming clear as anything, and I live on the ground floor! Went off his head, he did, sudden. Plunged through the window right down to the pavement. I rushed outside —I was among the first to view the remains, as it were— and he was lying there on his back, gone for sure, and the look on his face was awful. Enough to turn your blood!"

She lowered her voice, and a gleam came into her eye. "It was the tremens, I'd say. I had a lodger once was taken with the whisky horrors one night. Poor chap screamed the house down. Thought he was chased by animals, he did! Even tried to climb up the walls to get away from them, ripped the paper right off, and the next day I found fingernails in the plaster, would you believe it! They carried him off in a van, and that was the end of him. There's few as recovers, once the horrors get them."

"Yes," said D'Aquisto slowly. "I think you are right. It was the horrors."

❊❊❊ THREE

THE SOLITARY

1

When Captain Guzmán journeyed to Mexico City to gather information about the late Doña Dolores Cortés he carried with him a single page of facts and names supplied in advance by the police of the capital. Guzmán was irritated by its meagerness, yet delighted to have it proved once more that the haughty officials of the Federal District, who affected such superior airs, were in truth incompetent. "They know no more than I do!" he said proudly.

Their report began with such usual data as Doña Dolores' birth date, address, and the names of her parents and grandparents. Guzmán caught his breath when he saw that the lady's maternal grandfather was called Carlos Montejo. "Of the Spanish dukes, no less," he murmured, recognizing one of the most aristocratic surnames in his country's history. "No wonder prominent persons are concerned about her death!" It was at that second that Doña Dolores became the heroine of the melodrama Guzmán would later compose.

Reading farther, he found that she had been the last of the Cortés-Montejo line; there were no brothers, and her younger sister, Isabel Cortés, had preceded her in death by several years. Although weeks had passed since the spinster's violent demise, no one had yet located certain paternal cousins now living in Spain, who were presumed to be heirs. Her house was untenanted except for three servants guarding it.

The next item made Guzmán's eyebrows shoot upward. "She was interviewed by rural police some years ago in connection with the accidental death of the esteemed Conde Calderón in the city of Guanajuato. For more information, consult your files there."

"Jesus, Mary, and Joseph!" exclaimed Guzmán. He had been stationed in Morelia at the time of the Conde's fatal mishap, but he knew the story of the falling chandelier; it was another of the legends surrounding the Inquisitor's House. So the spinster's final visit to the Guanajuato mansion had not been her first; she had been present before, and on a notably grim occasion. "It will be in the files," said Guzmán, then remembered that three years ago he himself had ordered the destruction of all dossiers of old accidents, in order to clear space for a billiard table in the headquarters.

"Well, what does it matter if she was in Guanajuato or not? It is a coincidence and took place years ago." To pursue such a line of investigation was only fruitless. Guzmán, like a man plucking a thorn from his finger, dismissed this new fact.

The last line of the Mexico City communication described the dead lady's marital status as *soltera*, the Spanish word for spinster, which also means one who is alone, a solitary.

Beyond that there was only a list of her acquaintances, persons who "can doubtless provide you with data you seek. Authorities here have neither time nor funds to investigate a local matter for Guanajuato, and the responsibility . . ."

"Shirking bureaucrats!" snarled Guzmán.

Since domestic workers were the eyes, ears, and antennae of the police, Guzmán began his task in the capital by calling at the Cortés residence to question the servants, a cook, a maid, and an Indian man of all work, confident that an hour's talk and a brief inspection of the premises would explain the mystery of Señorita Cortés' presence at the séance. He went to the house, he asked his questions, and he learned nothing of value. The cook, who was the senior servant and by far the most articulate, could give no reason for the sudden trip to Guanajuato.

"No, señor, she never mentioned an acquaintance in Guanajuato, but then she spoke very little. . . . No, I know nothing of a Señora Laurier, nor a red-haired officer. . . . A hunchback? No, señor, no hunchback has ever come to this house, *por Dios!*" She crossed herself. "They are unlucky."

"Did she ever talk of ghosts?"

"Ghosts, señor? Never."

"Did she consult witch doctors? *Brujas?*"

"Ay, never! Last spring when I had an evil in my joints and my knees swelled, I asked for extra money so I could go to a *bruja* for a charm to cure it. Señor, she was furious with me! She sent me to the French doctor near the *Zócalo* and of course he did me no good at all."

"I see." Guzmán made a note in his book: "Subject detested witch doctors and all forms of unscientific quackery."

Guzmán learned that the lady often played backgammon alone, the right hand against the left; the maid reported that behind the closed doors of her bedroom she sometimes talked to herself, but no one could hear the words; she seldom went to the theater or concerts, seldom traveled, did not entertain at the Christmas *posadas,* and there were few callers. The lady's life, Guzmán concluded, was as colorless as her portrait and had no highlight except its peculiar ending.

He found the house so depressing that he decided to postpone his inspection of the letters and papers until the next day. A true provincial, Guzmán was never comfortable in these Spanish viceregal homes which lined older streets of the capital, rows of sunless mortuaries modeled on El Escorial. Their interior stairways were dark and hazardous; windowless rooms did not open into patios but were connected by a maze of dank hallways.

"How many rooms?" he asked.

"Thirty-four, I think. Most have been closed for years."

The most forbidding feature of the building was an enormous private chapel whose charnel-house atmosphere stifled the captain. "Gruesome," he said to himself. "She was a superstitious fanatic." Behind the altar hung a crucifix, a life-sized monstrosity with simulated blood, real thorns, and iron spikes which pinioned the hands and feet of a Cristo adorned with a wig of human hair. The eyes of the figure were painted in such a way that one could not tell whether they were open or closed, and at a quick glance they appeared to blink. Guzmán swallowed, and turned his back to it. Other walls were adorned with equally blood-chilling reminders of torture and martyrdom, and a glass reliquary displayed a bone, presumably human and holy. The captain scowled at the deeply worn grooves on the kneeboard of a prie-dieu and was thankful that in a few years advancing science would sweep religion away forever.

"The lady was a bit deranged and certainly morbid," he concluded, but this comment did not appear in his notebook.

After leaving the Cortés residence, Guzmán traveled across the city to interview the man whose name headed the list provided by the police of the capital: Victor Gil, a celebrated drama critic and the virtual dictator of theater and music in the country. An excellent witness, thought

Guzmán. Gil had not yet achieved his later fame as one of the world's finest writers of Spanish, but he was well known and widely respected, a man Guzmán could call "a distinguished and unimpeachable source." The captain did not suspect how frustrating their meeting would be.

The critic received Guzmán in his cubicle office at *La Prensa* and immediately became choked with emotion at the mention of Doña Dolores' name. After gaining control of himself, he veered from the subject to begin a long personal story, a tale involving Don Gregorio Gorgoni, the famed "mad billionaire." Guzmán, who had read newspaper accounts of the fabulous South American, was curious but could not help feeling that this was a waste of time. Besides, it was better not to inquire into the lives of important personages like Gorgoni. Safety lay in ignorance.

"Señor," he interrupted, "what you tell me is fascinating, but I am inquiring only about Doña Dolores. I have no authority to pry into Gorgoni's affairs, God forbid! Señorita Cortés does not so far appear in your story at all except as—how do you say it in your profession? An offstage character?"

The critic suddenly became thoughtful. "Interesting that you should call her that. An offstage character. Perhaps, in a way, Doña Dolores lived an offstage life. Is such a thing possible? Some of the great characters in drama never appear before the audience; they have no existence except through others, and yet—like Doña Dolores—they change lives and arrange circumstances. How little I really knew of the woman herself—or if she even *had* a self that counted. Yes, an offstage life. Clever of you to have realized this."

"Perhaps I am slightly confused," said the thoroughly bewildered Guzmán. "Do you mean that she had great influence because she was a friend of the billionaire? She acted through him and pulled strings?"

"She did indeed!"

"If you would be more specific, señor—"

"You must let me tell this story my own way. You can learn nothing of my dear friend Doña Dolores, who is now among the saints and angels, unless you hear about my meeting with Don Gregorio. In a way, it was the most narrow escape of my life, and I tell you truthfully that she saved me from Gorgoni. Now the story can be told; there is no reason for further secrecy."

Guzmán prepared himself for a story of hired assassins and tearful intercession, but Gil's tale was not like that at all.

At the age of twenty-four Victor Gil was a young man of intolerable self-righteousness. After studying *bellas letras* at the Universities of Madrid and Sevilla he returned to his Mexican homeland to work as a journalist and within a short time was the scourge of the stage, a puritan who believed it was his God-entrusted mission to cleanse the theatrical temple and drive out the money-changers. His scorn was so devastating and so cleverly phrased that soon his readers became convinced that they despised performers who, in fact, had amused them thoroughly. Gil was responsible for the bankruptcy of more than one repertory company, and in his zeal for excellence he took no account of reality: even dedicated artists are often forced to cater to the public as clowns, Tobys, or beleaguered virgins. Gil, who regarded the least commercial compromise as prostitution, became an unwitting menace to the very survival of the performing arts. Actors challenged him to duels and he was twice caned in dark streets. This was a pity, for despite a certain aloofness he was a likable young man, well intentioned and generous to everyone except the objects of his criticism.

When the theater failed to improve under his flaying, he decided that the only hope was a new company with himself as its producer. A company untainted by the box office, a theater devoted to no object but its own excellence! Although he had no experience as a producer, he at least possessed the advantage of being above commercial temptation. This dream obsessed him and he jotted down the names of prospective actors, drew up schedules, and finally faced the dire financial facts. A vast sum of money was needed, and here he faced his Zaragoza. Only a miracle could make the dream a reality.

Gil discussed the matter with his editor, who said, "Forget this! You are a fine writer and after a little mellowing you will be a splendid critic. What do you know about running a theater? Shoemaker, stick to your last!"

"But the capital needs a producer who will not sell his integrity for money! A man who will make no compromises!"

"And you are this man?" the editor inquired with deadly politeness. Then he thoughtfully drew ovals and circles on a sheet of foolscap. He liked Victor Gil and believed he had great potential, yet it was difficult to keep such an unbending young man in his present job. Outraged theater managements had already canceled their advertising, and some readers were howling for Gil's blood. The editor reached a decision. "There is only one person who is rich enough and perhaps mad enough to help you," he said. "Do you know Don Gregorio Gorgoni?"

"The South American? Of course I have heard of him."

"I have met him and we have a close mutual friend, a certain Doña Dolores Cortés. If I tell her about your project, perhaps she would arrange a meeting the next time Gorgoni is in Mexico. It is almost impossible to get an interview with Don Gregorio, but he is devoted to Doña Dolores. I will speak to her about your plan this afternoon."

During the next month Victor Gil plotted his assault on the billionaire's treasury, not only memorizing a glowing sales talk, but learning everything possible about the rich man's quirks and preferences, which seemed to be numberless and eccentric. He heard, for example, that Don Gregorio was a fanatic on the subject of mustaches, of all things, and this encouraged him, for he had recently cultivated a beautiful crop of hair on his upper lip in an attempt to conceal his youth. Mentally he scored an advantage to himself.

Never before had he given any special thought to his own appearance or personality; he had simply taken himself for granted. Now he stood in front of a looking-glass, practicing ingratiating smiles, studying his hand in the mirror as he rehearsed the momentous handshake. What he observed demoralized him. Why had he not long ago realized that his expression was chilly, that his voice conveyed no friendliness? "How the devil does one become charming?" he asked himself. "It is hopeless!" But when he tried out his new personality on various acquaintances, they responded at once, and to Gil's surprise some of his forced geniality became real. He found himself on the way to a modest popularity and enjoyed this novel experience.

One morning the editor said, "Don Gregorio will receive you tonight. Señorita Cortés told him of your plan for a theater and she says he is interested. God knows why!"

Gil's heart pulsed with excitement. "Tonight? I didn't even know he was in Mexico."

"Don't you read our paper? His arrival was announced yesterday on the financial page."

"Do I call at his hotel?"

The editor chuckled. "I can hardly imagine him staying at a public inn! He owns a dozen private houses here and always travels with an army of servants. Tonight he is entertaining guests at Number Seventeen Blessed Sacrament Street. Be there at nine—not before, and not one minute afterward. And I should warn you about something. Don Gregorio's housekeeper is a horrible hag, older than the first pope, but if you meet her, make a good impression. The señor is fond of the witch, and her opinion counts. Good luck!"

That night Victor Gil, dressed in clothes borrowed from more prosperous friends, stood nervously on a corner not far from a large residence that was imposing without being pretentious. Half a dozen expensive carriages waited in the street, their coachmen smoking and chatting among themselves. Two of them were speaking English, and Gil was tremendously impressed, for the employment of imported British grooms and drivers was an extravagant affectation which only the richest Mexicans could afford. As Gil watched, a prominent banker entered Number 17, and he was soon followed by other recognizable aristocrats, including the fabulously rich Conde Calderón, who had recently caused a scandal at the opera. Gil felt more and more like a rabbit approaching a lion's den, and only the purity of his artistic motives sustained him. When the hour struck he quickly added a dab of wax to his carefully trimmed mustache, hurried to the door of the house, and rang the bell with an unsteady hand.

His first shock came at the threshold. A tall butler with a head as patrician as a Roman bust appeared before him, dressed in a fashion Gil had never seen except in portraits or on stage: silk knee breeches with gold buckles, pumps, an embroidered waistcoat, and all of this topped by a powdered wig. Several other servants, equally dandified and no less antique, hovered in the background and Gil, after one glance at the ornate hallway, felt that he had stumbled into a dress rehearsal of a Molière classic. Obviously Don Gregorio fancied himself Louis XIV. "Whom shall I announce?" The butler's voice came from the grave.

"What? Oh? Why I am—Señor Victor Gil. I am expected at nine."

"At nine, señor?" The tone implied a misunderstanding

and perhaps a major blunder on Gil's part. Nevertheless the butler accepted the borrowed opera cape, holding it suspiciously at arm's length as though vermin might hop from the fur-trimmed collar.

Suddenly a witchlike screech rang through the hall, and Gil whirled to find himself confronted by a hag whose tousled hair was the exact red of chili peppers. "Who on earth are you, and why do you barge in at this hour?" she demanded. "I never interview salesmen after sunset. Besides, you should use the side entrance. Leave at once!"

Gil retreated from her, stumbling and bumping into the butler. "I am Victor Gil. Señor Gorgoni invited me—"

"Have you no card? Really!"

"A card? Of course I have . . . somewhere . . . I—ah, here it is."

She studied it with deep suspicion. "This proves nothing. Any rogue can steal another man's calling card. It's been done before."

They had reached an impasse. He could retreat no farther without actually falling into the street, and this harridan showed no sign of giving ground. She glowered at him, head tilted, with a cross-eyed squint that pierced to the bone. A true harpy.

"Señora, I am expected," he pleaded. "It was arranged by a Señorita Cortés."

"Oh, you're another pick-up acquaintance of Doña Dolores! I might have known."

"No, no. I do not know the lady. But she—"

"Worse than I thought! I suppose you are after the señor's money. The vultures Doña Dolores sends here give poor Don Gregorio no peace. And I have to keep a constant eye on the silverware. You people are capable of anything!"

"I certainly am not—"

"*Zut!* Well, you may wait while I make inquiries. Follow me!"

But this was not easy, for he had hardly taken a step when two servants seized his arms. "Not so fast!" said the bigger one. Quickly they ran practiced hands over Gil's entire body, searching him for weapons. "A routine check, señor. We take no chances." The man's gutter Spanish, throaty with the accent of the worst slums, was an odd contrast to his dazzling livery.

"This is outrageous," said Gil with no great conviction. Perhaps such indignities were customary when one was being received by a veritable emperor. Gorgoni must be in constant danger of assassination or kidnaping.

"If you don't like it you can leave," the hag snarled at him. "Small chance of that! Not when you can smell money!"

Cheeks burning with humiliation, he trailed her down the hall, remembering the editor's advice and holding his tongue. He could endure this, he thought. He could endure anything for the sake of the great theater he would one day build.

"Wait here," said the housekeeper, leaving him to cool his heels in a depressing closet that seemed part of the servants' quarters. It was lit only by a candle stub which threatened to expire at any second. The hag poked her head through the doorway a short time later, the ugly face puckered with malevolence. "Victor Gil! Your name has come back to me. You are the know-it-all who writes those vicious things in *La Prensa*. You should be boiled alive for what you said about that wonderful play at the Alcázar last week!"

Gil had been especially proud of that scathing notice. He had written, "On Tuesday evening yet another overdrawn Count of Monte Cristo chiseled the chains from his wrist and the pesos from his audience. . . ." Drawing himself up in defensive dignity, he said, "I am a critic, señora. That is true."

"Critic, ha! You are an assassin with no limit to your

conceit. Well, Don Gregorio will take you down a notch or two, never fear!" The head vanished and the door slammed.

It seemed then that eternity passed. The candle flickered out, and he waited in darkness until at last the butler appeared to announce in his death-knell voice that Don Gregorio would now receive him. On trembling legs Gil, guided by the servant, mounted a flight of stairs to a spacious second-floor living room, brilliantly lighted by chandeliers and gas jets. Gil, after the blackness of the cubbyhole, was momentarily blinded, then realized that there were at least a dozen men present, some seated, others standing, and most of them holding crystal wineglasses. They chatted in amiable tones, but when the butler loudly and mistakenly proclaimed, "Señor Vicente Gil," utter silence fell and all eyes turned upon him. He looked from one haughty face to the next, wondering who might be Don Gregorio—any of these urbane aristocrats would fit the part. Then, when he glanced toward the far end of the room, all doubt was removed.

The billionaire was enthroned in a massive Córdoba chair. On the wall behind him hung his own portrait, larger than life, and a mirror had been placed near a lamp to cast a white beam on the painting's features: a heavy lower lip so far outthrust that it met the drooping black mustache, narrowed eyes that were hardly more than two glittering dots beneath scowling brows set in a seemingly neckless head—Don Gregorio's hunched shoulders were almost level with his earlobes. The picture was striking, but it could in no way draw attention away from the man who sat near it, sprawling lazily, the careless and indifferent master of the world. Even before Gil heard the commanding voice, he was overpowered by the authority that radiated from this man, a dominance conveyed with no visible effort.

Yet Don Gregorio was absolutely nothing like the figure Gil had imagined; no theatrical producer would ever have cast Gorgoni in the role of a financial wizard, a manipulator of industries and even of nations. His ancient black suit, bulging over a sturdy paunch, was ten years out of style, and the half-buttoned linen vest somehow gave an impression of gravy stains. The shabby clothing was worsened by a diamond stickpin gleaming in his lapel, a jewel so enormous that it would have seemed vulgar on the turban of a rajah. The billionaire, at first sight, appeared to be a backwoods politician who donned frayed finery and a bogus jewel only for funerals, weddings, and his own saint's day. The big shovel hat, which he wore indoors as many middle-class Mexicans did, was an outrage against both manners and grooming, the untrimmed mustache needed wax, and his boots, partly unlaced for comfort, could have used polish. But in a room filled with debonair men and elaborately costumed servants, it was Don Gregorio Gorgoni who arrested the eyes and preempted all attention.

Gil, who had a keen sense of theater, appreciated the contrived contrast which made the billionaire stand out so vividly against his background. Everything about him declared, "I do not need fine clothes, I do not need good manners. I am who I am—and you know it!" Yet, stripped of all the legend of wealth, Gil knew, Don Gregorio would still have exuded force and attraction. He had magnetism, a compelling power so difficult to define that members of Gil's profession could describe it only as "star quality" or "quicksilver," for want of better words. Gil could not look away from the sullen face, the thick lips whose curl implied a terrible determination.

"You are Vicente Gil?" The billionaire, with a flick of his cigar stub, gestured for him to come forward.

"Sí, señor. That is, I am Victor Gil."

"Not Vicente?" The husky growl conveyed displeasure.

"Vicente . . . Victor . . . I am certainly Gil, all right." His baptismal name was suddenly of no importance. If

Don Gregorio called him Vicente, he would be Vicente forevermore. He was helpless.

Gorgoni smiled, the fierce mouth expanding and curving upward like a comedy mask. Now the face, so formidable a moment ago, glowed with kindness and goodwill. "Vicente, your plan for a new theater has been described to me by a dear friend. I find the idea most appealing. I am favorably inclined. Very favorably."

"Really, señor?" Breathless, Gil drew a sheaf of papers from his coat. "I have outlined every last detail. When you examine these pages at your leisure, you will find that—"

"What leisure, señor?" The eyebrows tilted sharply. "I have no leisure. I give instant answers, I take instant action. Besides, I never invest in plans or descriptions. I invest in *men*. Men who have visions and ideals! Men who are incorruptible. I rely totally on my instinct. Now, how much do you need?"

"How much? Well, we wish to be economical." Everything was going much too fast for him. None of the right cues for his prepared speech had been given, and now he floundered. "You see, we must import almost an entire company and build—"

"I am not concerned with the difficulties. I want to know only the solution. How much?"

Gil gulped and knew it was now or never. "Fifty thousand English pounds would start—"

"English pounds? I prefer to calculate in francs or rix-dollars. Hhhm. Fifty thousand times . . . Ah, yes." Don Gregorio bit off the tip of a new cigar and spat it across the room, narrowly missing Gil. "A lot of money. Still, it is less than I thought. Hhhhm." Pressing his fingers against his temples, he pondered the matter, his beady eyes never leaving Gil's face. Then he shouted, "Juanito! Bring me a pen and a bank-draft form. For francs or pounds or rubles. It doesn't matter."

"Señor, are you simply going to—" Gil's head was spinning. Could such a fortune be given to him just like this? It was incredible—yet it fitted with everything he had heard about the billionaire.

A secretary hurried forward with a tray bearing pens, inks, and printed forms emblazoned with a huge monogram. "*Gracias,*" muttered Gorgoni, but instead of commencing to write he stared at Gil, then asked, "Why do you wear that ridiculous mustache? It gives your face a shifty look. I do not approve at all."

"Really, señor? Perhaps you are right."

"No perhaps about it! Of course I'm right, and we must get rid of it at once. I cannot sponsor a man who resembles a Parisian pimp!" He thundered to the secretary, "Fetch a razor! At once!"

The mustache had become Gil's greatest pride and vanity. Now he spoke with his hand half over his mouth, as though defending the precious hairs. "Señor, tomorrow my own barber will—"

"I do not like procrastination! It makes me lose confidence!"

"If you insist, señor."

"I do *not* insist. You may do as you wish." Don Gregorio laid down the pen and pushed the bank forms aside.

"Oh, I agree absolutely," said Gil at once. "The sooner we get rid of it the better."

"I'm glad you see the light."

A servant dashed into the room, bearing a razor, shaving mug, and towel. Gil was dreadfully aware that the guests had crowded close; all of them stared, and he was sure their blank faces concealed laughter and scorn. Nevertheless he submitted, hoping his false smile was not so sickly as he feared. A brush was whisked across his upper lip, and he felt several swift strokes as the servant wielded the blade; then he was handed a damp towel.

"Much better, my boy!" Don Gregorio hugged Gil, an astonishing embrace of congratulation, then returned to his chair. "What was I doing? Oh, yes. Fifty thousand pounds."

"Yes, señor." His voice squeaked, and he watched wide-eyed as the billionaire began to write.

"Now there are one or two small matters before I sign this," he said. "I do not advance large sums without having motives, as I suppose you have realized."

"Right, sir. Ha, ha!" Gil had realized nothing, and his laughter was faintly hysterical.

"I have two nieces, beautiful girls who resemble me closely, and they are mad to go on the stage. Only as a lark, of course, and under assumed names. I have promised to give them an opportunity."

"Have they any experience, sir?"

"Naturally not. They are *ladies*, not actresses! But the younger girl would be a charming Juliet, and her lisp is hardly noticeable."

"Juliet? Ah, a difficult role."

"Talent is hereditary in my family," said Gorgoni smugly, but with an unmistakable threat. "'I hope we have no disagreement so early in our friendship, Vicente."

Hesitating, Gil closed his eyes and swallowed hard. It came with painful clarity that this was Vanity Fair and he was about to sell his integrity for riches. But what, after all, was one amateurish Juliet? There would be hundreds of productions, works of unmarred beauty. Don Gregorio was asking a small price. "I'm sure your niece will be magnificent," he said.

"Good! But she must be used quickly, she'll soon be too old for the role, she's graying fast. Now the other girl is more of a Dulcinea type. I assume you'll produce *Don Quixote* frequently. It is my favorite story."

"*Quixote?* A great classic, of course. But the dramatizations are unworthy. All attempts to put it on stage have failed to capture—"

"Nonsense! I saw a *Quixote* in Buenos Aires two years

ago, and it was a first-rate show! Real horses and a real windmill. Sancho Panza had a lop-eared burro with a white eye!" Don Gregorio guffawed, and slapped his thigh. "I don't have to tell you what the burro did right in the middle of the stage! The audience cheered for five minutes. Oh, your theater will have to do *Quixote* often, my boy. No two ways about it."

"Yes, señor," Gil agreed meekly, feeling something die inside him. Yet this second compromise was easier than the first had been. Don Gregorio was giving away a fortune; surely a short run of some miserable dramatization was not too much to ask.

The billionaire signed the draft with a great indecipherable flourish and handed it casually to Gil, who stared at the heavy slip of paper, unable to believe that his dream had come true. Not quite the same dream, not quite unsullied. But still—

"Very well, Vicente. You are on your own. Report your progress to me every three months, and at times I may make small requests. Now you must excuse me. *Buenas noches.*"

Outside the room Gil, in his excitement, almost fell down the stairs. He wanted to leap into the air, burst into song, yell and shout and pound his chest. Somewhere in the depth of his soul a voice whispered, "You are a whore like any other." But in the joy of his achievement he ignored this rebuke, he refused to listen.

"My cape and hat, please," he told the butler.

Giddy with triumph, he did not notice that a commotion had begun upstairs. Just as he stepped toward the door he became aware of two footmen racing down the stairs and Don Gregorio's voice shouting, "Stop that man! Stop him!" Before he knew what was happening he had been seized violently and was being dragged up the steps, back into the presence of the billionaire, who now stood in front of his chair, drawn up to full height, a terrifying figure of controlled rage. "Bring him to me and don't let him escape!" Not only the servants but the guests, their faces grimly menacing, surrounded him as he was impelled toward Gorgoni.

"What is this?" Gil gasped. "I don't understand."

"First, hand over that bank draft, you swine!"

"Señor, I—"

"Take it from him!" A rough hand plunged into Gil's coat pocket and extracted his wallet. The precious slip of paper, for which Gil had sacrificed his pride and his convictions, was snatched away and presented to the billionaire, who slowly tore it to shreds, dropping the pieces on the floor one by one. Don Gregorio, Gil decided, had gone completely mad, and his astonishment changed to real fear for his physical safety.

"You have something else of mine," said Gorgoni. "Admit it!"

"Señor, this is insane! I don't know what you mean."

"Oh, you don't? Look at me! Do you happen to notice that something is missing?"

"Missing?" Then Gil realized that the diamond stickpin no longer glittered on Gorgoni's lapel. "The jewel is gone," he murmured. Then, a dreadful apprehension dawning in him, he cried out, "You can't believe that I have taken it! This is ridiculous, señor!"

"We'll see. Search him!"

Gil, thoroughly alarmed but sure of his innocence, tried to aid the servants as they yanked off his cape and coat, but his least movement was taken as attempted flight. "You will see how preposterous this is, Don Gregorio," he babbled. "Never in my life have I—"

"Here it is!" exclaimed a servant triumphantly. "Thrust into his coat. Under the arm, where he could hide it with his sleeve!"

"No, no! Impossible!" Gil struggled against the arms

that held him. In some ghastly way the jewel had caught on his coat—perhaps when Don Gregorio embraced him. There had to be some reasonable explanation; they could not believe him a thief! But when he looked into the billionaire's face, he read his doom. Gorgoni was without pity, his sneer seemed carved in flint, the small eyes shone with fury. Gil saw the ruin of his career, his life—his whole future demolished in an instant. Visions of prison swam before him. What could a man like Don Gregorio do to him? There was no end to the horrible possibilities. Why had he come to this nightmare house, endured insult and humiliation? Could the money—which was gone now like everything else—have been that important? "I swear I am innocent, señor!"

"Innocent?" Don Gregorio addressed his guests, his voice ringing through the room. "Gentlemen, you see before you a man who will do anything for money! You watched him tonight. Do you agree?"

"Yes! True!" they shouted.

"With your own eyes you saw him sell not just his honor but his very mustache! True?"

"Yes! All true!"

"Señor Gil, this evening you have proved your character beyond doubt! You have proved"—Gorgoni paused, then went on very quietly—"that you are, in fact, just like all the rest of us."

Suddenly before Gil's unbelieving eyes the most incredible thing of this incredible night happened. The billionaire removed the black coat and tugged at the bulge of his stomach, and it disappeared, changing into a long skirt whose hem fell to the ankles. He pulled off the mustache, the protruding lip receded, and his eyes expanded to twice their former size. When the shovel hat was tossed aside, Gil saw graying hair combed neatly back and held with shell combs. The billionaire had dissolved, and in his place stood a middle-aged woman of obvious gentility, strong-featured but in no way masculine. She smiled at him pleasantly, with no hint of mischief.

"Good evening, Don Victor Gil," she said. "I am your servant, Doña Dolores Cortés. I have the honor to bid you welcome to my house, which is now your house."

"But—but—but—" Gil was speechless. Around him the room rang with laughter and applause; the servants released him, began to remove their wigs, and exchanged their outrageous liveries for modern clothing, which appeared from chests and closets. "Señorita, I—I—" Gil was unable to stammer out his utter consternation. "Never in my life have I— It is incredible! But the real Don Gregorio, does he know of this impersonation?"

Doña Dolores laughed, a warm laugh, nothing whatever like the raucous chuckle of the billionaire. "My dear friend, there is no Don Gregorio Gorgoni, and there never has been such a person. He exists only in this room as you saw him. Is that not fortunate? If he were real, think of the things men would be tempted to sell him."

"Yes. I understand." Gil looked away, unable to meet her clear gaze.

"Will you gentlemen bring champagne for our new friend?" she called. "He must be thirsty, and so am I!"

"*Por Dios!*" exclaimed Gil, recognizing a certain quality in her voice. "I have been doubly fooled! You were the housekeeper as well! Señorita, you are the world's greatest actress, I swear it!"

"*Gracias,* señor. From so fine a critic as you, that is indeed a compliment, but I am not an actress at all and I would be terrified on a stage. Now, if you have forgiven our joke, let us have a pleasant evening together. All these gentlemen are anxious to meet you, and your poor editor, I see, has at last come from behind the screen where he has been hiding. . . . By the way, you must pour your own wine tonight. We never have real servants in the house on these occasions. Those you saw are like myself—not quite what they appear to be."

So Victor Gil was welcomed into an informal company, a group of men who called themselves the Fraternity of Dishonorable Gentlemen. He learned that every man in the room had undergone an initiation similar to his own; each in one way or another had publicly sacrificed his pride on the altar of the mythical billionaire, exposing his corruptibility blatant and naked for all to see. And, in doing this, every one of them had purged himself of at least a little hypocrisy, a small measure of self-righteousness. They were comrades in embarrassment, closely bound in a fraternity that needed no officers or rules beyond the oath they all swore—a promise never to reveal the truth about Don Gregorio and always to perpetuate his legend. Not all of them were aristocrats, as Gil had at first supposed. The group included not only Gil's editor but three other journalists with whom he was acquainted and who had remained out of sight until the imposture had ended. There were also a painter and a well-known poet who had once been tempted by Don Gregorio into the promise of composing a fifty-canto epic about the billionaire's triumphs in the stock market. "I was invited here last year," the poet told Gil. "It was just after I'd published a furious essay about the poet laureate of England. I said that no true artist would ever agree to write poems on demand. . . ."

No one—not even the editor—pointed any moral to Victor Gil. It was unnecessary to remind him that the mote in his own eye was not unlike the beam in the eye of another. This had been brought home to him in a manner he would never forget. He felt exhausted and giddy from the experience, and the champagne went to his head. Several times during the next two hours he studied Doña Dolores, who now moved unobtrusively among her guests, an affable hostess, no longer the center of the stage. She encouraged conversation, started quiet games of cards and backgammon among those men not inclined to talk. Was she real now? Or was this the impersonation and Gorgoni the genuine character? He had believed equally in the housekeeper. Were all three perhaps false? Would Doña Dolores at any moment change into still another character? If this happened, he was sure he would go mad and run screaming into the street. When he attempted to analyze the methods by which she had carried out her impersonations, he failed totally. The costuming had been cleverly planned, of course; a red wig had served for the housekeeper, a mustache for Don Gregorio. She had a mobile face and a voice amazing in range and flexibility. Yet these added together did not explain her power to command absolute belief. Gil sighed, knowing he could never review the greatest performance he had ever witnessed.

Soon after midnight Doña Dolores bade her guests good night, arranging for Gil to ride home in the Conde's carriage, since the streets at that hour were unsafe for well-dressed pedestrians. Taking his arm, she escorted him to the entrance. "You must call often at this, your house," she said. "I am an admirer of your writing—such beautiful Spanish!" A mischievous twinkle came into her eyes. "Do not be disturbed by what that hag of a housekeeper said. Sometimes she is carried away and says things more forcefully than she means."

"Yes. The same thing happens to me, señorita."

"Are you terribly disappointed that there is no billionaire to sponsor your theater? I hope not. It is a noble dream you have."

"It would be a lie to say I am not disappointed—and just now I feel very truthful. Tomorrow I will think about the theater." Gil pressed her hand quickly to his lips. "I think I have been rescued from something. Thank you and good night, Doña Dolores." Then, smiling, he added, "Or whoever you are."

Victor Gil's character did not change overnight. A personality is seldom altered by the events of a single evening, and even the authors of Holy Writ, whose heroes do not always behave in conventional ways, suggest that instant conversion requires a miracle; the heavens open and a man is struck blind on the road. So obstinate is human nature that often one miracle has no effect at all, and a whole series of plagues and cataclysms must be unleashed before one stubborn Pharaoh sees the light—and then but dimly.

Nevertheless, something important had happened to Gil. He had always recognized other men's sins, but now he understood a little of their temptations. Although he did not lower his standards of art or conduct, he began to learn tolerance. Eventually he abandoned his plan for the perfect theater, wisely deciding that this was not the right country, the right time, and perhaps he was not the right man. His dream was not worth the risk of falling into the hands of another Don Gregorio. Doña Dolores had said it was fortunate that Gorgoni did not really exist, but Gil knew that the billionaire, in a thousand disguises, was omnipresent—he was the bureaucrat who offered security at the price of pride, the rich relative whose hopeful heirs wasted their lives in humiliating expectancy. Gil came to realize that Don Gregorio was a fraud in more ways than one.

2

This was the story the critic told Captain Guzmán that afternoon in Mexico City. Carried away by the memory, he acted it out, gesturing broadly, imitating voices and expressions, while the policeman stared open-mouthed, fascinated but not believing a word. "Loco," he told himself. "Next this man will claim that the lady traveled on a flying pink burro." Could it be that the critic had turned playwright and was using Guzmán as an audience to test the plot of a new comedy? When the tale had ended, Guzmán said, "Thank you. This has been most entertaining. Perhaps you will dramatize it for the theater?"

"No, señor. A play must be believable. Life has no such rule; it is free to operate as it chooses, and often it produces the incredible."

"It does indeed," said Guzmán. "Now I wish to speak to the editor you have mentioned."

"By all means. He was with the group longer than I. He can give you more details."

It proved that the editor could. Guzmán listened for more than an hour, heard everything Gil had told him confirmed and embellished, and left the office of *La Prensa* a thoroughly bewildered man. "In all the world there are no bigger liars than journalists," he muttered. But for once this well-known truth failed to apply.

That evening Guzmán returned to the Cortés residence, resolved to make a more careful search, to disprove Victor Gil's story. He felt persecuted by the two journalist tricksters, yet he was disturbed by the remote possibility that they had spoken the truth. "The tale is improbable," he told himself stoutly. "The odds are against it."

The cook, a funereal figure in her garments of mourning, fluttered about him, a giant raven, her fringed shawl spread winglike as she lighted candles and, in the larger chambers, gas jets whose hiss and whiteness of flame made Guzmán uneasy. In the morning the house had been merely shadowy and depressing; at night it was a pit of gloom.

"She lived here alone?"

"Sí, señor. All alone after her sister's death."

"Ah, yes, her sister. Describe her to me."

"I cannot. She died long before I came to work here. I know nothing of her."

The second-floor *sala* was exactly as Victor Gil had described it, lacking only the great portrait of Don Gregorio, and the captain noticed an iron hook mounted in the wall where such a picture could be hung. The Spanish throne-chair was in place, a little apart from the other furniture, and it seemed to await the billionaire's arrival. There was a locked closet to which the cook had no key. Did it contain the portrait? The outlandish costume? The liveries of spurious servants? Guzmán longed to break the door but, remembering the powerful name Montejo, decided to have patience.

"Do you enjoy working here?" he asked the cook. "Is it not dismal?"

She hesitated, wary of being led into indiscretion. "The lady was good to me. But I hope the new owners have children. I like the noise of children. The señorita was so quiet, so very quiet."

"Did the silence bother you at night?"

"Ay, I was never here at night. None of the servants were."

Guzmán was astounded. "But surely she did not stay

here alone at night! There must have been a watchman or—"

"There was no one. Now, of course, we sleep here. But when the señorita—bless her memory—was alive, we left at sunset."

"A miracle she was not strangled in her bed! Murdered by burglars!"

They left the *sala*, the cook holding the candle high to guide him. His spurs clanked too loudly in the corridor, and he was aware of the squeaking of his boots. He imagined Doña Dolores wandering these dark hallways, moving softly down the stairs to the chapel, praying alone before the crucifix, no sound in the house but the click of beads. *La soltera*, the spinster, the solitary . . .

"She was rich," he said. "I wonder why she did not marry."

The woman gave the familiar Mexican answer to the riddle of spinsterhood. "She was hard to please."

In the bedroom once occupied by Doña Dolores (alone, he thought, alone in the enormous bed), the captain studied a portrait near the bureau. In the dimness it resembled Victor Gil's description of Don Gregorio Gorgoni, the drooping mustache, the bulldog lips and squinting peasant eyes. But, looking closer, he realized that this was a funerary portrait, executed after the death of its subject, and the man was a dark-skinned Indian. In the lower corner behind the glass was a lock of the dead man's hair and on the right a sample of illegible handwriting.

"Who was he?" he asked the cook.

"I think he was the señorita's grandfather, Don Carlos Montejo."

"Montejo? Nonsense! This is an Indian peon!"

The woman shrugged and the candle flickered on the portrait. "Who knows?" she said.

3

In the year when Mexico seethed with the first of its great rebellions, a gunsmith named Carlos Montejo opened a modest shop under the eaves of a neighborhood market in the capital. This young man, despite his noble name, had no connection with the Spanish dukes, except that an ancestor must have been bound to them as a servant. He was a pure-blooded Zapotec Indian, and his grand patronymic was the same crude joke that is made by naming a slave Napoleon Bonaparte.

Only a few months before the gunsmith began his new enterprise, Father Hidalgo, the rebel priest who was later unfrocked and beheaded, had terrorized the country, and, although the rebellion was suppressed and the heads of the conspirators hung up to decorate the scene of their crime, no one felt safe. The wealthy, already armed, turned their homes into arsenals, while the peons attempted the same thing in secret. So great was the demand for weapons that Carlos Montejo employed a dozen men, then fifty, and soon enriched himself. His name remained a joke, but since he had also entered the field of moneylending, fewer people laughed at it, even though Montejo to the end of his life remained an Indian who spat on the floor and scratched where he itched.

Montejo suffered only one mortification: despite constant effort he was unable to beget a son. At first he blamed his wife, sure that her infertility was the result of her mixed Spanish blood. But his mistresses served him no better, and the only one who proved successful was the one he trusted the least. A glance at the pasty-skinned infant she produced confirmed his suspicion that she was consorting with a certain cavalry officer. "I am wearing horns!" he shouted. "This brat is none of my doing!"

Cursing the infidelity of women, he returned to his wife, and surprisingly a baby was born that same year, a scrawny girl whose dark complexion and heavy features proclaimed her paternity. The child was named Esperanza, which means hope, because he hoped to do better in the future. But when his wife went to an early grave, Montejo was left with no heir except this unattractive girl, who proved obstreperous from the cradle.

At the age of ten she disrupted the convent where her education was attempted by claiming to see visions of saints, and aroused scandal during Holy Week when she displayed bloody marks on her palms and forehead while she writhed on a cot, blasphemously wailing the seven last words of Christ. Esperanza might have achieved the first step toward sainthood had it not been discovered that the blood came from the arm of a younger girl who had been pricked with a sharpened quill. A century earlier Esperanza could have been burned alive for this sacrilege, but in this enlightened age she escaped with severe beatings, confinement, and a diet of gruel, none of which improved her character. In disgrace she was returned to her father, who bore his burden with Zapotec fortitude.

When she became fifteen, Don Carlos was anxious to marry her off and considered numerous candidates as potential sires of grandsons he hoped to breed. But Esperanza, to his shock, had a plan of her own, announcing one night that she had observed a young man strolling in a park near their home, a youth she described as "a fair-haired angel," and she would have him. Don Carlos, mortified by this conversation, berated her as a hussy and knocked her across the room. Privately, he investigated.

The fair-haired angel turned out to be Juan Marcos Cortés, a man as far above Esperanza socially as heaven is above a swamp, and the gunsmith was astounded by his daughter's even dreaming of such a union. But then he thought: Why not? This angel has his price, like everybody else. The notion of buying a Spanish aristocrat appealed to his ironic sense of history, and inquiries revealed that the Cortés family, for all their airs, had been ruined by taking the wrong side of every political question for twenty years. Their youngest son was as much on the market as their carriage and country house. Price for the commodity was the only consideration.

The courtship, conducted mainly by accountants and notaries, was brief, and before many months had passed Juan Marcos and Esperanza were joined in holy matrimony at an extravagant pageant in the cathedral. The bridegroom's family, grimly self-sacrificial, ignored the raised eyebrows of their friends, consoling themselves with the prospect of a comfortable retirement in the Castilian motherland.

After a honeymoon in Cuernavaca the young couple, whose quarrels had already begun, took up residence in the huge house the gunsmith bought for them: the gloomy building at 17 Blessed Sacrament Street, where Dolores Cortés was born, lived, and in the natural course of events would have died.

Her grandfather towered above her childhood like a colossus astride a harbor, dwarfing the landscape around him. Her parents, the Indian maids who were her nurses, the cooks, and the doorkeeper paled beside Don Carlos. During the early years, when she was the only child in the house, all the days of the week were spent in awaiting his Sunday visit. On Sunday she awakened before dawn, listening for the boom of the bells that would ring with the first light, and to Dolores their clang was not a summons to mass but a promise that soon her grandfather would hammer on the front door, shouting for the lazy citified inhabitants of the house to be up and doing. She leaped from bed, raced downstairs barefoot, clad only in her muslin nightgown. "Grandfather! Grandfather!" Lifting her high, he perched her on his shoulder.

Together they toured the house, Don Carlos flinging open doors to rout out yawning servants. Usually he found Esperanza red-eyed after a night of angry prayers. Refusal to sleep was a weapon she used against her husband when he was absent from the house, devoting the late hours to furious supplication, calling upon God and the saints to inflict instant misery upon Juan Marcos so he would be forced to quit his evil companions and rush to her side. She implored heaven that his mistress would burn with pox or strangle with consumption and that he would have such ill luck in gambling as to effect a permanent reformation. Saturday nights were a terrible strain upon Esperanza's knees and emotions, for Juan Marcos seldom returned home until an hour before dawn on Sunday.

Since the gunsmith's visit was as inevitable as the plague in August, Juan Marcos dozed in a chair, awaiting his early martyrdom, braced for Don Carlos to shout, "Wake up, *cabrón!* Time for breakfast. What weaklings you Spaniards are! I can drink all night and still be up to wake the chickens."

After breakfast he kissed his daughter and his son-in-law, commanded them to produce a male child quickly, and then led Dolores into the street, where they began their Sunday adventure. First, mass at the cathedral, and afterward any expedition which struck his fancy. Often they visited the wax museum, where Dolores' eyes bulged with fright at the beheading of Marie Antoinette and the murder of Julius Caesar. These figures were created at the same factory which provided statuary for the cathedral, and it was confusing to recognize Saint Peter as Bluebeard and to see Saint Teresa, dagger in hand, about to stab a naked man in a bathtub.

They strolled through the vast Santa Ana market, where anything Dolores could imagine was sold: shawls from India and Japan, bamboo cages aflutter with singing birds, pyramids of polished fruit, and great blocks of ice brought down from the summit of the volcano. The venders shouted and sang their wares, they haggled in the fierce joy of driving a bargain. Don Carlos paused frequently to chat with the stallkeepers, and no one was beneath his notice, not even the frightening *leperos* who lurked everywhere in their patchworks of rags.

"Grandfather, everyone talks to you! Everyone loves you."

"Yes, little one, everyone loves me because I have a magic charm I carry in my pocket."

"A magic charm? May I see it?"

"Here it is."

"But that's only a gold coin."

"Yes. And, being only one, it is not very magical. But if I add another to it and another and another, then the magic works. Everyone loves your grandfather. People take off their hats." He winked at her. "But if I lost the magic charm, they would see only an ugly Indian whose boots need polish."

She did not understand this then, but later she remembered it.

The residence of Juan Marcos Cortés was perhaps the only wealthy home in the capital which did not entertain a constant procession of callers. Even during times of mourning and Lent the prominent families of the city visited continually, and a meal without a half-dozen guests was a rare occasion. But Juan Marcos's relatives, who would have been obliged to make courtesy calls, had fled to Spain, and Esperanza had no family except her father, although she lived in dread that one day some barefoot, brown-faced Zapotec would knock on the door to claim the traditional hospitality of kinship. After her marriage she announced she would not receive social inferiors, which caused one Castilian dowager to curl a haughty lip and say, "I was unaware that the Indian's daughter *had* inferiors." This thrust was widely quoted, and Esperanza became a greater laughingstock than ever. Her invitations were ignored, and Juan Marcos's doorkeeper was an idle man.

For Dolores, consigned to a series of nursemaids, one uneventful day was like another until the joyous news came that her mother had again conceived. Suddenly the house bustled with activity and preparation. An elaborate nursery, crammed with male toys, was installed on the second floor, and she was told to refer to it as her "brother's room." Don Carlos became a daily caller, clucking and worrying over his daughter's health, adorning the walls of her room with charms and symbols so pagan and obscene that they had to be hidden when the priest visited.

As Esperanza's hour approached, the household held its breath, then, after a birth cry was heard, released it in a long sigh. "Four years of waiting and now another girl for my sins!" said Don Carlos. "There never will be a grandson, it is not God's will." The prophecy proved true, and when Carlos Montejo was laid to rest in a marble tomb twice as large as the house where he was born, there was still no male heir.

Dolores, nearly eight years old, grieved throughout the winter; then slowly her affections turned to her younger sister, Isabel, a frail child who cried often and was not expected to survive, although no one but Dolores seemed deeply concerned. Esperanza, ignoring both her daughters, withdrew more and more into her religious devotions, imposing a perpetual Lent on the household long after the year of mourning for Don Carlos had ended. She erected a private chapel, which she furnished with the most ago-nized symbols of martyrdom, declaring that such objects reflected her own sufferings at the hands of fate and her husband. Quarrels between the couple reached such a pitch that Juan Marcos, unable to bear his wife's mania, virtually lived abroad, making extended journeys to Europe with his friend the young Conde Calderón. During these years the two girls seldom ventured beyond the doors of the house. Esperanza, bitterly recalling her own disgrace, would not send them to the convent school but hired an elderly priest to instruct the children three times a week in catechism, reading, and the legends of the saints.

Sealed from life by gates and grillwork, the children created a universe of their own which Dolores peopled with a throng of characters. "Today," she would announce, "King Popo of the Mountain will visit us and drink chocolate, Isabel."

"Will he? Show me again what he is like!"

"King Popo is like the old man who sells charcoal to the cook, but he is fatter. Yet he walks the same way—on his heels, like this."

"Dolores, that is exactly how the charcoal man walks! But don't hold your skirt up like that. What if mama saw you?"

These fantasies, begun as a casual game, became a preoccupation. She observed the servants, venders at the gate, the priest who catechized them, and soon she could imitate his whining tone perfectly. Nor was it enough for her to ape the actions she studied. She set herself to determine feelings and causes. Why did the characters behave as they did? Why did the charcoal-seller walk in a peculiar manner? She decided it was because he rode a burro all day, an animal he had to prod constantly with his feet. "So he turns his feet this way," she said, moving slowly across her bedroom. "Yes, that is how it feels." As she struggled to make her voice another voice, her stance the stance of another, she found herself entering into the minds and sensations of the characters she created. "To sound like them, I must become them, I must believe." For Isabel's pleasure she still presented herself as a strange and fantastic personality, but secretly she felt that King Popo was really the charcoal man.

One day she said, "Isabel, can you remember our grandfather?"

"No. Hardly at all."

"I will try to show you what he was like." That afternoon, in an awkward performance which would years later be perfected, Gregorio Gorgoni was born.

No one entered the house, and no one left it. When the copper bells on the doors tinkled, it meant only that a tradesman or one of the servants had arrived. Then, when Dolores was nearly thirteen, Juan Marcos returned from a long sojourn in Spain because of the alarming state of his affairs in Mexico. One government and then the next had toppled violently, there were rumors that a monarchy was to be established, and no one knew who would control the chaotic land. Juan Marcos was in financial danger.

He arrived late at night and when, in the morning, the girls learned of his presence, they burst into his room at the first sound of his awakening, overjoyed by any change in the routine of the house and confident he had brought them presents from Europe. He greeted them affectionately, praising Isabel as his "pretty little doll" and then inspecting Dolores from head to toe. "How tall you have grown. Well, don't worry about it too much. Tall women are becoming fashionable in Europe."

Their presents, two Swiss music boxes, awaited them. "And there is something else. Something alive."

"A peacock?" cried Isabel. "Or a monkey?"

Juan Marcos chuckled. "A little of both, I suspect. I

have brought you a new friend. Your cousin Ricardo came with me from Madrid. He is twelve years old, and he will live here now."

Both girls paled at the thought of a stranger, a boy stranger especially, entering their world.

"You must be kind to him," said Juan Marcos. "His parents were taken by fever several months ago. He is, of course, in mourning."

"Will we be in mourning too?" asked Dolores. It seemed she had spent her entire life wearing nothing but black.

"No. His father was only my cousin, and since it happened across the ocean we will not count it. Later you will meet him, but I suppose he is still asleep now. Run along, your papa must dress."

In the corridor Isabel whispered, "He will spoil everything. I don't like boys. I'm afraid of the ones I see at church."

"Hush! He's our cousin. Do you think he's in our brother's room?"

"He couldn't be!" Isabel was horrified at the possibility. The second-floor chamber, still filled with dusty toys, belonged exclusively to their unknown brother who was still in heaven, waiting for the dilatory angels to bring him to Blessed Sacrament Street.

"Let's see if he is there."

"No, Dolores."

"Then I'll go alone!"

Unwilling to be left behind, Isabel followed to the closed door, holding her breath as Dolores lifted the latch. A sleeping boy lay on the bed, the blackness of his curling hair startling against the pillow. The girls stared silently a moment, then withdrew.

"Dolores, our cousin is pretty, not like a boy at all."

"Boys are not supposed to be pretty. He does not please me." Nevertheless, as they descended the stairs Dolores cast a quick worried glance into the mirror on the landing, wondering if it might be true that in Europe tall women were becoming fashionable.

Juan Marcos, doomed to spend several years without travel, took steps to reform his household. "I will not live in a cloister haunted by three female ghosts!" he told Esperanza. "Buy the girls bright dresses—they look like starved crows. I swear there will be some gaiety in this house!" Esperanza sobbed helplessly.

He purchased a harpsichord and engaged a music master for his daughters. Annoyed by the thinness of Dolores' hair, he ordered her head shaved in hope of producing a more abundant crop. For months she cowered when anyone glanced at the tight cap covering her bald scalp, and the suffering gained nothing, for the new hair was no thicker than the old; she still had difficulty keeping her shell combs in place. Juan Marcos, appraising her, sighed and inquired less subtly than he supposed if she felt any vocation for the religious life. "Wonderful women, the nuns," he said. "They do much good, and some of the orders are quite jolly." Shaking her head, she stared at the floor.

His attention soon wandered. Not only was he occupied by business affairs, but he began to devote more time to his second family, his mistress and their four children, who lived in a remote quarter of the city, a healthy band of half-breeds, far more entertaining than his pious wife and his legitimate but timorous daughters.

Meanwhile, the girls' lives had been altered by Ricardo. Within a few months he had established himself as ruler of the household, impressing Esperanza by his ability to recite the entire missal in Latin, charming her with sweet smiles, and joining her at times for prayer in the chapel. She did not notice that these displays of piety were always followed by requests for permission to attend the circus or to have a picnic at Xochimilco's floating gardens.

He assumed command of his two cousins, and they obeyed him willingly, having been taught from babyhood that males were born to command. The daily game of make-believe ceased, and the imaginary visitors were banished, for Ricardo enjoyed nothing in which he did not excel. "Anyone can imitate the doorkeeper," he said after Dolores attempted a demonstration. "Watch!" He performed an awkward parody.

Isabel clapped her hands. "Oh, Dolores, admit that Ricardo is funnier than you are."

"Of course he is," she said, hurt by Isabel's infidelity and resolving in the future to practice her impersonations in secret behind the door of her room.

As time passed Juan Marcos became aware that he should take steps to arrange a marriage for his elder daughter, yet he delayed from month to month, hoping the problem would solve itself. "She is no beauty," he admitted. "Still, the plainest shoe has a mate somewhere." But her sixteenth saint's day passed and no young men pursued her, no flowers were tossed onto her balcony, no midnight serenades were heard in the street. Only a handful of rich young blades or wealthy widowers were suitable prospects for a Cortés daughter, and these elevated gentlemen did not consider her a prize. An enormous dowry would, of course, change matters, but it was common knowledge that the family fortune had declined. Juan Marcos was again demonstrating his father's inability to recognize the winning side of a political struggle. In a year when everyone expected the powers of Europe to pounce upon Mexico to establish an empire, Juan Marcos was investing in government bonds and supporting an Indian politician named Benito Juárez for no reason except that Juárez resembled his late father-in-law, a man who had invariably succeeded.

Dolores Cortés had changed from a child to a woman. Now the servants called her "señorita," and her father's friends, on the rare occasions when they called, kissed her hand instead of her cheek. Management of household expenses had become her responsibility, since Esperanza could no longer be trusted with money. Coins set aside for the butcher and water-carrier vanished, and Juan Marcos accused his wife of secretly giving the money to the church. She, in turn, denounced the servants as thieves, driving one after another into the street with shrieks and crashing of crockery. At last Juan Marcos caused a strong box to be set in the floor under Dolores' bed and gave her the only key.

Ricardo had begun his apprenticeship in business, and now Dolores' days were again spent with Isabel. They attempted duets on the harpsichord, they played dominoes and backgammon, but although Ricardo spent little time with them he remained the center of their lives and they vied for his praise, embroidering shirts and vests, proud that despite his meager salary he was becoming one of the young bloods of the capital. His nights were occupied with entertainment, and usually he did not return home until long after everyone except Dolores had fallen asleep. She waited for him, concerned for his safety in streets infested by footpads and drunken soldiers, listening for the sound of his steps in the corridor below. During these hours she read by candlelight, but when he was unusually late no book could hold her attention. Then she stood in the shadows on the balcony until she saw him approach, frequently carried by reeling companions.

One night after he had entered the house she was surprised by a soft tap at her door. He stood in the hall, holding his boots in his hand, barefoot to avoid noise. "I saw your candle burning," he whispered. "Can you lend me twenty duros quick? I owe them to a man who is waiting in the street. If I don't give him the money, he swears he will shoot at the windows and wake up everybody."

"A moment." With the key from the cord around her

neck, she unlocked the strong box. "Here you are. Pay him and tell him to go quietly. Papa is sleeping at home tonight!"

She waited for him to return to explain this mysterious debt, but after a brief errand to the street he closed the door of his bedroom on the floor below.

The next day there was no opportunity to question him. At breakfast and again when he returned for siesta, Isabel was constantly present, making childish jokes, bidding for Ricardo's attention, and an unfamiliar anger welled in Dolores. She clings to him like a leech, she thought. There is never a moment alone. It seemed insufferable that she and her cousin should always endure the chatter of a twelve-year-old.

He did not appear at supper that evening, but not long after midnight she heard the quiet opening of the street door, soft footsteps, and then her name being whispered in the hall.

"Yes, I am awake. Come in."

He entered on tiptoe, holding a boot in each hand. "Is the señor in the house?" he asked.

"No, Papa has not come home."

"You saved me last night," he told her. "It was a debt from cards and had to be paid at once. Can you manage without the money for another week or two?"

"Yes."

His eyes sparkled and his face was flushed. "What an evening! Tonight I went with friends to a restaurant where they have Poblana dancers."

"Were the girls pretty?" she asked, hoping they were not.

"Pretty enough for what they are. We drank brandy, then started for the market to get soup. There was an old Indian asleep against a wall, so we tossed him into a fountain. You should have heard him yelp! It brought the nightwatch, so we ran down an alley." He described how they followed back streets to the market, where caldrons of chicken soup steamed all night over charcoal fires. She smiled at the pleasure he took in recounting these adventures. He was childlike, she thought, he did not realize how much he loved having an audience.

After he left her she went to the balcony and stood gazing over the neighboring rooftops. Although the hour was late, she was not sleepy. A glow of contentment warmed her as she reviewed Ricardo's visit word for word, gesture by gesture. She had thought of him as a child, but of course he was a man now. The soft prettiness had vanished; his face had become rather angular, and he was not a handsome man like her father. But he had a gaiety, a gift of laughter, and when he was near her she felt a strange and pleasurable stirring which no one else could evoke. She knew he was flighty, often careless of the feelings of others, and even vain. "But I could spend my life with him," she said.

When Maximilian Habsburg was proclaimed Emperor of Mexico, Juan Marcos was a man ambushed by history. The former government fled, and he sat at his desk staring vacantly at a stack of notes and bonds once worth a fortune and now waste paper. He considered suicide, then muttered, "I must think of my family, I must save what I can." The family that concerned him was his mistress and her children. Neither Cortés nor his dependents faced poverty, they had merely ceased to be rich, and on the day of Maximilian's triumphant arrival in the capital, Juan Marcos was occupied with selling a spare carriage and two matched mules he could no longer afford to maintain.

Dolores' understanding of what had taken place came from her midnight conversations with Ricardo. Nearly a year had passed since he first tapped on her door, and now he returned often, enjoying his audience, complaining that Juan Marcos's bad judgment had alienated him from the new monarchy and its resplendent emperor. Although he loved to tell of his skill and luck in gambling, he did not mention the twenty duros he had borrowed long ago, and his debt to the household fund had been increased by two more small loans.

One night when Juan Marcos joined his family for supper, she became aware that her father was studying Ricardo and herself with unusual thoughtfulness, and fear rose in her that their late meetings had been discovered. At the end of the meal Juan Marcos said, "Ricardo, take brandy with me. I have a matter to discuss with you."

Later Dolores lingered on the stairs, watching the door behind which the two men were talking. When Ricardo, his face troubled and frowning, emerged from the room, she called to him softly.

"You are still awake?" he said, surprised and not pleased to see her.

"Yes. Does Papa know?"

"Know what?"

"That you and I often talk together."

"No. We spoke of business matters. Good night, Dolores."

She did not fully believe him and when a month passed without his appearing at her door she became certain that her father had discovered and forbidden the private visits. Ricardo now spent even less time in the house than Juan Marcos did, and Isabel complained of his neglect. "He never is with us any more!" She looked at Dolores suspiciously. "Have you quarreled with Ricardo? Offended him?"

"Of course not."

"I think he is avoiding us. I think you have done something to turn him against us!"

"That is ridiculous, Isabel. Maybe he is tired of your chatter. It is enough to bore anyone."

Isabel's lip trembled. "You are spiteful! No wonder Ricardo stays away."

Anger between them was so rare that both were shocked, and the clash ended as abruptly as it had begun. Still, for three days the courtesy they showed each other had an edge.

A few nights later Dolores was awakened by an unfamiliar sound and nearly cried out before she realized the figure moving in the dimness was Ricardo. "What is it? You frightened me."

"I am sorry. I thought you were awake." He seemed confused, undecided, then sat on the edge of the bed beside her. A shyness linked with fear pervaded her, and, sitting up, she held the sheet to her throat.

"There is a candle on the table," she said.

"We can see well enough. The moon is bright." He fell silent, but his breathing was rapid.

"Ricardo, something has happened. Tell me!"

"Nothing, nothing at all. Only I am a little drunk."

She touched his arm, then quickly withdrew her hand, sensing a strangeness in him tonight. His eyes probed her face; then he said, "I want to leave Mexico. I want to leave here."

"Leave? No!" She spoke so loudly that he touched his fingers to her lips to silence her.

"What is there for me here? What future? It is your father's fault, and nothing can be done about it."

"You cannot leave us! You cannot mean what you say." But he did mean it, she heard the urgency in his voice, and a vision of her life in the house without him swam before her eyes. Month after month she would sit with Isabel, sewing, embroidering altar cloths; they would talk endlessly about nothing, not listening to each other, and the silence of the nights would be broken only by Esperanza's prayers.

"Will you help me to go, Dolores? Do you love me enough to help?"

"I cannot let you go! Stay for my sake. Stay because I

love you." Sobbing, she clasped him to her as though to hold him forever by the strength of her arms, and when he tried to speak she fell back on the pillow, pressing her hands to her ears. "I will not listen, I cannot bear it. I love you!"

"I am sorry. Poor Dolores."

His lips brushed her forehead, touched her closed eyelids, and her body shook as she felt the warmth of his mouth. She clung to him, terrified by the fever raging in her, still crying, "You will not leave me, you cannot."

"Don't be afraid. Hold me close, Dolores, closer. . . ."

Long after he had left her she fell asleep, exhausted and dreamless, yet feeling she still rested in his arms. She did not hear Ricardo return quietly to the room, then leave a second time.

When dawn broke through the mountains to the east of the capital, Ricardo Cortés had already passed the suburbs and was on the highway to Veracruz, riding a good roan he had secretly purchased several days before. Confident, eager for his future, he sang as he rode.

He did not fear pursuit. His pressing reason for fleeing Mexico would not be discovered for some weeks, nor was he worried that the hollow horn of his saddle concealed a pair of pearl earrings and a locket set with small rubies. Dolores, he was certain, could not report the theft of her jewelry without telling about other matters. Besides, he told himself, she would have lent it to him if she had understood how serious his plight had become. When he became rich he would repay her.

"Poor Dolores!" He had been quite fond of her; she was good company. But he would not dwell on this; he was too happy to have regrets. He had escaped from an impossible situation and from the house he had long ago nicknamed "The Madwomen's Cloister." It was a beautiful morning. As he spurred the roan toward the distant seacoast, his head filled with visions of the adventures lying before him, and he sang. " 'Oh, girls of Barcelona have honey in their mouths. Girls of Barcelona wear moonlight in their hair. . . .' "

When Juan Marcos read the letter Ricardo left for him he said one word, "Ingrate." "I can no longer be a burden in circumstances of your misfortune. I leave without speaking because the pain of such a parting would distress me too greatly. Express the love of my heart to your esteemed wife and lovely daughters, whom I cherish in my soul, dear kinsman. . . ." Juan Marcos added another word. "Hypocrite!"

Weeks passed, however, before he learned the depth of Ricardo's treachery. Tax-gatherers of the new monarchy, after examining Juan Marcos's financial affairs, confounded him with news that at least ten thousand duros were missing from Ricardo's accounts. "This shortage does not concern the government," they explained, "but we thought you should be advised."

When his family met for supper that night he descended upon them like a storm, shouting as though they, not he, had imported the culprit. "A viper! A thieving crow in peacock's feathers!" He glowered at Esperanza. "And you, fool, urged me to offer my eldest daughter to the thief!"

For an instant Dolores did not understand the words; then she covered her face with her hands while he continued, now to her. "Consider yourself lucky that he would not accept the dowry I offered, otherwise the scoundrel would be in your bed this very night." Rising quickly, she clutched at the table, upsetting a cup, then ran from the room.

"You have made her ill again," cried Esperanza. "She has been ill for weeks, and you have made her worse with your shouting. Add that to your other sins!"

"Be still! This is a family disgrace and I do not want it

to go beyond the walls of this house. To report a thief named Cortés is unthinkable."

There was silence in the room. Esperanza bowed her head and moved her lips in unspoken Aves while beneath lowered lids she watched the effect of this upon her husband.

Isabel spoke quietly. "Papa, did Cousin Ricardo really refuse to marry Dolores?"

"He did. He wanted more money than Moctezuma's treasure, money he knew I did not have. And do not call him Cousin Ricardo. Call him the sneak-fingered bandit he is." He realized that Isabel was smiling and supposed this was because of the cleverness of his insult. But it was a faraway smile, as though caused by something remembered or expected.

4

The Conde Calderón, who had a serpent's awareness of danger, always contrived to be abroad during troubled times, and he was basking in the sunlight at Capri when he learned of the collapse of Maximilian's empire. "So they shot the Habsburg," he said without emotion, although inside him was a twinge of regret, for the Austrian archduke had been so admirably tailored.

The Conde wished that his friend Juan Marcos Cortés could have lived to see justification of his faith in Benito Juárez, the Oaxacan Indian, who had now returned to power. Cortés had been recently taken by the plague, leaving a will which named Calderón guardian of his widow and two daughters. The Conde paid little attention at the time, but he instructed his Mexican attorney to do whatever must be done. Now, as he remembered the government bonds Juan Marcos had held, his eyebrows lifted and he pursed his lips. "So the Cortés daughters will be heiresses after all. I have been much too neglectful of them." Nevertheless, four years passed before the Conde found it convenient to return to Mexico.

After a week in the capital he called on a friend, the young editor of *La Prensa.* "I had an extraordinary experience last night," he said. "Have you heard of the Cortés sisters?"

"Cortés? Daughters of Juan Marcos Cortés? I thought the whole family had died."

"No, only the father and then his wife soon afterward. The daughters are very much alive, but everyone has simply forgotten them. I am their guardian, and last night I paid them the first social visit they have received in more than three years. There was literally moss growing in the entrance."

"Recluses, eh?"

"Yes. During the last years while troops marched in the streets and cannonballs sailed over the roof of their house, the two girls sat in their chairs doing needlework. Isabel can begin a remark, and Dolores will finish it, as though each knows everything the other is thinking. Several times last night they exchanged glances, and I felt that a whole conversation had been held. It was disconcerting."

"Are they attractive?"

"Physically, not in the least. Born to be spinsters. But Dolores has a definite charm, and I must say she rescued the evening."

"How so?"

"At first both girls were timid as fawns, but I brought along a bottle of cognac, and after supper the conversation became quite gay. Dolores performed a really amazing imitation of Carlota of Habsburg, although she had seen the Empress only twice. She caught every expression, the whispery voice, the way Carlota used to spread her fingers. The girl has an uncanny ability! She and her sister have invented a game, a pretense of visitors calling on them, and Dolores portrays the visitors."

"Rather childish for two grown women."

"They seem unaware of the oddity. One of her creations is a character called Gregorio Gorgoni. He makes speeches about how men will do anything for money. I understand she once put on an old suit which had belonged to her grandfather and actually deceived the servants into believing there was a male caller."

"Utterly mad," said the editor.

"Yet delightful. I refused to leave until Dolores promised to show me Don Gregorio in full dress some evening." The Conde paused, thoughtful for a moment. "It was most peculiar. When she did the imitations, all her shyness and awkwardness left her. She seemed to wrap herself in another body. Rather eerie."

The next month the Conde forced the editor to pay a call upon the sisters. "You simply must come with me."

"Very well. But I detest impersonations and I am never convinced by them. I must admit, however, that eccentrics do exert a certain fascination for me."

When they arrived at Blessed Sacrament Street, they were greeted by a nervous girl whom the Conde introduced as Isabel Cortés. Dolores had been taken ill, the girl explained, and the entertainment must be postponed. Still, she hoped the gentlemen would have chocolate or sherry with her.

They were ushered into an uncomfortable drawing room that had a musty smell, and a little later a third guest arrived, a blustering bumpkin whom the Conde seemed to know, an aggressive and insolent bore. "Your newspaper, señor," he growled, "is a tissue of lies and scandalmongering! You, as perpetrator, should be whipped through the streets and pelted with the garbage you wallow in!"

The editor sprang to his feet. "Your remarks demand satisfaction! You may suggest the time, place, and weapons!"

"Your villainy is deeper than I thought. What sort of coward threatens a lady who is also his hostess?" The black shovel hat was whisked off, the mustache removed.

"Jesus, Mary, and Joseph!" said the editor.

"Good evening," said Doña Dolores.

This was the beginning of the public career of Don Gregorio Gorgoni, a legend nurtured and shaped by the Conde and the editor. Items about the financier appeared in *La Prensa*, while Calderón spread the South American's fame at social functions. "I was chatting with Gregorio Gorgoni the other day. You don't know him? The South American billionaire. An eccentric genius." A prominent attorney was initiated into the secret, then a banker and a government minister. A new life had begun for Dolores Cortés.

The impersonation, although it required skill and discipline, came easily. She knew Gorgoni to the depth of his soul, she entered into him and became him with no sense of acting a part. For the space of the performance, Dolores Cortés had no existence, and she relinquished herself joyfully to the power and vitality of the South American, so lost in him at times she felt he was not her creation, but that she was his.

Isabel remained in her room during the impersonations, but sometimes appeared afterward to mingle briefly with the guests. Later the sisters would talk, but not about the events of the evening. Isabel reported on the health of the violets she had planted in the patio or the sweetness of oranges she had bought at the door that morning. Nothing beyond the house held interest for her, and often when Dolores listened and watched Isabel's face, she remembered Esperanza and was frightened.

The Fraternity of Dishonorable Gentlemen, as the initiates styled themselves, increased. Adornments were added—the liveried servants, the portrait of Gorgoni painted by the capital's best artist, and Dolores in the new role of the housekeeper. When the Gentlemen discovered that her art was not limited to the portrayal of Don Gregorio, they devised other hoaxes which she executed to their delight and her own. The Rani of Allahspur, a Hindu queen, was reported to be visiting the capital, and a certain hostess, a notorious social climber, was duped into entertaining her. The royal lady created consternation by demanding that her huge and ferocious Afghan hound be seated at the supper table in a place of honor between the hostess and the chairman of the National Lottery. In the midst of the meal the dog bayed mournfully and the Rani stormed out of the house, announcing that her canine companion had been poisoned by the food. *La Prensa* ran the story in full, and the Dishonorable Gentlemen chuckled for weeks.

Doña Dolores was no longer confined to Blessed Sacrament Street, and she began to attend the opera and the theater, for there was no lack of escorts among her new acquaintances. Yet few of these men called at the house except on nights dedicated to Don Gregorio. Once Dolores Cortés had been merely uninteresting, now she was awesome, and only the Conde felt completely at ease in her presence, although one widower and two bachelors summoned their courage and made tentative gestures toward courtship. "I am not interested," she told Calderón.

"My dear Dolores, have you never cared for a man?"

She was silent a moment, then said, "I am hard to please."

One August the rains poured unceasingly, flooding the streets, washing away graves in the low-lying cemetery. A dozen epidemics swept the city, and among the thousands stricken was Dolores Cortés, who lay in her bed for three weeks, alternately freezing and burning. When the fever abated she remained so weak that she could hardly support herself with a cane. Her physician advised her to go to the town of Cuautla to take the waters. "Winter will be here soon, and you cannot endure chilly weather."

At first she refused, but the Conde, alarmed for her health, offered a private villa he maintained near the famous springs. "You must go! Even your sister realizes this." Isabel also urged the trip strongly, although she herself would not leave Blessed Sacrament Street and had never in her life been separated from Dolores.

"I will manage very well alone," she said. "Perhaps the change will be good for both of us." Isabel had changed remarkably in the last weeks, acquiring a new cheerfulness, an air that could almost be called confidence. Never had Dolores felt closer to Isabel, more grateful for her companionship than during her illness.

The town of Cuautla nestled in a deep valley to the south of the capital, and after only a week there she was strong enough to write Isabel. "The villa is charming, set in a garden whose description can be found in the Book of Genesis. I endure daily parboiling in the mineral springs. If you are lonely, tell me and I will return at once." Isabel replied that all was well and on no account should Dolores endanger her health by an early homecoming.

In a shady corner of the garden, surrounded by bougainvillaea and roses of Castile, she often sat with an unopened book in her lap, eyes half closed, enjoying the sunshine and dreaming of the future. There was no reason they should not buy their own carriage, and now that Isabel was stronger and happier, they could share the sights and charms of the city as she had known them with her grandfather. She pictured small supper parties with Isabel and herself as hostesses, and perhaps at Christmastime they would open their home for the *posada* season, entertaining all who knocked. There would be quiet happiness and the deepening pleasure of each other's company. "No one has ever loved us, but we have ourselves. That can be enough."

As she thought this, the image of Ricardo came to her memory like a shadow between her and the sun. More than a dozen years had passed since his flight from Mexico, and she had schooled herself not to think of him, not to nurse her grief and hurt. Neither she nor Isabel spoke his name, yet often she felt him loom at the edge of their conversation, and when he drew too close they avoided each other's eyes, talked in strained tones, or fell silent. Time had dulled her pain, but it was not forgotten, not forgiven. If she had meant nothing to him, then he was the poorer for it; if he had taken nothing away from her room but a few pieces of jewelry, then he had indeed gone empty-handed; he, not she, had been robbed. "He was worthless, he was deceitful, but I loved him. At least I had that."

This memory was the one portion of her life not shared with Isabel; this was hers alone, and, for all the grief it brought her, it was still precious. "He could never really love anyone, but in his own way he cared for me. I was special."

A few days after the New Year the Conde paid a visit to Cuautla, his bacchanalias having left him in need of the waters of rejuvenation. His second evening at the villa, they sat on a terrace overlooking beds of *nochebuena*. "The climate has done wonders for you," he said. "You have color again."

"Thank you. I plan to return home soon."

The Conde's eyes twinkled. "I know the reason for your haste. Come, Dolores, I am your guardian, and you must not hide things from me."

"Hide things?"

"Do not pretend. I am certain that the Cortés family

will soon make a surprising announcement. During your absence I called on your sister twice, and both times your cousin from Madrid was perched in the sitting room. I know a courtship when I see one."

"Our cousin? You cannot mean Ricardo!"

"Ah, but I do. I remember meeting him years ago. I believe he was your father's secretary. . . . Dolores, what is wrong? Are you ill?"

The sisters faced each other in the *sala*. Dolores had not yet removed her traveling cape, and in the lower hall a coachman struggled with her valises.

"I did not expect you so soon." Isabel's hands fluttered like two white moths. "Your room has not been dusted."

"Where is he, Isabel? I hope he has had the decency to stay at an inn."

Her cheeks turned scarlet. "So you know. That is what brought you back so soon."

"Yes, I know. Well, is he in the house?"

"No, and of course he stays at an inn! He has gone to Puebla for a week to look at ranches. He is considering buying property."

"Indeed? Our prodigal must have done well. Or perhaps he reads newspapers and knows his Mexican cousins are not so impoverished as they once were. Why did you not tell me he had returned? Answer me, Isabel!"

"You would have spoiled things as you always did." Her voice trembled, but she lifted her head defiantly. "His letter came while you were ill. A letter for *me*, not you! He wrote me from Havana. Things had gone badly for him and he was unhappy and—"

"I daresay. Was it theft again or something worse?"

"You were always spiteful! You believed that story Papa told about the money."

"A sudden departure for an innocent man."

"Do you want to know why he left, Dolores, why he

really left? He ran away because Papa tried to force him to marry you. I know the truth now. And all the time, I was the one he loved."

Dolores sank into a chair, for a moment unable to speak. The hysterical voice seemed to be Esperanza's voice, and the twisting hands were her mother's. "You were a child when he left. What could you know of it?"

"Ask Ricardo if I was a child when he kissed me! Ask him if they were a child's kisses when we met in the chapel or the hall upstairs—any place where we could escape you. You were always watching, always interfering. He used to laugh about how jealous you were." Isabel turned away, gazing at the tall barred window of the *sala* and seeming unaware of her sister's presence. "I knew he would come back for me. I waited, never doubting it. When I embroidered napkins, I told myself they were handkerchiefs for him. Sometimes from the balcony I saw a man walking in the street and I was so sure it was Ricardo coming home that I could hardly keep from calling out. Then he wrote to me and I answered. I told him I was waiting."

"Then it was you who suggested my going away. You spoke with the doctor."

"I knew if you were here you would cause trouble. You always wanted Ricardo for yourself. Now we are going to marry and leave this house, and there is nothing you can do. It is decided, Dolores. Do you understand? It is decided!"

The shrill words struck like blows. What use was it to tell of the theft of the jewelry, of Ricardo's last night in the house? There would be an answer for everything. She felt helpless, and suddenly longed to become Don Gregorio, who had a strength she did not possess, who controlled all situations. She said, "You have misjudged me, Isabel. I have another life now. Have you explained that to Ricardo?"

"The impersonations? No. We have not talked of you, there have been other concerns. I thought you would someday tell him yourself. I want you and Ricardo to be friends, Dolores."

"Of course. We have always been friends—since we were children. All three of us." The words came gently and smoothly, as though someone else had spoken them, a stranger who, unlike Dolores, felt neither rage nor pain.

Two weeks later Ricardo Cortés began his second ascent of the mountain road leading from Mexico City to Veracruz, but this time he was not a young man in flight. He rode as a gentleman in a private coach emblazoned with a crest of nobility. The astonishing events of recent days, his incredible good fortune, had left him exultant and light-headed. "A miracle," he told himself. "I am Saint Jude's grandson."

The morning was cool and brilliant, sunlight glittering on the snows of a distant peak, an omen, he thought, of his own dazzling future. A perfect morning, marred only by the irritating silence of his traveling companion, a young man who had joined him at the last moment before the coach's departure from the capital. "I ride with you," he said, taking the opposite seat and giving no explanation. Nearly an hour had passed without a word being spoken, and Ricardo was fond of talking; he wished he had taken the train instead of accepting the Conde's offer of the coach. On a train one could always find congenial gentlemen and usually a card game. But Calderón said, "A man in your new position cannot travel by train except in a private car. Señor Gorgoni is adamant about maintaining appearances."

Ricardo studied the taciturn man sprawled opposite him, then chose a gambit to open conversation. "One sees few redheads in this part of the world. Are you Irish or Scottish, señor?"

"Mexican."

"Indeed? Permit me to introduce myself. I am Ricardo Cortés."

"I know."

"And you are—"

"Lieutenant Donaju."

"Ah, I wondered if the clothes you wear might be a uniform." He was dressed in a red-brown suit with a fringed shirt and dark sombrero. A pistol was strapped to his right hip. "I have been away from Mexico for a long time. I do not recognize the new uniforms."

"I am of the *rurales*. We are new but well known."

"Then you are not employed by the Conde or Señor Gorgoni?"

"No. But I am performing a task for the Conde today."

"Something special?"

"I am a specialist, yes." The lieutenant's sudden smile was engaging.

"Well, I am delighted to have company. There is a long journey ahead of me."

"There is?"

"Yes. All the way to Colón on the Isthmus of Panama. Have you heard of the canal the Frenchman De Lesseps is digging there?" Lieutenant Donaju nodded. "De Lesseps is failing, Lieutenant. The entire project will soon be controlled by Gregorio Gorgoni. He has appointed me to represent him there.'"

"You are an engineer?"

"I know nothing of engineering—nor does De Lesseps, for that matter. My position is more like that of an ambassador—at least, that is how Señor Gorgoni explains it."

Ricardo rested his head against the cushions and contemplated his amazing luck. Two weeks ago he had been resigned to marrying his cousin, ready to face the reality of his thirty-three years and his failure in each of a dozen careers. No wealthy widow had yielded to his proposals, and the money he won at cards always vanished overnight. His last adventure, an attempt to become a gentleman planter in Cuba, ended as a quagmire of liens, foreclosures, and bankruptcy. Weary of struggle, he had written Isabel as an attempt at finding security, a dreary compromise with fate. Then his future seemed settled until he encountered the Conde Calderón at an inn in Puebla.

Since the nobleman was Isabel's guardian, he expected opposition to his planned marriage, but the contrary proved true. "I am delighted!" said the Conde. "Isabel is a lucky girl, especially since her inheritance is none too secure."

"Indeed?" Ricardo asked sharply.

"Oh, the government is gradually paying its debts. An eternal process, of course, and perhaps an unreliable one the way these *juntas* change every few years." The Conde chuckled, then winked at Ricardo. "Let us speak frankly, my boy. We both know you would not dream of accepting such a bride as Isabel Cortés were it not for financial reasons." Ricardo began to protest, but the Conde overrode him. "Do not misunderstand! I am pleased by your ambition. Isabel means nothing to me, but I trust you have no false hopes."

After sharing a bottle of brandy, the nobleman became expansive. "You are excellent company, my boy. I cannot remember a better conversation. You must meet my dear friend, Gregorio Gorgoni." The Conde studied Ricardo thoughtfully. "Now, I wonder! It occurs to me that you might be the man he is searching for. There is a position open in his new company, and the one who fills it should become rich in three years."

"What sort of position?"

"He wants an urbane man, a gentleman, to go to Colón on the Isthmus of Panama. There he is to cultivate officials, join their card games and amusements, gain their friendship." The Conde waggled a jeweled finger at Ricardo. "Next year Gorgoni will swoop upon the French company that is building the canal and seize control. His man in Panama will have a magnificent opportunity. Gorgoni's associates seem to catch wealth the way other men catch the pox."

"You think I am the sort of man he—"

"You are exactly what he described! I will arrange for you to meet him the moment you return to the capital." The Conde lowered his voice. "I would not mention this to Isabel. If Don Gregorio should select you, you might have second thoughts about marrying. If she sought Gorgoni out and created a scene—well, you might appear less than reliable."

"You are quite right," said Ricardo.

In Mexico City Ricardo avoided the Cortés house while he made inquiries about the billionaire. At a newspaper office he was told the South American had recently financed a trans-Andean railway by reaching into his own pocket, and he was given a sheaf of clippings to read. Even Ricardo's barber recognized the famous name.

A bewildering interview with Gorgoni himself took place two nights later in the reception hall of the Conde's mansion. Ricardo entered clumsily, tripping over a footstool he had not seen because the lamps, heavily shaded with rose glass, were turned low. Don Gregorio, ensconced like a tarantula in the shadows, rasped out a series of confusing questions, then said, "I am impressed with your manner. Tell me, do you have any commitments to hinder your leaving Mexico?"

"None of the least importance, señor."

"Then you are the man I have been seeking. One might say I have been waiting for you. The Conde and my secretary will arrange the details. It is settled."

Now, as Calderón's coach bore him toward his future, he wondered why he did not like the Conde, who, despite all favors, was repugnant to him; when Ricardo recalled his eyes, it struck him that they were reptilian.

High in the mountains the coach jolted to a stop. "There is a spring here," said Donaju. "The driver will water the horses."

"Good. We can uncramp our legs." As they dismounted from the coach, Ricardo said, "Magnificent country! The Pyrenees are nothing to these peaks."

"Beyond that grove of pines," the lieutenant told him, "is a rock resembling a watchtower. From the top of the precipice one can see the whole valley of Mexico."

"Really? Is it far?"

"We can walk there in five minutes. The Conde suggested I show it to you."

"Very thoughtful of him."

"Yes." Donaju, smiling, rested his hand on Ricardo's shoulder. "Shall we go now, señor?"

Following the traces of a path which led steeply upward, they soon reached the place Donaju had described, and although the view was spectacular, it was a lonely spot, concealed from the road by trees.

Shivering, the Conde Calderón gathered his shawl around his shoulders and moved closer to the brazier. "Your house, my dear Dolores, is always infested with drafts. Well, to continue the story of the accident: Lieutenant Donaju says your cousin became giddy from the mountain air. At any rate he saw Ricardo faint on the brink of the cliff and stumble forward. That is the official report and the end of the matter."

"The end of the matter? You might have spared me the details."

Her large eyes studied him, but he could read nothing

in her face, and when she said no more he found her silence irritating. To his mind the scheme against Ricardo Cortés had been a work of art ending with the appropriate climax. There was no need for Dolores to pose as a tragic muse. She had not even thanked him, not once congratulated him on the role he had played in the deception. Instead of gratitude, her manner toward him was almost accusation, and he was determined to brook no nonsense. "You will admit everything went according to plan?"

"Yes."

"Well then?"

She turned from him, speaking so softly he had to lean forward to catch the words. "We should have allowed him to go to Panama. Months would have passed before he discovered the truth; Isabel would have seen him for what he was."

"We have been through all this," said the Conde sharply. "You agreed we could not risk his returning to expose Don Gregorio as a myth. It would have been Gorgoni who died."

"We agreed."

Surely, he thought, she could not be displaying this afflicted conscience for his benefit! Although the final disposal of Ricardo Cortés had been the Conde's suggestion, he was certain that she had had the same thing in mind from the beginning. Why else choose Panama for his destination? It was the graveyard of Europeans, so fever-ridden that travelers sped across it by rail, covering their faces with perfumed scarves to avoid inhaling its malarial air. Dolores had marvelous subtlety, but he had always found direct methods more reliable.

"It is possible that you are grieving for this fortune-hunter?"

"I am not grieving! He was nothing to me!" Then her voice faltered. "I am frightened for Isabel, for what this news may do to her. She has been sending messages to the inn where he stayed, she even went into the streets herself to search for him. Can you imagine Isabel going into the street alone? She is frantic, and I—I am afraid to face her."

"Then I will inform her of the accident," said the Conde. "Is she in her room?"

"Yes. She is not well."

"Do not distress yourself. I will manage tactfully and she will forget him in time." Before leaving, he paused, resting his hand on her shoulder. "My dear Dolores, sad as all this is, I must say it resulted from your most brilliant performance. Frankly, I doubted your ability to deceive a man who had once known you well. I admire you, and I am always at your service."

5

Spring came late that year, and it was May before the sisters could take breakfast at a table in the patio. "Let me move your chair from the shadow," said Dolores. "The doctor says you need more sunlight." Isabel nodded but did not speak, and Dolores felt a dread that she might have again withdrawn into silence, a mood which could continue for days. But this morning she appeared cheerful; her listlessness had gone, and Dolores noticed she had remembered to comb her hair.

She poured chocolate into Isabel's cup. "What do you want to do today? Practice music? Or are you still embroidering?"

"I finished the embroidery yesterday," said Isabel, and Dolores was relieved by the calm voice, which had no panic in it today.

"Were you decorating a scarf?"

"Yes. The peacock design."

"You finished quickly. May I see it?"

"I am sorry, Dolores," she said, "but it is not here. I gave it to Ricardo last night."

Dolores' cup rattled against its saucer, and for a moment she could not speak. Ricardo's name had not been mentioned since the day Calderón brought news of his dying, although Isabel had cried it in nightmares, cried it so loudly that Dolores had often awakened and rushed to her room.

Isabel smiled, her eyes clear and alert. "Do you remember the blue vest I made for him long ago? This scarf almost matches it. I am going to do another for his saint's day, silver on white with a monogram. Do we have silver floss?"

"Silver floss? I—I don't know." Dolores gripped the arms of her chair. "Isabel, you know Ricardo did not come here last night. You know that cannot be true."

"But he did. He often comes after you are asleep. We try not to disturb you."

Dolores rose, unable to look into Isabel's face. "You have been dreaming."

"No. Not dreaming."

She did not send for the physician who had attended Isabel during these months. His funereal voice, the knowing frown and solemn clicking of his tongue were more than she could bear. Of what use were the vials of medicine, the Latin phrases and the prescriptions for baths in sulphur water? Nothing could help but time, time for Isabel to regain interest in life, time for the new and frightening illusion to pass.

That night in her room she was haunted by Isabel's confident smile as she spoke of her dead lover's return. Dolores had never observed madness except at the close of Esperanza's life, and that had been a madness of shrieked prayers that set the teeth on edge. Esperanza too had received ghostly callers, but they had come in visions, bathed in radiance or infernal fire, and when she described them her eyes rolled and her hands twisted. Isabel had spoken so quietly this morning, so quietly . . .

"Of course it is madness! There are no ghosts." She was not an ignorant Indian, not like their cook, who believed Esperanza's chapel was haunted and every shadow was a specter. But what if the dead returned in another way, a way less material than superstition personified? Several times, when she had assumed the character of Don Gregorio, a strange sensation had come to her, a belief that Gorgoni's words came from her grandfather and were not spoken through memory or any recollection of her own, but derived from his presence; that Gorgoni's strength came not from herself but from Carlos Montejo, a presence, an incarnation of which she was the instrument.

At last she fell asleep, and she did not know what disturbed her hours later, but she turned on her pillow, sighing, thinking that it was morning, although no light showed against the shutters, that the cook had arrived early, had unlocked the door with the iron key she carried on a chain, and was now plodding across the patio toward the kitchen. In a moment she would hear the rattle of tongs as the charcoal fire was rekindled. She drifted into sleep once more, then, startled by some unfamiliar sound, sat up quickly, aware that it was not dawn and she had not heard the entering of a servant. Lighting the candle on her bedside table, she saw that her door, always open in case Isabel should call out, was now closed. A wind, she thought. But the night was still, the house utterly silent except for the creaking of beams.

Wearing a robe and carrying the candle in its holder, she went into the hall. "Isabel," she whispered. When no answer came, she hurried to her sister's room and found an empty bed, its rumpled sheets tossed aside and the net curtains open. She hesitated, frightened, unsure of what to do. Then, from somewhere below, came the sound of heavy footsteps and the closing of a door. "Isabel? Isabel, where are you?" As she ran through the corridor her candle flickered out, but she did not need its light on the familiar stairs that led to the patio. At the foot of the stairwell she halted, drawing into the shadows while she surveyed the deserted courtyard. No intruder moved in the darkness of the archways. A cricket sang near the arbor, and in a neighboring house a dog howled twice then fell silent. The open doors of the chapel glowed faintly red from three votive candles that burned night and day.

The entrance hall to the street was blackness, but she moved through it swiftly and when her hands found the front door lock she gasped, discovering it was unlatched, although she herself had secured it at sunset. "Isabel! Isabel!"

"I am here, Dolores."

Whirling toward the voice, she saw her sister, a dim figure in the chapel doorway, barefoot, dressed in a white nightgown, her uncoiled hair falling to her waist. As Dolores approached, Isabel neither moved nor spoke, but the candles behind her cast a wavering light, giving her features a fragile loveliness, a strange beauty Dolores had never seen in the pale face.

"Isabel, what are you doing here? I heard something— and the door was unlocked."

"I unlocked it for Ricardo. He left only a moment ago. Perhaps you saw him?"

Against her will Dolores cried out, "Ricardo is dead! He can never come back! Do you understand he is dead?"

The smile did not leave Isabel's lips. "You would like to believe that, Dolores. Why does it please you to hurt me? We have always loved each other."

"I have never wanted to hurt you. What I do—what I have done—is only for your happiness."

"Is that true, sister?"

"I swear that is true!" She gripped Isabel's arms, gazed into her face, and saw that her words did not reach her. "Come to bed, I will help you to your room."

For an hour she sat in a small rocking chair beside the bed, watching until Isabel slept. "I did it for her," she told herself again and again. "I saved her from him." But she could not stifle the memory of the rage that had shaken her at the Conde's villa when she first learned of Ricardo's return, nor could she forget Isabel's words, *Ask Ricardo if I was a child when he kissed me.*

"I did it for your sake, Isabel," she whispered to the sleeping woman on the bed, but the words were hollow. "I did not realize what he meant to you."

As she was leaving the room an impulse, an uneasiness, made her open the cedar chest where Isabel kept embroidery and needlepoint. But although she searched, she did not find the blue scarf with peacock embroidery. The next day she searched again, ransacking the house room by room, questioning the cook, and scattering the ash heap to hunt futilely for any charred scrap of cloth. But the blue scarf had vanished and was never found.

6

It has been said that the Conde Calderón was a conniver, a man who delighted in hatching plots and staging charades. When, in the autumn of his last year of earthly existence, he paid a call at 17 Blessed Sacrament Street, it was for the purpose of conspiracy. He intended to perpetrate a hoax.

As his carriage entered Doña Dolores' neighborhood, it occurred to the nobleman that he had not called at the Cortés house in daylight for a dozen years, not since the death of Isabel, a woman he had found insipid even in madness, but whose life had been somewhat redeemed by her funeral. He himself had made the arrangements for this lovely rite, since Dolores had been prostrate with grief. A beautiful funeral, he recalled. One of the most artistic he had ever arranged. Banishing all natural flowers, he had insisted on silk and wax lilies artificially scented, and for reasons of fashion she had been laid to rest in the habit of a Dominican nun. To the Conde this did not suggest an attempt to slip through the gates of heaven in disguise. On the contrary, the uniform of a religious enhanced the ceremony, and he intended to wear either Franciscan brown or Jesuit black for his own final appearance. A ruby cross would be striking against either color.

In recent years the Conde had spent much time in Spain and had had little contact with Doña Dolores. Twice he had attended gatherings of the Fraternity, enjoying himself thoroughly, although afterward he had felt a coolness in Dolores' manner. "She has resented me ever since I helped dispose of her wretched cousin. That is the reward for being a Good Samaritan." He was offended but still admired the lady's talent. Nowadays, he had been told, she seldom went out, entertained rarely, and it struck his imagination that she had become a marionette, reposing lifeless on a shelf until an audience assembled. Yet there were rumors suggesting her life might not be inactive. One of the Dishonorable Gentlemen had caught sight of a figure which he believed to be Gregorio Gorgoni strolling alone in the Alameda one evening, and there was a report that the billionaire frequented the Santa Ana market. Was it possible that Doña Dolores had been swallowed up and consumed by her own creation? The Conde could not quite accept this, but it was an intriguing fancy and reminded him of his favorite English story, *Dr. Jekyll and Mr. Hyde*—a fascinating idea that the evil in one's soul should become separately embodied. Calderón was too practical a man to be truly superstitious, but his imagination inclined toward the preternatural. He could not, for instance, dismiss tales of vampires; such creatures were simply too delectable not to exist and he often pictured them hovering bat-winged over the beds of certain pale acquaintances.

The carriage halted, and his footman helped him dismount. A few minutes later he was seated opposite Doña Dolores in the upstairs salon. "You must forgive me for not calling on you last spring when I returned from Europe," he said, accepting the sherry she offered.

"I have not felt neglected."

"As you know, I am disposing of all Mexican holdings. My next departure from here will be the last one." The Conde sighed and clicked his tongue. "I had no idea I was so encumbered by property. There have been a thousand details to arrange—removing squatters from certain ranches, having surveys made. But all is going well now, thanks to the admirable man the President has assigned to my service. Captain Donaju has become indispensable to me."

"Donaju? Yes, I recall the name."

The Conde looked uncomfortable. "Enough of my affairs! I called on you today for a purpose apart from the enjoyment of your company."

"Indeed?"

"I want your aid in a certain project which has caught my fancy, something I think you will enjoy. Perhaps you know I have always been interested in spiritism."

"Spiritism? You mean—the summoning of the dead?"

"Yes. I am fascinated by the tricks its practitioners use. Highly intelligent people have been deceived. Well, I have planned a most unusual entertainment, a demonstration and test."

Warming to his subject, the Conde leaned forward, his eyes bright. "Not long ago I entertained two gentlemen for supper at my house in Guanajuato. One of them you may know, Señor Ramos, the jewel merchant. The other is an American doctor who lives near Guanajuato, a most peculiar man, but we share a fondness for chess. The subject turned to spiritism and both men, it seems, are followers of it. The American pretends to be skeptical, but he admitted consulting a dozen mediums in two countries. That, to my mind, sounds like faith. Now the other man, Señor Ramos, is a perfect fool but likable enough, and he told me of a famous medium who established some communication between him and his dead son. Her name is Señora Laurier. Have you heard of her?"

Doña Dolores lowered her eyes, looked away. "I remember remarkable stories about her several years ago. I was interested."

"You didn't by chance consult her?"

"No. I have no faith in such things. Still, one wonders." She did not tell him that years before she had gone twice to the street where the Lauriers resided, and twice she had turned back, afraid to request the audience she sought. "I understand those who believe in— Sometimes it seems to me that Isabel is standing near my chair, and if I glance over my shoulder I will see her. But I do not look. I—I do not want to be sure. I should be sorry to discover that her nearness is only my imagination."

"Curious," said the Conde, throwing a quick look of appraisal at her. "But to return to my subject, I am convinced that the Laurier woman and her husband are swindlers, although they must achieve some impressive effects." He rose and refilled his sherry glass, excited now that he had come to the point of the plot he had concocted. "I propose to hold a séance at my house in Guanajuato with Señora Laurier officiating. There is a legend that the place is haunted, though I find it merely drafty, so it is the perfect setting. The Day of the Dead should be the date to give the whole proceeding a supernatural aura. I shall invite only two or three guests. I am sure it will be an excellent evening, and as a climax we shall prove the medium is a fraud."

"We shall?"

"Oh, the séance will be the usual thing, no doubt—a floating wand, mysterious rappings, bells. We will detect certain tricks of the trade by observation. But the joke will be having the medium deliver spirit messages to a man who does not exist: Don Gregorio Gorgoni!"

"Don Gregorio? You cannot be serious!"

"Oh, I am! We will not expose Gorgoni at the end, of course. That the medium has been fooled must be a secret for ourselves and several of our Dishonorable Gentlemen who, I understand, were duped by the Lauriers years ago. Can you imagine their consternation when they hear of this? Delicious!" The Conde lifted his glass in a toast to his own cleverness.

Doña Dolores hesitated, then said, "I am not sure Don Gregorio can accommodate you in this."

"My dear lady, whatever do you mean?" The Conde, who had expected enthusiasm, was astonished.

"I realize you regard him as a hoax," she said slowly. "But to me he is more than that. Can he meddle in such matters?" She was quiet a moment, then continued, "I am curious about Señora Laurier. Certain people I know have found a strange consolation through her. I envy them; I too need comfort. But perhaps it is dangerous to traffic with what we do not understand."

"Come, come! This from an intelligent woman like you!

Do you think this Señora Laurier will really produce ghosts? Perhaps raise Satan?"

"Satan exists." She looked at the Conde, a hard unblinking gaze. "One can be in league with him, have him at one's service without knowing until it is too late."

"Really, Dolores, I don't understand this nonsense. I insist you accept my invitation. You owe that much to me. After all, Gorgoni is partly my creation too!" He was petulant, but when he saw her expression change he realized a shift of tactics was demanded. "You say others have been consoled through Señora Laurier. If you appeared to her as yourself, could you be sure that what she told you was not surmise? That she might have knowledge of your life, your family? But if you were presented to her as Don Gregorio and then a message was spoken to Dolores Cortés, you would know genuine communication had occurred. What would any of us not give for such an assurance?"

"I would give all I have," she said slowly. "And yet—" She faltered, moved toward the door as though to leave without making an answer, then turned back. "Very well. I shall do it as a favor to you. And then we shall be even, our bargain ended."

"Excellent! I knew I could count on you."

As he descended the stairs he was pleased by how well he had managed the interview. He had been right not to tell her that his plot was double-edged. A story told by Captain Donaju had convinced Calderón that the peculiar American doctor had engineered the murder of his own wife, and his visits to mediums were the result of being guilt-haunted. Guilt delighted the Conde, and he was eager to observe Esterbrook's reactions during the séance. The Lauriers' illusions were reputed to be most effective, and what would the doctor do if an accusing ghost appeared? It would be fascinating.

He was still annoyed with Doña Dolores as he climbed

into the carriage. What was that nonsense about being in league with Satan, of all things? She should be happy to aid him in this new project; she owed him a favor. Had they not together saved Isabel?

He was smiling as he rode away, satisfied with the completion of his plan and blissfully unaware of its consequences for himself and the woman he had just left, who now sat alone in the Córdoba chair that belonged to Don Gregorio Gorgoni.

FOUR

THE PATRICIO

1

There is a belief that some men inherit features and character from the land of their birth—that mountains influence stature, northern lakes and fjords produce eyes of a frosty blue, and men of the torrid zones are hot-blooded. Francisco Patricio Donaju, born in the rugged Mexican state called Guerrero, apparently brought this folklore to mind, for both Tomás D'Aquisto and Captain Guzmán described him as a man marked by his birthplace.

In an embarrassingly lyrical passage of *True Facts* Captain Guzmán (or perhaps the professor) tossed science to the dogs and reverted to myth in picturing Donaju: "A true son of Guerrero, that fierce state whose proud name means 'warrior,' he was endowed with the strength of its rocks, and in serving our Beloved President he showed the courage of the pumas who roam beneath blue Guerrero heavens whose color was reflected in the major's eyes. . . ."

Guzmán did not mention that pumas prey on the helpless, and the soil of Guerrero is noted for its sterility. Privately he detested the region and all its inhabitants. "It is Mexico's Sicily," he confided to a friend. "Its only products are cactus spikes and jaguars. Where else could Donaju have come from?"

Tomás D'Aquisto, pondering the life of Donaju to find a link between him and the dead, was struck by the same thing and wrote in his manuscript: "Donaju was reared in a desolate and savage land. Perhaps this accounts for him. I myself cannot understand what forces combined to produce such a monster, for if what I have heard can really be true, then Donaju was of a breed not seen since the Dark Ages and perhaps not then. . . ."

The magician, in learning part of Donaju's story, had accidentally stumbled onto a tale so horrifying that it was almost beyond his belief. D'Aquisto could comprehend slaughter in war, and even entertained romantic notions about it, but the idea of planned genocide, the systematic destruction of thousands of helpless persons, shocked him so profoundly that he assumed creatures like Donaju and his cohorts were unique, without past or future parallel. He assured himself that such atrocities could happen only in a backward land like Mexico, and that no advanced country such as France, England, or Germany would ever tolerate the wholesale coldblooded destruction of innocent people.

D'Aquisto's naïveté is understandable, and he was no more ingenuous than most men when he wrote: "Modern civilization could not foster a Donaju. He was a leftover from savagery." Every century discovers anew the magnitude of evil and always looks upon it with fresh astonishment.

2

A broad and beautiful road runs from the high valley of Mexico southwest to the Pacific, where it ends at the ancient seaport Acapulco. Today this road is a great highway and in various forms, as a path, then a trail, it has been an important route for more centuries than history can remember, familiar to generations of travelers before the first Aztec armies followed it to search out victims for the altars of Tenochtitlán. Coffee-colored men, their ankles clicking with shell bracelets, wore a path there when much of Europe was impenetrable forest, and Indian explorers stood awed by its beauty a millennium before an upstart Spaniard impertinently claimed the discovery of the ocean which is its western terminus.

The road begins in magnificence, climbing to a crest where it is said that three thousand peaks are visible, then winds giddily down to flowering orchards in a valley of perpetual spring. Far to the west, at the brink of the Pacific, it has a splendor which is different but not less.

Between the east and west lies a barrier: a rocky stretch of wilderness gouged by dry stream beds, slashed and scarred by gulches where the thin crust has been torn away to reveal the ribs of the earth. This is Guerrero, a country of crags and canyons whose infertile slopes tolerate only plants armed with spikes and bristles, life which seems neither to give nor to receive sustenance. It is a land without pity.

This vast waste has long been the natural resort of fugitives and renegades. Once entrenched in its mountain fastness they have been immune to pursuit, and in those narrow valleys that will support life at all peculiar communities have sprung up, settlements of clannish people isolated by choice and geography.

In the last days of the viceroys a group of runaways founded a village three hours' ride north of the Acapulco trail, a location from which they could range forth to prey on pack trains and travelers. The leader of this band was a burglar from Puebla, and he named the town—which was little more than a robbers' roost—the Glories of the Virgin of Soledad, honoring the patron saint of his calling. The

Dark Virgin was protector and intercessor for housebreakers, and no burglar would dream of working without first addressing a special prayer, the *Oración del Justo Juez*, to the Lady and promising her a share of the loot.

The sons and grandsons of these founders more or less continued their families' occupation, but they took up other activities as well. The women planted maize and maguey, tended scraggly flocks of sheep and goats, while the men became breeders of horses, a natural development since on the trail they chose from the finest stock in Mexico. Only a few remained full-time robbers, and these did not prosper. Travelers had learned to move in armed convoys, so the game became risky and the pickings lean. To this village, in the year 1854, came an Irishman called Michael Donahue, a formidable giant who arrived in a dramatic way.

Among the thugs of Soledad were three men who worked in concert, boastfully calling themselves Los Tres Tigres, but since all three had the given name Francisco and were more like weasels than tigers, the villagers referred to them as "the three little Panchos." The Panchos stalked only in darkness, choosing the weakest victims, and usually returned empty-handed, but one night on the road near Iguala they waylaid and robbed a private *diligencia*, a lone coach without an escort. They murdered the driver before the horses had reached a full halt, then stripped and shot the male traveler, whose wife, a stringy dowager, they raped without interest as a matter of form and a proof of masculinity. Then it was time to dispatch her too, and she knelt horror-stricken, staring into a rifle muzzle, when suddenly a voice interrupted.

"Drop your guns, señores, or I will kill all of you." An incredibly tall man with a thick red beard had materialized like a specter in the moonlight and now stood covering the bandits with a brace of revolvers. He spoke with an odd accent, but his Spanish was clear and his authority unmistakable. The astounded highwaymen glanced at the revolvers, heard his deadly tone, and obeyed while visions of the gallows tree flashed through their minds and they were too terrified to wonder where the stranger had come from or how he had managed to approach in utter silence.

For a moment the kneeling woman was unable to comprehend what had happened, then, seeing deliverance, she cried out, "Thank God you have come!" Rising, she stumbled toward her rescuer, wringing her hands as she wept. "The devils were about to kill me. My husband is already—" She got no farther. The man with the revolvers did not flicker an eyelid, but a shot rang out. The woman stood still, a look of bewilderment on her face, then crumpled to the ground. "Like yourselves, gentlemen," said Michael Donahue, "I leave no witnesses. Dead birds don't sing. Besides, I am easily described." When he tilted his head they saw a liver-colored scar on his right cheek, the letter D seared there with a branding iron.

The Irishman holstered his revolvers, and as he did so one of the Panchos glanced at a rifle lying on the ground. "Don't think of such a foolish thing, *amigo*," said Donahue. "I would put a bullet through your skull while you hunted for the trigger. Besides, you need me. Tonight I watched, and although you are brave men"—the cowardly Panchos took heart at his flattery— "your methods are awkward. You rode out here on the mere chance that a coach would pass, true?" They admitted this was so. "But I, you see, knew it would come. When it stopped at the Posada Santa Fe, I persuaded the driver that night was safer than day, since bandits expected no travelers after dark. I was waiting for them here when you interrupted."

"Ay, señor," said one of the Panchos timidly, "we had no idea it was *your* coach! I swear by the Virgin we would never—"

The Irishman laughed, a hearty roar. "A small thing among friends! You are men of honor just as I am. We will do well together. You need me, and I am tired of working alone. Pick up your rifles, señores, we trust each other. But on the other hand"—again his voice was deadly—"it would be a pity if you had rash thoughts." Then, turning to business, he became brusque. "The *diligencia* is not worth keeping and too dangerous to sell. The horses look spavined. We'd better start them down the road with their passengers and be content with money and luggage. I suppose your camp or village lies nearby? Good! I can think of nothing but eating." As an afterthought he added, "Tonight I want no share. In the future I will make the plans and take the greatest risks. For this, I expect one half after we've paid the Virgin and whatever authorities you bribe. I am not selfish, but I kill any man who cheats me of a centavo. Is this agreeable, señores?" It was not agreeable, but they agreed.

During the next year, when Donahue's leadership brought them prosperity, they were glad none of them had tried to carry out the treacherous thought which had been in every mind.

Michael Donahue, called in Spanish Miguel Donaju, was not welcomed in Soledad, but he won acceptance and even grudging admiration. Early, he was forced to shoot two residents, first a hag who, mistaking him for the red devil, attempted to poison him with a brew of toadstools; later a sniper who fired at him from ambush. Neither victim had relatives obliged to avenge them, so no blood feud was begun.

The Irishman selected a lonely plot of land three miles from the nearest neighbor and built himself a hut of adobe and wattle. After careful inspection he chose a tall olive-skinned girl to live with him, giving her father a mare and an embroidered shirt. Two months later he took the girl to Chilpancingo, where they were married by a priest, an almost unheard-of event. Soledad women considered themselves wives, and certainly they were mothers, but their matrimony was informal. None had a man who was as cautious as Donaju about Purgatory's punishment of carnal sin.

Although the villagers admired Donaju's strength and ruthlessness, he was never admitted to their community, was never called Don Miguel or even Señor Donaju. He remained a foreigner known as El Patricio, "the Patrick," a name given all those Irishmen—and English, Scots, and Germans—who deserted the American army to fight for Mexico when the northern republic robbed its neighbor of her lands in 1847.

He never talked of his past, believing no one in this remote place could comprehend his story. Not one person in the village knew that such a country as Ireland existed, and the few who had heard of Europe supposed it was a province of Spain. Donaju was mistaken. Suffering and oppression are universal, and the ingredients of his life and of the lives of these people were the same. Comedy, not tragedy, suffers most in translation.

Like the males of Soledad, Donaju had taken a wife while in his early teens, and like many Mexicans he had first worked as the servant of a foreigner. He was first a stable boy and then second groom for an Englishman who owned the land on which he, his family, and his bride's family were born. It was at this time that Donaju developed his love for horses and his contempt for men. At the age of sixteen he was ordered off the estate, accused of having an insolent air and a cheeky tongue. When Donaju protested, his employer threatened to set the dogs on him, and indeed this was done. Three bull mastiffs, yelping and leaping, charged toward the boy, surrounded him, and fought each other for the privilege of licking his hand. The dogs followed him joyfully down the lane while the infuriated Englishman shouted that if Donaju did not turn them back at the gate he would charge him with theft of his animals.

That winter his wife died in a Dublin slum while giving birth to a son who survived only a few hours. Her death was also a thing the Mexicans would have understood, for it was really due to starvation, and hunger was a constant fact of their lives. At seventeen Donaju became a strong-arm thief and footpad, always hoping his victims would cry out in English accents.

The next spring he sailed for New York, his passage paid by a labor recruiter after he marked a contract he could not read. During the voyage he dreamed of having land, animals, and a house of his own, but he arrived to find himself trapped for three years in a Connecticut mill, working to pay back the passage money. On the last day of this enforced labor he celebrated by breaking the jaw of a foreman who had named him "thick Paddy" and insulted the Catholic Church. After six months in the workhouse he drifted west, sometimes taking employment on railroad gangs, but always moving on. Then, in the distant land called Texas, a territory belonging to Mexico, he discovered a town named San Patricio, a place which was a startling oddity on the North American continent.

In 1823 ten thousand Irish families suffering famine and persecution pleaded with the Mexican government to allow them to settle in this uninhabited area. The Mexicans did not answer the petitions, but in the following years many of the Irish simply came and took up residence, gradually founding the community of Saint Patrick. Miguel Donaju, big and good-looking, found an immediate welcome there. He quickly learned to handle firearms, to break cow ponies, and to herd the cattle that foraged among the stones of the dry prairie. His neighbors lent him money to buy two mares and build a corral. Suddenly, miraculously, Donaju was a rancher, the owner of land and animals.

The revolt of the Texans against Mexico brought terror to San Patricio. The Irish knew too well the consequences of unsuccessful rebellion; besides, they had no quarrel with their Mexican neighbors and little in common with the Protestant towns of Texas. Although Spanish was not their native tongue, neither was English, and those Irishmen who had sampled the doubtful freedom of New York and New England were unmoved by slogans that inspired other men. Some joined the Texans, others helped the Mexicans, and Miguel Donaju wished only to be left in peace. But the land was in turmoil. Bandits roved the hills, and the Apaches, whose power had only recently been broken, threatened to rise again. One night Donaju's ranch was burned and his herd slaughtered. He blamed the rebellion for his ruin and never forgave the Texans even after they were successful and he found himself, to his surprise, a resident of their new nation.

The Republic of Texas soon joined the United States. Free from the bondage of Mexico and members of the great northern democracy, the Texans could now legally own slaves and thus exploit the land properly. In San Patricio there were constant rumors of a new war with Mexico. No one believed that the Americans would allow the rich land of California and the vast territory between it and Texas to remain in the hands of a weak neighbor. But when the inevitable war came no one in the community, least of all Miguel Donaju, was prepared for what happened.

Miguel and every able-bodied man of his acquaintance were suddenly members of the United States Army—a totally illegal impressment, for not only was there no conscription law, but moreover they were Irishmen who had emigrated to Mexican territory. But nothing could be done. The generals needed men, and San Patricio was in the path of the advancing army. Donaju was taken away from the ranch he had finished rebuilding.

During the first two weeks he considered flight into the western wilderness. He was horrified when forced to stand at attention while a Methodist preacher harangued the troops about God-given duties, and it dawned on him that a rumor he had heard was true: this was a war of Protestants against Catholics, and he, against his will, was to fight on the side of the devil. As the troops moved south, he heard about drunken soldiers profaning a church and beating a priest. Now he was sure, and his anger mounted daily as he watched the confiscation of cattle and horses from the Mexican ranches, horses that might have been *his* horses, and he bit back his rage when he heard himself called "Paddy" by the adventurers and soldiers of fortune who comprised the army.

On a moonless night Miguel and four other men, all from San Patricio, slipped away from the camp and joined the Mexicans. They were only five among many; within a few weeks a full company was formed, and by the end of the month enough men had deserted to form the Saint Patrick Battalion. For the first time in years Miguel Donaju was completely happy. He had found his natural place in life and was no longer a victim but an aggressor who could strike back. At the battle of Saltillo every American who crossed the sights of his rifle was the English landowner or the Connecticut foreman. He fought his private war confident of victory, and he was a superb fighting machine, fast and fearless.

The battalion was moved east to help meet the threat of General Scott's advance upon Mexico City, and in the darkness before dawn on the day of the battle of Churubusco, Donaju was exultant, proud of the battalion and of his Mexican comrades who today would cut the invaders to pieces and drive them to the sea. Far behind the lines the thousand churchbells of Mexico City were ringing victory before the first shot was fired. No one yet knew that a Mexican general, vain of his own glory, would refuse to bring reinforcements into battle, willing to see his country crushed if he could humiliate a rival. The defenses crumbled, and Donaju's companions fell to the left and right of him. He saw a Mexican brigade wiped out, the last survivors fighting with cutlasses and clubs when there was no more ammunition. The encircled and decimated Battalion of Saint Patrick at last surrendered. Donaju was too dazed by his captivity to be aware of the march into the capital, but he heard the churchbells pealing the false victory and he muttered, "Someone should tell the priests." He paid little attention to the military court that tried him immediately, knowing already that the sentence would be death by hanging.

On a bright morning, the thirteenth of September, 1847, he was led manacled into the Plaza San Jacinto. There was still fighting in the city, shots and cannon fire echoed from the direction of Chapultepec Castle, and at the moment when Donaju first saw the makeshift gallows a boy, little more than a child, was hurling himself from the heights of the castle, his body wrapped in the Mexican flag—death before surrender, a foolish and gallant gesture whose unexpected nobility casts light. Dozens more followed him, the child heroes, plunging to death and immortality in the memories of their countrymen.

Donaju's companions died in an uglier fashion, kicking the air, dangling from ropes when the cart on which they stood was driven from under them. He watched familiar faces contort in death—William and Francis O'Connor . . . James Mills . . . Lawrence McKay. His own turn would be soon.

Forty-three men of the Saint Patrick Battalion were hanged that morning, but Donaju was not among them. With several others he gained a last-minute reprieve when it was discovered he was not an American, had taken no oath, and his induction into the army had been illegal. Since he was innocent, he was sentenced only to be lashed, have his face branded with "D" for deserter, and forced to wear an eight-pound yoke around his neck while he labored as a blacksmith's helper. Then, when the Americans were ready to leave Mexico, his head was shaved and he was drummed out of the army of which he had never officially been a member. Donaju bore the humiliation, endured the pain in silence when the searing iron was pressed against his cheek and he smelled his own flesh burning. None of those around him realized that quietly and secretly something had given way in the Irishman's mind.

The invaders departed. Donaju was left penniless in Mexico City and, by his own choice, alone. Two months later, with the scar still livid on his face, Donaju became a lone bandit prowling the country from the northern desert to the jungles of the south.

This was the man who after several years of wandering settled near the village of Soledad, married, and soon became father of a healthy male infant whom he proudly named Francisco Patricio Donaju.

Patricio's first cradle was a straw basket strapped to the saddle of his father's horse. "You will kill him," the mother wailed. "You'll break his bones or addle his brains."

"Shut your mouth, woman. My son rides with me."

The señora, herself little more than a child, suffered much during these years. Miguel's love for the infant was worship, but then black moods came upon him and he cursed the child, saying things his wife did not understand. "My son in Dublin makes two of this half-breed bastard!" She supposed he had fathered children elsewhere, but his vehemence alarmed her, although she had no idea that the Dublin baby had lived less than a day. When seized by these spells, he imagined that others of his dead were still living and seemed to expect hanged comrades of the battalion to visit him. Once he ordered his wife to clean the house before his friends arrived. "Put flowers on the table! White flowers!"

Patricio was born with pale blue eyes and the flaming hair of his father, but the midwife said, "All babies are light-eyed. They will darken, and his hair will also become a Christian color if God is merciful." Donaju, frantic that his son might not resemble him, took the child to a hag called La Bruja Verde, a witch who practiced various rites with entrails of chickens and blood drawn from vampire bats. Señora Donaju, forced to go along to feed the child, grew faint with horror when the witch slit open the body of a vulture, then pushed the crown of the baby's head into the bleeding crop while chanting prayers to the devil and to Indian gods. Silently Donaju's wife implored the Virgin not to let her milk be poisoned by what she witnessed. Patricio's hair and eyes did not darken, and in gratitude Miguel sent a silk skirt to the hag.

The next year, when the child lisped his first words, Miguel realized that his son would grow up speaking Spanish, the language of the contemptible Panchos. He began talking to Patricio in Gaelic, forbade his wife's relatives to come near the house, and tried to force her to learn strange and unpronounceable words. It was a doomed attempt, yet so great was Miguel's persistence that he marked the child's speech and gave it an oddity which created another barrier between the boy and those around him.

The world, as Patricio discovered it, was a hostile place, and he and his father were its only real inhabitants. His mother counted for little except to serve him as she served his father, for women were creatures to be used. They ranked below horses, which were animals one had to care for and respect. Women were more like burros, serving in a clumsy way and easily replaceable.

The three small dark men who rode with Miguel on journeys Patricio was forbidden to join belonged to his father; he commanded them and owned them just as he owned the eight horses in the corral and the herd of bony goats. Once a month, sometimes oftener, the three Panchos arrived at dusk. His father strapped on the beautiful revolvers with silver handles, knelt for a moment before the statue of the Virgin and the glassed portrait of San Patricio, then strode to the door, boots and spurs gleaming. On these nights his father had a clean smell of leather and saddle soap, and Patricio watched in envy as the four men rode away, his father tall and straight, a splendid giant flanked by dark dwarfs. Sometimes there would be new and fascinating things in the house the next morning —shell combs edged with gilt, jade necklaces, watches of various sizes, whose use Patricio could not understand, since no one had told him that the day was divided into hours. On other occasions his father returned at dawn empty-handed, and then Patricio hid with the goats or spent the day in the arroyo, having learned that his father would be dangerous and might knock him down or beat him. Beatings were not uncommon. Patricio was whipped until blood ran down his legs on the day he showed fear of the sorrel stallion his father had placed him on, and was punished as severely when he ran home in fright after a village boy pelted him with stones. The blows hurt, but he harbored no resentment of his father. Miguel was all-powerful; he could do as he wished. One day Patricio himself would have force and strength, and then he too would have the right to strike. Such power was the gift of manhood and the privilege of administering pain the sure mark of ownership. He had always supposed Miguel owned the Panchos but was not certain until one morning when he was awakened at dawn by cries and curses from the direction of the corral. He rose from the straw mat, went to the door, and looked outside.

The night before his father and the three Mexicans had ridden away, and now they had returned with nothing to show for their effort. Two of the Panchos were binding the wrists of the third to the corral while Miguel stood nearby watching, a rawhide quirt in his hand, and although the man wept and begged, he did not resist. When he was securely tied, Miguel said, "Now I will teach you a lesson. Because you did not obey orders we have come back with nothing. You are an unruly burro and now I am going to break you." The first slash of the rawhide laid open the man's shirt and ripped the skin beneath it. "There will be ten like that. You will count them aloud so I can hear you."

When the punishment was over Miguel said, "Take him home. His woman will clean him up."

"Sí, señor," said the two Panchos together, and Patricio heard the awe in their voices. Miguel saw Patricio in the doorway and when he came into the house he said, "What do you think, boy?"

"Is he your blood enemy now, Father? Will he try to kill you?"

Miguel laughed. "No. He will want to for a while. But then he will obey me because he is afraid. If I had not done what I did, I would have had three enemies, for none of them would respect me. Learn that, boy, and someday you will command men."

Patricio grew up alone, wild among other wild things. From the time he could run without stumbling his mother lost control of him, and by his eighth saint's day he could defy her, clawing, kicking, and biting like a mountain cat. He avoided the village, knowing he was different from its inhabitants, but often Miguel took him to the cantina. While his father drank and played dominoes, Patricio sat in a corner sipping warm cinnamon water, watching and listening. No one spoke to him, for although Miguel was proud of his son, he would permit no one to be familiar with the boy. It was in the cantina he learned the all-important word *macho*. A jaguar was *macho*, a burro was not. Bulls, stallions, hawks, and eagles were *macho* and must be admired, but chickens and pigs were contemptible—although a boar, if fierce and evil-tempered, might be *macho* too. To be *macho* was the ideal of all men, and the cantina was the scene of constant struggles to prove this quality. Challenges were hurled; small men attacked big men to show they were not chickens but fighting cocks. Pistols were drawn, knives flashed, and bottles were shattered. Only Miguel was aloof from this. No one insulted him, no one dared him; all knew better.

Patricio learned the ways and habits of animals. He could smell rain or duststorms and knew where to search for birds' nests and wild honey. But only in one way did his imagination stretch beyond the mesas and rock slopes which bounded the horizon: very early he was told about God and the devil.

These two forces, with their servants and ministers, ruled the earth. When a certain man of Soledad, a notorious seducer and *cabrón,* was struck by lightning, Señora Donaju explained that he had been snuffed out by the finger of God. She often used this expression—God's finger flicked the Morales family from the world by sending down an avalanche; with the same careless but mighty gesture, He unloosed a flash flood to drown the Vargas brothers who were suspected as police informers. When she spoke of such things, even Miguel listened respectfully, for he too believed that fate was governed by a very personal Presence and Its allies or enemies. One had to watch out for such forces and try to placate them.

The mesas, the great arroyo, the groves of stunted trees were peopled by mysterious beings who were neither God nor Satan yet had connection with both. In caves gouged by wind and water lived a race of dwarfs only two feet tall who had faces of babes and the souls of rattlesnakes. They carried off young girls to unimaginable futures, although why they wanted such weak things Patricio could not fathom. Worse, they stole the best ears of corn and snatched the fattest sucklings. But if worshiped, these creatures could bring gentle rain, "grazing rain," which watered the soil without tearing away young grass. More frightening than the dwarfs were the were-tigers, human beings who sprouted the fangs and claws of jaguars. They ripped open the bellies of watchdogs, sprang upon men and horses, and pawed away dirt from graves in order to attack the newly buried.

But nothing, not even the were-tigers, were as terrifying as the hordes of Unquiet Dead who rose from cemeteries to float like wind-borne mist. The Unquiet Dead froze the blood by their mere presence and entered the nostrils to assume the bodies of living men. They prowled during the dark of the moon and during the hours between Good Friday and the dawn of Easter when God was dead and nothing stood between men and the ghosts.

Patricio, like his father, often heard banshees wail in the storms, and he had caught sight of disappearing shadows when he opened a door or rounded a corner quickly. He also knew that his red hair and pale eyes, the outward marks of specialness, had been preserved by the magic of a witch, and he wondered if this might draw specters to him.

The invisible ghosts, imps, and demi-gods were difficult to understand, but he often considered their power and strangeness. A mile from the house there was a place he had chosen as his own, a rock shelf fronting a shallow cave. From here he could view the open country to the north, a sweep of barren land without a hut, a corral, or any sign of human presence. Here he enjoyed the freedom of being utterly alone.

The arroyo lay below him, and if he leaned over, cupped his hands, and shouted, his voice rang back hollow and magnified. God's voice, he was sure, sounded like this, but it would thunder down the canyon, shaking the rocks. He liked thinking of God, but after a moment the picture of his father astride the sorrel stallion always intruded. Miguel, of course, was not God, yet, if the creatures of

Soledad were men, he was more than human. Perhaps he was like Cristo, God's amazing son, who when a year old had reached out his baby hand to break an oak tree. He always imagined Cristo as tall and muscled, a *macho*, with hair and eyes the color of his own.

Patricio's life changed little until one night during his eleventh year. That evening Miguel rode out with the Panchos but did not return home at dawn. Late that morning the three Mexicans approached the house, leading Miguel's riderless stallion and a pack mule dragging two poles with a blanket stretched between them. The Irishman, raving with pain, was lashed to this. "An accident, señora," they told Donaju's wife. "We halted a coach on the road, but its horses suddenly bolted. He was trampled, and a wheel went over his back."

They carried Miguel into the house, but when they loosened the first rope he screamed in such agony that he had to be left as he was, and two more straps were added to hold the shattered bones. "He is dying," said the señora. "We must call the *padre*."

Soledad had no real priest, but there was a defrocked renegade who knew the rite of extreme unction and who presided at funerals although two missionaries from Acapulco had pronounced anathemas against him. Señora Donaju summoned this man, but instead of confessing, Miguel cursed and spat in his face.

"Your husband will go to hell, señora, but I can't help it. I suppose he would have gone there anyway. You owe me a silver peso for my trip and half a peso extra for the Latin words. If you prefer, I will accept payment in tequila or rum."

For five days Miguel lay screaming and babbling, unstilled by the opium his wife forced between his jaws. Squatting on the floor, Patricio stared at his father, astonished at the way one leg was bowed and twisted—like the foreleg of a mare who had stumbled into a gully that spring. Patricio, with Miguel steadying his hand, had shot the animal through the skull. The mare was beautiful, lean-flanked and strong, with a chestnut coat that gleamed in the sun. He felt an almost choking pain when his father said, "Squeeze the trigger. Never pull, squeeze. Are you ready? Now!" The explosion jerked his shoulder, and his eyes smarted with smoke as the mare shuddered and died. Then, looking at the lifeless animal, a sense of power swept through him, leaving him giddy. His finger had done this, taken away in an instant the life of a creature a hundred times his strength. Like the finger of God, the power to end things . . .

Now he wondered why God did not reach down to remove his father as the mare had been removed. This was the order of life. The maimed should die quickly or be destroyed, as coyotes destroy one of their own pack who has been too badly wounded.

He had never loved his father; he had never felt love for anything except the freedom of the arroyo and its great space of clean sky. But he had revered Miguel as the visible sign of God and the sign of what he himself would one day be. Now Miguel had betrayed him. He should have known the horses might stampede, he should have leaped in time, he should have been faster, more clever, and Patricio burned with shame. The weak Panchos could now sneer at Miguel. They would be right, but if they laughed he would kill them, and his eyes wandered to the revolvers, which were again in their place on the house altar, where they absorbed the power of the statue and the votive candle. Soon the revolvers would be his, and with a quickening pulse he imagined holding their hard, beauti-ful weight in his hands. . . . The three Panchos knelt before him, gibbering in terror. They did not say "little Patricio" now, but called him "señor" as they begged for their lives. "You joked about my father," he said, then slowly squeezed—he did not pull—*one, two, three!* They lay in the dust at his feet, dead like the mare, and he was sorry they could not return to life to tell him how clean the shots had been, to admire him for standing over them powerful as Cristo before he killed them. He yearned for them to admire and love him for what he had dared do, and he grieved that they were dead. . . . In the dim room he watched his father. Soon, he thought, soon.

But Miguel did not die. On the sixth day he began to recover, and Patricio got no closer to the revolvers than touching their silver handles in the dark. Over the weeks the Irishman's pain subsided, but his legs did not straighten and his back mended crookedly. He would never walk or ride again. The Panchos, learning their former leader was helpless, avoided the house, for they owed Miguel his share of the last robbery. Cursing them, he strapped the revolvers to his hips. "Someday they will be curious," he said. "Someday they will wander too close, and then!" He never took the revolvers off, day or night, and their holsters left long scratches in the dirt when he dragged himself to the corral to watch the horses, whose care now became Patricio's task.

Summer came, the season of rain, and for a month there would be good grazing on a slope two miles from the house. Each morning when the boy led the horses from the corral he was aware of his father's angry face in the doorway. Miguel said nothing, but sometimes Patricio heard a contemptuous laugh and, glancing back, saw the sneer on his father's lips. He believed Miguel was mocking the way he rode, and his temper flared, for he was a good horseman and deserved a better mount than the pinto gelding Miguel told him to ride. The gelding, the only bad animal in the herd, should have been sold or traded long ago, and Miguel, for an unknown cause, was taking vengeance by putting him on such a horse.

To guard the herd he was given an ancient musket

whose recoil would have knocked him from the saddle, although there were half a dozen good rifles locked in a chest in the house. This was further punishment, and when Patricio looked at his father's revolvers or at Valiente, the great sorrel stallion, his blood rose in rebellion, and one day he said, "Why do you treat me this way? Have I done wrong?"

"Wrong? Could such a fine specimen as you do wrong?"

"Why must I ride the gelding? Why do you—"

"The gelding is like you, it has no balls. The horses are mine, and I still command here, whatever you think. Now do some work. Valiente needs currying."

"Tell me what—"

"Shut up! After you finish with Valiente, go with your mother to Soledad. She is selling some things from the chest."

That afternoon in the village, when Patricio saw a boy no older than himself practicing quick-draw shots with a pistol, envy and rage welled in him. He did a man's work but was not permitted to be a man, and this because of a helpless creature like his father! "I would rather die than crawl forever on my belly," he told himself. "I would go to the arroyo and put a bullet through my head." He despised his father as a weakling not *macho* enough to behave like a man.

For a week he said nothing, contenting himself with the small rebellion of slipping out one night to ride Valiente while his father slept. Two days later, when he brought the herd to the corral at sunset, Miguel was lounging near the gate, his back propped against a rock, his misshapen legs stretched out. The ground was damp, and when Patricio saw that the silver handle of one revolver was caked with mud, he could hardly control himself. He unsaddled the gelding, then faced his father. "It is time I learned to shoot. Will you lend me the revolvers and teach me?"

Miguel spat. "They are for a man."

"I am almost a man."

"You are a whelp and you think you are as good as I am! You should see yourself on a horse, you fool. A clown, a show-off! Every morning you leap into the saddle like an acrobat. You swing your leg and put on airs. A fancy boy in a grand rodeo! You do it to taunt me!" His eyes blazed and there was a mad look in them. "You took Valiente from the corral two nights ago, didn't you? I saw you sneak out, laughing at me. You think it funny that I have to crawl to the door to watch you ride my horse!" Miguel's arm streaked to his side and suddenly there was a revolver in his hand. "If I shot you through both knees, you'd learn some crawling yourself, you scum! Do you think I won't do it? Do you think I've lost my guts?"

Patricio stared at the black hole at the end of the barrel, while his mouth went dry and his skin prickled with fear, knowing if his panic showed, Miguel would press the trigger. *"Bueno, señor,"* he said, praying his voice would not break. "Afterward, when someone shoots you in the back or steals the horses or puts horns on you with my mother, who will pay the blood debt? I am all you have. Kill me then, cripple!"

Miguel hesitated, confusion on his face, then lowered the revolver, dropped it. Slowly tears formed in his eyes and rolled down his cheeks and he slid from the rock to lie sobbing, his forehead in the mud at the corral's edge. Patricio stooped to retrieve the revolver, slipping it into his own belt. Then, changing his mind, he replaced it in his father's holster. Now he could wait; now Miguel would give him guns of his own and let him ride the stallion.

"God forgive me!" Miguel pulled Patricio to him, clasping him in powerful arms, crushing him against his chest. "Ay, it's not your fault that I'm as I am. You're my son and it's only the two of us against everyone. Oh, we must love each other, boy! It was the devil who possessed me, the devil who spoke!"

Patricio's body went limp in the strength of his father's embrace. He felt the hardness of Miguel's muscles, the roughness of the red beard which seemed to burn his cheek and forehead. He had never been held this way, never imagined the fierce sensation which poured through him, bringing panic. His face was afire, he could not catch his breath, and he knew he must break from the encircling strength. When he closed his eyes, the picture of Miguel holding the gun flashed before him, the steady hand, the eyes unyielding as flint. Miguel would have killed him, would have watched his son die because he willed it. His father was *macho*, but he himself was even stronger. He released himself from Miguel's arms.

"It's getting dark," he said. "I will help you to the house."

Miguel said anxiously, "You know it was the devil? You do forgive me, son?"

Patricio nodded but felt disappointment. It was degrading that his father should ask this, but he was pleased that Miguel respected him—respected him because he was afraid. He glanced back to make sure the corral gate was barred and wondered why he suddenly remembered the morning when one of the Panchos had been bound there.

The dry season, bringing gales and dust storms, came too soon that year. The ribs of the horses poked against their skins, and forage was sparse even for the goats. When the gelding sickened and died, Miguel grew alarmed. After days of brooding he decided to keep only Valiente and the strong young mare Patricio now owned. The other five animals would be taken to Chilpancingo and sold. He sent for his brother-in-law, a greasy youth whom he hated, and commissioned him to handle the sale.

"You will go with your Uncle Javier," he told Patricio. "Keep your eye on the bastard. Especially after he gets the money."

"You think my uncle would steal from you?" Patricio asked in mock innocence.

Miguel snorted. "Even the Holy Cross would steal if its arms weren't fastened! I'd rather send you alone, but you're not old enough and you don't understand money. Go with God, and if that swine Javier tries to visit a whorehouse or gambles, threaten to shoot him. Then do it."

The trip to Chilpancingo, the provincial capital, was the most exiciting event of Patricio's life. Although he was twelve years old, he had never been farther from home than a three-hour ride. He wore his tooled leather boots and on his hip he proudly strapped the gleaming nickel-plated revolver Miguel had given him, secretly hoping that Uncle Javier, whom he hardly knew, would commit some folly. After leaving before dawn they rode all day through bleak unchanging country, arroyos and knolls broken here and there by cliffs whose red rock faces were scarred and pitted by the wind. They slept in a dry gully, and Patricio shot a wolf that was alarming the horses. The next day the land softened and they passed small ranches whose golden maize fields seemed astonishingly rich to Patricio, but he felt contempt for the men working there, men doing a woman's labor of digging and hoeing. Late that afternoon they reached Chilpancingo, a squalid collection of adobe houses, a dozen streets surrounding a government palace, and a stone church whose dome and towers made Patricio gasp. He had not imagined there was a building of such size in the world. Nor had he supposed that so many people could be gathered in one place— hundreds of them, perhaps thousands. Their voices and their smells pressed on him until he felt stifled and dizzy. Narrowing his eyes, he glared at the townsmen as he and his uncle rode through the narrow street toward an inn where they would spend the night.

Passers-by and loiterers stared with open curiosity,

angering him until he realized that it was his red hair and light complexion which drew their attention. Then he was proud of being different, of being set apart from these stoop-shouldered town dwellers. They were weak and womanish; it was no wonder they admired him, gawked at him. Tilting back his sombrero, he sat ramrod straight in the saddle, scowling fiercely.

At the inn they tethered the horses and rented sleeping space on the floor of the dormitory, where they unrolled the blankets and straw mats they had brought with them. To conceal ignorance, Patricio copied his uncle, smoothing his hair with the iron comb which was chained to a wall, then waiting in line to use the public toothbrush, also chained between the water jug and slop jar. He was pleased to discover the use of the toothbrush, for although his father had brought several such brushes home from the highway, their purpose had never been clear.

He slept badly that night, finding it distasteful to be crowded in with fifteen strangers, the closeness of their bodies oppressing him and stale human odors assailing his nostrils. At dawn his uncle said, "Come on. We'll eat at the market, then see about the horses."

As they entered the plaza, Patricio was startled by the blast of a bugle. Across the square in front of the government palace he saw a double line of uniformed horsemen, brass buttons and epaulets gleaming, light shining on the studs of polished scabbards and rifles. Twenty-four men sat proudly at attention on identical mounts, big dark chestnuts with white hoofs and blazes. Regimental colors fluttered in the breeze, but the men themselves were motionless, statues chiseled from rock, forbidding and magnificent. Never had Patricio seen a sight so stirring, and he stood marveling at the sheen of their round leather helmets trimmed with buckles and silver braid. "Who are they?"

His uncle's lip curled. "Pigs of soldiers."

"No! I've seen soldiers. Remember, four soldiers came to Soledad two years ago. My father helped kill them. These are different."

"They're a cavalry guard, you hick," snapped Javier. "There's a new general in power, and I suppose it means trouble. Come on! Don't stand there staring like a ninny."

"I want to look—at their horses. I'll meet you in the market."

Instead of crossing the plaza, Patricio approached them obliquely, moving through a gathering crowd. The horsemen, now that he was only a few yards from them, certainly bore no resemblance to the four ragged soldiers who had fatally wandered into Soledad. These were big men, tough and sturdy, not so large as Miguel but far taller than anyone else he knew. Their helmet straps, worn not under their chins but against their upper lips, made a ferocious and unnatural stripe across their faces, and black mustaches bristled under the straps. Their skins, he noticed happily, were far lighter than those of the people in the plaza, and their noses were thinner and straighter. Three officers in white and gold uniforms stepped onto a balcony above the horsemen, one of them holding a paper in his hand, and he read from this, shouting angrily through a megaphone, although the crowd in the plaza was absolutely silent.

"Citizens of Chilpancingo, give attention! All honorable men pay heed! The sentence of death passed upon the outlaw and rebel Joaquín Patino and his fellow malefactors will now be carried out that all men may see the sure hand of justice. Death to traitors! *Viva Mexico!*"

Five men, their arms weighted with chains, were led from a doorway, while an oxcart bearing a double gallows was moved into place. The captives struck Patricio as runty and despicable, their frail bodies hardly able to support the irons that manacled them. He looked again at the stern, handsome horsemen, and above them the officers standing tall, resplendent in white. Whatever such men chose to do was right. The captives were loathsome, mere vermin who were privileged to die in the presence of noble witnesses.

His blood thrilled to the long roll of drums. The first two prisoners plunged through the trapdoor floor of the cart, and there was a loud snap, clear and sharp above the drum rattle. Gasping, Patricio sank his teeth into his own lip. He glanced quickly toward the nearest cavalry officer, afraid he had betrayed himself, that his surprise had been noticed. The man stared straight ahead, hard eyes unblinking, at the two scarecrows who still squirmed at the end of the ropes.

The ceremony of death was slow and prolonged, as it was meant to be, but Patricio stood rooted to the spot, forgetting his father's orders and his uncle's untrustworthiness. At the finish, after the corpses had been hung by their ankles in the plaza, the bugle sounded once more, then a fife played while the drums beat a new and exciting rhythm. The cavalry lines wheeled, moving as one man, the horses prancing, and as they disappeared into the great gates of an armory Patricio longed to run after them, to seize their stirrups or the leather greaves and cry out, "Let me come with you! Oh, please! I am one of you!"

At the inn he found his uncle leading the horses from the courtyard. "Enjoy yourself?" Javier asked sourly. "Admiring the pretty soldiers? Go get the bedding. I think I've found a buyer. The price is not good, but everyone is selling animals."

To Patricio's disappointment, his uncle was a model of reliable behavior. The horses were sold, the money was counted three times, and Javier said they should return to Soledad immediately. "I have a new woman at home. I want to get back before the bitch puts horns on me."

Javier, like all Soledad people, had a violent hatred of soldiers, so Patricio did not dare ask the questions that

crowded his mind, but that night, when they camped and
built a mesquite fire, his uncle volunteered some information. "Too many soldiers! There will be trouble and probably raids." Patricio nodded, his heart pounding as he
imagined the cavalrymen, sabers flashing in moonlight,
charging down a slope upon a sleeping village. He saw
flaming houses, and his head rang with gunfire, horses
whinnied and stampeded, men and women ran screaming
into the streets to fall beneath the gleaming blades while a
drum rattled and the bugle sang.

His uncle looked at him suspiciously. "What's wrong?
You don't have a fever, do you?"

"No."

"You're sweating."

"I'm near the fire."

"Then move back, idiot. Your face is as red as your
hair." Javier yawned. "Let's sleep. I hope I dream about
my new woman." They both dreamed that night, dreams
that had different features but were of the same nature.

3

In the next months Miguel squandered the money
from the sale, using it to pay witch doctors who performed
rites in the house night after night, smearing his shattered
legs with foul unguents, creating blue and green fire whose
fumes made the brain reel. He ate almost nothing except
herbs and potions they prepared, and gradually all
strength ebbed from him, but he said, "Soon I'll be on
Valiente again! I can feel the bones straightening." Patricio's mother, terrified by the witches, fled the house and
lived with her relatives, taking with her the last valuables

from the chest. "Should I go after her?" he asked his father.

"No," said Miguel. "Good riddance! We'll be better off."

Late one night a dust storm swept down the mountain slope, its winds howling. Patricio, in his sleep, confused its voice with the bugle and lay dreaming on his mat when Miguel gave a terrible cry. Patricio stumbled to his feet. "What is it?"

"The candles! Light the candles! Hurry, boy, hurry!"

Patricio took fire from the charcoal jar and lighted the candles and the two bowls of grease which had floating wicks. Miguel, his face drawn with fear, clasped Patricio's hand. "Is there no more light? They are coming for me—I heard my father call, he spoke to me!"

"Who spoke? You were dreaming. It was the wind."

"Not the wind! Don't I know my father's voice?" Miguel's body trembled. "Listen! Listen!"

Patricio heard the storm rushing over the house like a torrent; the door strained on its hinges, and the wooden bar creaked. Yet when he looked at his father's face he knew Miguel heard something he could not hear. He has gone mad, he told himself, he is dying and has gone mad. Miguel's fingers, cold and wet, gripped him, and his voice fell to a whisper. "My father spoke, and Jamie Mills who was hanged in the square. They were here, and—" Miguel's shoulders suddenly jerked and he mumbled, "Father, Father." Patricio did not know whether Miguel spoke to his natural father or whether he thought there was a priest in the room. "Father . . ."

Again the wet fingers searched for him, clutching his wrist. "Bless me, Father, for I have sinned," begged Miguel. "I confess to Almighty God, to Blessed Mary ever virgin . . . to the saints Peter and Paul and to all . . ." Miguel's teeth chattered and no more words came. He lifted his head and his eyes widened as he stared at some presence he recognized, a presence Patricio could not see but whose nearness terrified him. Miguel's head sank back, the chatter of his teeth became a deeper, harsher sound; then the fingers lost their grip.

"What was it?" Patricio cried. "What?" He shook Miguel's arm but knew there would be no answer. His father was dead, and he felt the room filled with unseen menace. He fled from it, running outside, leaving the door open behind him, dust blinding his eyes as he stumbled toward the shed which served as a stable.

He stayed there until morning, when the storm died. Then, strapping on the silver revolvers, which were now his, he mounted Valiente and rode to Soledad to tell his mother what had happened, shuddering as he remembered the look of recognition on his father's face, not daring to think of the hours in the stable when he had burrowed into the straw, cowering, believing he heard strange sounds from the house where the dead man lay, his blood cold as he awaited a visitor who had not come.

4

Now he lived alone. His mother would not return to the lonely house, and this pleased him. Her family tried to rob him of his inheritance, foolishly thinking that because he had not quite reached his thirteenth birthday he was merely an overgrown child. He drove his uncle off at gunpoint, and for the first time Javier realized that his nephew was already taller and stronger than he himself was. The quarrel was settled when Patricio gave his mother the Palomino and five of the ten goats.

There were beans and corn meal in the house, enough to feed him for several months, and he felt it would be prudent to wait a while before going to Chilpancingo to join the soldiers. He longed for this constantly, but feared they might turn him away as too young. It was better to wait until the end of the next rains. This was his plan, but he had no chance to carry it through. A few weeks later his future was decided for him.

Throughout the winter there had been unusual activity in the Guerrero wilderness, bands of armed men, soldiers and rural police, roving the hills. They entered villages that had been undisturbed for a generation, approaching stealthily at night, arresting men for no apparent reason or on charges that made no sense. Those taken did not later appear in the jails of Acapulco or Chilpancingo; they simply vanished. Not only men: whole families disappeared from isolated homesteads, departing so mysteriously that they might have been snatched away by the baby-faced dwarfs. But hoofprints of cavalry near their deserted houses revealed the truth. Alarming rumors reached Soledad, but Patricio, who kept to himself, heard nothing.

Late one morning he saw a cloud of dust approaching from the direction of the village—horsemen, at least half a dozen. Quickly he led Valiente from the corral and tethered him out of sight in the gully; then he concealed his revolvers. There were too many strangers to fight, and he did not want to tempt them to robbery.

Running back to the house, he reached the dooryard just as the horsemen galloped through the gap in the cactus hedge, coming so close before halting that he leaped against the wall, afraid of being ridden down. There were eight, heavily armed, but Patricio had eyes for only one, their leader, a broad-shouldered man in a blue uniform whose brass and gold braid gleamed like those in the plaza of Chilpancingo. This officer was one of Them, and Patricio was delighted. Could it be possible that somehow he had attracted favorable notice that morning and this man had been sent to recruit him? The other seven, in baggy cotton clothes, were a shabby crew, and Patricio ignored them to gaze up at the stern *macho* face of the officer. "*Buenos días, señor,*" he said, lifting his hand in a self-conscious salute.

The officer eyed Patricio in silence, thoughtfully running a finger over his bristling mustache. Patricio was painfully aware that he had outgrown his clothes, his wrists protruded, and his matted hair needed cutting. When the man spoke, his voice was the commanding rumble Patricio hoped it would be. "Where's your father, boy?"

Wincing at the word "boy," Patricio drew himself up tall. "I live alone. I am the man here."

"Search the place," the leader told two of his men.

"*Sí,* Lieutenant." So he was a lieutenant—a rank of great importance, Patricio supposed.

Again the sharp eyes inspected him. "You're odd-looking. Are you Mexican?"

"*Sí, señor.* My father was a foreigner, one of the Patricios, and I am one also. He served in our army like yourself. He—"

The officer grunted. "Show me the deed to this land."

"Deed? I do not know that word, señor."

"This land is property of Don Salvador Fundes, given his family by colonial grant in 1760. You've been living here without paying rent. Can you pay now? It will be three thousand pesos or more."

"Three thousand? No, I don't—"

"You are under arrest." The officer gestured to the man at his left. "Bind the prisoner."

Escape flashed through his mind, but two rifles pointed at his chest and a moment later his hands were bound behind him and a halter was thrown over his neck. "Señor, there is a mistake! You must—"

Leaning from the saddle, the officer raised his leather

crop and slashed it across Patricio's face. "We do not make mistakes. That is your first lesson."

Nine men, including the youngest of the three Panchos, were taken from Soledad that day, and there would have been many more had not most of the population fled to the hills. The ropes holding the prisoners were exchanged for iron manacles locked to a long rod so no man could move without all moving, and for a week they were herded across country, following no road, but over a rutted trail winding south and east, at first marching, then stumbling, and at last dragging the weaker ones whose legs would no longer support them. Along the way they were joined by other guards and other captives until the column numbered more than a hundred prisoners. In the blaze of afternoon sun it seemed to Patricio that the ground buckled and shifted, cactus and mesquite danced, and the sky lifted, then lowered, a metal canopy white with heat. The pain in his legs was agony, for although his body was hard and his arms were strong he had never walked any distance since the year he learned to ride. Those not used to horses fared a little better, but one man from Soledad died on the fourth day, and because they had been dragging him all morning no one realized he was dead until nightfall. A dozen more were left beside the trail the next afternoon, a few shovelfuls of dirt thrown over them.

"Where are we going?" The question was shouted, then whispered, then mumbled, and when a man went out of his head from the sun it was shrieked. Always the answer was the same. "Who knows?"

Patricio did not ask. The shame of his abasement was nearly as painful as his tortured muscles, and he could not bear speaking to his fellow captives. Talk would link them, make him one of them. Common suffering created no bond between Patricio and the others. Their whimpering disgusted him, their smell sickened him, and he kept telling himself, "I do not belong here. Someone will see!"

He did not hate the officer who had arrested him and who now, with an air of perfect disdain, commanded the march. Patricio's lips were still swollen from the slash of the crop, and he knew that honor demanded he kill the lieutenant if a chance arose. Yet he felt that he himself was at fault. In some way he should have forced the officer to recognize his superiority, to treat him as a comrade, and despite the humiliation and pain of captivity he hungered for the lieutenant's admiration. Remembering the upraised arm, the fire of the leather across his face, he said, "Filthy bastard! The swine!" But he knew the lieutenant had done only what Miguel would have done—what Patricio himself would do. Without hardness the officer would be worth no more than the Indian scum who limped behind him. Each morning Patricio tried to stand straight, to look *macho*, hoping that the proud man at the head of the column would glance his way.

On the seventh day they arrived at a railroad junction; there was no town, only a barracks, a storehouse, and a great pen fenced with thorn branches. Their manacles removed, they were driven into this corral, where a score of prisoners already huddled in the thin shade of the fence. Several of these were women, and there were three small children.

"Where are we going? How long have you been here? Why?" All answers were confusing.

"I was arrested when I visited my brother in jail." "It was something about my burro. . . ." "Something about papers . . ." "I don't know."

"We went into an employment office and they told us to wait in the back room. Three men with guns came in and bound us. Now we are here. . . ."

That night Pancho from Soledad approached Patricio, trying to sound friendly, although there was fear in his eyes. "Well, redhead, did you enjoy the walk? Now don't snarl like a mountain cat! We come from the same place, we're *compadres*."

"I am no man's *compadre*. You stole my father's share one night."

"Ay, you're a devil! The Patricio's son, no doubt of it. But we're among strangers, maybe criminals who will take the pants from our behinds. We'd better stick together. Besides, I have information."

Patricio decided the man might be useful. "What?"

"I talked to an old man who says these railroad tracks lead to El Hule. That means we're being sent to Valle Nacional!" There was horror on Pancho's face as he spoke the name.

"What is that?"

"Valle Nacional! The tobacco plantations. It's the place of death."

"Tell me."

"El Hule is its entrance, that's why people call the town 'Graveyard Gate.' They say no one has ever come back but a few walking corpses, and no one stays alive a full year there. You cannot even die decently. Before you're dead they throw you to the Hungries."

"The Hungries?"

"Alligators! The swamps around the plantations swarm with them. After the fever or the foreman's whip kills you, the Hungries crack your bones." Gooseflesh rose on Pancho's arm; his voice trembled as he repeated other tales of horror, stories of slavery, starvation, and inevitably of death.

"Why are we being sent there?" Patricio asked.

"Because we can work, of course! Work until we drop dead. The owners and bosses pay so much a head. They try to catch Indians in the north, but men die so fast on the plantations that they have to take anyone they can get. That's why we're here. Someone bought us."

"I see. Now leave me alone. I want to think."

"Think about escape! That's what I'm doing."

He did not doubt what Pancho said. Things overheard when Miguel had taken him to the cantina now came back to him. There was a joke—or was it a song? "Siberia is hell frozen and Yucatán is hell aflame, but nobody from either place would go to Valle Nacional." All that Pancho said seemed likely, and of course this was a sensible way to get workers for the plague-ridden hot lands. Patricio's eyes wandered over the gaunt men who shivered on the ground in the pen. The night was as chill as the day had been burning, and they clung together for warmth, thin arms and scrawny legs intertwined like the tangled brown worms he had often turned up when raking the corral. If they went to Valle Nacional, that was their affair. He, Patricio, would find a way out. In unconscious imitation of the lieutenant he ran his finger thoughtfully over his upper lip, stroking the few thin hairs that had recently sprouted there.

Two days later the train arrived. They were herded into cattle cars, urged by prodding saber tips and a bullwhip cracking at their heels. The car into which Patricio and Pancho were shoved had been half filled before it stopped at the junction. The occupants were different from the Guerrero prisoners—wiry, darker men and women with rags of sweat bands around their heads. "Yaquis," whispered Pancho angrily. "White men like us are put with this Indian filth!" Patricio glanced at Pancho's coffee-colored hands but said nothing, although it was he, not Pancho, who was suffering the indignity.

He heard two guards talking outside the car. "If we get these Yaquis to the valley alive, it'll be the work of the Virgin!"

"Have you had trouble?" The second man had been guarding the pen at the junction.

"*Dios!* We took them by gunboat from Guaymas to

Acapulco, and out in the middle of the gulf they started throwing their own children overboard!"

"Savages!"

"Then the parents jumped after them, and not one could swim."

"Suicide!" The guard crossed himself.

"The bastards wanted to cheat us out of our commission money. We fished a few dead ones out. There's a reward for dead ones now, but you have to present his ears to collect your money, and that's a mess."

"Well, that's the army for you."

They rode all that day and most of the next, a sleepless trip, for as soon as the train was in motion the Yaquis began a weird and tuneless chant which someone said was a death song. The air in the car was so foul that Patricio, sickened, did not mind the lack of food or even the shortage of water. When they arrived in El Hule, they were locked in a pen larger than the one at the junction, and again there was no hope of escape. In the morning a stir arose among the prisoners when it was discovered that an old man called "the grandfather" had been murdered in his sleep, strangled with a rag of twisted cotton.

"That's what comes of having Yaqui killers around!" said Pancho loudly, but he winked at Patricio and later sidled up to him. "Redhead, I have a gun hidden in my shirt."

"A gun? But they searched—"

"The old man, the grandfather, smuggled it in some way. I saw him slip it into his sombrero, so I visited him last night. It's only a small pistol, but it will do. I have an escape plan, but we'll need two or three more good men." Pancho scowled at him. "You understand that I command the escape?"

"I understand any man who has a pistol."

The next day when they began the long march into the valley, Patricio realized that any plan was doomed. The road wound along a swift river with impassable jungle on both sides, and beyond the jungle rose sheer cliffs of gray rock. There were guard outposts and three villages to be passed. Ten pesos' reward was offered anyone who brought in a fugitive prisoner, and Patricio had no doubt that the villagers would sell their own brothers for half that price.

Pancho whispered, "It will be easy. I have talked to three good men, all *macho*."

"Fine, *compadre*," said Patricio with a twisted smile. His own plan began to form in his mind.

They were fed at sunset and the prisoners were allowed to mingle. Pancho assembled his group. "There's no pen here, so they will chain us for the night. We strike then. I cover the guards with the pistol while you four clap chains on them."

"A good plan," said one of the recruits, "and a bold one."

Pancho smirked. "In my home town my nickname is Tiger. We are friends and you may call me that."

The plan was executed an hour later, and it worked with astonishing smoothness. All happened as Pancho predicted; the guards, careless now they had entered the valley, worked in groups of three, carrying lengths of chain which would lock four prisoners together. Pancho whipped out the pistol. "Move and you die!" In an instant they had seized the guards' rifles, snapped handcuffs on them, and were breaking toward the jungle. "Run, run!" yelled Pancho. Already alarm shots were being fired in the air a few hundred yards away.

There was a new moon, enough light to see thick tree trunks, but the twisting roots and vines were invisible. They fled noisily, stumbling, their feet often entangled. "Hurry up," Pancho urged. "We've got to go faster." But Patricio, pausing to listen, realized there was no pursuit.

The guards were not fools like Pancho, they would not plunge into the darkness to chase five armed men who had no chance of getting far anyhow. Patricio said nothing. Let them run, he thought, let them wear themselves out. He trailed a little behind, holding a rifle in one hand and in the other a length of chain with handcuffs he had seized from a guard.

At noon the following day Captain Carlos Cruz of the rural police was in the office of a guard outpost at the head of the valley when he heard a commotion outside and went to investigate. "Good God, what now?" he said.

Crossing the narrow drill field and approaching the building was a peculiar group of men, obviously prisoners being returned, a scruffy hangdog quartet fastened together with a regulation chain. They were in no way remarkable, but in back of them strode a tall boy with a rifle over his arm and three more rifles in a bundle on his back. He was dressed, except for his boots, like any peon, yet his skin was lighter than the captain's own pure Spanish complexion, and his hair was a flaming color Captain Cruz had never before seen. When they neared the building the boy shouted, "Prisoners—halt!"

He came quickly forward, ignoring the guards, and addressed himself to the captain, standing rigidly at attention. "You command here, señor?"

"Sí. I am Captain Cruz."

"I am Patricio Donaju of Guerrero, son of Miguel Donaju of the Battalion San Patricio." The boy saluted. "I am returning four escaped prisoners."

"Indeed?" The captain's tone was dry, but he was amused. "My report said five prisoners fled last night. Are you by chance the fifth?"

"Formerly I was a prisoner. But I have promoted myself, and, as you see, I am now a guard. I have come to collect my reward and join the army."

"How did you get those guns? You look like a walking arsenal."

"I disarmed the captives, señor." The boy's smile was winsome. "It was quite easy. You see, I look younger than I am, and they didn't suspect that I could—"

"Humm," said the captain, and turned to the guards. "Give those four men the usual lashes, then lock them up. Come to my office, boy. This is all irregular, but I want to talk to you."

As the men were led away, Pancho, his face contorted, shouted over his shoulder. "Burn in hell, traitor!"

Patricio, still smiling, lifted his hand in farewell. "*Adiós*, Tiger."

Captain Cruz was a shrewd man who knew a good recruit when he saw one. A thirteen-year-old boy with the gall to "promote himself" by bringing in four adult prisoners was not to be wasted for the few months of labor one could wring from a plantation slave before he dropped dead. Besides, the lad was tall, white-skinned, and European-looking. One stroke of a secretary's pen wiped out the back rent Patricio had been charged with owing, and two years were officially added to his age. He was enrolled not in the regular army but in the captain's own organization, the *rurales*, the provincial police force, which had been changed recently into an elite military corps to serve the dictator and act as a counter force to the army. The dictator had a well-founded distrust of army generals, having been one himself.

Patricio became the captain's personal orderly, little more than an errand boy, but he consoled himself with his new uniform, russet wool trousers and a suede shirt dyed the same color—not so eye-catching as a cavalry uniform but smarter and handsomer.

Now he lived in a barracks, and never had he imagined a room so clean, so purified by smells of soap, sand, and lye. His comrades, some of them only a few years older than Patricio, were a pugnacious gang of men, braggarts and bullies all. Patricio expected to fight them to prove he was *macho,* but this did not happen. They avoided him, sensing something strange, and for his part he neither liked nor disliked them: they were only to be observed and occasionally imitated.

Although his pay was low, he did not lack pesos for long. When not on duty, he scoured the trails and jungle thickets for escaped prisoners and in the first four months he caught three, proudly offering them to the captain as a cat presents dead birds to its master. "You are uncanny!" exclaimed Cruz. "Do you smell them out like a bloodhound?"

"Often I can smell them, sir." The captain laughed, mistaking Patricio's serious remark for a joke about the unwashed fugitives. Afterward he was struck by the picture of the redhaired boy standing in his stirrups, head tilted to the wind, nostrils quivering like a wolf's, and it made him rather uneasy. Once he said, "Do you do this searching just for the rewards, or do you enjoy the hunt?"

"I like money, Captain," he answered, unwilling to talk about the thrill of discovering tracks in the soft dirt or detecting a furtive movement in the thickets. He had never forgotten that triumphant morning when, at dawn, he had suddenly leveled his rifle at the unsuspecting Pancho and said, "I command now. Obey me or you are dead." He had timed it well. The four men, exhausted, had paused to rest in a clearing, their guns lying at their sides. If all had attacked him at once, they would have had a chance. But they knew at least one would die in the attempt, and each feared it would be himself. They submitted to him, trembling as they locked the irons on each other's wrists, surrendering themselves. Then they were his, he owned them even more than his father had owned the three Panchos, and as he marched them to the guard post his blood was vibrant, he felt taller than any tree in the jungle. Now when he brought in a fugitive, always a cowering skeleton of a man, he relived that morning, tasting again its heady sweetness.

He was happiest when he considered the dangers around him. An endless stream of humanity poured into the valley, most of them young, many tough and rebellious and these had to be broken, crushed until they were glad to obey. The Yaquis were hardest to subdue, but a Yaqui, if conquered, might last as long as two years—twice the usual lifespan of a Mexican slave on the plantations. Yet these northern Indians were so troublesome that Captain Cruz was pleased when most of them were sent to Yucatán, which was outside his jurisdiction. Secretly Patricio imagined a great rebellion sweeping the valley and saw himself suppressing it with whip and saber. Such a thing never happened, and he could not understand why so few prisoners chose the quick, honorable death of resistance.

Captain Cruz, who foresaw a brilliant future for the boy, undertook his education about this and other matters. "They cling to life day by day because each one thinks he is an exception. No one believes in his own death, not any more than you do or I do. They have hope, and that is their weakness. It is hope, not despair, that paralyzes men."

After a visit to the laborers' compound in the valley, the captain gave him another lesson. "This morning you saw a man punished. How was it done?"

Patricio was surprised, since the captain had seen it himself, then realized he was being tested. "It was as usual, sir. The man was taken from the ranks at morning roll-call. Four men bound him; then the foreman gave him twelve lashes. After that the prisoner kissed the foreman's hand and thanked him for the punishment—the way they always do unless they want another twelve, which would kill them."

"Why was he made to kiss the hand and say 'Thank you, señor'?"

Patricio frowned. "I think it shows the other men who are watching who is boss. The whipped man cannot be a hero afterward. He has humiliated himself."

"Yes, but more than that, the man who was punished will believe the same thing. He will not forgive himself for what he did. That is important."

Patricio nodded, now understanding things his father had once tried to teach him.

In time he learned a new set of words, a special language. Since slavery was illegal, the tens of thousands of men and women who toiled for the plantation owners until they quickly died, were not slaves but "contract laborers" or "debtors." Yaquis and other Indians were "immigrants for resettlement." These and a hundred other elaborate terms were a necessary nuisance, legal cosmetics to mask the face of oppression.

The valley was a vast cemetery. No one kept records of the unnamed dead; their number was uncounted and countless. The living entered daily—by tens, hundreds, sometimes a thousand at a time. A special group of men called "catchers" operated throughout the country, spreading nets for the unwary, setting up false employment offices that would advance a hungry laborer money for a meal. When he finished eating, he was seized for owing the cost of the food, sold to the valley or a similar place, and sent to join the thousands taken from jails and prisons. Whole families were sold by petty officials; every month one great corporation, owned largely by Americans, legally adopted nearly a thousand children, and these unlucky sons and daughters became part of the human river flowing into the valley—flowing, like all rivers, in but one direction. They came on foot, in wagons and railcars, but the valley's population did not increase. The living and the dead were a monthly equation, one man arriving because another had perished, and soon the newcomer, like his predecessor, would fall in the fields because it was cheaper to replace him than to keep him alive.

The dead were everywhere. Patricio's horse could not go a mile without treading on one makeshift grave after another. As Pancho had said, some were indeed devoured by the Hungries; a few, their usefulness burned out, were permitted to crawl to the edge of El Hule, where they died on the dirt floor of a shack called the House of Pity, and gradually the graveyard of the little town became a necropolis. Yet Patricio gave these dead no thought. All his life, ever since first hearing of the Unquiet Ones, he had been sensitive about phantoms, but the slaves, unlike Miguel, had no souls, and only souls could return as specters. For Patricio this valley of death was not haunted.

He learned and grew, but only once during that year of training did he have an experience that moved him deeply. One day the captain said, "Ride to El Hule and spend the night. There is a merchant living there, a man named Campos. Last night he and his two daughters and their servants were arrested for sedition. I hear he's richer than lard and I don't want the local police stripping the house of what may become government property."

When Patricio arrived at the only impressive residence in the squalid town, he found three policemen prowling the patio like coyotes. He evicted them, presenting an order neither he nor they could read; then he locked the gates and began his private search of the premises.

The secret police had swooped upon the suspected rebels in the night, but Patricio found little evidence of struggle. At the far end of the patio was a carved stone fountain rising from a pool filled with hyacinths, and, kneeling beside it, Patricio examined the stiff body of a watchdog that had been shot above the left eye. A pity, he thought, to kill such a beautiful, useful animal. Near it lay a torn silk slipper, a little girl's, and he supposed it had been kicked from her foot when she was dragged from the house. He remembered the captain's saying that Señor Campos, the arrested man, had two daughters.

In the first room of the house Patricio stopped still, gaping. Never had he imagined such luxury, such opulence of brass, silver, teakwood, and mahogany. The humblest object shamed any valuable Miguel had stolen from travelers. Room after room was rich with canopies and velvet draperies, a softness of comfort and beauty he found awesome at first, then stifling. Impressed yet resentful, he touched a silver vase holding vermilion plumes, he glowered at row upon row of books, associating them with the weakling clerks who toiled in the *rurale* headquarters, squinting creatures whose fawning courtesy did not conceal the arrogance of literacy. An Oriental carpet silently reproached his manners, telling him he must not again unconsciously spit on the floor—so he spat deliberately.

"Jesus, Mary, and Joseph!" he said, looking at the walls. "They own more painted pictures than a dog owns fleas!" Nor were these like the paintings he had occasionally seen, the religious portraits people hung to bring luck or safety. He could understand the use of those. But the paintings he now scowled at had no purpose at all, and some of them were disgusting: a nude woman showing big ugly breasts and buttocks whose soft fatness sickened him. Only one painting held his interest. A boy, too frail and light-boned, knelt peering into a pool of still water. Patricio had done this several times himself, although the mud puddles of Guerrero were poor reflectors. Studying the picture, he remembered the pool near the patio fountain and decided that after he finished his exploration of the house he would go there. He longed to see himself in his uniform. The sheet of metal nailed to the barracks wall to serve as a mirror showed only a hazy outline, and it was pocked with bullet holes where someone, apparently infuriated by his own appearance, had emptied a pistol point-blank.

As Patricio moved from one room to the next, he found himself hating the graceful lines of chairs whose fragility made him feel loutish and hulking. He despised their owners—these people who bought gilt frames for their stupid paintings, ate with forks, slept in beds raised off the floor. They pampered themselves, thought themselves elegant. By next week, if they were lucky enough to be alive, they would be slaves like other slaves in the valley. Maybe they would look up from their toil to see Patricio ride by, proud in his saddle. He drew his knife and swept the blade twice across the polished surface of a table and was pleased by the jagged scars.

At the end of a second-floor corridor he opened double doors, and as he entered a dim ballroom he caught sight of a movement. "Who's here? No one is—" Then he realized that the walls were adorned with four mirrors, one on each side, reaching from the floor to the high arched ceiling. Slowly recognition of the four figures surrounding him came like dawning light. Himself! Better by far than any pool or sheet of metal. He opened the doors wide to admit the sunshine.

The separate features of his face were well known to him. Often he had studied himself in a tiny looking-glass at home. But, being the former property of a dainty traveler, it was so small he could see only one eye at a time. His mother owned a bigger piece of broken mirror whose cloudy glass distorted all shapes and made skin appear greenish. He could not bear the sight of himself in this; even a mud puddle was better. Now, for the first time, he beheld Patricio Donaju, a clear complete figure, marvelously multiplied by four. It was magnificent and strangely frightening.

He advanced cautiously, moving to meet the redhaired stranger who came toward him with the same hesitant steps. The stranger's eyes widened; he lifted his hand in greeting, then touched his forehead, his ear, ran his fingers down his cheek and over his smiling lips. The face in the looking-glass grinned, charming eyebrows rising in delight. He chuckled, self-conscious in his own revealed presence, yet glowing with pleasure, a little giddy. The young stranger was captivating, the neat uniform stretched taut over a strong, slender body, polished boots planted wide apart, hands on narrow hips, fingers just touching the handle of a revolver. Light streamed through the door behind him, and the young man smiled in half-silhouette, eyes shining—were they blue or green? They changed miraculously when he tilted his head to the light and away from it. He was—the word came instantly—beautiful. Patricio had found his first friend.

He laughed in pure pleasure, and, once laughing, he could not stop. When he threw back his head his shoulders shook—how gloriously they shook! He slapped his thigh, then again, delighted by the way his hand flattened when it struck. Wonderful! Suddenly he wanted to weep like a woman, and he moved so close to the glass that a mist clouded the stranger's lips. "Who are you?" he whispered. "You are Patricio."

He stepped back, his eyes steady as he fixed each feature in his mind. He ruffled and fluffed his hair—this was how Patricio looked when, without a sombrero, he rode in the wind. Now Patricio was reaching, nodding, frowning. Even his hand fascinated him as it untied the leather laces at his neck, then unbuttoned his cuffs. He pulled his shirt over his head and dropped it to the floor, then took off his boots, holster, trousers, and cotton underwear. The stranger stood naked, the muscles of his hips and legs flexed under white skin that was untouched by the sun. Patricio gazed silently, his breath rapid, his eyes dropping, then moving slowly upward, pausing to study the curve of a knee, the shape of a thigh, and his hands, pressing and vibrant, moved to follow his gaze. He lost consciousness of the house, the noises from the street; he stood rapt while his blood throbbed with a dizzying excitement, not unlike the joyful sensation of his triumph over Pancho and the moment of his first victory over his father. He felt Miguel's arms gripping him, his face crushed against Miguel's chest, the roughness of the shirt, and a button scratched his cheek. Suddenly his heart hammered, blood rushed to his head. The taut lips in the mirror parted; the mouth opened as it gasped for air while his body shook in an uncontrollable spasm. His knees gave way, and he sank to the floor, limp, panting, and drenched with sweat.

For a moment he was unable to dress himself, then, hands still trembling, he fumbled with his clothes, keeping his eyes averted from the mirror, not daring to look again, feeling he had seen what he should not have seen, felt what he should not have felt. If he turned again he would be undone, although he did not know how or why. With head bowed he ran from the room and fled down the broad stone stairs to the patio, where he breathed its air and openness into his lungs.

Later he stripped and washed himself in the cold spray of the fountain, not glancing into the pool, carefully scrubbing every inch of his body as though to cleanse himself of a defilement.

That night he slept near the fountain, having ripped a lace curtain from a window in the house to use as a net against swarms of mosquitoes and night-flying insects. Spreading down his mat, he kicked aside a child's slipper he had seen there earlier, giving no thought to its owner, a small girl named Elvira Campos, not suspecting that one day in another place they would meet and she would accomplish what all other enemies failed to do. She would destroy him.

5

Patricio Donaju became a corporal at sixteen and a sergeant three years later, an astonishing achievement for a young savage with no political connections. Unlike the regular army, whose officers seemed to outnumber its men, the *rurales* had few promotions. Even a modest rank carried power, importance, and the opportunity to enrich oneself by bribes. Captain Cruz commanded fewer than five hundred men, yet his least word meant life or death to a hundred thousand people in a broad territory. He was police, prosecutor, jury, and judge. To his regret the great landowners in his district were beyond his control unless they made the fatal mistake of offending the dictator, and Cruz often chafed at limits imposed on him by army generals and politicians; nevertheless, his rank was sufficient to make him a god within boundaries.

In the ranks jealousy was bitter, competition intense, and frequently men who had been passed over for advancement shot their successful rivals, then turned the gun on themselves. Yet Donaju's quick success caused no complaint. Everyone admitted his worth, even though few liked him. He brought honor to the post by winning third place in two events of the national military riding contest at the age of eighteen. There were endless arguments as to whether Donaju or Captain Cruz was the best marksman in the region, but there was no question about who was the fiercest hand-to-hand fighter. "The Patricio is a maniac!" they said admiringly. "Like two jaguars! Did you see how he broke the arm of that cavalry man from Jalisco? And he smiled while he did it!" It was at this time that the nickname "the Smiler" was first applied to him.

Yet there was secret grumbling about his private life, and some of this reached the ears of Captain Cruz, who summoned Patricio to his office. "Sergeant, I am not sure if you are a saint or a machine. Why don't you drink more?"

"It weakens a man, sir."

"Humm. Why don't you go to the whorehouse?"

"Sir?" Patricio had never considered such a thing. He had not the least interest. "I don't want the clap."

"Nonsense! You've been listening to a *padre* or that fool Dr. Gomez. I tell you frankly you're getting a bad reputation among the men. Next Saturday night go to El Hule. Get drunk in front of witnesses, then have yourself a whore or two. By God, if you want to be an officer, you'd better *act* like one! I want no more bad reports about you."

Three nights later Lola María, a girl working in a house called Aunt Isabel's Delights, had a strange experience, one of the rare pleasant surprises in the fourteen years of her unlucky life. A few months before, Lola María had been kidnaped from the streets of Oaxaca while on her way to the market, where she helped her mother at a vegetable stall. After her virginity had been auctioned off at a city brothel, she was brought to El Hule, where she would be kept until her body was exhausted. In the last four months she had become inured to revulsion, past caring about any indignity. She longed only for rest and to be left alone with her constant dream of steaming bowls of Oaxaca beans and chilis.

That night she and a dozen other girls sat on a bench in the fetid barroom at Aunt Isabel's. Saturday was always the worst night; already she had made eleven trips to a cubicle at the rear of the patio, and it was still early. A dozen *rurales* were there that night, and she watched their carousing without interest, her eyes not flickering when one of them drew a pistol and shot two cockroaches crawling on the wall. At times she glanced toward one young sergeant whose hair and complexion were so unusual that she wondered where he came from. He was handsome, although this meant nothing to her. Suddenly this man, who talked louder and laughed more boisterously than any of his companions, strode to her and seized her hand roughly. "Let's go," he said.

As she led him toward the cubicle, he shouted back to his companions and slapped her buttocks, a blow that made her stagger. Bad luck, she thought; he is one of the worst and so drunk he will take forever.

But once they were behind the curtained doorway an instant change came over the sergeant; all trace of drunkenness vanished. She said, as she had been taught to say, "You are handsome and *macho*. I love you a lot." She was slipping off her dress now. "Do you want the candle or the dark? The candle costs ten centavos more."

"The candle." He inspected her, standing a yard away, then shook his head, and a sigh escaped him. Clearly he was disappointed, and she was alarmed that he would complain and she would be punished. "Sit down," he said, squatting on the floor. He was silent for a time, then asked her name. "Tell me, Lola María, do men who lie with you ask you about other men?"

"Sometimes." She had heard this before. Now he would question her about her life. It was wearisome, but saved work.

He went on quietly. "If anyone asks you about me, you will tell them that I am more man than anyone you have been with. It will be worth your while to do this." Then his tone altered; he put his hands on her throat, and it chilled her. "If you say anything else, you will be very sorry. Now we will wait a little."

When they returned to the crowded room, he was instantly drunk again. Leaping onto the bar, he fired his pistol to command attention. "Listen, *cabrónes!* Lola

María is the best lay in the republic! She is mine now, and I will pay for her and keep her here for myself alone. If any man takes her and puts horns on me, I will cut his liver out." The *rurales* hammered the tables, shouting, "*Viva el Patricio!*" Lola María's head reeled, and she could hardly believe her good fortune. Now she could rest. No man would touch her. She gazed up at the young sergeant, who stood poised on the bar, unsteady, waving a tequila bottle, pouring the liquor over his own head in a crazy self-baptism. The other *rurales* again cheered him. Lola María's face shone with gratitude. He was giving her this gift of life and he did not even want her; she did not believe he would ever want her. He is a saint, she told herself.

Almost every Saturday for the next two years Donaju came to the brothel. He seldom bothered to pretend drunkenness; his point had been made. But he took care that everyone noticed when he and Lola María retired to the curtained room, where they sat at opposite ends of the straw mat. They did not talk, and Donaju seemed unaware of her presence. Sounds of other inmates of the house came through the thin partitions, the groans and gasps of coupling, and sometimes Donaju's hands clenched and turned into white-knuckled fists. When the noises were especially loud she saw sweat break out on his forehead, and once he put his hand to his mouth as though to hold back sickness. Their sin disgusts him, she said to herself. He should have been a priest. Perhaps he will become one—God works slowly and in unknown ways.

As months passed she realized that a change was taking place in the sergeant. His eyes were harder now, and frequently when he had forgotten she was in the room she saw pain and longing in his face, an expression not unlike that of men who came to the brothel but had no money to buy a woman even though their need was unbearable. They drank, they watched hungrily, and when they left they left suddenly without looking back. He was lonely, she decided, and could have wept for his unhappiness because she worshiped him. Others said he was cruel, that he had ice water for blood and the heart of an alligator. She alone knew his complete goodness.

One night in the second year of his visits she was forced to speak to him, although it frightened her for she knew he did not like to talk. "Señor, I have heard a rumor that you are going away, that you have been transferred." Her voice quavered.

"True. I leave in three days."

"You have been good to me, señor. Without you I would have been dead long ago. Of the twelve girls who were here when I came, only two are still living. Now you will go. I do not know what will happen to me." An instinct told her to smother the sob that formed in her breast.

Silently Donaju looked at her. He had already decided that she could not be left here alive to expose the legend he had built. Was it better to send her to the plantations or to kill her now, at once? Afterward he would say she had confessed being unfaithful to him, and there would be no questions. Who cared what happened to Lola María? Who had ever cared?

He sat frowning, unable to make up his mind, although he knew it was safer to take care of things himself and have done with it, as he had planned to do from the first night he came to this foul place. As he pondered, she spoke again. "Whatever becomes of me, señor, I will pray for you each day as I have done for two years now. I pray to all the saints whose names I can remember, but especially to San Patricio."

"You have done this? When you pray for me what do you ask?"

"For your happiness, that peace will come to your soul. I can give you nothing, señor, but God gives all."

Donaju stood up quickly. "I must leave. I will see that

you are sent to your family in Oaxaca." He did not know what weakness caused him to make this promise. What did her prayers matter? No one listened to the pleadings of Lola María—least of all God. He left abruptly, before she had a chance to shame him with her gratitude, to make him further repent his impulse. But he kept his word, and years afterward, while men heaped curses on Donaju's soul, a candle still burned in Oaxaca under a crude portrait of the Irish saint.

Donaju's travels and his swift rise to prominence began with the special assignment that took him from Valle Nacional. On the recommendation of Captain Cruz he was loaned to the *acordada*, the secret police whose name inspired terror not only within the country but far beyond its boundaries. The members of the *acordada* were kidnapers and assassins, and their work, performed in disguise and darkness, was to weed out rebels and concealed liberals even though these agitators had fled Mexico. Hundreds of political fugitives had escaped to the United States, and it became the *acordada*'s task to hunt them down, to arrange with the Americans for their extradition by legal fictions, or, failing that, to kill or kidnap them. These violent measures were seldom necessary, because the government of the United States supported the dictator, hailing the neighboring tyrant as the protector of industry and civil tranquillity. Twice when armed rebellion threatened, American troops rushed to the border, ready to intervene on his behalf, and American police could usually be counted on to send any liberal exile back to certain death in the political prison of San Juan de Ulua.

Individual Americans, however, tended to be as erratic as their government was predictable. Maverick judges scoffed at the extradition cases, throwing them out of court with remarks that embarrassed everyone but the joyful defendants. Political kidnapings, although often aided by the police and the Texas Rangers, were risky; if word spread, a mob of outraged Americans might free the victims, as they had in St. Louis and in Douglas, Arizona. So the dictator's agents in the United States acted with caution and secrecy. Donaju was invaluable, for, dressed properly, he could stroll down an American street and pass for a native. If forced to speak, he could repeat a few words of English learned with an Irish accent, then fall back on his scanty knowledge of Gaelic. He was merely another Irish immigrant who had not yet learned the language. No one paid attention to Donaju, and no one connected him with a series of unexplained murders and disappearances that took place among exiled Mexicans in every city he visited.

The work was exciting, its dangers suited him completely, and he enjoyed outwitting the gringo police, never realizing that their investigations were less than halfhearted. The police could not be bothered if a spick was killed by another spick or some greaser vanished from a cheap hotel. "Another quarrel about women," they said, shrugging their shoulders. "Let them fight it out among themselves."

Donaju was secretly lodged in curtained rooms at various Mexican consulates, and he went out only on assignments. The idle periods between tasks were a punishment to him. He spent hours pacing the floors of the cramped, airless rooms, from each of which he always removed the cot or bed to give himself more walking space. Also, he detested mattresses; they were like quicksand: one sank. After a few months he violated orders by going out late at night to prowl the streets, listening to the harsh rattling language of passers-by. He was lonely, yet he did not want company; incomplete, but he did not know what he lacked. On certain nights, the longing, the sense of emptiness and need, became a physical pain, a throbbing in his chest and head. I will ask for a transfer, he told himself. Being indoors so much is the trouble.

The exiles he preyed upon were men he despised—editors, professors, writers, most of whom had been important in their homeland, famous attorneys and heads of schools. In the United States they were ignored or treated with contempt. This pleased Donaju and led him to think that Americans shared his own scorn of intellectuals. It did not occur to him that Americans thought all Mexicans were lumps from the same tortilla dough and the notion of one of them being a scientist or a doctor of laws was as incongruous as that of a mule in a top hat and as unlikely as the idea of a talking dog.

One night in southern California Donaju and two other strongarm *acordadistas* waylaid the editor of a small exile newspaper, ambushing him on a sidestreet in San Diego. Bound and gagged, he was tossed into a closed wagon, then spirited across the border near Tijuana. After several hours of painful questioning, they took him to a lonely place to hang him. "Señor! I have two daughters. I beg to send them a last message."

"Certainly," said Donaju. "I will see that it is delivered." Such a message might contain useful information, so this promise was always given but never kept. "What do you want to tell them?"

"That I love them."

"Nothing more?"

"There is no more."

A memory stirred in Donaju; he recalled the house he had explored in El Hule. Its owner, whose name he could not recall, had also had two daughters. "Did you ever live in El Hule?" he asked.

"No. You know I am from Guadalajara. I published a paper there, the largest paper in—" The man saw that the noose was ready and Donaju had lost interest in questioning him. "Why do you ask that?" he shouted. "What is the difference? Who cares?" Now he was screaming, babbling a jumble of sentences, anything to prolong these last minutes.

"Get on with it," said Donaju, and they finished their job.

That night a dream troubled him. He was again in the deserted house, moving from room to room, gazing at the pictures and furniture. He saw himself walk down the corridor, open double doors, and then, compelled and unable to stop himself, he entered the ballroom. He caught only a glimpse of the figure in the mirror, but it filled him with terror and he was instantly awake, damp and trembling on a mat in the Tijuana hotel. For years he had not thought of that house, had not permitted himself the memory of the boy in the looking-glass. Now he could not drive it from his mind, and he paced the room, holding his head. He put on a poncho, for it was raining outside, and left the hotel to walk the muddy unlighted streets of the town.

Soon after this he returned to Mexico and to the *rurales*, his usefulness in the United States over. Many exiles had become suspicious of the bogus Irishman, and a printed description was circulated, so he was of no further value as a secret agent. But his work had been distinguished, and in recognition of his merit and loyalty he was made a lieutenant. He was then twenty-two years old.

This time the promotion created difficulties. Very few captains cared to harbor an assistant of such well-known ability, and for two years he was shunted from post to post, always doing better than anyone else, always sped on to the next place at the first opportunity. He had special duty in the capital for several months and earned extra money by accepting certain private assignments, such as a task he performed for the Conde Calderón.

Now his rank was high enough to admit him to society —not the venerable Spanish society, but the class just below this, the politicians, merchants, and highly placed civil servants who ran the country and supported the dictator with fanatical devotion. He had just won another medal for horsemanship, and this added greatly to his social attractions. The fact that he was a barbarian with no manners harmed him not at all, since he made no attempt to conceal his roughness. The ladies were shocked and enchanted. "A noble savage," they said, sighing. "Delicious!" One woman, unable to capture the handsome officer's attention by any usual means, circulated a faintly scandalous rumor linking her own name with his. Others tried the same approach, and thus arose a whole series of stories which later confused Captain Guzmán when he wrote Donaju's biography.

At last a niche was found for the admirable but troublesome lieutenant. He was given his own command, assigned to an unimportant town in the highlands, a place called San Miguel de Allende, which had been a thriving city in colonial days and had since declined—a backwater where great buildings were beginning to decay. It was an occasional stopover for travelers bound for the city of Guanajuato, which lay not far distant. "A beautiful spot," Donaju's acquaintances assured him. "Lovely hills and charming old houses." He did not care; the important fact was that now he would command, no one would interfere with him.

Within two hours of his arrival in San Miguel, Donaju displayed one of the quiet rages for which he became famous. Everything he saw scandalized him: the headquarters were strewn with garbage, and he found cobwebs on the gunracks, a moldy taco in a desk drawer. Far worse, the twenty men of the San Miguel post were flabby and soft. Donaju turned to the sergeant and said, "Who was the former commander? Tell me the name of the chicken-ass."

"What? Why, it was Lieutenant Guzmán, señor. He left

yesterday. He is a Guanajuato man but is now stationed in Morelia."

"He should be stationed in a pigsty, and you should swill at the same trough. Line the men up for inspection."

When they were assembled, Donaju walked slowly back and forth. "This is a *rurale* post? You are sow-bellied, slack-jawed apes. You there! Stop scratching your fleas, you're at attention. All of you stink like Indians." A murmur rose; eyes flashed while fingers itched for pistols. "You are insulted? Any man whose honor is offended can meet me on the drill field in an hour." The Smiler smiled murderously, and no one accepted the challenge.

Some men were foisted off on other commanders, others discharged; two were arrested for stealing equipment and shipped to Valle Nacional, "contract labor, criminal class."

His investigation uncovered one serious case: a man of the post was exposed as a traitor in the pay of an underground political group engaged in smuggling fugitives out of the country. The threads of the conspiracy were impossible to unravel, but Donaju learned that it involved a nearby ranch owned by a strange woman called Madre Juana, who was not, as the name suggests, a nun, although she devoted her life and fortune to work usually performed by religious orders. On her ranch she established a refuge and school for unfortunates: blind men, mutes, cripples, the pitifully deformed or handicapped; and here they learned skills to enable them to earn a living. Some people thought Madre Juana was a saint; others said she was simply a fool; still others, like Donaju, suspected there was concealed profit in her charitable work. "You give and you get," said Donaju.

One night he mounted a raid against the ranch, intending only to search the place and bring in a few residents for questioning, but a demented cripple mistook the *rurales* for bandits and fired a shotgun, killing two men. Hell erupted as the *rurales* took vengeance. A dozen people were slain outright, and others perished horribly, trapped in a room filled with blazing looms, spinning wheels, and bundles of wool. Since the Madre herself was among the victims, a public clamor ensued. Had Donaju not found and fabricated enough evidence to link the ranch remotely to a conspiracy, his career would have been damaged. As it turned out, he was commended for vigilance and the scandal died quickly. A particularly gruesome but traditional method of execution was ordered for the traitor within the *rurale* ranks—a hideous polo game, of which we shall hear more later.

Life and duty in San Miguel had no resemblance to serving in Valle Nacional. Here there were no slave camps, no masses of festering prisoners. This was ranch land, too dry for richness but productive of cattle and maize. The *rurales* kept order among the peons, enforced the will of employers, and patrolled the roads for fugitives from the Guanajuato mines. They rounded up men for the lowland plantations, pursued highway bandits, and remained alert for rebellion. For nearly a year while he rebuilt the demoralized post, Donaju was contented.

Then, with the coming of the rains, the longing and restlessness that had plagued him before returned suddenly. He did not live in the barracks but had a house of his own in the center of town, and, lying alone at night while the July torrents beat on the roof tiles, he found sleep impossible. During the day his temper flared for no reason; subordinates were assigned impossible tasks, then punished for inevitable failure. "I am unfair," he told himself, and this alarmed him, for he had never before questioned his own conduct.

Several times when his loneliness gnawed him, he joined his men at a local brothel and cantina, buying drinks for everyone, even drinking himself, although the taste sickened him. "Play music!" he shouted. "I'm paying!" Guitars strummed, an Indian boy with a sweet sad voice sang,

"Life has no value in Guanajuato . . ." And he thought, Not in Guanajuato, not anywhere. Nothing mattered. . . .

He longed to talk, to share what he thought and remembered. There were urgent things he must communicate, although he did not know why they were important. But who would listen? Who would answer him? The barrier between himself and others was impassable. He neither liked nor respected his men, and his attempts to join the society of the town were disastrous. Several merchants invited him to supper, and their simpering daughters entertained by twanging on a harp or mandolin. It was unendurable.

Seeking a friend, he began to observe his new assistant, Sergeant Lomas, an athletic young man whose swaggering manner was an imitation of Donaju's own. He fell into daydreams involving this sergeant, picturing the two of them in Guerrero, sitting on the ledge above the arroyo as he had done in childhood. They took turns shouting into the depth, listening to their echoing voices. Perhaps he would describe Miguel's dying, telling of the presence he had felt enter the darkened room.

Sergeant Lomas soon received special treatment. He did not suspect his friendship was being sought, but he was delighted to be relieved of some unpleasant duties. "I've made a good impression on that Patricio son-of-a-bitch," he told a companion. "For almost a month he hasn't threatened to tear my guts out. Well, he knows I'm a good man." He swaggered more outrageously than ever.

One night Donaju followed the sergeant to a favorite carousing place, then entered casually to join the table where Lomas and three other *rurales* sprawled. They sat up straight immediately, and all conversation stopped. "Señores, enjoy yourselves! We are not on duty, and I am human too." They doubted this remark. "A bottle of tequila," he called. "No, make it good rum."

Several whores lurked in corners of the room, and when

the other men danced with them Donaju and the sergeant were alone at the table. "You are thoughtful, Lomas," he said. "What's on your mind?"

"Nothing, sir," said Lomas with complete honesty.

"I don't believe it. I've noticed you often are thoughtful. What do you think about?"

The sergeant, encouraged by the friendly tone, chuckled. "Why, I think about the same thing you do."

"And what is that?"

"Women, of course, sir! Like everybody. I was just noticing that little dove over there, the one with the high tits. She'd give you a ride for your money!" He nudged Donaju, then was suddenly aware he had overstepped a boundary. "But I think of other things too. Deeper and more important matters."

"For instance?"

"Well, I often think about the telephone. Once in the capital I spoke over one, and it's the coming thing, sir. If we had a telephone we could talk to Querétaro and Guanajuato and inform each other about fugitives. We could . . ." The sergeant warmed to his subject, not realizing he had lost his audience until Donaju interrupted.

"It takes one rifle shot to cut a wire, Sergeant."

"What? Well, yes, I suppose so. Clever of you to think of that, sir." Although deflated, Lomas did not give up hope of impressing the lieutenant. "Another thing. We should have a regular *rurale* for chief clerk at headquarters. It's bad to trust civilians. Now, I have a brother-in-law, highly educated, who can—"

"I will consider the suggestion. Good night."

"Don't rush off, sir! You see that girl by the bar? She's a wildcat! I had her just last week, and if you—"

"*Adiós.* Report early to headquarters tomorrow. There's extra work. We've been lax this summer."

Outside, he mounted and let his horse walk slowly, bitter at having been a fool. At a mansion near the plaza the daughter of a family was being serenaded; guitars whispered and a violin cried with an unbearable loneliness, while a young man sang: " 'Beloved, when shall I see thy face? I spend my life waiting, blind and in darkness. . . .' " Donaju listened, his head bowed, his hands limp at his sides, and at last the horse, sensing the rider's helplessness, found its own way home.

The next morning Donaju finished his duties quickly, changed his uniform for cool clothing, and started toward a place just beyond the town, an open meadow near a stream, abandoned land hidden from the trail by willows and laurels, where an unused corral made a good practice ring for Valiente, the stallion he had named after a predecessor. He crossed the stream, then paused in a laurel thicket, surprised to see that another rider was there before him. *"Qué bonita!"* he exclaimed, his attention arrested by the beauty of a white mare, a mount of uncertain breeding but of superb gait and appearance. The long tail and flowing mane were groomed to perfection; the satin coat was dazzling. Her owner sat on the top rail of the corral, his back to Donaju, calling soft commands, which the mare obeyed instantly. She trotted, circling faster, and as she passed, the man sprang lightly astride her bare back to ride Navajo style, heels clamped to her sides, his unshod feet pointing straight out. Then, with a quick movement, he stood, knees bent a little, arms extended, balancing himself easily and gracefully. "A circus boy." Donaju sneered, but when he heard the young man laughing in pure delight he knew the performance was given for love.

The rider, now in full view, was as unusual as the horse. He wore the white cotton trousers of a peon, no shirt, and a red checked scarf knotted at his throat. A sombrero concealed his hair, but the skin, though suntanned, was as light as Donaju's own. A Spaniard, he thought. The young man leaped from the horse to the rail, poised uncertainly for a second, then jumped to the ground to take something from a basket. The mare neighed happily and began to munch from his hand. He rested her for a moment, then produced a harmonica from the basket and played a rollicking tune. The mare pranced and pawed the ground coyly, demanding to be coaxed. The music stopped, a gentle reproach was given, and when the tune started once more she danced and performed airs, awkwardly, by no means perfectly, yet Donaju had seen poorer exhibitions acclaimed at contests. Grinning, he kneed the stallion and rode forward.

"*Holá!*"

"*Buenos días, señor.*" The young man lifted his sombrero in greeting. Yellow hair tumbled over his forehead, and Donaju was startled to look at eyes that were almost the color of his own. Although there was no other resemblance, he suddenly recalled the boy in the mirror at El Hule.

Swinging down from the saddle, he said, "I've been watching. The mare works well."

He was so unused to giving even faint praise that he bestowed the compliment as if it were a treasure and was taken aback when the boy said, "No, not good at all. Usually she is wonderful, but not today." The contradiction was delivered with such honesty that Donaju was not offended. They looked at each other; then both said the same thing at the same time. "Are you Mexican?"

"Yes," said Donaju. "From Guerrero."

"I also am Mexican, but I was born in Guanajuato. Often people think I'm not Mexican because of my hair—I'm *rubio* like you. My father was from the United States, and I'm told I look like him."

"How are you called?"

"Daniel. Daniel Jérez. I think it is a common name among my father's people, but it is written with different letters in their language. You are called—?"

The words "Lieutenant Francisco Patricio Donaju" were on his lips, but he said, "Patricio."

They shook hands formally. "You came here to ride, Patricio?"

"Yes."

"Good! Then we will ride together."

Suddenly Donaju felt younger; half a dozen years slipped away. Perhaps it was merely the sound of his name spoken in such an easy, relaxed way by a youth who was not more than eighteen. He could not remember when anyone had called him by his first name, and it had a good sound, a pleasant sound. He returned Daniel's smile, liking the confident way the boy held his head. "Has your mare any speed?"

"Speed? Jesus, Mary, and Joseph! Estrella—that's her name—goes like a mountain wind. Come on, Patricio, climb on that stallion and we'll give you a race! He's a big fellow, but she'll show him her tail."

"You've met your match, Daniel! Over to that ruined church and back, *verdad*?"

When Daniel shouted, "*Vámonos*," Estrella lunged forward, ears back, nostrils flaring, and gained two lengths before Valiente was under way. Daniel crouched low, streamlining his body against the wind, molding himself to the flying animal. "*Dios!*" Donaju exclaimed, spurring the stallion. "He's the devil on horseback! A rider—a real rider!"

The mare was swift, but Valiente's strength told. Neck and neck they circled the tumbledown church, Daniel laughing, shouting inaudibly above the pounding hoofs. Then Valiente pulled ahead, his long powerful strides outdistancing the smaller rival.

At the corral, when they dismounted, Daniel ran to Donaju and threw his arms around him. "Patricio, you are magnificent! Never have I seen a man so beautiful on a horse. You should ride in the capital at the *charreadas*."

"I have," said Donaju, awkwardly breaking away. He was thrilled by the praise and the depth of Daniel's admiration, yet it puzzled him that Daniel did not mind having lost the race. "You ride well too."

"Yes, I am very good. But nothing like you! The way you took that turn, leaning to help the horse! Oh, I do that too, but not like you." He extended his hand again. "I am proud to be your friend, Patricio. It is an honor to ride with you." There was neither flattery nor humility in his tone.

"We'll wash at the stream," said Donaju. "We're a dusty pair."

Afterward they sat on the bank, the willows shading them from the noon sun. "You live in San Miguel, Daniel?"

"No. Guanajuato. I work for a Spaniard who is visiting here this week. You may have heard of Señor Pérez. He has a famous stable."

"You are a horse trainer?"

"No. But horses will do anything I am clever enough to tell them. So will dogs—someday I must show you my dog, Patricio! But that is not my work. I am a secretary."

Donaju frowned. "You write letters and things? I would not like doing that."

"Neither do I, but the pay is good. It is expensive to keep Estrella, and I could not part with her."

"Of course not. I suppose people try to buy her—or steal her."

"I will not sell. And for the stealing—well, it has been tried." Donaju's eyebrows lifted at the unexpected fierceness in Daniel's voice. This boy was still coltish, but there was steel in him.

"You went to school to learn this work?"

Sighing, Daniel slowly stripped the leaves from a willow wand. "I was in school most of my life, God pity me. After my father died my mother gave me to the Jesuits to be a priest. It did not work out. I have an unconquerable vice."

"A what?"

"A vice, a sin one commits over and over. The *padres* say a vice grows and wraps itself around your will like a boa-constrictor. Well, the toils of my vice were too strong for me. I could not control my mind or my body."

Donaju thought gloomily of the previous night, of Sergeant Lomas. "I suppose it would be bad for a priest to want women all the time," he said.

"Women? Oh, you thought I—" Daniel shook his head. "Everyone thinks priests suffer most from lack of women. For me that would be an easy sin to conquer—at least I think so, although I've had no real experience with it. My vice was pride."

"Pride? That's no sin!"

"Maybe pride is the worst of the Seven Deadlies because it affects everything you do—it even poisons obedience. Sometimes it's as bad to obey unwillingly as not to obey at all. I could never submit, I couldn't be like a dead body in the hands of God. Father Ignacio said I didn't conquer my vice because secretly I loved it. He was right, and two years ago I gave up."

Patricio spoke roughly. "Good! I don't know anything about sins and vices. A man does what he does. To hell with priests. Let's talk about horses."

They did. They spoke of palominos and pintos, of the stubborn Yaqui ponies that lived almost without water and found forage where goats perished. Gradually their talk drifted to other things, and the words stored in Patricio's head began to pour out. He became excited and he told Daniel of the summer torrents sweeping down the arroyos in Guerrero, floods so swift that stones floated on them. He described the echo, "God's voice speaking without a body. Listen, it was like this. . . ."

"I know," said Daniel. "I have done the same thing. There is a mine shaft in Guanajuato, it goes to the middle of the earth, I think. I have called into it."

The heat of day had passed, and they realized they had talked for hours without thinking of time, that soon evening would come. "When do you leave here, Daniel?"

"Tomorrow or the next day—whenever the señor decides." Hesitant, he looked away. "I am sorry. I would like to ride with you often, Patricio. You see, it is not always easy for me to speak with people. Perhaps that is why I spend time with Estrella and my dog. I am often lonely. Have you ever felt that you were the only one of your kind in the world? I know this is foolish, but—"

"Not foolish. I understand." Donaju was thoughtful; then he said, "I am a lieutenant of the *rurales*. I command the post here."

"That's very good, isn't it?" Daniel seemed pleased at his friend's good fortune but unimpressed by the title.

"Something occurs to me. We have trouble with the civilian clerks in our headquarters and—" The picture of Daniel riding beside him in a russet uniform loomed in his mind. "I was considering bringing a young man into our post. He would join the force and do a lot of riding, see action, of course. But he would also make sure the clerks answered letters the right way. An important job. Maybe a corporal's rank could come quickly."

"Are you asking me to do this?"

"Yes, I am."

"I know little of the *rurales*. I don't think I—" He gazed at Donaju, his face troubled, then smiled. "Tonight I will tell my employer that I want to work for you." The smile became a grin. "Do you always get your own way, Patricio?"

"Yes," said Donaju. "Always."

6

The magician wrote in his manuscript: "Donaju was a man who never gave or received friendship. His never knowing devotion may have brutalized him. Perhaps this lack of love and the weight of his conscience made him turn from the living to seek the dead. . . ."

Captain Guzmán put it differently: "His dedication to duty was total. He denied himself those personal relationships lesser men enjoy."

Daniel and Patricio rode in the hills on Sundays, a reddish dog called Pícaro trotting beside them. ("Pícaro's hair is the same color as yours, Patricio. And he looks at you so lovingly that I begin to think you're related." "Whose mother do you insult? The dog's or mine?" This was the first joke Donaju had ever made, and he roared at it, amazed he had not realized he was witty before now.) They attended fiestas in remote villages and traveled to Querétaro to see the Hill of Bells, where the Emperor Maximilian fell before a firing squad. Often they slept in the fields or in the sparse groves that dotted the highland, their horses resting nearby, the dog keeping watch. On cool nights they built campfires, and Daniel sometimes played his harmonica. ("Why don't you sing, Patricio? I'm sure you can sing." "Don't be a fool! Do I look like a canary?" But he did sing and was surprised that he had somehow learned the words of a dozen songs.)

South of San Miguel a rancher had built an earthen dam across a stream, and they swam in the reservoir of brown water, Daniel swift as a trout, but Patricio did not resent this superiority as he would have resented it in any other man. There was no competition between them; their talk was filled with mutual praise and wonder at each other's accomplishments. Donaju learned the smallest details of his new friend's life, anecdotes of the monastery, jokes about the Jesuits, but when it came to revealing his own story he was evasive. Daniel is childlike, Donaju thought, and does not understand the thing men must sometimes do. He was proud, not ashamed, of all of his career, but intuition told him not to speak of it. Their pleasures and talk remained boyish, and Donaju now enjoyed a childhood and youth he had never known.

At the *rurale* post no one was aware of their friendship, although Sergeant Lomas complained privately that the commander showed favoritism toward this blond recruit. "Prejudice! Both have skins the color of sour milk." This was unfair. In public Donaju hid his partiality under coolness, and, boylike, they took a delight in concealment.

"No one must know we are as close as brothers," he told Daniel. "The men would make your life hell, and you would have to fight every day. I'd have to give you extra work to show I was fair." Daniel accepted this explanation, which was true as far as it went. But Donaju had another reason for secrecy, realizing that if their friendship became known it would raise eyebrows and cause whispers. Such Spartan societies as the *rurales* have always given rise to love affairs between men—indeed, perverse love is their principal by-product. Donaju's stomach still turned when he recalled certain men in the barracks at El Hule, swaggering males by day who at night crept from their own sleeping mats to the mats of comrades. Once he himself had awakened to find callused hands caressing his body, and although he had smashed the face of his would-be lover and was not bothered again, he did not forget his revulsion. His love for Daniel had nothing to do with such things; he knew its purity and was proud of having such a friend, although he did not suspect that what he felt was not the pride of friendship but the more dangerous and intense pride of possession.

In May, during the hot weeks before the rains swell the dry streams, Donaju made a circuit of his district, accompanied by Daniel, who acted as his orderly. "They will be ambushed going alone," said Lomas, but he admitted the trip was a *macho* gesture.

However, the journey was uneventful until the last place Donaju visited. This was a village called Las Jacarandas, a mining camp so far from San Miguel that it should not have been Donaju's responsibility, being nearer to Guanajuato. He suffered this nuisance because he was a junior commander and nobody else wanted the job of supervising the mining company's police, who kept order, prevented slowdowns, and guarded against the escape of three hundred contract laborers.

In midmorning they ascended rugged hills at the base of a mountain ridge, passing the picked skeletons of burros that had fallen under the weight of silver ore, and came at last to a bullet-riddled sign that said in both Spanish and English: LAS JACARANDAS, TWO MILES. PROPERTY OF NEW ENGLAND MINING & SMELTING CO. ARMED PATROL. TRESPASSERS WILL BE SHOT.

A moment later they met the chief of the company police, who was riding toward them with several men. "Cristo, a miracle! Who sent for you, señor? We were just now on our way to San Miguel."

"No one sent for me. Is there trouble?"

"I was coming to report the death of a foreigner. Also, the Devil's Doctor has gone crazy, and since he's a gringo we don't know what to do with him."

"The Devil's Doctor?"

"His name is Esterbrook. The company sent him here to take care of the men—foolishness, of course. Anybody would die before consulting him." The policeman lowered his voice. "He cuts up corpses, and some of them may not even be quite dead. Anyway, he has at last gone completely crazy."

"And who is the dead foreigner?"

"His wife, the Señora Olivia. The doctor says she is entombed in an abandoned shaft—Mine Seven. If she is not dead now, she will be in a day or two. The husband is raving mad, and I don't know if we should tie him up or leave him alone."

"He speaks Spanish?" Donaju asked this as they rode toward the houses clustered on the mountain.

"Miserably, but some. We have a German engineer who speaks all languages. He can interpret if you need him."

"Did Señor Ruíz send you to fetch me?" Ruíz, a man Donaju's age, was manager of the mines.

"No, the *jefe* has been gone since yesterday, and I'm not sure where he is. Maybe Guanajuato. That has made things worse."

Beyond the shacks of the village were several large residences, then, past another ridge, the black mouths of mines that had long since been abandoned for more productive work farther up the slope. At the farthest of these cavelike entrances was a sign: MINE SEVEN. DANGER. KEEP OUT.

"The Devil's Doctor is in there now with men he has hired to dig the woman out. It is hopeless, of course, and he is paying the men a fortune because Mine Seven is dangerous and haunted. No one goes there willingly."

After dismounting, they entered a dank corridor, the policeman following reluctantly, shivering as he felt the chill breath of the shaft, casting a longing look backward as the sunlight vanished. "This one was always trouble," he said. "Always unlucky." Far away Donaju heard shouts and hammering, blurred echoes in the tunnel. The corridor was perhaps ten feet wide and so low that Donaju had to duck his head under the rotted timbers supporting the ceiling. Water dripped on the stone floor.

Daniel whispered, "It is a crypt, Patricio. I feel like a trapped bird."

The passage veered, then widened into a large chamber lit by lanterns and candles. Half a dozen men, naked except for loincloths and sweatbands, toiled here, demon figures in the uncertain light as they struggled to move slabs of new-fallen rock that sealed off the far end of the cavern. "Patricio, we are in hell!"

A light-skinned man, a foreigner, was directing the men, shouting frantic commands while he labored with an iron pry-bar. "That's the Devil's Doctor," said the policeman. "Mad as an owl."

"The woman is behind those rocks?"

"So he says."

"Is there a chance of getting her out?"

The man shrugged. "A hundred men working a month, maybe. If the rest of the roof did not fall on them—which it would. The mine runs back another mile into the mountain, but there is no way out. The woman is done for."

A rivulet of dirt and pebbles rattled down. Dropping their picks, the workmen threw themselves backward, arms raised to shield their heads. The doctor panicked at the sound but retreated only a few steps. Then he flung aside the pry-bar and clawed at the rocks with bloody hands. "Livia, Livia! God, can you hear me?" Again small stones and earth pattered to the floor, shaken loose by the vibration of his cries echoing in the vault.

"Get the men out of here," said Donaju. But already the workmen were pushing past him, fleeing in terror. Donaju seized the doctor's arm, spinning him around. "*Vámonos, señor!* We go!"

"Go?" The man's eyes rolled as he struggled against Donaju. "No, I can't leave her here. I—"

"*Vámonos!*" Donaju swung his fist and knocked the man unconscious, then carried him from the mine, wondering at each step if the ceiling would give way, wondering why he bothered with the hysterical gringo who hung limply over his shoulder. Outside, he said to the policeman, "Take him to his house and tie him to the bed. You were a fool, señor, to permit him to endanger those workmen. They are worth fifty pesos apiece—maybe more, these days."

During the next hours Donaju gathered information about Dr. James Esterbrook and his wife, Olivia, Americans who had lived in Las Jacarandas almost two years, people who were well known and little understood. "Why should they come to this place?" he asked. "The doctor cannot earn much money here."

The chief of company police had no answer, but the German engineer offered an explanation that made no sense. "The doctor is a man who wishes to suffer for humanity. There are people like this, and many of them are Americans. They go to China, to Africa—they come here."

"Like the Franciscans?" asked Daniel.

"Yes, but no. They work not for God but for themselves. They feel they owe something to the world. Myself, I go where the money is."

Donaju shook his head. "I will write to the capital. Maybe the doctor is a fugitive criminal."

The German laughed at this notion. "A criminal? He has the conscience of a Lutheran! And Olivia is—I mean was —even worse. She started a school here and was doing all sorts of good things. Myself, I do not like saintly women."

The police chief gave Donaju a meaningful look and later drew him aside. "I am sure the doctor is not a criminal, unless it has to do with cutting corpses. But everyone has his faults, and the doctor's weakness is women. When he goes to Guanajuato to buy medicines, he always visits the gallant señoritas. His wife was a good

woman—still, I saw her several times look at our *jefe*, Señor Ruíz, with mare's eyes. Maybe she put horns on the
doctor. Who knows?"

The facts of the accident were no less puzzling than the
Esterbrooks themselves. The doctor had rushed into the
mine office, shouting that his wife was trapped in Mine
Seven, entombed alive by a cave-in, and demanded an
army of men to dig away the fallen rock. He had been out
walking, he said, and from a distance he saw her enter the
abandoned shaft. "She was exploring. She collected unusual stones." He had followed her and just as he reached
the entrance he heard a deafening roar and her voice
crying for help. "He could not have heard her," said
Donaju. "It does not make sense." He wished Señor Ruiz
would return to help explain things, but the manager was
still absent, and no one could find him.

That night Daniel and Donaju slept at Esterbrook's
house. The doctor was no longer bound, but lay in a coma,
drugged with hemp from his pharmacy. An hour after
midnight he twisted on the bed and began to speak ago-
nized words neither of the watchers could understand.

"He talks to his wife," Daniel whispered. "Twice he said
'Olivia.'"

Suddenly the doctor sat up, eyes open, staring ahead,
and his face was ashen. He listened, raised his arms then
as though to shield himself from blows, at last fell backward with a shrill cry and collapsed on the pillow to lie as
one dead. Daniel, shuddering, crossed himself. "*Dios!* He
looked as though a ghost had come!"

The bedroom was stifling, and Donaju felt he could not
breathe its air. They went to the patio, and after a moment
of silence he said, "I have seen that look before. My
father . . . " Haltingly he told the story of Miguel's
dying. "He believed something had come, and I believed it
too. Have you known of such things?"

"Yes. There is a woman called Candelaria who lives in

the mountains near Guanajuato. She is a great *divina* who has visions and raises spirits from their graves. When I was small my mother took me there one night. I remember a fire whose smoke made you dizzy; then I saw shapes like rainbows—only brighter—and I heard my father speak."

"What did he say?"

Daniel hesitated, studying the lantern on the table. "He said my life would be happy, but I would join him too soon. And my dying would be painful."

Donaju stirred uneasily. "It was the smoke you breathed."

"No. They were sad words, but ever since I have known that if my father could return to me, then it cannot be terrible to die. Dying is not the end." Reaching out, he clasped Donaju's hand. "The sadness of death is parting, but maybe we do not part altogether. I promise I will not leave you behind, my friend. I will speak to you as my father spoke to me. Will you listen for me, Patricio? Will you swear that you will listen?"

"I swear it, Daniel." They spoke no more, but they felt communication as they gazed up at the motionless stars, heard the night wind on the mountain and the lonely, faraway cry of a wolf.

A week later Lieutenant Donaju dictated a report which Daniel wrote, edited, and dispatched to the capital. One section dealt with events at Las Jacarandas, and, after giving much of what has been told here, Donaju continued:

. . . The next morning the doctor was recovered of his senses. He made no attempt to continue the futile rescue, saying he was now certain his wife was already dead and further effort was useless. When asked why he was now so certain, he answered with great emotion, "I know. Isn't that enough?" He became so disturbed that I did not press the question.

The subject was urged to return to his homeland, but he said he owed it to his wife's memory to remain at his work. Since Esterbrook is employed by an important company, I did not insist. He seems to do neither harm nor good. Because he has performed autopsies—legally—the inhabitants avoid him except in desperation. A local priest condemned him for mutilation of corpses and for sacrilege but, under the new regulations, that is not a police matter.

A certificate of accidental death was issued. However, we are in doubt about filling in the line "Time of Burial." She was presumably buried before death, and such a statement would look strange on the certificate. We left it blank. Kindly do NOT return this form as you have returned others! All this paper work interferes with important duties. Every month the red tape is worse.

Another matter concerning Las Jacarandas: the manager, Roberto Ruíz y Tola, seems to have absconded with company money. He has been missing for some days, and I am told his accounts reveal a shortage, although the amount is rather small. Name and description are listed in the Wanted For Questioning bulletin.

I announce the promotion of recruit Daniel Jérez y Gomez to the rank of corporal. . . .

Corporal Daniel Jérez used part of his increased salary to rent a room on the second floor of a private house, thus escaping the rowdy life of the barracks. Secretly Daniel despised the men he worked with, although outwardly he was good-humored and helpful. Moving into new quarters seemed the beginning of an adventure to him, and the day he brought his few possessions into the room he was struck by a premonition that something important was about to happen, some experience that would end the restlessness he had suffered in recent weeks, moods of discontent when even Patricio's company had not satisfied him, although he would not admit this to himself. It did not occur to him that he was now enduring the pangs of growing up, which most men pass through at an earlier age.

From the windows of his new room he could look across a narrow street into the living room of his neighbors, a family named Campos, newcomers who had lived in San Miguel only a few years. Señor Campos owned a small shop stocked with unlikely merchandise—books, writing materials, musical and art supplies, things of little interest to most people. With his two grown daughters he lived on the two floors above the shop. When the shutters were open, Daniel saw that the apartment was crowded with expensive furniture, the leftovers of more prosperous days.

One night Daniel heard tinkling music and, going to the window, saw that the living room was bathed in the light of half a dozen lamps and a tall candelabrum, a scene that had the brilliance of a stage. Señor Campos, gray-haired and frail, was entertaining several guests. Daniel noticed a young woman who resembled the señor; then his eyes moved to a girl seated at a spinet piano, her small hands first drifting, then darting above the keyboard. She wore a lace dress of so light a blue that it seemed almost white, and, although she was clearly of a good family, she had put a rose in her brown hair in the manner of a fandango dancer—a saucy touch that Daniel found charming. Perhaps he had seen girls more beautiful; he neither remembered nor cared. He knew only that his heart suddenly ached as he watched her. *"Preciosa!"* he murmured.

Until now no woman had stirred him deeply. He found harlots disgusting and, being a young man with no money or family, he seldom allowed himself to think of the aristocratic goddesses he glimpsed in carriages or saw strolling in the plaza, eyes modestly lowered, always accompanied by *dueñas*. They were not real to him, not flesh and blood, even though their slender ankles and ripe breasts made him look twice. Once, while riding with Patricio, he had noticed a peon girl sitting on a stone wall, her bosom bared as she nursed a baby, and he had felt a twinge, sharp and painful. He longed to continue staring at her, but he turned his head quickly away, his cheeks flushed, hoping Patricio had not read his thoughts. Patricio, Daniel was sure, had the chastity of a priest and was never disturbed by carnal temptations. Such feelings were not to be discussed with him.

The girl turned from the spinet, smiling as the guests applauded, and when Daniel saw the beauty of her in full face he fell in love, instantly and completely, an unchangeable fact, as sure as his sudden decision to leave the Jesuits or the moment when he gave his friendship to Patricio and altered his life on an impulse. But what he now felt was not like his love for Donaju, not a deep and quiet devotion. This was a pounding of his heart, a singing in his ears.

She moved among the guests, laughing, making small jokes, and when she tossed her head there was a flash in her eyes. "She has the devil in her," said Daniel proudly. "I will have to tame her, but not too much." At her father's urging she returned to the spinet to play again, and he held his breath when the light of the candelabrum shone on her lips. He expected to hear some melody he would not understand, the foreign music he heard from pianos when he walked past great houses. But she played a song he had known since childhood, one that street singers and peons sang, "The Traveler," a song about hills and roads and distance. "She loves what I love," he said. "And she will love me."

In the next weeks everyone except Donaju noticed the change in Corporal Daniel Jérez. Often he gazed into space, daydreaming, and Sergeant Lomas said, "Are you catching flies, Corporal? Your mouth's hanging open." On a sheet of paper he wrote a single name over and over in different styles of penmanship: "Elvira Campos . . . Elvira . . ." And then: "Elvira Campos de Jérez . . . Elvira, Señora de Don Daniel Jérez y Gómez . . ."

There had been no problem in meeting her. He had spied on the shop until he was sure she was alone, then entered and bought a dozen sheets of paper. After a moment of awkward silence he blurted, "Señorita, you are the most beautiful girl I have ever seen. I love you and wish to marry you. If you knew me, you would love me. But I do not know how to bring this about."

"Señor," she said, astonished, "you are crazy."

"Yes. Ever since last night when I watched you through the window."

"Through the window? This is outrageous! I will keep the shutters closed."

"They will be closed forever and you will die of heat while I die of longing. I will never stop looking, señorita."

That night the windows were open as usual, and when she entered the living room alone and played "The Traveler," he was prepared and accompanied her on his harmonica. She arose angrily and slammed the shutters, but could not quite hide a smile. "What a woman! She is perfect!" He sat on the sill, legs hanging out, and played the tune over and over, knowing she could not help hearing.

The following day she exchanged a few grudging words with him in the shop, but when, a week later, he attempted a quick kiss, she rebuffed him. "This is impossible! Do not come back, señor."

He paid no attention. "There is a promenade in the plaza on Sunday evening and fireworks afterward. Will you walk with me?"

"No! This town is small, and although you wear no uniform when you come here, do you imagine I don't know what you are?"

"You do not like my work? Well, neither do I. But it will take some time to change it." Frowning, he said slowly, "There is a friend I must not hurt, not in any way and not ever. I must manage carefully and take time." Then, smiling, he bowed as he had seen gentlemen bow. "I am an honorable person and I love you. Since you cannot get rid of me, you must learn to enjoy me. *Hasta la vista, mi vida!*" Going out, he was exultant that there had been tears in her eyes. "Little by little," he told himself.

Three months later Sergeant Lomas was granted a private interview with his commander. "A confidential matter, sir, about Corporal Jérez. Last night I talked with him more than an hour."

"Where?" asked Donaju.

"At a plaza restaurant. He'd been drinking, which is unusual for him, and he wanted to talk about personal problems. It surprised me, because we're not really friends. I think he was desperate to talk, and I happened to be there."

"Desperate? Why was the corporal desperate?"

Lomas chuckled. "A girl—what else? He has fallen in love with a town girl named Elvira Campos. He is crazy in love."

For a moment Donaju did not speak, but when he did his voice was steady. "Why tell me, Sergeant?"

"Two reasons, sir." Lomas squirmed under the gaze. "Jérez made me promise to say nothing to you, and that seemed suspicious. But more important, he meets the girl on the sly because her father hates the *rurales* and won't have one in the house. So they sneak into the cactus somewhere. I asked myself, Why should that be? Jérez wants to marry the girl, although I'm sure he's already cut her flowers. Still he can't go to the house. I'd understand if the family was rich or important—they'd want something better than a *rurale,* even a corporal with a good future. But these people are just educated nobodies who run a store, and half the time they eat beans like everybody else. So why not accept Jérez? And why does he talk about quitting the force? It sounds political, sir. Maybe there's even a stink of sedition somewhere." Glancing at Donaju's face, the sergeant panicked. What in the name of the Virgin had he said that was so terrible? The commander seemed thunderstruck, and Lomas recognized signs of beginning fury. "Maybe I shouldn't bother you with this, sir. Probably nothing in it, but I thought we might do some checking." He spoke too rapidly and knew it, but Donaju's expression terrified him. "I'm sure the corporal isn't mixed up in anything. But he's the innocent type, and—"

Lomas flinched when Donaju's fist struck the desk top. The lieutenant strode to the window and stood with his back to the sergeant, silent for a long time. When he spoke it was in a monotone, his jaw hardly moving. "Learn everything possible about this family. Borrow unknown men from Celaya and put a watch on their house. Send a letter— no, not a letter; go to Mexico City and search the records. You have a month for investigation, and do not report until you are finished. Above all, Jérez must suspect nothing."

Lomas brightened. "You think it's important, sir?"

"Yes. It is important."

Donaju did not interfere with the sergeant's investigation, but he made inquiries of his own and quickly learned that Daniel's love affair was exactly as Lomas had claimed. The night watch had often seen them slipping through the streets after midnight. Bound for where and for what purpose? The sergeant's words repeated themselves in his head. "They sneak into the cactus. . . . He's already cut her flowers. . . ."

Donaju concealed his hatred, making excuses for not seeing Daniel, and when the boy accepted readily, he told himself, "He is thinking, Good, I have more time for my girl. More time—" He could not bear to finish the thought, and the image of the girl tortured him. He knew now that Daniel would be punished, whatever Lomas reported. If it could not be done under regulations, then he would do it privately, take Daniel to some lonely place. . . . He remembered standing in the sunset near the corral in Guerrero, staring into the barrel of the revolver in Miguel's hand, remembered the fear that had seized him, yet he had never loved his father until that moment, and now as he lived the scene again the gun was in his own hand and Daniel stood before him. When he imagined the punishment, it ended in forgiveness and a strange conversion. Even now he could not think of life without Daniel, and he despised himself for this.

Lomas made his report two days early. "You were right, sir! This thing is bigger than anyone except you suspected. The Campos family comes from a small town near Valle Nacional, a place called . . ." He struggled to decipher the printed letters of a note.

"El Hule," said Donaju. "A dozen years ago they were arrested for sedition."

"Yes, sir. How did you know?"

"I was there. I had forgotten their name until now. Go on."

"There was strong evidence, but they were released after a few weeks. They were rich then, and since they have no money now, it's plain enough how they escaped justice. Later Señor Campos served six months in San Juan for owning illegal books. There's always been suspicion, but never enough proof to nail their skins to the door. Not until now!"

"Now there is?"

Lomas could hardly contain his excitement. "The Celaya men who've been watching the house have spotted a hidden guest. Sometimes he ventures out after dark, and they're certain he is that editor from Oaxaca who's described in the last bulletin. The Campos family is harboring a fugitive right enough!"

"And what is the corporal's part?"

Lomas spoke softly, glancing at the closed door. "Up to

the neck, I'm afraid. His love affair now has unexpected success. Twice this month he has had supper there on the señor's invitation, and one of our men, watching from a rooftop, saw him sit at the table with the secret guest. It's clear they've come to trust the corporal as one of their own. God, how sex can twist a man! He and the girl still have their nightly meetings. They slip away—"

"The traitor's rutting does not concern me!" Was he to be spared nothing? A chill like dying came over him. "Raid the house two hours before dawn and arrest Corporal Jérez at the same hour. You are in charge, Sergeant. When you bring the prisoners here, I will question the Campos family. I leave the corporal to you. Get all information."

Lomas's chest swelled at this proof of his chief's confidence. "About questioning Jérez, sir. If he is difficult shall we—I mean, he has been your own orderly and—"

"We show no favors, Sergeant. Do what you like. I have no interest."

7

The excerpts given here are from a report dictated by Lieutenant Francisco Patricio Donaju and submitted to *rurale* headquarters in the capital. Most of the actual wording is the work of a civilian secretary. Being an official document, it is replete with half-truths and omissions.

. . . Sergeant Lomas did well in carrying out the investigation, which the undersigned officer initiated, but he bungled the final job. The Campos residence was raided at 4:07 a.m., September 12, Lomas attempting to storm the barred front doors, thus alerting the suspects, who proved to be armed and dangerous. Two *rurales* were slain in the gun battle.

(See attached citations.) Lomas has been fined two months' salary.

Manuel Campos y Arías, owner of the house: taken alive but died of wounds within a few hours.

Juan Escobar y Moreno, fugitive editor: died either by *rurale* fire or by his own hand to elude capture.

Angela Alicia Campos, a daughter of the owner: perished in the same uncertain fashion as Juan Escobar.

María Elvira Campos, a daughter: escaped, fleeing over an unguarded rooftop. (See attached official reprimand of Sergeant Lomas.) Her capture is expected daily.

Two servants: confined to civil jail after questioning.

Quantities of subversive literature were found on the raided premises. (See attached inventory of confiscated property.)

Arrest of *rurale* traitor Corporal Daniel Jérez y Gómez was marked by violent resistance and injury to personnel. His guilt, indicated by previous evidence, was further confirmed by seditious statements uttered at the time of arrest. Moreover, pieces of the literature mentioned above were concealed in his room. These items, overlooked in the original search, came to light when the undersigned officer personally inspected the room two days after the arrest.

The undersigned officer took no part in the questioning of Jérez. Lomas, the interrogator, was apparently a friend of the corporal, and it seemed probable that Jérez might respond more honestly to an acquaintance; he did not, no confession was obtained.

Evidence was submitted and the Post Commander acted as judge, maintaining strict impartiality by avoiding all communication with the prisoner from the time of arrest. The mandatory death sentence was publicly carried out in a traditional way two weeks ago.

Efforts are being made to trace further threads in the network of rebellion. Most former connections of the Campos family have long ago fled the country or have been imprisoned for years. Corporal Jérez has no surviving family, and it appears that the seeds of sedition were implanted in him here in San Miguel. It was recalled that he once mentioned a woman called Candelaria, the leader of a cult near Guanajuato. Since cults are always suspect, the undersigned officer intends to make a private inquiry, visiting this woman to see if her followers are hiding treasonable work behind the mask of superstition or witchcraft. . . .

Since beginning this report, word has been received that a girl resembling Elvira Campos is being held in León. The undersigned officer will himself go to complete the identification, traveling via Guanajuato to investigate the above mentioned matter at the same time.

Lt. F. Patricio Donaju
Post Commander
San Miguel de Allende, Gto.

P.S. (For Col. Rodriguez.) Some of the difficulties in the Campos case may be due to the fact that I have been suffering from an illness, the first in my years of service. It came on suddenly the night of the Campos raid and appears to be malaria—fever, chills, sudden shaking. I am still able to perform my duties, but later I will request recuperative leave. At that time another officer must be sent here, since Sergeant Lomas is not competent to handle this or any other post.

A week after Donaju's report was dispatched to the capital Sergeant Jorge Lomas spent two long evenings struggling to write a letter to Jesús Orca y Lomas, a minor bureaucrat in Mexico City who until recently had been administrator in San Miguel. The letter was printed in childish capital letters and contained many misspellings, which are corrected here in translation. Because of the dangerous nature of his remarks, he did not dare dictate the message to a public scribe or a *rurale* clerk.

Dear Uncle Chucho,

As I wrote before, I'm really in the pigpen over this Campos business and I hope you're doing everything possible to speed up my request for transfer from San Miguel. I almost think Lt. Donaju has gone crazy. Well, maybe not crazy, but there's at least one shoe off his horse. For the love of God, don't quote me! It'd be my *neck!* Crazy or not, he hates me and I can't figure out why.

Right now he's away, gone to León to claim a prisoner who's almost sure to be Elvira Campos. I hope so—maybe it will improve his disposition. He went alone as usual. He's got nerve, all right. On the way he'll hunt up a witch called Candelaria—he thinks she has something to do with the case. It's plain silly, because everybody's heard of Candelaria and she's just a crackpot—conjures up spooks and so forth. But I don't question the lieutenant!

Catching that editor, even dead, was a big thing, and last week I tried in a roundabout way to remind Donaju that I ought to get some credit for starting the investigation, and even a reward. What I was really thinking about was a trick horse that belonged to Corporal Jérez. The horse was confiscated and put to pasture with orders that nobody's to ride her. Well, I mentioned that this was a waste, and I was just getting around to the fact that she ought to be given to me, when Donaju gave me a look that would fry your liver. Then he turned on one of those alligator smiles and said, "Don't worry, Sergeant. I haven't forgotten you. You'll be rewarded." When? The horse is still in the pasture!

I know you say Donaju's tough but fair. Still, this time he's really got a bird in his sombrero. Maybe it goes back to the morning Jérez was executed—a funny thing happened then. We led Jérez out to this field where a lot of people had gathered to watch, and Donaju was there sitting on that big stallion of his—oh, very elegant, like one of those statues at Chapultepec. Jérez wasn't in good shape, because I'd given him a hard time during questioning. I couldn't help it—the damn fool wouldn't say a word and duty's duty. But when he got to the field, he suddenly straightened up and stared at Donaju. He said, "Go with God until we meet, Patricio." Just that. In the calmest voice you ever heard, and I don't know why there was something terrible about it, but there was.

Well, Donaju looked like he was going to fall off his horse or have a stroke or something. I never saw anybody turn so white. He opened and closed his mouth and for a minute I thought he was going to stop the execution. Then he pulled himself together—the big stone *idolato* again. He watched what went on, but he didn't take any part in it, although it was one of those old-fashioned *rurale* executions of a traitor where everybody gets to do something. You've probably seen it—the prisoner's buried up to the neck and the men ride back and forth with poles, taking swings at his head. It looks like that horseback ball game they play in Mexico City. It's kind of a mess. When I get my own command, I'll stick to shooting.

Donaju seemed all right for a day or so afterwards; then he got a touch of malaria or something. He gets chills and I guess he can't sleep, because the night watchmen have seen him walking the streets at all hours and they're nervous—they think he's checking up on them.

Anyhow, he's made life hell for everybody and especially me. I've gone on and on about this even though I hate to write letters—*can't* write them, I guess! But I want you to know how much I need that transfer. So pull any strings you can, dear Uncle Chucho. The sooner the better.

My wife sends her best, and a big *abrazo* from your little great-nephew, Marcos.

Your most humble and affectionate servant and obedient nephew,

Jorge

The sergeant's transfer was approved in the capital two months later. It did him no good. That same week he was felled in his own doorway, the victim of an unknown sniper who was believed to be either a rebel terrorist or, since Lomas was a woman-chaser, a wronged husband taking vengeance for his horns. The marksman fired from a great distance but with deadly aim.

8

The man and the woman sat facing each other, he on a chair, she on the edge of a bed in which, until a few minutes ago, she had lain in a drugged sleep. Her eyelids were heavy, her brain was still numb, and for this she was grateful. Letting her head fall forward, she tried to sink once more into the pleasant haze where there was no memory, no consciousness.

Donaju spoke sharply. "Wake up! You've slept a night and a day. It's enough." When she felt the sting of his fingers on her arm, she forced her eyes open. Surely he was the devil himself, and she still feared him, although there was little he could do to her now. They were all dead—her father, her sister . . . Daniel. What became of her now mattered nothing, had not mattered since the moment when she had awakened in the night, terrified by the crash of rifle butts on the doors, the whine of bullets in the patio, believing for an instant that this was only a dream, the same dream that had tormented her since the night long ago in El Hule when the soldiers and police had battered their way into the house. Her father always said they might someday come again, but she had not really accepted this. But when she knew an attack upon the house was actually happening, she fled by instinct, crawling through the tiny window, running across the roof as she had been taught to do. Her only thought had been to reach Daniel, who could somehow save them. Then, from a rooftop near the corner, she looked down into the street and saw them drag him from his house. He was bound, but still they beat him, kicking him to the cobblestones. She screamed at the sight, but no one heard her. There were so many people screaming and shouting from windows, so many horses, and so much noise. She knew that everything was lost, knew she had caused Daniel's destruction, but still she kept going and found refuge with friends, who smuggled her to León, where she was arrested. . . . She should have stayed in the house that night. . . . She should have died with them.

"Are you awake, Elvira?"

"Where are we? Yes, I remember."

It was a large room, its decorations expensive but tawdry—a canopied bed, a chandelier with purple tassels, a long mirror framed by gilt cupids and roses. The mattress and the sheets reeked with the perfume of previous occupants.

This house, which stood on the edge of a city not far from Guanajuato, was a brothel for the rich, one of several such places owned by a politician, a man indebted to Donaju for past favors and now further obligated by the unexpected gift of this girl Elvira—not a virgin, but eighteen years old and beautiful enough for several years of service in the better houses, then adequate to use in poorer establishments catering to workmen and soldiers, and, at last, briefly, for the cribs that served peons.

Ornate grillwork barred the windows, and the house was operated much like a prison, but only new arrivals were closely guarded, the owner having learned that regular doses of opium and other drugs soon guaranteed the fidelity of the inmates. This expensive practice shortened the usefulness of a girl and lessened her value, but it gave the owner absolute control. Those who fled always returned soon, ill and shuddering, begging to be taken back. Elvira Campos did not know any of this, nor did she yet suspect why she had been released from the jail in León and brought here.

When Donaju had stood at the door of her cell, she had seen immediate recognition in his eyes. But he said to the jailer, "This is not Elvira Campos. I have made a useless journey."

"But señor, she was boarding a public coach with no papers, and the description—"

"You doubt my eyesight? I tell you it is not she. Now I wish to speak privately with your commander. Maybe something can be salvaged from this wild-goose chase."

Not long afterward she was taken from the jail to the

street, where Donaju awaited her, and although she believed herself beyond hoping, for a moment she was seized by the thought that this man, whom Daniel had loved and feared, was arranging her escape—perhaps for Daniel's sake. Why else had he lied about her name? Then he said, "Hold out your hands." He bound her wrists with a leather thong, mounted his horse, and led her away as if she were a tethered animal.

Once, when they halted briefly on a country road, she questioned him, begging for news of Daniel and her family, although she had known for days they were dead, word having traveled swiftly through the underground network to the jail cell; yet she had not resigned herself to the news. At first he seemed not to hear her; then he said, "If you speak his name again, I will kill you. Later we will talk of him, but not now. I am not ready yet."

At sunset they came to this house, and a pockmarked woman forced her to swallow a liquid that was at once sweet and bitter. Then Donaju told her that her family and Daniel were dead. "You already knew this, of course. He is dead, but you are still alive. A pity, is it not?"

He sneered when she said, "I would have died in his place. At least he has no more suffering."

"No. The suffering is saved for me—and for you, señorita."

The pock-marked woman brought her to the room where she drifted into heavy sleep with dreams that were strangely beautiful, and now she recalled them with guilt.

"Why did you not kill me yesterday on the road?" she asked. "Murder me as you murdered them?"

"I need you alive. But we both know you should die for what you have done."

"What I have done? It was you! You were his friend, and he loved you. He told me many times."

Donaju leaned toward her, his shoulders tense. "What did he say of me? What were his words?"

"Does it matter? Does anything matter?"

"Yes!" When she covered her eyes, he jerked her hands away. "It is what I have left. What he said, what he did. And there is no one but you to whom I can speak of this. No one else mourns him—soon no one else will even remember him. We will share this. You too destroyed him."

Crying out, she sprang to her feet, trying to strike at him, to claw his face with her nails. "No! I told him to go away! It was not my fault! It was you—" He thrust her backward onto the bed, where she lay helpless, her strength ebbing away. "Could I help it if he returned each time?"

"Could you not?" Donaju's voice was a whisper. "You knew how you endangered him. You will think of this many times—whenever we speak of him."

For a long time both were silent, both remembering. Then Donaju said, "I am going now. You will remain here, and I do not think you will find life pleasant. From time to time I will visit you and we will talk. You have much to tell me, and you must remember everything. Before long we will make a short journey together."

"To San Miguel?"

"No. To a place I visited three nights ago." He remembered the hut clinging to the bald rock of the mountain, its dark interior cluttered with the white skulls of animals and men, the piercing smell of incense, and the eyes of the woman who crouched near a fire, mumbling incantations. She had told him to return in three weeks, when the moon had waned. And he would go, not knowing it would be the first of many such journeys. To Elvira he said, "You will meet a woman called Candelaria . . . a *divina* . . . *a woman who summons the dead.* . . ."

FIVE

THE DAY OF
THE DEAD

1

One night four months after the explosion in Guanajuato the captive magician was performing for a crowd of ruffians in the Dragons of the Queen when a messenger entered and held a private conversation with El Lobo, the bandit general. Afterward El Lobo, a black scowl on his face, summoned D'Aquisto to his table. "*Compadre,* you have hidden the truth from me. Why did you not admit that the police are searching for you?"

"The police?" Hope rose in D'Aquisto. He had been missed; at last someone had informed the authorities.

"Captain Guzmán of Guanajuato has circulated your name and photograph. His men have inquired for you at every lodging house in the city."

"I am not without fame," said D'Aquisto. "My absence from civilization would hardly pass unnoticed."

"True, my friend." The bandit paused, then slammed his fist on the table. "Especially when the police want to question you about the deaths of five persons!"

"The deaths of—"

"Naturally I have heard about it." El Lobo tapped his

ear with a blunt finger. "I am a wolf, and news is howled to me across the hills! Four months ago five souls were snatched by the devil from a mansion in Guanajuato. There is a rumor that they were destroyed by ghosts, but even that fool Guzmán knows better. You had a hand in this, my friend, and that is why Guzmán wants you. I have been harboring an assassin under my roof! It is an outrage!"

"Then turn me over to the Guanajuato police. My presence endangers you."

El Lobo's massive frown vanished. Leaning back on two legs of his chair, rocking with laughter, he pounded D'Aquisto's shoulder. "You are devilish clever to have blown up five of them in a way Guzmán cannot explain! *Magnífico!*" He shouted to the barmaid, "Drinks for everybody! Tonight we toast the man who has turned Major Donaju into *carne asada!* Magician, I love you. We will never part! You are safe here. Guzmán's men never venture north, and long ago I took steps to protect you."

"What steps?"

"In Guanajuato you stayed at an inn called The Three Crowns, no? Soon after your arrival here I sent word to the proprietor of that inn, a man who owes me many favors, to remove all record of your presence there and to conceal any baggage you left behind."

"*Dios!*"

"Your possessions are safe; the proprietor will keep them a hundred years if necessary."

A hundred years, thought D'Aquisto, a cold lump forming inside him.

El Lobo grinned. "Guzmán will be utterly baffled!" He pulled his chair close to D'Aquisto. "Tell me privately, did you come to Mexico to kill Donaju? Others have tried and failed. They lacked your cleverness."

"I did not kill Donaju."

"Ha! And I am Columbus!" El Lobo pointed to his eye.

"Well, it is a good riddance. Donaju never entered my territory, but I knew much about him, and once our paths crossed."

"How?"

The bandit made himself comfortable, loosening his gun belt, opening the top button of his trousers to free his paunch. "Above Guanajuato, near the caves where the mummies of the Old Ones are buried, there lives a witch called Candelaria; she has been there a hundred years, perhaps two hundred."

"She is of advanced age, then," said D'Aquisto.

El Lobo shrugged. "This witch is the daughter of a former one, or a granddaughter, or who knows what? There has always been a witch called Candelaria, and she has always been old. She may change from one body to another, but the witch remains and does miracles. She draws devils from the liver and spleen, casts and breaks curses. Also, Candelaria finds lost objects and speaks with ghosts."

"Ghosts? Tell me."

"Two or three years ago I visited this witch. We had liberated a ranch west of here, and it was notorious that the owner had thousands of pesos. My duty was to obtain his money for the revolution, but the old fox had buried it and would not tell us where, although we tried everything—candles to the soles of his feet, tying his arm in a sack with a starved rat. No use! He went to hell without uttering a word.

"So I went to the witch to learn where his treasure was hidden. Now, it is dangerous for a well-known patriot like myself to go so near the city. If Guzmán's men recognized me, I would be hanging by my thumbs in an hour. So I disguised myself as an Indian peon. You would be astonished at how easily I can pass for an Indian."

"Amazing," said D'Aquisto.

"It was night when I climbed the slope to the lair of the

witch—and may Blessed Guadalupe protect us from such hellish places! The wind has carved the rocks into unnatural shapes, and as I followed the path I thought there were devils and devil-beasts around me. Things moved in the dark, and I did not know if they were ghosts or men, but they proved to be others like myself who had come to consult the *bruja*.

"At the top of the path is a stone hut concealing the entrance to Candelaria's cave. Inside, half a dozen men and women sat on the floor, waiting, and although it was dim I saw that one of these men was different from the others, bigger, and he had light-colored eyes. I sensed he was dangerous, so under my serape I kept a pistol in hand, and I am sure he did the same thing. We did not look at each other, but we both watched, if you understand me.

"One by one we were summoned into the cave to speak with the witch. When this man was called, he went in with a woman who was sitting beside him, a beautiful woman, I think, but it was difficult to see. They were with the witch a long time, and I noticed that when they came out the woman was not able to walk by herself. The man held her arm, so roughly that I knew he was not her lover —although he might have been her husband. Now, the door of the Candelaria's hut is low and shaped like the doors of temples the Old Ones built in ancient times. As the man was leaving, he did not bend enough, and the sombrero was knocked from his head. *Dios!* He had hair the color of red chilis!

"I had never seen Donaju, but I knew instantly who he was, and I thought I had walked into a trap. As soon as he was gone, I seized the old man who is the *bruja*'s servant. 'The one who just left,' I said, 'tell me about him.'

" 'He and the woman come here often. He will cause no trouble for you. Let me go, señor!'

"It was true. Like the rest of us, Donaju had come only to consult the witch. Later I learned more from the servant." El Lobo, small eyes gleaming, leaned closer to D'Aquisto. "Donaju went there to speak with a ghost!"

"Did the ghost appear?"

"Only to the woman who always accompanied him. Those who summon spirits go through a special rite; they inhale the smoke of herbs and drink a potion which opens their souls to admit the dead. Donaju himself could not do this—too many men would have been happy to slit his throat while he was in a trance. He stayed on guard and listened while the woman and the ghost talked together."

"What did the ghost say?"

"It talked through the woman's mouth, and the servant could overhear little, but there were words about flowers and stars and much about love. This makes me think it was a female ghost, since men seldom mention such things. The woman was eager to receive this spirit and always wept when it left her. But its presence made Donaju tremble; his teeth chattered, and the servant said his breath came as harsh as a dying man's rattle.

"This story puzzled me. It was dangerous enough for me to go to that place, but worse for Donaju. So the ghost had to be someone he had loved deeply. But then why was he afraid? We fear our enemies, not our sweethearts."

"We fear those we have wronged," said the magician slowly. "And whom do we wrong more than those who love us?"

El Lobo frowned. "That makes no sense. I am very good to my women even after I grow bored. I always get rid of them in a kindly way." He finished his drink and called for another. "The witch did not help me find the treasure. She said, 'Dig beneath barley,' and there were two hundred hectares of barley on that ranch, so what sort of spirit help was that? She also warned me I would be deceived by a woman with a cast in her left eye. This proved true.

"I informed *compadres* of the revolution about Donaju's visits to the slope, and one night they fell upon him from ambush. He killed all three of them. Nothing could touch Donaju. He had the twelve lives of a weasel until you came, my friend. Just between us, how did you manage it?"

"Are you sure I did?"

"It is clear. Donaju dies and Guzmán seeks you. Would you have me believe you came to Mexico as a mere traveler? I am no child. I still have my eyeteeth!"

"I came because a certain woman was here. A woman I had to see again."

"Foolishness," said the bandit. "One woman smells like another. Still, I understand. Her rope was around your neck and you could not get free. I once endured the same thing."

"So I came to Guanajuato. But matters did not end as I hoped."

"She deceived you? With Donaju! I knew it! So you arranged an explosion, using hell's own trickery, and avenged your honor. It is exactly what I would have done."

"Believe what you like," said D'Aquisto, rising.

"Sit down! Have another drink with me!"

"Impossible."

"Why?"

D'Aquisto looked down at his straw sandals, then glared at El Lobo. "Because my feet are too cold. *Buenas noches,* General."

In the courtyard of the inn the magician leaned against a wall, turning up the collar of his cape to shield his throat from the wind, a wind that blew nightly, nudging tumbleweeds, rustling the thatch roof of the stable. Was it possible that a police official in Guanajuato believed he had engineered the destruction of the Inquisitor's House? That he, Zantana the Great, celebrated on three continents, was a multiple murderer? Incredible, yet no more insane than his captivity in this forsaken place. "When I make my escape I will go north to the United States," he said. "Anything to avoid these mad Mexicans! In God's name, what led me to this wilderness?"

He had searched Europe in vain for Margot Laurier, always arriving too late in cities where there had been news of her. From recent clients he learned that prosperity had at last come to her: all of them complained of her outrageous fees, while admitting her talent. The séances seemed to have become more theatrical and perhaps less genuine than the one he had attended in London, where the very dinginess of the proceedings had alarmed him— the ordinary gone mad, specters borne on air that reeked of cabbage and bacon. But in Rome, Margot was reported to have materialized a silvery ghost that splashed water from a fountain. "Her husband's death has changed her," he said. "She avoids what she fears may be real." Abandoning his own efforts, he employed private investigators, who eventually discovered, to his astonishment, that Madame Laurier had returned to Mexico.

D'Aquisto was not proud of the letter he sent, a letter both pleading and reproachful, reminding her of a promise made in London. After several weeks a reply came:

> You are not unfair to ask that I keep our agreement, and your kindness is well remembered. Although my career as a medium is now over, I have plans to hold séances in the city of Guanajuato at a certain house which I once described to you. I am inviting special guests, whose names you have also heard. This is a thing I must do, and I have planned it for a long time. Neglecting my debt, I had not thought of including you, and it will be difficult. Still, if you wish to attend at least the first of these meetings . . .

D'Aquisto did not consider the strangeness of Margot Laurier's letter until he was aboard a steamer bound for Mexico. Why was the medium returning to a city that could have nothing but terrifying memories for her? And when she wrote of "special guests" could she mean those persons who had attended the earlier séance? It seemed incredible that she would associate with those who had once brought disaster. Incredible—and rather sinister. "But it is perfect!" he said. This reunion was the ideal experiment, and it occurred to him that perhaps Margot Laurier, plagued by doubts about the reality of her own powers, was arranging a final test. "She is determined to learn if what happened with those people in that house and in that city was real or an illusion. She has overcome her loathing for the sake of the truth. I am proud of her."

So he made his journey not with misgivings but in anticipation, a confidence that here at last would be the ideal demonstration, the proof. In Guanajuato he went to the Inquisitor's House without foreboding, feeling no menace. And then, in the darkness of the séance, the voice had spoken. . . .

He shivered in the courtyard of the Dragons of the Queen. "The dead have no voices. It cannot be like that. The others heard nothing; they swore they did not." He clung to his thought for a moment. "But they were lying."

Wearily he went to his room only to find that sleep was impossible. He lit the candle and forced himself to work on his manuscript, trying to relieve his thoughts by writing them on paper:

Consider the phenomenon of telepathy, which the American psychologist William James feels has been proven. If there is contact with the spirit world, then telepathy is necessary. The body is doomed to decay, and not all the art of Egypt can preserve the organs of speech. Spirit communication must be by Direct Thought (although Thought in an unknown way might form itself into sounds; Signor Marconi has drawn sound waves from silent air). Great men such as Immanuel Kant have received mental messages over a distance of miles. I myself, in a humble way, had an experience which I relate for others to examine. . . .

One part of the performance of Zantana the Great had been a demonstration of mind-reading. Miranda, dramatically costumed, sat blindfolded on a silver throne while D'Aquisto roamed the aisles of the theater, requesting her to identify various objects offered by the audience.

"What is this?"

"A key," she answered, because keys were always available and this would be the correct reply to her husband's fourth question, just as the eighth object was always a fan and the twelfth opera glasses.

But in addition to this simple system, D'Aquisto worked out an enormously complicated code for other replies. The inflection of his voice and the rhythm of his words had exact meanings, and during the mind-reading performance his apparent asides to the audience gave Miranda information. If he brushed against a spectator and said, "Pardon me, sir," the answer to the next query had to be "A cameo brooch," while omission of the word "sir" meant a white cravat. There were also codes used to spell entire words, letter by letter.

The tremendous difficulty of remembering the signals and keeping the sequences in mind was increased by the fact that performances were given in four different languages, each with its own nuances. D'Aquisto, gifted with an astounding memory, had small patience with Miranda's problems and no understanding of the torture she endured in her struggle for perfection. "How *could* you make such a mistake? The fifth question always involves women's clothing, and we use only eleven items. Did you not hear me cough to show gloves? An idiot could remember that much! Are you really so stupid, or do you merely refuse to try?"

"I am sorry," she said. "It is my fault." He agreed with her fully.

Then one night, while performing in Dublin, the magician himself erred when he accidentally trod on a man's foot and said without thinking, "Pardon me, sir." He was already asking the next question when he realized the error, and hopelessly he awaited the wrong answer, "A cameo brooch."

Miranda's voice came clearly from the stage. "A necklace." And this was true.

Afterward he rushed to the dressing room. "How on earth did you do it?"

"Do what?" A look of apprehension came into her eyes. "Did I make a mistake, Tomás?"

"Why did you say 'A necklace' when the code answer was 'A cameo brooch'?"

"Did I? Forgive me, I must have been confused. But I heard nothing from the audience. Strange they did not notice that—"

"I am speaking of *my* error! I gave you the wrong code, but you answered correctly! How did you know?"

"I don't remember. I thought all was as usual." She laughed uncertainly. "How lucky! You made a mistake—which you never do—and, without realizing it, I made another which set things right."

"Miranda, that is impossible! Some thought wave entered your mind."

"I was aware of nothing."

"Try to remember. Something prompted you. What was it?"

She shook her head. "I made an error, nothing more."

D'Aquisto groaned. "Tonight we gave a demonstration of genuine telepathy! It must have been that! Do you realize the odds against such a series of mistakes? What came to you? Was it like a voice whispering? Or only an impulse?" When she could make no answer, his temper exploded. "Is there no way I can make you understand the importance of this? No! You stare at me with the eyes of a hurt dog and mumble that you made an error! My life is spent listening to your apologies!" He stormed out of the theater and did not return to their hotel that night, unable to forgive her denial of his miracle.

In the performances that followed he eagerly awaited a second demonstration of telepathy, but none came, and eventually he decided to abandon the mind-reading display, although it pleased audiences, and Miranda, delicate and ethereal, was effective in the role of a telepath. In fact, he felt resentment when the audience applauded her. "It is a mistake to allow the attention to be divided. It is bad staging," he told himself. But more than this, he detested using the code when he was convinced that genuine thought transference was so close to his grasp, yet unattainable.

. . . And so on this single occasion we achieved telepathy, although there is no proof except my own word. But if this could happen between two minds, then why should Death's silencing of the tongue end communication? If the Soul, if the Intelligence, survives, then—

Recollections of Miranda flooded over him: he saw her on stage as an Oriental princess, light glittering on a jade necklace, then swathed in white as she floated in John Maskelyne's theater, "Flying Angel"; and he remembered her slender body the night when he, little more than a boy, had first taken her to his bed. And there were memories familiar and homely: her quiet face as she brewed coffee in a hotel room; her hands as she sewed a new buckle on his cape. The buckle and her stitching had survived her; he could touch them now. Then he saw her lips as he had last seen them, waxen in death, and the words of the séance spoke themselves again. "*I loved you. Why did you destroy me?*"

The pen dropped from his hand. "It was not her voice. It was not meant for me!" Donaju, the doctor, the woman Doña Dolores—one or all of them stood accused. Even the medium herself, for had not Margot Laurier destroyed her husband by the illusion or the force she had created? If a ghost had tormented him to his death, it was Margot who unleashed it. Why, if D'Aquisto was guilty, had he been saved from destruction? "I was spared. I alone!"

Spared for what future? He gazed at the crumbling mud plaster of his room, the ceiling smoke-blackened by a thousand candle flames. "I want to talk to someone who can understand my thoughts. I want to read a book, listen to an opera! I want to see tall women in elegant clothes. I want a warm room and a clean pillow!" His head sank to his hands, and he sat numb and despairing, hearing the roof tiles creak as a lizard scurried across them, and listening to the dry breathing of the wind.

The bandits talked of spring, but D'Aquisto could detect no change of the season. Nights were not so cold now, but the landscape remained the same, the gray mesas unsoftened by a single blade of sprouting grass. He pondered a dozen plans for escape, realizing that the first requirement was to improvise durable footwear. "I will make myself shoes of some sort," he said, trying to recall the ingenious methods of Robinson Crusoe. "A discarded saddle will provide leather, fishline will do for stitching, and I can sharpen a strong nail for an awl."

But in this impoverished place there were no discards. Every scrap of material was hoarded by an owner, and the rubbish heap outside did not contain so much as an inch of string, let alone a fishline. "Robinson Crusoe was fortunate," said D'Aquisto bitterly. "He contended with a desert island, not a Mexican hotel."

Then one night, while he was giving his usual performance, there occurred an unprecedented event that caused D'Aquisto's dead hopes to flare to life: El Lobo yawned, an unconcealed and unmistakable expression of boredom. D'Aquisto had thrilled to the applause of thousands of spectators, had reveled in the gasps which followed his miraculous escapes from a locked chest, but no tribute from an audience had moved him so deeply as the bandit's yawn. "May it please God he is at last tiring of me!"

For nearly a month there was no further encouraging sign, and D'Aquisto was growing frantic when late one morning the bandit requested his presence at breakfast. "*Compadre*, I apologize that I am forced to bring up a certain matter," El Lobo said, his frown and the severity of his tone denying all apology, "but I really must ask just how much longer you intend to be my guest? Not that you have exactly overstayed your welcome. However, any visit has limits. Putting it bluntly, when do you plan to leave?"

D'Aquisto's mouth fell open, and he mentally gasped at the man's effrontery. He was about to burst into an angry tirade against his captor but decided on a more malicious reply. "Oh, I have no plans. I find it agreeable here, and you yourself, General, have assured me that your house is my house."

El Lobo looked uncomfortable. "And so it is. But I have decided not to learn juggling. It is perhaps not the thing for a national leader to do."

"You are quite right," agreed D'Aquisto. "Beneath your dignity. You have more important affairs to occupy you."

"Exactly." The bandit looked at the magician expectantly, but D'Aquisto said nothing. "You are not making this easy for me, my friend. Frankly, your presence is likely to be an embarrassment for me in the future. We are moving toward revolution, important figures may be coming here to confer—"

"Please say no more," said D'Aquisto haughtily. "I know when I am not wanted. I would not dream of imposing on you."

"Please, *compadre*. This is painful." El Lobo bit into a red chili and munched it thoughtfully. "I am sending a party of men north toward the frontier, where they will buy the new-style American rifles. I do not mean to turn you out, but would you like to accompany them?"

"I should be delighted. When do they leave?"

"Soon. Any week now. I warn you, it is not an easy trip."

"I am still delighted."

As El Lobo rose from his chair, he grinned. "A rumor has reached my ears. One of my men reports seeing a horse that resembles the one stolen from you last winter. I would not be surprised if it turned out to be the same animal."

"Was this horse by any chance wearing a pair of Spanish leather boots?" inquired D'Aquisto politely.

The bandit's grin broadened. "That would be peculiar. But who knows? One must not question miracles."

2

In the autumn of 1909 a London newspaper announced that Zantana the Great would emerge from retirement to begin a year of theatrical touring. "The celebrated stage conjurer will present a performance entitled 'A Thousand and One Ghosts,' a programme combining illusion with an educational lecture. Zantana, who has unmasked spiritist swindles, will demonstrate and reveal the trickery by which frauds are perpetrated. He promises to expose the famed Spirit Cabinet of the Leighton Brothers, a hoax which has baffled the public on both shores of the Atlantic. . . . Many readers will recall that Zantana figured in the news several years ago when a company of American soldiers patrolling the Mexican frontier found him wandering in the desert, one of the few survivors of a bandit attack upon a party of travelers. . . ."

More than one reader exclaimed, "Zantana the Great? I saw his show before I had long trousers! He must be older than God!" Actually, the magician was little more than sixty.

Theatrical managers were also surprised. "Why is he doing it?" asked one. "Surely he can't need money!" But he did need money. The disastrous journey to the Texas frontier had broken his health, and he not only fell victim to Europe's most expensive physicians but also suffered extortion at the hands of innkeepers in Vichy and Baden-Baden until the hardy constitution that had enabled him to survive the desert eventually overcame the twin hazards of medicine and mineral water.

During his convalescence D'Aquisto refused to listen to any conversation concerning the occult. "I have had enough, I no longer care." Like Saint Augustine, he imposed an iron discipline upon his thoughts, but, also like that saint, he had dreams that outwitted all defense. In sleep he relived the séance, saw again the blazing mansion, heard the voice of the medium.

One day he received a tangible reminder of his journey to Guanajuato: a package and a letter that had been forwarded many times to different addresses.

Esteemed Sir:
    At one time I made efforts to communicate with you regarding a tragic occurrence in the City of Guanajuato, State of Guanajuato, Republic of Mexico, whose special police I have the honor to command. My attempts met no success.

What a pity! Having learned of your world-wide reputation as an authority on such matters as I was investigating, I am sure you could have cast Brilliant Illumination on obscurities involving the deaths of Major F. Patricio Donaju and the Honorable Doña Dolores Cortés.

By application of scientific police methods, the tangle has since been unsnarled, and I take the liberty of sending you a published copy of the final report on events in which I believe you had an interest which has never been quite clear to me. Whatever your connection, I am certain it was thoroughly commendable.

Because of inside knowledge, you might wish to offer corrections to this report, and if so, I urge you to write to me directly, rather than bothering with authorities in the capital who might misunderstand your remarks. Comments should be made to me personally. *I urge this strongly.*

A newspaper account suggests that you had difficulties on a journey from Guanajuato to the Texas frontier. I assure you that such unpleasantness is untypical of this Republic and certainly of my district, which is a peaceful area inhabited by orderly citizens who are known for their unfailing hospitality to all travelers.

I extend salutations and the hope that you will enjoy my humble volume and address any comments to my own attention.

> I remain yours truly,
> your attentive, very
> affectionate and con-
> stant servant,
> Captain José Guzmán

"The man is mad!" exclaimed D'Aquisto. "Fortunate that I avoided him!"

On opening the leatherbound copy of *True Facts,* he studied the frontispiece, a photograph of the author glowering behind the bushy ramparts of his mustache. D'Aquisto hesitated, reluctant to open a Pandora's box of memories, yet knowing he would eventually be compelled to learn what the policeman had discovered. Could this man

Guzmán prove that Margot Laurier's séance had been an exercise in fakery or at best in self-delusion? One had only to glance at the first page to see that the captain had no patience with "occult balderdash" and "spiritist humbug." Could one trust an investigator who simply dismissed the instinctive beliefs of the human race?

Unwillingly D'Aquisto began to read, and at the end of the fifth page his lips twitched and he said, "Preposterous!" Yet there was much here he had not known. The revelation that the billionaire Gorgoni was purely a creation of Doña Dolores astonished him, for although he had spoken to the lady the day after the first séance in Guanajuato, he had no suspicion of her career of impersonation. "Then it was the same circle that the Conde once arranged. All who survived were present."

And the book, despite its absurdities, affected him, leaving behind a sense of incompletion that was curiously like nostalgia or loneliness. He felt guilt, for, although Guzmán was an ass, he had plodded to the end of his task, while D'Aquisto had given up. "If inquiry is left to idiots, it is small wonder that mysteries remain."

That evening, when he attended a performance of *Carmen,* he was unable to concentrate on the music. Stage settings for the walls of Sevilla brought the fortress buildings of Guanajuato to his mind; the Spanish cigarette girl resembled Elvira Campos; and the strings of the orchestra made him hear the hunchback's violin. "The hunchback, of course!" exclaimed D'Aquisto aloud, and a lady on his right gave him an angry stare. Little Brother, according to Guzmán's report, had survived the explosion, but the policeman had dismissed him as a "mute imbecile." The Hunchback could be found; he could be questioned. D'Aquisto thought of the detectives who had discovered the whereabouts of Margot Laurier. Someday I will speak to him, said the magician, this time to himself. I will go back, I will learn the truth. . . .

The magician's international tour of "A Thousand and One Ghosts" was a professional success and a personal affliction. The young man and the pretty girl who assisted him on stage were bumbling and incompetent, the girl especially provoking wrath. "You walk like a spavined camel! Have you no grace? Glide, glide!" But neither instruction nor scarcasm could transform her into a second Miranda. His valet, perfectly competent in London, was unequal to the demands of theatrical touring, and daily the magician found himself plagued by small nuisances, details Miranda had always managed in her quiet way. Even the applause of the audience, once music to feed his soul, meant little, and he marveled that his happiness had ever depended upon public praise. "They would cheer louder for a talking pig," he said.

His final engagement was to be in the Mexican capital, where he planned to bid an unaffectionate farewell to his assistants and then proceed alone to Guanajuato to mark the anniversary of the Day of the Dead. This done, he would visit a convent where, his investigators informed him, Little Brother had for several years been a servant of the nuns.

But during the last week of his appearances in the United States this schedule was upset by a telegram from a Mexico City impresario: INCREASING CIVIL DISORDER HAS DIMINISHED AUDIENCES. ALL PUBLIC GATHERINGS UNSAFE. REGRET WE MUST CANCEL YOUR ENGAGEMENT HERE.

So the reports he had read in newspapers were true: the aged dictator who had held Mexico by the throat for nearly forty years was at last tottering; the revolution was under way. Sighing, D'Aquisto folded the telegram and pushed it aside. He would postpone his visit for a year or two, return to Europe to spend a comfortable winter on the Mediterranean. He gazed at his own face in the mirror above his dressing table. The sharp frown lines had deepened; all his features had become more hawklike. His hair, brushed back dramatically, would have shown streaks of white if he had not taken steps to disguise nature: his satanic guise was an asset on stage; it would not do to let the public see that Lucifer was turning inappropriately gray. "I am no longer young," he said. "If I do not go now, I shall never go. My love of ease will overcome my love of adventure, and then it will be too late. I will sit forever on the terrace of a villa. But no matter how the sunshine dulls my curiosity, I shall always wonder. . . ."

A week later D'Aquisto embarked for Veracruz. His American manager accompanied him to the gangplank of the steamer, shaking his head sadly. "Why go to Mexico now, of all times?"

"I have an appointment," said D'Aquisto.

3

At sunset on the Day of the Dead a patrol led by Captain José Guzmán halted on a high promontory near the Valenciana church, a few miles outside the city of Guanajuato, an observation point that commanded the gorge, the terraced city with its domed towers and spires, and beyond it the scattered ranches of the river valley. "Give me the binoculars, Sergeant," he said.

Guzmán surveyed the landscape, his gaze moving east to west, pausing briefly to study the ruins of the Méndez hacienda, a ranch house sacked and burned a year ago. Its charred buildings stood deserted, the corral empty, and a flock of vultures who had completed their foraging were now settling to roost. It seemed to Guzmán that in the last months the gaunt birds had doubled in number; they were everywhere, a prophecy in the sky.

Past the Méndez ruin lay other abandoned ranches, pillaged and stripped, their owners long since fled to the cities, leaving the vast acreage idle, fields unplowed, pastures ungrazed. Here and there adobe huts had sprung up, mud shacks of peon squatters—women, small children, and the very old. Their men and boys had vanished, gone north to join a brigand general who called himself El Lobo; or they went east, west, south. A dozen armies of tatterdemalion rebels had formed.

"Is all well, Captain?" inquired the sergeant.

"Everything is as usual." A world is crumbling, thought Guzmán, but everything is, of course, as usual. It was a war of ten thousand skirmishes and, as yet, not one battle: a raid against a ranch, the derailing of a train, a bomb exploding in a police station. The rebels seized towns, and by the time troops arrived to expel them they had vanished to the mountains or jungle, a phantom army. There were strikes, there was arson; the enemy was everywhere and nowhere. The senile dictator lashed out at them in vain, a blind, doddering bear, harassed by pit dogs. Three of Guzmán's junior officers had been slain from ambush last summer, and there were no replacements for them, which was why he himself led the patrol today, although such duty was beneath his rank. *Major* Guzmán, he thought. The orders for his promotion were being drawn in Mexico City; any day he would advance in command. But in command of what? No one was even sure that the dictator was still in the capital; there were rumors that he had fled the country, or was now fleeing, or would soon flee. The rumors, whether past, present, or future, agreed that he was taking the entire national treasure with him. In Guanajuato no one knew. Two weeks ago the telegraph lines had been cut, and no trains were arriving.

The light was fading rapidly as he shifted his gaze

toward the outskirts of the city, focusing the glasses on the graveyard of Saint Gabriel the Angel, where torches were beginning to flare among the crypts and monuments. "I am looking at the rebel army," said Guzmán.

"What? They're marching?"

"No, they are celebrating the Day of the Dead. How many people have gathered in the cemetery today, Sergeant?"

"I don't know, sir. Perhaps four thousand. Mostly women and children."

"And how many rebels? I will tell you: three thousand nine hundred and ninety-nine. The last one has not quite made up his mind. And they are all thinking about how you and I will look with our throats cut."

The sergeant chuckled uneasily. "You are joking, Captain."

"Of course. Most merely want to shoot us." Guzmán watched the confused scene in the graveyard, the brown-skinned crowd milling and shifting. "Have you noticed that there are almost no fireworks this year?"

"Yes, sir. My wife has been disappointed."

"Tell her to be patient. They are saving the gunpowder for other purposes. She will hear it before long."

As Guzmán spoke, a figure crossed his line of vision, a tall man wearing a cape with a winged collar who almost instantly disappeared into the crowd. "Is it possible?" exclaimed Guzmán.

"Beg pardon, sir?"

"Nothing. I thought I recognized someone. I must have been mistaken."

But as the patrol made its way back to the city the conviction grew in him that the man in the cemetery was Tomás D'Aquisto, and, recalling how he had once suffered the delusion that the magician had materialized in the blackness of the Governors' Palace, he said to himself, "A slippery character. Now you see him, now you don't."

At nine o'clock Tomás D'Aquisto, walking silently through silent streets, approached the Inquisitor's House and halted in the shadows of a doorway, the same doorway which seven years ago had concealed Pablo Sanchez, the terrified candy-seller who cried out his prayers when he saw the devil. That night had resounded with fireworks; rockets had shrieked into a smoky sky, and a hundred clanging bells echoed among the rooftops. Tonight, its anniversary, was pervaded by a waiting stillness. The massive buildings, shuttered and barred, revealed no life, and the magician had walked a mile through hushed streets, hearing no sound except his own boots on the cobbles. There were no passers-by, no candles flickered behind opaque windows, and the streetlamps were unlighted. Although the moon had risen, he had to feel his way like a blind man, and once he tripped and fell at an unexpected curb.

"The people are still at the cemeteries," he said. "They will return soon." Yet he was uneasy not to hear the whistle of a night watchman or a sound of hoofbeats, it was as though he had entered a necropolis, the only living man wandering by moonlight among the immense tombs and temples—not unlike the nightmare Margot Laurier had described to him when in her trance she fled to the balcony of the Inquisitor's House and discovered not this city but a darker city where no footsteps fell, no voices were heard.

D'Aquisto gazed at the façade of the mansion, its marble gargoyles gleaming faintly, cold-skinned, reptilian. The second-floor windows had been sealed with boards; the heavy front doors were closed. No one, even in a country where shelter was scarce, would live there. The policeman who wrote *True Facts* could preach about coincidence and the probability of accidents, but what man had such faith in science that he would take up residence in this infamous house and tempt fate to make him yet another link in the coincidental chain? An older logic, an inborn voice, whispered, "This place is unlucky. Stay away!"

As the magician scanned the blind windows he was filled with sudden anticipation. "Something must happen here tonight." He had no reason to believe this, the Day of the Dead was endowed with no special power, yet his breath came quickly and his attention was so fixed on the Inquisitor's House that he did not notice two quietly moving figures who had entered the street until they were almost opposite him. They moved furtively, staying close to the walls and avoiding the moonlight: a woman shrouded in a black shawl, followed by a man in a dark serape. D'Aquisto drew into the shadows, waiting for them to pass, but at the entrance to the mansion they stopped, looked left and right. Behind them the great doors, as though in answer to an unheard knock, swung open, and they vanished into the darkness inside. Then the doors closed again, not with a creak of hinges, but soundlessly. The magician watched and listened, but no light appeared in the house, and it was hushed, as seemingly untenanted as before. Moments passed, and when no sign came he stepped into the street, determined to seek entrance himself.

"Good evening, señor," said a voice near him.

D'Aquisto, startled, saw a stocky mustached man in a brown uniform approaching. "What—"

"Good evening," the man repeated. "I have the honor to address Señor Zantana? Or do I call you Señor D'Aquisto? I have never been sure."

"D'Aquisto. Forgive me, I do not remember—" Then the magician recalled the frontispiece of *True Facts*. "You are Captain Guzmán?"

"I am."

"A most unexpected meeting. Yet another remarkable coincidence."

"I saw you today in the cemetery of Saint Gabriel the Angel. I presumed you would come here tonight. It is an anniversary, no?"

"I am keeping a religious vigil," said the magician, anxious to be rid of this companion. "Margot Laurier, regardless of your book, was a friend of mine. I have come to say Aves for her repose."

Guzmán chuckled. "I am impressed by your piety. You must not blame me for my remarks about the medium. As a man I am unusually honest, but as a writer, I did what I could."

It occurred to the magician that perhaps the captain was not the fool his book made him appear. Guzmán's eyes were shrewd, and his tone suggested a man not easily taken in. "I apologize, Captain, for not writing to thank you for the report you sent me. It involved a matter which concerned me deeply."

"And still concerns you?"

"Yes."

The policeman glanced toward the dark house. "There are questions which bother one. I myself, although I know better, am never quite comfortable in this street. For a long time I avoided it, but now I am often drawn to this place. Ridiculous, is it not? Lately a new legend has grown around the mansion. A cult of Indians—and others—gathers there on certain nights. We have threatened them with jail, and the *padres* have promised them hellfire, yet they come back, they break in, they hold their rites. I no longer try to stop them. I have other worries." Guzmán took the magician's arm. "We should not stand talking in the street. The night air of Guanajuato is notoriously unhealthful, especially just now. My house is only a few streets away. Come, señor."

"Excuse me, but I must finish my prayers and then return to the inn. Tomorrow I have to make a journey."

"A journey?" Guzmán's eyes narrowed. "Permit me to

guess that you plan to go to the Convent of the Holy Child."

"How did you know?" Clearly he had underestimated the captain.

"Logic. You did not come to Mexico to mumble a few Aves in a doorway. No doubt you learned that the nuns gave shelter to a hunchback known as Little Brother."

"You are right."

"Then, señor, you really must come with me now. I will save you a useless trip."

There were apparently no servants in Guzmán's house, but two armed guards lounged in the patio. "We will go to my library. It is the most comfortable room. You must forgive my poor hospitality, but I live the life of a bachelor now."

"You have no family?"

"My wife and three daughters are in the capital, where it is safer. I had two grown sons, both *rurales*. They were killed in the south last year—an uprising of workers on one of the plantations. I am told they died bravely."

"I offer my sympathy. Such a loss must be hard to bear."

"I have found it so."

The library was a large, sparsely furnished room with a vaulted ceiling. Guzmán lit three lamps, turning the flames high. "I cannot get enough light these days. No matter how many lamps I light, it is never enough. Sit down, señor. I cannot offer you rum or brandy—we live off the land these days—but there is tequila."

One wall had portraits of two young men, broad-featured youths resembling the captain. Mounted above them was a pair of crossed sabers. "My sons, Corporal Juan Guzmán and Sergeant Jorge Guzmán," he said. "The paintings were done from tintypes, and the likenesses are not good. The artist made them handsome, and they were not handsome boys. I wish he had drawn more truthfully."

Near D'Aquisto's chair stood a tall bookcase containing several legal volumes, a few patriotic works, and almost a hundred copies of *True Facts*. "As you see, my library is well stocked. I have the world's largest collection of the works of José Guzmán."

The magician smiled, surprised to find that the policeman had a sense of humor. He had imagined the author of *True Facts* as a different personality. This was a beleaguered man, his eyes haggard, his uniform rumpled, and D'Aquisto noticed the captain's unconscious habit of glancing over his shoulder. "You must be proud of your book. Not many men in your position are authors."

"At one time I took pride in it. I thought it would earn me a promotion." Guzmán's voice became fretful. "I have a promotion, by the way, only it is not confirmed. I do not understand why it takes so long. There is no news at all—it is maddening!" He poured two glasses of tequila, drained his own at a swallow, and poured another. "You and I know, of course, that most of my book was nonsense."

D'Aquisto, hesitating, said, "I am surprised to hear you say so. Your frankness does you credit."

"Frankness is easy for me now." Guzmán walked slowly back and forth in the room, pressing his fist into his palm. "What does it matter whether the book was truth or lies? I did what I was asked to do. The important people were pleased. I have made a successful career by pleasing important people. Soon I will reach the rank that Donaju held, and I have none of his ability." Guzmán paused. "Nor do I have his talent for evil."

"Yet he was the hero of your report."

"Politics. Unimportant now—nothing is important any more. I stay at my post, still obeying orders, worrying about a promotion, when I should be concerned about saving my head. The revolution is coming like a flood down the canyon, and I will be the first man to drown. I tell myself that any day the American Army will cross the frontier to save the government. They have always supported us; it is in their interest. But this time I think they will not come. Maybe I do not really care and welcome the end. I no longer know." Near one of the shuttered windows he halted his pacing. "Everything is quiet outside. Strange for a fiesta! But I am not deceived by it. At any moment the city can explode; an army will pour into those streets."

Guzmán sank into his chair and with a wave of his hand dismissed the future. "You are not here to listen to my troubles. We were to speak of what took place in the Inquisitor's House. Tell me, how were you involved in the affair? I had no idea, and I always feared you would publicly contradict what I wrote. A few years ago that would have been serious, so I appreciate your kindness in saying nothing. Now we can at least satisfy one another's curiosity."

"I am an investigator of spiritism." D'Aquisto spoke slowly. "Half of my nature has always believed in it. The other half is the devil's advocate, so I am at war with myself. You may find that difficult to understand. I judge from your book that you dismiss all such things as nonsense; you are a materialist and an atheist."

A smile flickered across Guzmán's face. "Of course I am an atheist. I swear it by the Blessed Virgin of Guadalupe."

"Think what it would mean, Captain, if I could show the world that the least shred of this nonsense was true! The faintest whisper, the smallest sign is the proof there is no death! And so I come to the story of Margot Laurier."

Guzmán listened quietly, his face expressionless, as D'Aquisto outlined the history of her life and described his own experience at the London séance. "Then I came to

Guanajuato. I joined the circle at the Inquisitor's House, and in the darkness a voice spoke, a voice I believed I recognized."

"What words were said?"

D'Aquisto avoided the policeman's eyes. "I did not catch them. It was only a tone, a feeling." He sipped the bitterness of the tequila, then continued. "I thought perhaps it was not I but another person who was addressed, even though all of them denied hearing anything. During the next two days I sought them out, questioned them, begged them to tell me of their experiences—what they had learned, if they had achieved some communication. Three of them spoke with me; the fourth would not."

"I suppose Donaju refused."

"Yes, but I did not need him, for I managed to see Elvira Campos. She was dazed, confused by drugs, and I am not sure she knew what she said or even to whom she spoke. I had a glimpse of hell that day, Captain."

"And it was not pleasant?"

"What must it be like to love and be loved by the dead?" asked D'Aquisto.

Guzmán stirred uneasily. "Another tequila?"

"Thank you." D'Aquisto held out his glass. "As a policeman, you had only one question: was some crime committed in the destruction of those five? I needed to know more than that. I learned that Elvira Campos believed herself possessed by a dead man and that on at least one occasion—at a séance arranged by the Conde Calderón— Major Donaju also felt the presence of a ghost. But were they good witnesses? I think not. Doña Dolores Cortés told me nothing in a most gracious way. Yet she had been deeply moved, shaken as I myself was shaken. Then there was Esterbrook, the American doctor."

"A peculiar character," said Guzmán. "At the time of my investigation I did not know what to make of him. Since then I have learned something."

"You discovered that he was a murderer?"

Guzmán raised an eyebrow. "If you suspected that, señor, it was your duty to inform the police. We might have arested him and prolonged his life a little."

"I was not certain he murdered his wife. But he could not stop speaking of her. He was obsessed by the woman, haunted by her. I called on him in midmorning, and he was already drunk—drunk and in agitation. I am sure he heard the same voice that startled me. But he talked only of his wife, praising her as a saint and then damning her for being unfaithful. If she deceived him, I think he purchased his own horns."

"It seems unlikely," said Guzmán.

"No. He spoke frankly of his affairs in the brothels of Guanajuato. I think he felt guilty in the eyes of his wife, and he encouraged her infidelity to ease this guilt. Then, when what he had abetted took place, he was furious."

"*Qué cosa!* He admitted this?"

"Not in exact words. And at the end he insisted her death was an act of God. A special God, I daresay, who resides in Massachusetts and dispenses immediate punishments—with a little earthly aid."

"I have information for you," said Guzmán. "Last year some miners searching for a new vein tunneled into the shaft where the Señora Esterbrook was entombed. They found what remained of her, and she was not alone. There was another skeleton whose clothing was that of a certain manager who had disappeared years before. The investigation was reopened; we listened to old gossip and heard that he was her lover and they used to meet in this tunnel. There was a rumor that the doctor engineered the avalanche which buried them. If so, I gather he repented his act."

"He repented it," said the magician. "He was in torment."

For a moment both were silent. D'Aquisto heard the

faint clink of spurs as a guard walked in the patio. Guzmán bit off the tip of a cigar and lighted it with a paper twist he had held over the lamp. "We are short of matches. It is ridiculous." He blew out the flaming paper, stared at the smoke curl. "You did not agree with my report that the séance had a political purpose?"

"No. They gathered for a personal reason."

"And what was this reason?"

D'Aquisto hesitated, then spoke the conviction that had slowly formed in his mind. "To atone to their dead."

The captain considered this, puffing on a cigar while he studied D'Aquisto. "You had a narrow escape. You might well have attended the last séance, the fatal one."

"I did not know there was to be a séance that night! I cannot understand it. Margot Laurier promised me that I would be informed, but no message came. Can you imagine my excitement during those two days of waiting? I was convinced I was on the verge of discovery, sure I would find tangible evidence. The end of my search was at hand!" The magician's emotion carried him to his feet; he moved close to Guzmán, and the words poured from him. "I had examined hundreds of cases, hundreds! All were frauds or imaginings. With Margot Laurier I was approaching the truth; and it was not only the medium, it was the circle. They were special, all of them. They possessed some gift, some power I did not have, but which I felt that night.

"Have you read Pascal, Captain? He says we understand nothing of the works of God until we learn that He wishes to blind some and enlighten others. I have always been blinded, but during those two days I lived in the hope that I would at last see.

"Late the second evening I rode to one of the cemeteries to watch the festival. On the way I saw Elvira Campos and Donaju in the street. Only later did I realize that they would not have been together unless there was to be a séance. I raced back to the city, toward the house. I must have heard the explosion, but I do not know—there were so many explosions that night, so many bells, so much shouting. When I saw the flames, I knew they were destroyed, gone, I was cheated of my answer. I would have given myself to the destruction to know what they must have known in that last hour. An explosion? An accident? Not for an instant did I think so. They were demolished by a Power, a force I sensed in that house, a Power they called down on their own heads."

"Do you still believe this?" asked Guzmán quietly.

Closing his eyes, the magician turned away. "I believe it. Whatever I may say and however much I may doubt, part of me clings to this. My one encounter with a miracle! I cannot give it up. It is my faith."

The captain nodded, his face thoughtful. "To atone to their dead. Then you have traced a thread binding them together. There is a pattern, and the pattern is guilt."

"It must be. It is clear."

Guzmán sighed. "Señor D'Aquisto, your version is even neater than *True Facts*. You are talented at constructing perfect explanations, and I begin to think you should have been a policeman. But your pattern unravels. I, for one, do not think Dr. Esterbrook was guilty."

D'Aquisto was astonished. "Why, you yourself said—"

"You would hang a man on such evidence? Perhaps you should not be a policeman after all. There are already enough of us willing to convict without proof. The doctor may well have had a weakness for women, and his wife probably had a weakness for the mine manager. But his career at Las Jacarandas was more like that of a saint than a murderer. Is it not possible that he sought his wife's spirit because of love? That he forgave her and longed for her?"

"I cannot accept such a thing."

"Why not? Because it shatters perfection? Come, señor,

admit that he may have been an innocent man, a victim of odd circumstances that caused gossip and such surmise as your own."

"Then he should not have been at the séance."

"Nevertheless, he was."

"But he—" D'Aquisto faltered. "If he was innocent, his presence was only a coincidence. No more than that."

"Coincidence?" Guzmán's eyebrows shot upward. "I reject coincidence. It is the refuge of the unscientific mind."

"I still believe he was guilty," said D'Aquisto. "He must have been."

The captain nodded. "This sort of logic is familiar to me. Very well, we will say he was like the others. Then all who went to that house owed atonement—except one, of course."

"Except one? Which one?"

"Why, yourself. Naturally! Your interest was purely scientific and impersonal."

The mockery was spoken gently, but D'Aquisto's hands tightened on the liquor glass. "You are shrewder than I thought, Captain. I think you imply that I am a fraud."

"No. You are an honest man—and a good one."

"I am neither of those things," said D'Aquisto harshly. "I too am haunted. My wife, Miranda—"

"I am not questioning you, señor," said Guzmán.

The magician seemed not to hear him. "After tonight we shall probably not meet again, Captain, so I make you my confessor. I have never talked of Miranda since her death, but she is always in my thoughts. When I first saw her she was a child, a terrified child, frightened every waking hour of her life. Her eyes showed that she expected to be hurt, and God knows what she had suffered. But because of an old man named Cantari, a man who was a father to both of us, she was changed by love from a whimpering creature into a beautiful young woman. There was a gaiety about her, a lightness and a love of laughter.

"I married her when we were very young, not loving her, but because marriage with her seemed the natural thing. We lived together and we worked together for more than twenty years. Can you imagine what she was like at the end of that time, Captain? She had become again that crushed child I had first known. The laughter was gone; the fear had returned to her eyes. I did that to her; she was my creation! I did it day by day and year by year without even knowing it. I destroyed her in a thousand small ways—sometimes because of vanity or from selfishness, often because there was rage in me and I needed to strike out and she was there to take the blow." The magician's voice trembled, but he spoke quietly. "Small neglects, small hurts, but they were endless. That is how Miranda was broken—each hurt adding to the last until I could hurt her no more, she was beyond my reach.

"And she bore this because she loved me. I loved her, although I was not aware until it was too late. Since her death I have tried to remember anything I ever did to show my love. And I can think of nothing! Not one single kindness that I did not somehow extract payment for. And so I destroyed her." D'Aquisto returned to his chair, sat with closed eyes while Captain Guzmán silently refilled his empty glass. "She died suddenly in a Paris hospital. Of pneumonia, they said. Even at the last moment I did not think to tell her I loved her, although I realized it then. I would like to tell her now."

Guzmán stubbed out his cigar, twisting it among the gray ash in a plate near him. "You are too hard on yourself, my friend. We all live as though there would never be an ending. Life is made of unkindnesses, and none of us spares another for long. I think of much I should have done differently, but I do not dwell on this." Suddenly he smiled. "Neither do I learn from it."

"You have been a good listener, Captain. You must forgive me for being disturbed tonight. When we met in the street you said you would save me tomorrow's journey. How is this?"

"I recently had word from the superior at the Convent of the Holy Child. The hunchback you are seeking died quietly there some weeks ago."

"Did he say anything? Did he tell anyone of—"

"Nothing. I am afraid that your investigation—and mine —is closed. There are no other witnesses."

The magician appeared stunned. "Then there will be no proof?"

"No. You have proof enough of your miracle. Be content with it."

After the magician had gone, Captain Guzmán unlocked a cabinet and removed an envelope containing several finely written pages. At his desk he looked once more at the surprising Italian penmanship of Little Brother. The superior at the Convent of the Holy Child had found this document among the hunchback's possessions and forwarded it to Guzmán. The captain had planned to show it to D'Aquisto tonight, then changed his mind during their conversation. "Let him keep his miracle. He needs it."

Convent of the Holy Child
August 18, 1910

For the Reverend Mother María Immaculata
Esteemed Mother in God,

I, Agapito Véloz, known to you as Little Brother, write this on the eve of what will be my last saint's day on earth, the day of Saint Agapetus the Martyr. Mindful of approaching death, aware that I am at war with God, I remain unrepentant of certain sins and unfit for final confession. But here I write the truth, unstained by any lie, and I write for honorable reasons which I shall make plain.

You have commended my gentleness, esteemed Mother, and once said that I resembled the good Saint Francis in that I would not destroy even the red ants that bit me or the rats that plagued me in my room in the stable. Yet I, who vowed to harm no living creature, am guilty of the deaths of six persons. And although I regret the causes of these acts, I do not regret the acts themselves. I must explain from the beginning.

I have no clear memory of my first years of life, yet sometimes in nightmares fragments of scenes loom in my mind and I know they are from childhood, when my parents, who had not the gift of speech, were beggars in the streets of Mexico City. I see a stone chamber, windowless, with wet straw on the floor. Men and women lie on this straw; some are legless, some have no hands or no arms, and there are those who are mad. I see my mother and myself kneeling at a trough; we scoop something soft into our mouths, then others hurl themselves upon us, beating us away from the food.

It was from a life of such horror that a woman called Madre Juana rescued us. Madre Juana was not a nun, but, like yourself, Reverend Mother, she was a saint on earth, and she welcomed us to a refuge she had built on a ranch near San Miguel de Allende. There were food, clean mats to sleep on, and animals for me to tend and play with. But most of all there was a love that encompassed us.

Here at the convent one of the mothers, less holy than yourself, once shouted in anger that I was too ugly for salvation. Always my face has been a monkey's face, but as a child I had no suspicion of this. At Madre Juana's no one was ugly. No one spoke of another's affliction, and because she was proud of us we took pride in ourselves. The blind held their heads high because their hearing and fingers were more sensitive than those of sighted men, and a handless weaver could boast of making baskets with his wrists and toes and teeth and challenge others to equal his skill. My parents were taught the manual language of mutes, and for the first time they, and later I, could converse. The child of two beggars learned to read, like a priest or scholar, and I was instructed in writing the Italian Hand, for Madre Juana hoped I would become a scribe. I also learned music, both the guitar and violin, and my violin later brought me much consolation.

Our complete happiness continued until I was twelve years

old. Then one night a company of armed men led by an officer named Donaju swept down upon us to commit acts so horrible that even now, as I remember them, my hand shakes. The Madre, the best, the kindest of women, died by fire. My parents were slaughtered. I myself, in trying to defend them, was trampled by the hoofs of Donaju's horse. My back broken, I grew into the deformed creature you have known and on whom you have taken pity.

I swore I would not forget my dead. I went to the hilltop shrine of the Blessed Virgin of Guadalupe, wrapped my legs in thorns, and crawled up the steps, cursing Donaju and imploring torment for him.

Many years later, while I was serving my master Señor Laurier, the Virgin afforded me the opportunity to avenge those who had died at the refuge. Donaju was our escort on a journey to Guanajuato, and I thought of approaching close and firing a pistol, or plunging a knife into his heart. But I knew punishments would follow, and I was afraid. They say that suffering inures us to pain, but the pain I have endured has only left me terrified of its repetition. I could not bear the thought of torture. I knew I must make up in cunning what I lacked in courage. In a mansion called the Inquisitor's House I attempted his life by releasing an iron chandelier, thinking it would crush him. I failed, and the Conde Calderón died in Donaju's place. Although everyone believed it was an accident, Donaju was alerted and I did not dare make a second attempt. Still, I told myself that God is not forgetful and someday the time would come. . . .

Esteemed Mother in God, I cannot describe the love I felt during those years for Don Pierre and Señora Laurier. I loved Don Pierre because he was what I could not be. When I followed him in the street, it was *I* who was handsome, *I* whose smile caused ladies to blush. His elegance became mine. Later, I loved him even more, because he needed me, and there is no greater cause of love than this. And the Señora Margot—I say only that I adored her as you, Mother María, adore God. Yet deep as my love for her was, I think it no greater than the love she felt for Don Pierre, and I know that in his destruction she met her own.

After Don Pierre's death I fell into despair, and it was only devotion to the señora which kept me alive. But she, although never happy, grew in strength until at times I did not know her. I continued to serve her, always watchful, always listening, but could not divine the source of this strength. Only when we returned to Mexico and she told me we were going to the Inquisitor's House did a suspicion of the truth enter my mind. When I learned the names of those who were to attend a séance there, I became certain.

My lady always believed that those who had once been guests of the Conde were the cause of Don Pierre's ruin. I knew now that she planned some vengeance upon them, although I did not know the nature of it. She neither confided in me nor asked my help, which I would gladly have given, for my hate was as great as hers and rage against Donaju burned like coals in my stomach. Whether her plan involved the power of the séance or some physical means I cannot tell.

On the day of the first gathering of those people, my lady called me to her and told me I must soon begin a new life of my own, that we would no longer be together. She spoke gently, but it was like hearing the judgment of doom. I could not comprehend parting, or imagine life without her. I begged her, but she would say no more. Then I realized that, after she had done whatever she must do, she would end her life and suffer a suicide's damnation.

That night, when the circle gathered, I was in terror of what might happen, even though there was a stranger there, a man to whom my lady meant no harm. But as I stood in the next room, playing my violin, a spell came upon me, darkness and a sound of rushing waters, and there were voices speaking, the voice of Madre Juana and of Don Pierre, calling me, telling me what I must do.

On the third night, when again the circle gathered, I opened the jets and lighted the candle. . . .

Esteemed Mother, I do not write this as an act of repentance, for how can I regret taking my lady's damnation upon myself? I am content in the destruction of Donaju, and I believe that the others too were evil.

But terrible and frightening rumors have reached my ears. There is talk that my lady was a witch and that on the last night of her life she summoned hellfire and even Satan. She does not lie in holy ground, but in an unblessed grave near the suicides and the Jews. Nor is she left in peace there, but has suffered desecration at the hands of persons who have gone in the night to drive the witches' cross into her body. Three times I have stolen away from the convent to replace the disturbed earth. When I am no longer here, who will care for her? I beg you to intercede with the fathers in Guanajuato that she may be removed to a consecrated place and masses may be said for her soul, for she perished not by the fire of the devil, nor by her own hand, but by mine.

I also implore you, Esteemed Mother, to broadcast what I have written so that all blasphemies against her may be dispelled. I swear she had no power for evil and no power over the dead. It was only Memory she evoked, and this was not wicked but beautiful. Always when I played my music while she was lost in her dream, I felt the souls of those I have loved, my mother, my father, the Madre Juana, and they spoke to me in silence, they caressed me and left the warmth of their kisses on my cheeks, coming not as ghosts come, but as when in our deepest prayers we know the presence of the saints and feel their hands reach forth to give us peace.

Thy child in God,
Hermanito

P.S. There is money for what I have asked you to do. You will find it buried in the stable under a tile in the stall of the mare with the little brown colt.

Captain Guzmán folded the pages and replaced them in their envelope. This, then, was the last word, the refutation of the miracle D'Aquisto had believed in and the accident which he himself had proved. "I write the truth, unstained by any lie. . . ." For a moment he sat lost in thought, troubled, and his eyes rested on the crossed sabers and the portraits beneath them. He tapped the corner of the envelope on his desk. "Can one be sure? He had reasons to say these things. I wonder . . ."

4

Although its doors were ajar, the mansion seemed deserted when, a few minutes before midnight, Tomás D'Aquisto entered and moved cautiously through the gloom of the corridor, finding his way past a stone bench, moving toward the rectangle of moonlight in the patio beyond. He knew that at the end of this passage there would be a flight of marble steps leading to the second floor, gray marble with a Moorish balustrade. Now he saw them, as he had so many times when in memory or dreams he had revisited the house.

Slowly he mounted, then paused at the top of the stairwell. Below lay the open courtyard with its dry fountain, moss-grown, and the weeds with gentle but eternal persistence were prying apart the rock-slab flooring. Was there a scar on one of the slabs where a chandelier had fallen? He looked for a moment at the narrow iron door which led to a strongroom where the first inhabitants of the mansion had breathed their last, dying, he wished to believe, with words from the Torah on their lips. Behind him was the room where Margot Laurier's circle had met obliteration, the closed doors still smoke-blackened, their casings charred.

The hunchback was dead; the police captain knew nothing more. There were no avenues left to follow except the one that led back to this mansion, the place of the beginning, and tonight, surely, of the end. No sound came from the room where his search must terminate, but he tapped softly on the panel, feeling an excitement, a tingling of his blood. Farther down the balcony corridor another door opened, and a woman bearing a hooded lantern approached him, her bare feet noiseless on the tiles.

"Who is it?" Her voice was a rattling whisper, the Spanish words hoarse with gutturals of an Indian tongue. In the gleam of the lantern D'Aquisto saw matted white hair falling to her waist—ashen, stark against the black shawl. "I do not know you," she said. "Why do you come here tonight?" Her face, webbed by wrinkles, was the red brown of the Guanajuato earth.

"I seek entrance, old Mother."

"You are a stranger. Leave us in peace."

"I am not a stranger." She shook her head silently, and her eyes, strangely brilliant, fixed on D'Aquisto, challenging him. "Tell me, old Mother, are you called Candelaria?"

"I am Candelaria."

"I have heard much of you. I come as a friend and *compadre* of El Lobo. I ask admission in his name."

"El Lobo?" Lifting the lantern high, she studied the magician. "Follow me, then. But our rite ends at midnight, and that is soon now."

She led him into the small chamber where the Conde had once enjoyed his late suppers, the room in which Margot had received D'Aquisto, and from here they entered the ruined salon, not by a door but through an opening cut in the wall and concealed by a scorched tapestry. The moonlight, striped by shadows of half-burned beams that had once supported a roof, threw pale patterns on walls and floor tiles whose blackened gilt had been washed and faded by the rains of seven summers. Two braziers heaped with incense and charcoal glowed red on their pedestals, wisps of thin smoke drifting upward, and a dozen communicants, both men and women, were gathered, some kneeling as in prayer, others sitting on the floor, hands folded and heads bowed. None spoke and none turned to see the stranger who now knelt among them.

The magician breathed the sweet sharp fumes of the incense and, forcing his eyes to dilate, he stared at one bright coal, shutting out all that surrounded him, erasing all images from his mind, that it might receive whatever would be given. He breathed more deeply, and slowly the shapes in the room wavered, then converged and dissolved while his blood rang in his head and he struggled to thrust himself through the curtain of darkness, to enter a world of his vision, gray but luminous, from whose mists would emerge a silent caravan that had neither beginning nor end, a procession moving eternally, without origin or destination, but now it would not pass in stillness as it passed in his dreams. The shrouded figures would approach, hands raised in greeting, a familiar voice would call his name and he would answer. . . .

A bell rang midnight, long strokes echoing from a faraway tower. D'Aquisto's eyes opened, and he saw Candelaria, her arms stretched high, fingers extended, while her lips moved, twisted. The communicants swayed and bent and rustled, a cornfield swept by the wind; their bodies shuddered while in moaning unison they cried out a chant, and D'Aquisto, trembling, prayed aloud. "Let them come now! Let them come to me!" His head thrown back, his hands clenched, he waited.

The tolling bell ceased, and the medium's arms sank to her sides as the cries of the communicants died away. Silence returned to the room, a silence broken only by the sound of one man weeping. Candelaria spoke softly. "They have left us. The visit is ended, and now we must go."

The magician rose painfully to his feet and, unsteady, with his head bowed, made his way outside, where he leaned against the marble balustrade, unmindful of the ragged men and women passing quietly behind him as they left the house. "I have done all that can be done," he whispered. "There is nothing more."

Step by step he descended the stairway, the faces of the five who had perished here looming in his mind, a faint smile shimmering on their lips before they vanished. He walked slowly into the courtyard, where he sat for a moment on the low wall of the fountain, gazing upward past the arches and pillars of the house to the sky and the great stars, incredibly brilliant in the thin air. "The silence of space frightens me. I am engulfed in infinity and afraid."

From the street he heard muffled laughter, the strumming of a guitar as a group of merrymakers returned from a cemetery at the end of the Day of the Dead, and D'Aquisto thought of the grotesque revels he had watched that afternoon in the graveyard of Saint Gabriel the Angel, the gay crowd elbowing one another for room to sit on the inscribed slabs, where they munched sugar skulls and drank punch the color of blood. Urchins clambered over the tombs of moldering aristocrats, a brass band played fandangos, while children in death's-head masks capered and fought and danced. The necropolis, like all cities, had its slums, and in a quarter where there were no sculptured saints or obelisks the picnics were spread on the graves of those who had no permanent claim to the earth where now they lay; their bones lodged in rented land, and at the end of five years they would be disinterred from the costly precincts of holy ground, evicted, as in life, from estates not their own.

Alone in the courtyard of the Inquisitor's House, the magician listened as the noise of the passing celebrants faded away. "The fiesta goes on. They jest with the dead, they placate them with bribes of bread and sugar. They flout Death himself or claim him as a comrade. But no one is deceived, and Death plays the final joke. Unless

. . . unless . . ." He gazed once more at the closed doors above him.

The old woman, appearing from beneath the balcony, entered the patio. "Señor, you must leave now." When he did not move or reply, she said, "You are troubled? They did not come to you tonight?"

He turned to her, anger in his voice. "Do they ever come? Ever? Tell me, for the love of God!"

"They come."

"Your word is not enough! How do you know?"

"How?" Her hands remained folded in her shawl, and she spoke quietly. "I know because I have seen them."

He searched her face, seeking any sign, any mark of wisdom or knowledge or even deceit, but there was only quietude and an ancient peace.

"Are you tired, señor? Have you had a long journey?"

"Yes. But it has ended. I can go no farther."

Rising, the magician moved slowly through the moonlight, a tall, slightly bent figure, the flowing cape and black sombrero casting a strange silhouette on the pale stones. Then he merged with the shadows, groping his way through the dim corridor toward the darker streets of the city beyond.